M L CHAMBERS

two-date warning

M L Chambers

Quarterback Scramble
The Marriage Offensive
Two-Date Warning
Flag on the Date
Red Hot Zone
Ineligible Receiver
The Heart Hand-Off
Champagne Problems
On the Rocks
Fools Dive In
Kendry the Vicious

two-date warning

Book 3
Mountaineer Footballers

M L Chambers

"I'm glad you are here with me."

Frodo Baggins {Return of the King}

CHAPTER ONE

A CHUNKY, CHEAP STREAMER. Abrasive crepe paper that when wet, congealed into a nasty dense paste, folding and sticking, making demented zags in an otherwise tolerable drape.

A flimsy party adornment hung by mothers with the best intentions. A last-ditch effort for when the rented princess suddenly dropped out of the birthday appearance, because they're too high to drive.

Yes, a streamer. In one of those unwanted but still mass-produced colors. Chalky black, dismal gray, sickly green, or the ever-unpopular taupe. Yes, that's precisely what Lauren felt like as she stood among the excess of Nightingale.

In front of her in line, a blonde wore more leather than a cow, with precariously placed cutouts to nix bovine comparisons. But it wasn't only the blonde. As she emerged from the vampire-esque vestibule, Lauren's heart stuttered with a pained awareness this one was not like the others.

Nightingale was of a caliber she'd never before witnessed in sleepy Burlington, Vermont.

Hair was everywhere. Big luxurious hair, shackled into waves in thrilling shades of blonde and pink, glittering black. Micro skirts were honed tools to display toned, tanned legs, ignorant to the subfreezing temperatures outside. Corsets and crop tops, and mesh. Backless jumpsuits, dresses with gaping holes in the stomach and thighs. Clothes that looked like they were held together with prayers and dreams and hundred-pound fishing line.

When old God-fearing Mrs. Luisa Lopez relayed Maddie the date information, Lauren wondered if the widow had known she was throwing Lauren into her own personal hellscape.

She laughed bitterly. Odds were high the old biddy was doing needlepoint in her glider, cackling at the thought of Lauren Peck inside Nightingale's tinted doors.

Maddie had known, was probably still laughing.

Lauren should've taken her sister up on the one-time, nonrefundable makeover.

The words echoed in her mind. "It's your first date since Eric," Maddie had said dryly. "You should put in a little effort."

Lauren hadn't heard anything over the smack of Maddie's Flamingo Pink nail polish bottle against her palm. Flinching, she'd stared in the mirror and asked, "Why put in effort for a guy I don't even know?"

"What if he's your soulmate?"

Lauren had swallowed back a snort. "Then he won't care."

"Yes, but *you* will," she'd insisted, irritation rising, bottle thumping. "You don't want this to be the look you remember ten years from now. Banana Republic khakis? Do you work at Best Buy?"

"They're Express."

"Oh sorry. I didn't know Express made depressed stepmom clothes."

Luckily, their oldest sister Kayla had leaned into the bathroom doorway to say plainly, "Back off."

A swift swell of relief came with the rescue from Maddie's constant browbeating. But then Kayla leveled hazel eyes on Lauren and said, "She's right though. You really should do something with your hair."

She *had* done something. Washed it. A feat akin to summiting Camel's Hump. Not that either of her sisters understood the task of wrangling such gnarly, frizzy curls.

Conditioner, deep conditioner, leave-in conditioner, styling mousse, Moroccan oil on the ends. Curbing it into a non-limb-devouring dirt blonde wall was harder than keeping her mouth shut about Viggo Mortensen's busted toe.

Nigh impossible.

"Do you need to use the phone?" the hostess asked when the line moved, smiling through the pain of her flawless ballerina bun. On her left boob, a name tag said *Carissa* in signature Nightingale plum, the same shade of pleated fabric dripping down the walls.

"Oh." Lauren's brows knitted together. "I have a phone." She raised her purse as evidence, unsure if she could be heard over the pulsing Chainsmokers' remix pricking at her ears. Music she'd never learned how to dance to, but everyone else had. Secret city-wide dance classes every Tuesday after Lauren went to bed to update her AO3 page.

Don't worry about me, guys. Who'd ever take me dancing anyway?

Foot tapping, she tucked a hunk of still-wet hair behind her ear. The first bit of icy panic wiggled into her stomach.

Nightingale wasn't a club exactly, but it wasn't a restaurant either. Definitely not a bar.

Bars didn't have green leather couches or medieval chandeliers, candles instead of filament.

It was gothic and quirky. Cool, in the overconfident cocky way some people wore Crocs. Disco balls shot beams of pure color at dancers, regal navy fabrics covered tables and chairs like it was Versailles in the midst of re-foiling the gold leaf.

To add to the absurdity, negronis and whiskeys and lime-accented tequila shots permeated the air, a pungent mix of overly rich liver punchers served by black silhouettes with plum name tags.

It was a place without inhibitions, which made Lauren feel very... *crepe-y*.

"Can I help you with something, then?" Carissa offered. "Or ..." She let her question drag as she clocked Lauren's cream button-down, the neat bunny-eared shoelaces. "Are you here to meet with Michael, the owner? Do you two have a meeting?"

Oh no. A sudden rush of mortification thickened Lauren's throat. One glance and Carissa assumed Lauren was here for an audit, to conduct a health inspection, interview for bookkeeper.

"No, I'm actually meeting someone." She forced her chin up as she swallowed the urge to tuck tail. "I have a date. He made a reservation. I think. Do you take reservations?"

"Oh, honey." The hostess's lovely features contorted with pity. "This is where he invited you?"

"It's a blind date," Lauren returned, shoulders dipping to suppress a cringe.

Carissa didn't hide hers. The neat fold of her silver dress seemed to revolt at the sympathetic flinch. Bending in her heels, the hostess lowered her voice. "If you need a rescue, I work until one, and I'm happy to pretend to be on the phone with a friend who has a broken leg or your sister in labor."

So it was that kind of place, that kind of man. The one who couldn't hear *uninterested*, or *no*. Needed an elaborate scheme for dismissal and evasion.

Great.

Start the countdown clock.

"Do you think I'll need it?" Lauren asked as a quiver of anxiety made her eyebrow tick. "I thought Nightingale was a restaurant. This little old lady set us up. Her husband passed away last year so I've been helping her with the yard, because she's my neighbor. Has been for ten years, and when she suggested a date—well she didn't suggest it, she commanded it—I said no. I don't want to date.

"But then she went on and on about how hard it was to be alone now that dear, dear Ricardo is dead and buried and told me love is the only thing worth living for. Obviously, I had to say yes."

"The guilt trip."

Bingo. "She did seem genuinely sad." The crux reason for Lauren's apprehensive agreement. "The trouble is she told my sister, who ratted to the whole family that I had a date. Then any chance of catching a last-minute cold or working late excuse vanished." Her hands pulled at the sunset orange sequins on her clutch.

"They're drama queens. So it's been a couple years since my last date. I'm busy."

Busy avoiding men.

"This is not a first-date place. Not for a girl like you."

Not for a girl like Lauren. Right.

She nodded, unable to form words around her pounding eardrums, and the heavy lump of expectations met threatening to choke her. A girl like Lauren was most easily explained as a girl not like Maddie or Kayla, or even Carissa, who were beautiful, eyebrows plucked into neat arches, not flat across the eye. No one would describe their hair as dingy or their elbows as rib crackers. Their waists nipped in where Lauren's was two-by-four flat, and she'd bet they never got asked if they were attending a meeting at eight on a Friday night.

"Tell me the name of the guy," Carissa said, removing an iPad from behind a wall mount and entering the passcode. "Maybe I know him."

"Yes." Quickly, Lauren grappled for the itty-bitty zipper on her—Maddie's—tiny clutch. Apparently, stuffing your pockets with crap, that is, useful everyday objects, made her ass look lumpy. Which was harsh. But also, Lauren liked the iridescent sparkle of the clutch, even if it only fit a ChapStick and credit card.

Maddie had insisted men paid on the first date.

Had Brian?

"He might have left," Lauren warned, smushing her fingers into the narrow pocket and grappling for Mrs. Lopez's note. "I'm late, because ..."

Because she'd hoped he had the patience of a gnat. Because she'd dawdled on the walk over, looped around the block, weighing the level of intolerability her sisters would be if she bailed. Conclusion: endlessly.

"Here is it," she said, ripping the cardstock's edge free to hand it over, happy to be rid of it.

A squint through the macabre, disco lighting. "Santos?" Carissa read, eyes widening. From parted lips came a short, surprised laugh. "Miles Santos." She shook her head. "That's who you're meeting?"

The shocked tone didn't stir good thoughts.

Home.

She'd go home. Put a rice and bean burrito in the microwave and eat it before the center totally unfroze as the roof of mouth seared from fake lava cheese product.

No. Already, she heard her sister's uppity voice, "You didn't even try. Do it again."

And there was no hope Maddie's selection would be any better than a maniacal neighbor's.

"Well"—Carissa laughed again, staring at the note, rereading the stumped cursive—"there's no need for a call. Not with Miles."

Because he wasn't coming?

Miracle of miracles. Wish granted. She'd been stood up.

The grin that spread her lips felt foreign, a smile of another time as excitement galloped through her. As the music took on a jovial beat, the lights became whimsical rather than intimidating.

With the smile, came a laugh. A ringing, spine-bending laugh of pure joy. Pure vindication.

Carefully, Carissa asked, "Are you alright?"

Lauren snapped her mouth shut. Right. Stoic. Lauren was known for her quiet, feckless manner. She'd taught herself to exude indifference. Forced herself, rather. Sometimes she could pretend it came naturally, as if there was no ever-brewing storm raging under her skin.

Tucking her face down, Lauren focused on low, even breaths, restricting the flare of emotion whipping to get free. Emotions. Pointless fluid things she hated having, things she wanted to snare in a net and sink to the bottom of Lake Champlain.

Disjointed lights, grating noise, the sting of the rum-soaked floor, the scratch of sequins over cold fingers. There. Better.

Being stood up. Nice. Fit squarely into her plans.

Why then did she feel unworthy, stupid, and humiliated? Why was she thinking of her nails plucking hair off Brian's beige couch, knees clenched together, back bowed. Pathetic. Obsessed. Delusional.

Her skin burned, but she wasn't warm.

Fifteen minutes into her non-date, and she was flaying, losing her discipline. Reverting back to *her*.

Forget Nightingale and Mrs. Lopez, Maddie and her ludicrous bag. Lauren blinked stinging eyes, tightened her mouth, and charged for the cold night air.

Hit a wall.

"Lauren?" a velvety smooth voice curled over her name.

Her hands rested on something hard and warm, smooth. A stomach. With a startled yelp, she yanked back, accidentally whacking said stomach with her purse.

"Sorry I'm late?" That voice, that tingling fresh spring rain on sunburned skin voice poured cement into Lauren's stomach, hardening until she couldn't think at all.

She could never have guessed the voice would belong to a devil.

But sweet Gondorian Eagles, Carissa's shocked response was warranted.

This man was not her date, could not be. He was ...

A lesson in opposites.

Alluring and threatening. A lazy, self-assured grin and a chin made to break glass. Finely handsome in the way of runway models and the kind of ruggedness that belonged on a motorcycle. No helmet.

A dark, decadent Gucci floral T-shirt. No jacket. An ornate gold cross dangling at his neck.

Observations seen and forgotten, battered aside as Lauren absorbed what lay underneath. Muscle yes. Leagues and leagues of it. But the tattoos consumed her interest. She counted seven, eight, nine, more. Swirling black lines carved over his body. Impossible to tell where they started, ended, if they made a bigger puzzle, or if the hash marks and curls were pictures all of their own.

Bold lines and delicate spirals, words and numbers, a cross, a claw, each molded to brown skin like chocolate dipped over a strawberry, filling each seed spot and hardening to a mouthwatering shine.

She followed them up his arm, under his shirt, rediscovered them poking out his collar, reaching for his neck like vines stretching up a wall, desperate to touch the sun.

Her cheeks heated, and an invisible weight tugged at her guts.

He had the sweetest face. Rich brown curls fell over his fore-head, nestled around pierced ears. Full lips. Smooth bare cheeks. A nose that might've been hard to look at if not for the crook in the middle. Dark eyes reflected the plain white of her button-down.

Absurdly, Lauren wondered if he'd gotten the tattoos after he'd had his nose readjusted. If someone had noticed just how beautiful he was and made fun of him for it. Beat him down for traversing the line between feminine and masculine beauty.

And in retaliation, with a swollen nose and black eye, Miles Santos had sat down at the nearest tattoo parlor and demanded they cover him, mark him.

Needle jagged edges to his petals.

"Do you like what you see?" His voice, the flare of smug amuse-ment, the wicked confidence, sliced through the technopop to wrap around her, cloak her in warmth, slow the pulse in her throat.

Speed it up.

From behind them, Carissa cooed, "Miles."

Lauren jolted free of her gawking, closing her mouth, pushing away from his chest.

She was acting like she'd never seen a man before. Like a gooey-brained princess. Like she'd never learned. Never felt drag-on's teeth on her ankle. Heart racing, she stumbled back further. The floor went out from underfoot. A stair.

Miles caught her, held her steady without pulling her closer. In fact, he barely looked at her.

"Carissa," he purred, using his free arm to wrap around the hostess's small waist. Kiss her cheek.

As he easily balanced two women, Lauren felt a spike of ice center her, knock her out of her admiring haze.

Carissa tapped his cheek, a little too close to the mouth. "Miles," she repeated. "I told you I got a new job."

The devil smiled, smoothing the collar of Carissa's dress between his fingers. "The color suits you."

He was still holding Lauren's forearm, grip sure but gentle. Hand warm. Tattoos there too. Sneaking down his hand, reaching for his fingers.

That wasn't what held her stare.

Intersecting white scars riddled his knuckles.

On top were cuts, still raw and open, pink patches struggling to close.

No. This was not a man for a girl like Lauren.

Burrito time.

Carissa unwound from Miles, folded Mrs. Lopez's note and handed it to Lauren. "I have just the table for you two."

"Oh actually." Lauren wiggled out of Miles's hold to address Carissa. "Weren't you just saying that my sister called, and I had to—"

"No," the hostess returned sharply, eyes bright in the glow of betrayal.

Lauren felt all four wheels of the bus trample her back. "Then maybe I could borrow your phone."

"Sorry. It's not for customers," Carissa returned, chin upturned, prepared to parry any escape attempts.

Between the reed-like hostess and Miles's intimidating frame, Lauren was herded to an ink-blue suede couch, rectangular cushions tufted, hugged low to the floor. In front of it, the stout dark stone table looked to double as a footrest.

Miles sat first, knees spread indecently wide, draping thick arms along the back edge with the bearing of a king.

"Sit down." Carissa pressed knuckles into Lauren's shoulder, tone sharp.

Struggling to bend in her stiff pants, Lauren's hips creaked as she collapsed next to her date. *Date.*

Don't lose it; don't you dare lose it.

"Something to drink?" Carissa asked, suddenly amenable.

Lauren turned and found her date's attention pinned over his shoulder, staring at the dancers, dark gaze sorting them into mental yeses and noes. In Lauren's case: charity projects.

"Champagne," he ordered, watching a redhead gyrate in the strobe. "We'll split the nicest bottle."

"Only the best for you."

Then the traitor was gone.

And Lauren Peck was on a date. With a man. With tattoos. A man who ordered for her. A man who had yet to look at her. Even when he turned, he avoided her, following Carissa through the throng of bodies, hanging on every swing of her hips.

Vomit.

Is this some kind of weird foreplay? she wanted to ask. *Are you two the actual couple? And tonight you're pretending to be strangers to reignite a long-lost spark?* How long before Lauren was a voyeur in their twisted sexcapade?

Miles's arm slid across the soft fabric to trail a finger up her shoulder. "Lauren."

That voice. She winced, pulled away like he was dangling a worm in front of her. SOS. She'd send an SOS. Her fingers dug into her clutch, wrapped around her phone.

No.

No, she couldn't. That was for emergencies. She was twenty-six, she could stick out a bad date. Survi ved worse, she thought ruefully, no hibachi grill to burn her hair on. Again.

A pause. A chuckle. "Jumpy," Miles noted.

Lauren stiffened, reined in the storm.

"You didn't answer my question, Lauren."

Question? "We haven't even introduced ourselves."

He grinned at that, like the bite in her tone was flirty, not intimidating. Bending forward to plant elbows on his knees, he offered his hand. "Miles." When it was clear she wouldn't shake, he made a fist, knuckles straining. "I presume, since you sat with me and look exactly like the type of woman my Tia would want me to date, that you are Lauren."

What type? she hungered to ask, but that implied she cared what people thought, invited judgment, conversation. Lauren straightened the pleat running down her calf. "*Tia* means 'aunt'?" Why did she think German would be useful in high school?

"Yes. But we aren't quite related. At least, not by blood." A smile again, straight white teeth.

Champagne glasses appeared in front of them, Carissa's gentle touch uncorking a green bottle without a sacrificial drop. She poured with flourish, letting bubbles fizz and hiss before depositing the cloth-wrapped bottle in an ice bucket to chill. No words. A shadow.

Really committing to the ruse.

"Will you answer now?" Miles asked, sounding smug as he set a glass on her knee, left her to catch it from falling.

Palms awkward on the thin flute, Lauren lamented the sparkle caught in her grip. "I don't drink champagne."

Rather than rile him, Miles seemed intrigued by her rejection. "Lauren," he mock chided. "Your hesitation is giving me a complex. Answer the question."

Her nose tickled, her annoyance expanding. "You haven't asked one."

"Do you like what you see?"

Could he be more vapid? Lucky for him, with the storm on permanent lock out, she didn't throw her drink in his face. Just sent him a cold up-down. "What if I said no? You don't look good."

"Then I'd pay the bill, and we'd part ways. No point in a date without some initial sexual attraction." Not a hint of anger laced his tone. Too cocky for that, too assured of his sex appeal. "Can't say we didn't try."

An out. Agree and she could—"No point?" she heard herself ask. "What about connection or love?"

"Love corrodes," he returned simply, rising to stand. "Nice meeting you. Drinks are on me."

"Wait. Stop." She grabbed his arm, spilling bubbly on her thigh. "I like it. Don't leave." She felt the muscles around her mouth tighten with frustration. At herself. He'd given her a clear out. Why'd she keep trampling them, speeding past the exit?

To her luck, he didn't argue, didn't comment, just laid his intense stare on her hand over his forearm. She flinched, yanking away. Clingy.

New record.

Eyes lingering on the spot she touched, she watched a flash of confusion erode his cocksure attitude. Less than a second, then he was next to her, closer than before, lifting his glass. "To liking the view."

She nicked her flute against his and abandoned it.

His glass stopped short of his mouth. "It's bad luck not to drink after a toast."

"I'm not thirsty."

"A sip."

"I don't want to."

"It's not spiked," he argued, glaring at her glass on the table, careful demeanor shedding. "Drink mine if you want. I'll order a new bottle and you can slug from the rim."

"No, thank you." She was careful to enunciate every syllable.

"A taste."

A muscle under her eye spasmed. Lightning struck her chest. She dug fingers into the suede, feeling individual hairs flick the vulnerable skin under her nails. "No."

"No?" he asked angrily, stretching a hand to her. "Seven years of bad luck because of 'no'?" He pressed his glass to her lips. "One drink."

Two outs. And now this. "Listen to me, I said no!" The words left on a determined burst as she shoved him, sprayed champagne across his face.

"*Dios*, what is—"

"I'm not being fucking coy," she snarled, thunder in her voice. "I'm asthmatic. The bubbles mess with my lungs and my inhaler didn't fit in my bag. Stop asking or I'll figure out how to stuff your detached balls into the sequins."

CHAPTER TWO

A TENSE MOMENT PASSED. Balls and sequins. Miles gave the threat points for creativity. And delivery. Words flung with weight.

He rubbed a hand down his face. "I am completely fucking this up, aren't I?"

He watched as his date smoothed thin hands down her pants, as if Martha Stewart was about to emerge from the toilet with a steamer, searching for legs to burn. Irritation had caused the tips of her ears to redden, but at least she was no longer a robot caught in a feedback loop. Inhaling, exhaling, the occasional blink.

A human only in technical terms.

"You're what?" she asked, voice back to monotone.

Thanks, Tia, what a catch.

"This date," Miles explained, wondering how the explosion and the robot coexisted beneath all that starch. Was it just wires and frayed ends? "It's going tits up, right?"

Her nose scrunched. "Tits up?"

"Do you feel romanced?" he asked rhetorically. "Do you even want to be here?"

She blinked.

"Fuck." Miles tossed back the rest of his champagne and took her glass for a repeat down the hatch. He wasn't much of a drinker. Then again, he wasn't much of a dater. Especially not with uptight bureaucrats like Lauren.

Tia Luisa overdosed on horchata setting this up.

And now he was fucked. He couldn't give another ditch attempt with the black cloud hanging over his head.

Seven years bad luck, all his busting ass, his investments, he'd be off the team and still suffering with seven years. Shit. He poured himself a generous topper. Would a fake sneeze and a chilled splash of Perignon on her lip count as a drink?

Thoughts of a splash zone radius receded, drowned by an intoxicating scent. Sweet and heady. Somewhat floral. What was that? He peered down the end of his glass to Lauren, eyes flat, lips drawn. And his stomach clenched.

Her?

"I'm sorry," he said, leaning in, trying to pinpoint the delicious fragrance. "You're allergic?"

"Asthmatic," she corrected.

Yes floral. He blinked in surprise, blood heating. An illogical reaction, potent enough to plant odd thoughts in his head. He pulled back to look at her, cocking his head. Dark blonde hair getting larger with each passing moment, sticking out at her ears, her hairline. Light lashes, sea glass irises. Bland but citrus. There was citrus in the smell. Layer after layer he uncovered, intoxicating.

"I'm sorry," he repeated, feeling himself staring. Unable to stop. "I didn't know. I thought—I didn't know."

He'd thought she was being purposely difficult. Fitful. He'd thought she was having a snit because he hadn't asked her what she wanted or taken her to the right place.

Nightingale was by no means high-end.

But he'd had to come. Had to see Carissa. Carissa, yeah, and the bad luck. Fuck. He cast the utterly feminine perfume from his mind, though it lingered in the cracks, a constant enthrall.

He signaled Carissa with the flick of two fingers. An adept server, she was at their table before his hand hit his knee, smiling coquettishly, not a hair out of place.

"Lauren needs a drink."

Move back, he ordered himself, *slide away. She's not for you.*

His knee brushed Lauren's. He forced himself to focus, to pay attention.

Carissa was nodding, and Miles noticed she had a bit more meat on her bones, more color in her cheeks. "A different bottle? We have a California sparkling rosé that is very sweet—"

"No carbonation," Miles interrupted.

"Water," Lauren said, voice free of the spray of fire, back to a stilted whisper. "That's all I need."

His knee jumped. "No, we can't do water. Water's bad luck. What about a rum and Coke?"

"Carbonated."

"A mojito?" Carissa proposed.

"No."

"Is there anything you can have?" Points to him that he didn't add, *you difficult, contrary, exasperating woman.*

Eyes the color of wilted iceberg lettuce leveled him. "Water." Prim as a dagger at his jugular.

"Juice," Carissa mediated. "Peach juice. Sweet and refreshing."

"Juice," Miles seconded. "Something."

The downward curve of Lauren's mouth deepened. "Fine. I'll take a double vodka with lemon over ice."

He and Carissa flinched at the same time. From abstinence straight to a death sentence.

"There was that so hard?" he gritted as Carissa flitted away. Reminded himself to move the fuck away.

Sank deeper into the cushions, slugged more bubbly. A third-no fourth refill.

"Would've been easier if I could have water."

"You're on a date, don't drink water."

"And what a date it is. Will you be in my lap by the time my drink comes?"

Shit. He folded his big body away. Two hundred and eighty pounds of muscle was never subtle. "Sorry," he muttered, wanting to kick himself. "And the water—I'm—I'm a little superstitious."

Her response was a single brow arch.

"Fine," he admitted, voice like a growl. "More than a little. But you could have just explained you didn't want champagne before the toast."

"Oh yes," she quipped acerbically. "I had so much time to express myself between answering how hot you are and getting plied with liquor."

"Fucking hell."

"My sentiments exactly." She rubbed at her forehead, and he imagined a headache there big enough to rival his.

A long moment thundered by in silence. She flicked her eyes over him. "Love corrodes? Really? It's a first date."

"You'd rather I lie?" He scratched his jaw and filled his cheeks with champagne. Dry, bitter, but crisp as it slid down the back of his throat. Refreshing in the stuffy heat of the club.

She must be boiling in here, he thought wryly. Only her hands and face clear of thick fabric, not a single button undone on her shirt. *Good.* He mused childishly. *Roast.*

He didn't even want to be here. But now he was stuck, at least until she drank, until the curse lifted.

"Mrs. Lopez said you were looking for someone serious."

In that case, she'd hit the nail on the head with Lauren. Shit, his Tia would kill him if she knew how badly he was butchering this.

He'd warned her, told her no, he didn't date. Didn't want to. It wasn't like that for him. There was no woman-shaped hole in his life.

"Tia will maim me if I do this wrong," he admitted. "She hustled me into this, crying, holding her wedding photo. But I'm not good at it. I don't date much, especially not women like you."

A dark shadow moved across her face so quickly he wondered if he imagined it. "Then, you're not looking for—"

"Anything," Miles filled in. "Nothing. I want to tell Tia I tried and never speak of it again."

Her lips pursed and for all of his supposed observation skills, it was the first time he noticed her mouth was quite nice. A dark pink that didn't smudge when she chewed on her lip. "I don't for one second believe that."

He poured the last drops of the bottle into his glass to make a sad piddle of fizz. "It's true. When Tia suggested this, I thought she was pulling my leg. But she was very adamant about us getting together." He dragged a hand through his hair, drew her eye. "Which makes me wonder if she should be put in a home."

"Definitely not interested in love then?"

"No." Vehement no.

"What about long-term commitment? Marriage? What about kids, and vow renewals, matching gravestones? None of it appeals to you?"

"Oh, marriage," he trilled sardonically. "Yes. A legally binding contract to force two people to stay together or burn in hell. No. No to all of it." Like it mattered. He was going to hell regardless.

"You act like it's a choice," she returned, an oddly light edge filling out her voice. "Who would marry you? Cocky, assertive, self-absorbed, you think loudly stating your opinion is acceptable because you call it the truth."

She snorted. And the sharp discordant sound reeled him in.

"Said the woman who saw me and immediately tried to bail." He caught her perfume again, stronger, as he leaned over to taunt her. "How long between seeing the ink and your tragic escape was it? Two seconds? Three?"

Her eyes rolled, but then ... then that sweet, plump mouth transformed into a smile. Soft and pink. Not a stitch of makeup. Which meant that dusty rose of her lips was her, the vibrant shade enchanting, lighter at the high cupid's bow, darker in the center of her bottom lip.

When she smiled, he understood why Tia Luisa picked her for him. The curly dark blonde hair, round sea glass eyes, lips like a sunrise. Despite trying to hide it, Lauren was pearl earrings and faded watercolors beautiful, an elegance made for a gilded frame and murmured admirations. A canvas of old hung in a private gallery left untitled. No words able to capture the simple allure of each feature. The sum greater than its parts.

Plus she had the Catholic show-no-skin-unless-you-want-to-be-a-harlot thing down pat. Drab black pants dragged on the floor, an ill-fitting button-up, with the wrists clasped tightly, collar licking her throat. Even her shoes were lumpy and anonymous.

She chipped clear nail polish off her thumb.

Miles scratched his chin. Around them there was laugher, come-ons, hooting, thumping music, the hiss of the windows trembling. Noise. Crushing noise and he still felt the urge to fill the air between them.

"So," he said, saving the last of his Dom. "You work in an office?" A guess, based on ... everything about her.

"Yes. I'm the building manager for City Hall."

"Wow, that's—"

"Boring," Lauren interjected, saving him from a flat-out lie. "Dead end, hopeless, fill in the blank."

"Do you like it?" he asked stupidly. How much longer before—

Carissa floated by on an invisible breeze, dropping Lauren's vodka and spinning away before her grin turned into a laugh.

No doubt she thought it was hilarious he was here on a date. Miles Santos dating.

An oxymoron.

"The work is work." Lauren lifted a shoulder and let it drop, pointer finger teasing the rim of the crystal glass. "My coworkers are mostly nice."

He drank.

They sat.

Music, dancing, laughter. Life.

Between them, it was so uncomfortable a vacuum formed, air fleeing.

Drink, he thought viciously, *drink the disgusting vodka you ordered so I can find Carissa and leave.*

"Work is work," she said and then her face dropped into her hands. A groan rose from her hunched form. "Nice. Clever. Inspiring. No wonder I'm alone," she hissed to herself, tone dark and lethal.

With a jolt, she snagged her lowball glass, bit into the lemon wedge and drank back the double. No breath.

Average height. She had to be one thirty soaking wet. Another drink and he'd be carrying her to the car.

Eyes glistening from the burn of alcohol, she wheezed. Coughed, and then word vomited to him, "This is my first date in two years, and I wore a button-down." A terrifying laugh. "And you're my date!"

In a state of pure fear, Miles stared, unsure how to respond. Escalation seemed mean. Agreeing to the button-down disaster cruel. He flicked the stem of his flute. "We've established how unappealing you find me, but please go on."

"Please"—she chuckled, tapping the end of his nose with her free hand. Cold—"it's not that. We both know you're painfully handsome."

Smiling again, long lashes fluttering, beckoning his deeper into the endless green of her gaze. Why had he wanted to leave? The tip of her tongue wet her lips, she leaned closer. "Too handsome," she told him.

"And you're a lightweight."

"I just"—she drew a finger between her third button and his gold cross—"us? You and me? What was Mrs. Lopez thinking? Have you ever even worn a button-down?"

"For work."

"What do you do?" Her head tilted further. Soon she'd be upside down. "Bounty hunter? Skydive instructor? No. Assistant manager at Arby's?"

He caught her arm to steady her before she was counting the cork dents on the ceiling. Yes. A lightweight. Miles felt a smile spread. "I'm a running back."

She stared at his hand on her for a long moment and then frowned at her empty glass. Shook her head. "Am I drunk? Is that like a bag boy or—"

"Yes, you are." He led her upright, ended up close again, inhaling. Drunk. Yes. Him too. Had to be. "And I'm a football player. I play for the Vermont Mountaineers. I'm the starting running back. Lucky number seven."

An extended silence.

"What the hell was your aunt thinking?" She was laughing again. Full-on, spit-flying, hair-puffing laughing.

In brief, it was not at all how he expected the night to unfold. He'd anticipated banter, seduction, an invite back to her place that he would decline like a well-heeled gentleman.

Dios forbid Tia accidentally hear about his exploits.

Then he'd wipe his hands of this gap in his routine. Forget Lauren, make sure Carissa had a ride home and properly fuck off. Mandatory date complete.

He'd thought he'd been coerced, but Lauren had been hogtied and dragged inside. Perhaps she wasn't completely uptight, but just unwilling.

He leaned back as he finished his glass. She did look quite like a clerk. A jaded IRS agent or a bank teller approaching postal.

And she probably had no idea he made enough money last weekend to buy Nightingale and everyone in it. Had no idea the power laced in his bones.

Hell, she'd literally been repelled by the sight of him.

Did a more ill-suited pair exist?

"Hobbies?" she asked airily, leaning to match him and watch pink and blue beams cross. Shoulders scrunched, her spine took on an awkward curve on the couch, caved her stomach, pushed up her hips and thighs. No sexual arch, no suggestive stretch.

Carissa delivered a fresh vodka lemon and removed the empty bottle of champagne.

Miles caught the glass and set it in Lauren's cold hand as he scooted closer to her. Wanting to peel her back more, find what Tia had on her.

The perfume was her hair, saturated in exotic flowers and—lemon. Her hands smelled like lemons too. Had she drunk before coming? Or did she like lemon on everything?

"Hobbies," he repeated, thinking, examining her profile, the jut of her nose, a rounded chin. "I like working out."

She nodded.

"Hanging with friends."

Another nod.

"Going out."

Her smile grew to a grin.

"What?" he asked defensively. "What's so funny? You don't approve?"

She sucked her teeth, shrugged. "I think those are great hobbies."

"Yours are better, is that it?" He twisted to rest on an elbow, watching her squeeze lemon into the clear liquid, juice making fog clouds behind the glass. "Tell me them."

"Hmm." Her head dropped back on the couch, trapping her hair, exposing a small line of exposed white skin at her throat. "I like to write *Lord of the Rings* fan fiction. I like doing 5Ks and 10Ks. Bonus points if they're for a good cause. Not running though. I'm not a runner. Just walking. I sit all day. Oh, you know what's the best, my favorite thing?"—fingers gently caressed her heart—"walking around barefoot right after you vacuum."

Drunk.

Hammered maybe.

"You know"—their gazes locked, clashed—"real hobbies."

Challenged. His traitorous heart skipped a beat. "Wow. You really put me in the deep end right away." His cheeks hurt from smiling. "What's fan fiction?"

"Exactly what it sounds like. Fiction for fans. I take characters from the movies and put them into my own stories. Usually in an alternate universe." She sipped this time, pouring eighty proof down her throat. "It's very embarrassing and I very much enjoy it."

"And then you publish it into a book?"

"Hell no," she exclaimed, her expression aghast. "I don't even use my real name for any of it. I don't tell anyone."

He held still, waiting for her to realize the misstep. When she only drank more, he pointed out, "Except me."

She waved indifferently, chin on her sternum, sitting like she was in the back of a darkened movie theater chomping popcorn, not at a VIP table in Vermont's most popular nightclub.

"Tell me, honestly," she said seriously. "Do you think we'll ever cross paths again? Do you think tomorrow you'll even remember my name? No. We both agreed to the date. You've said there's no chance for more. Well, I agree, and I don't see the point in pretending I'm not who I am. I just don't have the energy today." She nodded to him. "Go again. What are your real hobbies?"

Something about the freed look glowing from the gentle green irises seemed to strip Miles of his eagerness to leave.

It was unsettling. Fascinating.

He should be watching Carissa, making sure she was safe, happy, scoping the place out for sketchy suspects. Worrying about his girls, their well-being. Not getting tipsy with an insurance agent.

Skating his knuckles across his bottom lip, he smiled. "Alright." He cleared his throat. "I like having sex. A lot."

"Revolutionary."

She thought him simple, plain? "I like winning fights. Especially when I'm outnumbered. Especially when they take the defeat hard."

"One more," she said, watching his hand fist into a tight ball.

He eased off, glanced at his scar-laden hands and then down at his shitkicker black boots. Understood the image he cast. An image he'd honed to be intimidating to men, approachable to women. A fine line. "OK, I like to eat standing over my kitchen sink like a gremlin sneaking food."

"Oh, I do that one too." A throaty chuckle. "It's so sad when one of my sisters walks in and gives me the lecture about how too much sodium is going to kill me."

"Sisters?"

"Three." A saccharine smile he knew well. "We live together. Our parents left us the house when they became snowbirds."

"I'm liking this," Miles confessed, adjusting until they were both resting on their shoulders, face-to-face. The music and lights and clang of drinks acting like a personal veil of privacy. "Ask me another question."

"Biggest fear?"

"Losing a fight."

She made a face. "No. It's finding someone in the shower when you pull back the curtain and you're already naked."

"Crocodile in the toilet."

"Cliché." She tsked. "Dream date?"

"We're on a beach—"

"Awful!"

His jaw dropped in feigned offense. "What's wrong with the beach?"

"I could list a thousand reasons. Sand, sunscreen, sweat, wet hair. Seeing each people in what's essentially their underwear."

"You're getting naked eventually, why not make it easier?"

"Not all of us want our bodies to be on the table for discussion day one. He needs to know me better before he's subjected to all this." Her hands moved wildly over her body, like she was marking a bad rash.

"Subjected?"

She nodded firmly. "Subjected."

Staring at her disgruntled face, he felt an argument brim his lips, a rebuttal to change "subjected" to "honored." But this wasn't a date. He cleared his throat. "Can I get back to my date now?"

"Go on. Tell me your dream. Tell me my nightmare."

Cankerous woman. "Beach. Picnic with checkered blanket. I teach her how to surf. We spend hours sharing the same wide board until her thighs ache. Come back. Eat. Sex, right on top of the food."

"Seagulls would watch you do it and the ants—I can't even begin to talk ants."

"What's yours, stick in the mud?"

She finished her glass, cheeks darkening. "I can't tell you now."

"Why not?" Now he had to know. He leaned forward, eager. "It's lame, isn't it? What's the opposite of the beach?" he wondered aloud, pulling on sluggish nerve endings. "You attend a public forum together?"

"Concert in the park," she corrected smartly. "It's free on Thursdays in the summer. I'll concede to a checkered blanket. But no food. Just a bottle of wine."

"Duh." Miles hit his forehead. "You can drink wine. We should've ordered wine."

"We'd drink wine," she continued like he'd never spoken. "Listen to music, sit together, and feel the warm breeze. It'd be relaxing and romantic."

"A date where you don't talk. I thought you were into 'connections'?" He made air quotes and her lips pursed again. And he thought he liked them the least that way. "Favorite food?"

Lauren didn't hesitate. "Buffalo mac 'n' cheese."

"Band?"

"Miley Cyrus."

"Season?"

"Fall."

They looked at each other. Her hair knotted up at her neck as she turned on it, a smile slowly unwinding. "What?"

His gaze moved gently over her bewildered features. "Tamales, Black Bear, summer." He shared a slow smile. "Do you think we should tell my Tia she's the worst matchmaker in the history of the world?"

"Nobody's this bad. Maybe it's a prank. She's in the crowd right now. Disguised." Her eyes glittered with amusement. "The bro with the fake gold chain."

He should be tracking the staff, ferreting out dark corners, sweeping the back rooms. Instead he was laughing, drinking with a woman he had—down to every atom—nothing in common with.

"Do you want another drink?"

Lauren twisted, brown eyebrows lifting, as if surprised to find she'd finished hers.

"No." She pushed up sloppily, fingers gripping the couch. "I don't know why, but I thought we would be having dinner, so I haven't eaten. And I think if I stand, I'll pitch forward into your crotch."

"Dream date."

A sharp laugh shot from her throat.

Miles felt an odd, pleasant chill coax the steel in his spine. "I'm sorry, I did this wrong. Dinner would've been smart, but I don't know any places around here."

A hand wave, fingers colliding, catching on her wild mane. "It's fine," she assured, swaying slightly in her seat as she checked the time on her phone. Frowned.

"Are you late for something?"

"Early," she groused, puffing out a breath. "I told my sisters I wouldn't be back until midnight."

Midnight. He could suffer her until midnight. "I do know one place," he said. "We could go as friends."

"We're not friends. We're pawns on Luisa's chessboard." She bit into her lemon, prying the rind free. Ate it. "Hungry pawns."

Miles found his feet and swayed. Shit. "Come on." He took Lauren's hand in his. "It's close, I won't let anything happen to you."

CHAPTER THREE

NOT A RESTAURANT. NOT a bar. Not even another club.

A strip club.

The first thing Lauren did was search for the flashing red exit sign. She'd been an odd duck in Nightingale; in Pink Persuasion, Lauren was a fish on Mars.

A slightly drunk fish on Mars. And the vodka was working magic trimming the smug corners off her date.

But she'd need a hose of Grey Goose to shine this.

She lived with three women—three—and she'd never seen so many boobs. Not one alike. Purple glitter pasties, double-stick tape red hearts, tassels, strings—a pair were covered just by an arm. That's it. Like she'd forgotten she had nipples and was Mac-gyver-ing.

It smelled like body odor and hairspray.

Having oh-so-generously paid the cover charge, Miles guided Lauren to a linoleum table with stairs at the end. An extra-special gleaming silver pole perched right where the ketchup ought to sit.

Was this real? Had she thrown back the second vodka, stepped outside and smacked her head on black ice? Were medics asking her what year it was?

"Wake up," she hissed under a stream of DJ announcements.

"Next to stage, Poppy Rocker."

Pink Persuasions' only redeeming quality was its worst quality. No privacy. She could see every dark wall, every table with the turn of her head.

Smaller than Nightingale. No less crowded. Tables spilled over, foldable chairs ran two rows deep along the main raised stage. Pitbull played as Birdie ended her show grinding a phallic-shaped balloon in a gold bikini. A black spiked collar with chains stretching to her hands.

How did she wipe with that?

She'd ask Miles during her speech about the plight of women's rights and the true dark core of sexist fantasies. That is, if she could get a word in edgewise.

Hand secure on her elbow, he greeted every passing body, every beer-guzzler, each bowling-shirted, glazed-eye pervert by name. Voice a dark roll, stern, brisk as he led Lauren determinedly forward. Like a principal stalking through the cafeteria, singling out the reprobates.

"Don." Miles nodded, stopping Lauren to let a parade of slutty mechanics wiggle by. "Brandy, Cindy, Jem." He used a softer tone for the dancers, a gentler look that didn't rove from well-contoured faces. "Capri, Jade, Meadow."

Smiles poured in. Choruses of "Hi there, Miles." Purrs of approval, whispers of longing. Hands dusted his chest, patted his shoulders. Lingered.

Bad had shot past worst to the eighth circle in a ten-minute walk.

Stupidly, drunkenly, she'd thought they'd reached an understanding. They weren't compatible but they could make the best of it.

His making the best of it was ruling his kingdom of humping naked women while Lauren's stomach ate its lining. As she bounced across the plastic seat cover of booth 12B, she checked the time.

Ninety minutes.

Rather than allow her a semblance of personal space, Miles sat his hulking, tattooed body right beside hers, sending her shoulder into the bumpy black wall. From the stage, trapped behind his bulk, no one would guess she was with him.

Clever asshole.

Again, before Lauren could voice dissent, use her nature-made rib crackers, a redhead smacked cardboard Heady Topper coasters on the table. She was dressed as a maid without a skirt. No obvious cleaning products.

"I thought you weren't coming in tonight." Her tone was not that of a maid caught with her pants down but a truck-stop waitress, harsh, judgmental, too familiar.

"Change of plans," Miles told her, stretching back to reveal Lauren. "Chasity, this is Lauren."

"Miles," Chasity hissed. "You didn't."

"We're hungry and I don't know a place with better fried chicken. Could you please get us two buffet wristbands?"

"I should get a magazine to swat you with." Her lips barely moved as she spoke, nostrils flaring. A jerk of her chin and blue eyes pinned Lauren. "Hey, baby girl, can I get you a drink?"

Trying not to look directly at Chasity's black bow tie areolas, Lauren croaked, "Water."

No more drinking. Another drink and she'd be participating in an underground fight club, stealing dolphins from Sea World.

Would it be worse to hold a wet leash?

There'd be no lasciviously looming men, dirty green bills crumpled in clammy hands waiting to grope any who dare to claim it. Disgusting.

Revolting. She felt her stomach turn.

Born and raised in Burlington, Lauren had steered clear of Pinks since conception. The only quote, unquote gentlemen's club in Vermont, she walked past it daily for work, avoiding her reflection in its blackout windows.

Red hair bobbing, Chasity delivered two waters, muttering to Miles as she caressed ample cleavage, "Millie didn't come in today."

He nodded acknowledgment, jaw tight, passing her a twenty for the turndown service.

For a man who didn't date, he certainly got around. Carissa, Chasity, Millie ...

Like you're surprised? Look at him.

Even stumbling through a haze of tipsy edges, Lauren's pulse registered the hard body beside hers, the subtle flex in his bicep as he gripped his cup, his thigh warm and thick. She dipped her gaze to his hands and slowly, inexorably imagined the warmth of his grip on her bare skin, gliding along her waist, fingers like hot stones on her numb skin, palm a furnace, he'd cup—

"You stay here," he told Lauren as Pitbull's greatest hits played. "I'll make you a big plate. Don't leave the table."

Any warm feelings evaporated.

Lamentable that he was too good-looking to have a personality to wet his whistle.

"I can get my own food."

"I don't want you walking around here. It's not safe."

Funny. This might be the safest place for her. She was invisible next to the sexy player and voodoo seductress.

"I'll be fine."

Miles's wide hand came down on her thigh, pinned her. Plastic creaked. He smelled like oversweet sugar, as if he'd already acclimated to the cloud of body spray.

"No," he repeated, fingers crushing the pleat of her slacks. "You'll stay here where I can see you. These men are animals and ..." Midnight eyes dropped for a fraction, held on her mouth of all places. The energy between them changed, shifted from reluctant seatmates to ... to something yearning.

She flushed red, had to close her eyes and turn her head away.

Vodka goggles. *Quit drinking on an empty stomach.*

He stood, cleared his throat, straightened his cross. "You'll stay."

"Why did you bring me here if it's dangerous?"

"You're hungry and this is the only place I've eaten at in Burlington."

"What? You've been in town for a day?"

"A little over a year."

She made a small noise in the back of her throat. Surprise and disgust rolled into one.

"I have my priorities," he said dryly. "Really the food's not bad. Though, I wouldn't recommend the salad bar; I never know if it's Caesar dressing or—"

"I lost my appetite." And any remaining hope for eating salad.

"What are we at?" he asked as she checked her phone. "Eighty minutes? That's when you're free of me?"

More like free of her sisters' interminable nagging, but yes—she nodded.

"Come on," Miles said in that velvet voice, the voice that got Lauren drunk and whisked her into a nude bar. He stood and spread tattooed hands on either side of the pole.

An apt picture, Lauren thought ruefully.

"We can get along for an hour." He almost sounded reasonable. "Listen to the music, indulge in the tap water. Jade makes the cheesecake, but you can eat around the glitter." A smirk.

Her lips thinned. "Why do you come here?"

"I'm kidding about the glitter. I found one blue hair, one time, and I have a slice every night."

Every night? Lauren's mind swam. "I don't get it. You've got money, you're a good-looking guy. When you're not trying to kill me, you're tolerable adjacent. Why hang out in a sketchy strip club?"

"Why does anyone?" He let his attention drag to the stage.

She scoffed. "You don't need to pay to see anyone naked."

"I like a certain type."

"Uninhibited?" she guessed, stifling the urge to undo her buttons. Rather, she pressed the one against her throat, checking her fortifications.

"No," Miles replied carefully, taking her collar and popping it, offering her the smallest bit of extra coverage. "Emotionally unavailable."

Dear God, they really were the worst match possible.

Lauren collapsed back in the seat, ignored the smell of sweat and closed her eyes. "I went on a date," she said, tugging on her empty belt loops. "Back in high school, before—" She stopped. Cursed herself. Tried again.

"On our way to dinner, he stopped at his friend's house." Her eyes opened to find him tilted in, hanging on her words. "He left me in the car, got ridiculously high for a half hour and when he came back, he said they'd split a pizza and asked if I could drive myself home. And honestly, I had more fun on that date."

Miles seemed to swallow hard, the cocky puff of his chest falling. "I can't be that bad."

"What's a stronger, more negative way to say we have nothing in common."

"Opposites," he answered, eyes bouncing to the stage. Glowing lights lit his teeth as he moved, revealed the curve of a cocky smile. "You know what they say about opposites." A flash of a grin. "Chicken or cheesecake?"

Lauren sighed. Seventy more minutes. "When in Rome."

She didn't watch him leave but felt it, felt the energy of the room cling and follow him. Strip from her. Her finger hovered over those two letters on her phone.

Was it worth it? To pry her sisters from their warm beds. To destroy her first opportunity in months to get them off her back.

One week.

She wanted to go one single week without the question, "Aren't you over him, yet?"

No questions. No speaking looks. No pity. The thought conjured a wave of anticipatory relief. She could stick it out, she decided as Miles returned.

She might not like him, but the stuffy stagnant air loved him, it coated him in a breeze that said, if shit goes down, I'll get you out.

He sat. Thighs touching. Sixty minutes.

The chicken, Lauren suspected, was from KFC. As were the biscuits, and the cheesecake was surprisingly tart. Fresh cherries in the drizzle. With Miles's bulk beside her, peeling the skin off his drumsticks, Lauren couldn't see the stage or cash or wandering hands.

Not that she wanted to of course.

Ha. The way she leaned, spread over the table for a glimpse each time Miles stuffed cash into glittery, perfumed fingers, was losing its subtly.

She waited, but there was no lap dance. No polished nails on the pole, no service for Miles's payments.

Thirty minutes.

She licked her fork clean. "So—" She reached blindly for a benign, time-consuming topic. "Where are you from?"

Biffed it.

"Raised in LA. Played ball in Vegas."

Full, tired, a little tipsy, she rested against him, head on his shoulder, hair tickling her mouth. "Hot."

"Thanks." He nudged her with his elbow. "I didn't think I'd miss Vegas, but do I. Twenty-four-hour strip clubs. Showgirls. And that's just what's above board, I hardly had a spare moment."

"I give up," Lauren groaned. "Let's do the last twenty minutes in silence."

"Why not leave? You got your food. Ride stops here. I'm not inviting you home." He didn't sound mean but part of her died.

"As if I'd say yes," she snapped.

"Why are you still here, Lauren, when you've done nothing but stare at the exit and check the time? I'm not holding you hostage. Climb on over if you want out."

She'd really rather die than traverse his powerful thighs. "Because I need to be able to tell my sisters I tried, to stop them from mentioning my descent into spinsterhood or a lifetime of loneliness."

"Being alone doesn't mean you're lonely."

She stared at him like he'd turned water into wine. The first non-misogynistic, non-self-absorbed thing he'd said. "I agree," she admitted, wiping her thumb around the Fiddlehead label on her water. "The only thing a man has ever done for me was make me question myself."

"Then on behalf of all men, allow me to apologize." He twisted, fingers rapping on the plastic seat back, dark eyes drifting down the line of her jaw. "Sands running out. We're almost done. What are you going to tell your sisters? Men are still trash?"

"I'm leaving nothing out. My date flirted with our hostess, tried to poison me, brought me to a strip club buffet where he spent upward of a grand."

White teeth sank into his bottom lip, his voice coming out sheepish. "How much of that can I blame on nerves?"

"Zero," she returned flatly. "But it's good." The more she thought about it ... "Actually, it's perfect. You've proven my point wonderfully. Men and me do not mix."

"You've served your sentence gallantly. Our time's up." He slid out from booth 12B and offered his hand for the second time.

This time, she took it, marveling at the warmth buried in every bend of skin. "Wait."

Oh God, was she going to do it? Could she? Her stomach twisted, a red heat scored up her throat. She had to do it. Last nail in the coffin.

"There's one more thing," she told his back as he escorted her between cocktail tables, held open the door.

The bitter winter night slapped her cheeks, stole her breath and luck have it, extinguished her nerves. She spun, a shiver already wracking her frame. "We need to kiss."

Pink Persuasion's neon open sign gave Miles a demonic red glow. Lucifer himself. White clouds spilled from his mouth with every exhale, not a hint of the cold penetrating his bare arms.

"Kiss?" He sounded appalled. Like she'd pulled out a gun and said, "Give me your wallet."

"You want to kiss me?" His gaze dripped to her mouth, fastened there.

Self-conscious, she wet her lips. "I promised I'd give you a fair shot, so if we could just very, very quickly kiss before we say goodnight ..."

A long moment passed. "You want to kiss me to prove you don't like me?"

It sounded dumb when he said it like that, but ... "Yes."

"And what if you're wrong?" he asked roughly, eyes curiously pinned to her mouth. "What if you like the kiss? What if you kiss me and it all changes? What if our bad date ends and a good night starts?"

"Just a peck."

He stepped closer, a cloud of sugared breath hit her cheeks. "Between pawns?"

"If we don't," she said, her hands skating up his chest, her thumb on the dark seeds of a wilted sunflower, "next week, they'll set me up with one of the fine men in there."

A dark look crossed his face, stealing his beauty and twisting it into jagged edges and steep slopes. Dangerous trails. He hated the idea. Could he not understand he was the same as the other men inside? He covered both her hands with one of his, curling his fingers to grip. Peeled her off. "I ordered you a car."

Oh, it was a no. No to the kiss.

Embarrassed, Lauren wrapped her arms around her waist to squint at the empty street. "I don't need it. I live close."

"It's not safe for you to be walking this late."

"I walk this street every night."

"Not at midnight on a Friday when it's about to snow. Take the car. It'll go wherever you want."

She spun, chewing on the inside of her cheek. "What about you?"

He nodded over his shoulder, curls staining blue under the half-moon's shine. "Cover lasts all night."

Of course he was going back in. Of course midnight wasn't the end of his evening.

A black Mercedes pulled to the curb, near silent, engine a tense hum. The window rolled down.

"Santos?" the driver asked. Miles nodded and left Lauren to flounder down a hole of humiliation. Was she still drunk? She made weak fists with her hands, trying to cast the stolen warmth away. A headache slammed into her. Too soon. Christ, couldn't she have a few hours' sleep before the regret and shame balled in her chest?

Miles spoke to her back. "About Tia—"

She didn't turn, not with a terror of emotion rising. Voice a rasp, she said, "I'll tell her you were a gentleman, but we have nothing in common, we're … opposites."

"Opposites attract," he said. Then his deliciously warm hand was covering her nape, pulling her around, up. Into him.

Romantic, she'd dare say, sweet. The end to a fairy tale. Cue music and a happily-ever-after banner.

Except her shoe slipped on a patch of smooth ice, his fingers caught in her web of thick hair. She yelped. He stumbled.

Her mouth smashed into his teeth. Her cheek struck his. Bones screamed. Blood coated her tongue, her teeth stung. She tried to recover, threw her hand out to balance and punched Miles directly in the dick.

He released her, ripped back, doubled over.

"Fuck," he wheezed, holding his crotch, gasping, eyes wet with pain.

Lauren wiped her lip, horrified to see her fingers come back red. Her eyes burned, ribs twisted to claw at her lungs. Watching the asphalt for other traps, she hobbled forward.

"I'm sorry I didn't mean to—"

Cupping his package like it was on fire, her date snarled, "Good *night*, Lauren."

Chapter Four

Miles tilted his chin back and planted his cleats at the white hash next to the fifty. Ten paces to the left lay the angular, white Mountaineers logo of dramatic peaks and valleys—roughly the size of a sedan. The peaks, dusted with snow to match the season, were painted with a weekly adjustment as fall overturned to winter.

If he kept playing like he had today, the team's owner would add a cap of gold to his helmet. And Miles would happily carry the weight. He felt high. Wired but relaxed. An excess of adrenaline and comfort, especially after that last play.

Three touchdowns. One hundred and seventy-six yards.

The best game of his career. The best game of his life. The best he'd thought would ever be possible for him.

He never wanted to leave the field, never wanted the game to end, wanted another sixty thrown on the clock and to go again. Ignore the screaming in his thighs, the shaking in his hands and push. Pound out another hundred fucking rushing yards.

But it wasn't that simple. Seven days stood between him and his next display. His next check.

Seven days to settle his racing thoughts, a week to recover and retrain muscle. A hundred and sixty-eight hours to complete his list. To prepare his luck, to polish and shine to pristine condition before the ref's coin flipped in the air.

Running backs had notoriously brief careers. Hard on the body, being torn to the ground, trampled. Men burned out, unable to maintain the sheer power required to play. A short career.

Seven long days.

These minutes. Alone on a field, in a stadium not two years old, he savored them. Be it under the distant New England sun during a frost warning, or the sweltering heat of the Vegas practice field, Miles found peace on the sprayed white lines.

For a handful of time every Sunday, Miles felt like he was doing enough. Today, he'd done more than enough.

It'd been a year since the team expansion, since the Vermont Mountaineers were born, since Miles signed his name to the green and silver, but The Peak felt brand-new. Curls of heat wafted between the turf's blades, mixing with the exposed mountain air. He could smell the trees, the water. Never thought he'd miss the climate-controlled Raider Stadium.

He'd been terrified the cold would make his thighs seize, thin the air in his lungs, slice his performance to practice squad levels. But he'd worked smarter, not harder. Going on fourteen months, he'd kept every moment of his pregame identical to those in Vegas.

And when he could lie, cheat or steal for some extra luck, you bet your ass, he was a good liar, a clever cheat and stole only the best.

Cameras and microphones, long black merino wool coats and the smell of hairspray deluged him as a semicircle of reporters invaded his sacred spot.

No stop for Warren Rose, the quarterback, or even Burton Kilbride, the most likely player to provide a crass, headline-catching soundbite. No. Today, this Sunday, they cornered Miles on the grass, and in his bones, he knew he'd be thanking Coach Foss for the game ball.

MVP.

"Untouchable," one reporter called him, reciting his stats, notes flapping across Miles's stomach.

An older, dark-haired woman elbowed up next to him. "Miles, what is the secret? What good luck charm have you found and are you planning on keeping it?"

He flashed a moneymaker to the wide, fisheye lens, adrenaline taking its second loop in his system. "No secret. I think I've finally found the right routine and today it lined up for me."

"Well I'm sure Coach Foss wants you to do that exact routine every game. With a performance like today, the Mountaineers are destined for their first-ever playoff game. What do you say to those who pitched your name as the league MVP?"

The speculation didn't end there. More suggestions, more references to Miles's secret charm.

He answered until his heartbeat slowed, until the cold broke through his pads and clawed into bare skin.

His thighs quaked, forming deep knots in the muscle. Happenstance when his position was to sprint and evade. The tops of his shoulders ached from the weight of his pads, a dense plume of exhaustion rolling thicker than a brutal Vegas sandstorm across the 15.

League MVP. If he made MVP, he could give every girl at Pinks a six-digit salary.

For life.

"Can you share one of your pregame routines for the fans?" someone asked, the black fuzz of a mic tickled his chin.

He wasn't secretive about his success. His … superstitions, as many had dubbed them. Every player possessed a few. Filling up the gas tank with regularity. Brushing his teeth twice. They hid innocuously in the open.

Miles was just aware of his. Noticed them and collected them.

Shower before the game. Eat three cookies 'n' cream protein bars, two right socks on his left foot.

Habits adopted and nourished to elevate his body, his mindset, to the perfect gameplay.

"It's a long process," Miles said promptly, "that starts the night before each game."

"Anything special for this game?"

An oversized hand clamped down on Miles's shoulder.

"He had a date." Burton Kilbride, the Mountaineers' oversized tight end. Under his crazy sweat-soaked beard, teeth formed a wicked smile. Forced the reporter back a step. He might be the only fucker on the team who was scarier without his helmet.

Aside from the scraggly beard he kept getting fined for, Burton's dead eyes could chill the warmest smile, and the deepening of his mangled Irish accent made him seem more beast than man.

"That's what he's done," Burton went on, a glutton for air time, even with red eyes and uncombed dark hair. "He met him a girl."

There came a harsh pinch of Miles's pads under Burton's prodding fingers, as if to say, *you dumbass. Only an idiot deals with women.*

Burton had half a foot on Miles, but his towering height would only be a disadvantage if they ever went toe to toe. Since he'd started young, Miles never relied on bulk to win a fight, only skill and calculated movements, mental manipulation.

Smiling into the camera, Miles shifted his cleat to the left to press spikes into the top of Burton's shoe.

A hiss.

"Lady luck," the reporter jeered, overjoyed to have a scoop. "Is it serious? Will you be seeing her again?"

Three mics where one used to be.

With a meaty paw, Burton took ownership of the biggest one, drawing it to the gap of hair on his face. Allegedly a mouth.

"Aye. Boy mentioned it on the plane, gossiped in the locker room how he iced his balls after."

Miles was going to pour antifreeze into Burton's whiskey for the next month. He crushed Burton's foot.

The big bastard grunted and added, "And the kid's not going to be MVP, that's me." He wiggled his foot free, shoved at Miles's ribs. "So tell him he can stop air drying around the locker room."

"I will when you stop taking your fill," Miles returned with a bite, poking around blindly to stamp on his toes without making more headlines.

Feasting on Burton's candor, questions came like a thick fog, slipping from every corner to bury Miles in a haze of white.

"Do you have a girlfriend?"

"Who's the date?"

"What's the name of your lucky charm?"

"When are you going out again?"

Miles spiraled. A smile pinched on his face, eyes stuck ahead, locked on nothing as his cleats became too small. A pulse started in his toes. His fingers became loose on his helmet, almost let go.

No answers, no replies. He didn't bother to keep the smile as he parted the barrage and strode for the team tunnel.

They were wrong.

He'd done everything right. The normal routine, just as his body liked. Spaghetti Saturday night. Make the rounds at Pinks. Drive Steph home. Get up late. Drive fifteen over to the stadium with no underwear or shoes.

Each box was ticked. The same as last week, the one before.

But today, he'd played on a new level.

It *was* the date.

The terrible date. The date that tried to castrate him, had head-butted him.

Lauren.

Fuck. Fuck. Fuck.

"Hey." Cole Seeder caught Miles's shoulder as shadow swallowed sun. His low voice echoed on the arched cement walls. "What's the rush?" the tackle asked, a furrow in his dark, bushy brows.

Cole's tangle of long, thick hair, his tattoo, wide neck, and dastardly frame drew the attention of most. But Miles stared at the ring on his friend's finger. The wide band of black ink. A part of his wife he carried. A reminder of the weight and price of love.

The required sacrifice.

Late at night, when Burton and Miles were too shitfaced to take a woman home, they mused about what Cole would do when his sweet Canadian wife divorced him. Cut the finger off? The whole hand? As lovesick as he was, Cole might carve out his heart.

He didn't know better.

Hadn't felt the brutal slap of love yet, the strangle it wove around your throat until you felt the tightness in your every vein.

Love wasn't eternal or forgiving. Love was rounded corners and gentle tones until someone messed up.

Then it was hatred. Violent, pulsing hatred, coiling black ready to whip. Throw-you-out-of-the-house-by-your-hair hatred.

Only love could produce such darkness. He and Burton knew, bore the scars of love's wreckage.

Lauren loved love.

The walls went sideways around Miles, his stomach fell to his shins.

"Whoa." More hands, two gripping the hard plastic of his chest pads. A flash of golden eyes.

"Whoa." Warren pushed Miles to the wall, brittle cold scoured his elbows.

"He's having a panic attack," Cole's voice came from behind the quarterback, or his side, maybe across the hall.

Miles couldn't pin it with the echo. Couldn't hear anything but his hammering pulse.

He batted his two captains' hands away, temple-smacking cement.

"Stop shoving," Warren drawled, knowing Miles wouldn't hurt him, not even as the walls caved. "Do you want everyone to see? What is it? Did they ask you something?"

"I'll talk to them," Cole vowed in a quiet, firm tone. A hero drawing his sword.

Miles's vision blurred, melted together green and gray, the yellow lines painted on the floor and the flickering LEDs guide lights.

"No," Warren cut back, knuckles forcing Miles's chin to raise. "Don't draw attention to him."

Cole leaned back on his heels, narrowed his dark gaze. "Then should I hit him?"

Both men stared at him.

Miles tasted blood in the back of his throat. Laughed. Wanted to make fun of them for worrying over him. The stoic tackle and irreverent quarterback.

Warren contorted his pretty-boy face, high cheeks making shadows of his jaw. "Don't hit him," he said, southern twang sliding through. "Kiss him."

That sliced through Miles's haze. He shoved at the quarterback, vision splintering until he saw a wide patch of yellow frizz. Lauren.

Lauren was the key to success. Lauren who never wanted to see him again. Lauren who had to get piss drunk to tolerate him.

Awkward, purse-lipped, boring Lauren.

Fuck.

Prim and proper and pissed. Even when she asked him for a kiss. *Asked.*

Was that how sexual appeal worked in her world? *I find you mildly arousing, do plant one on me. Stretch those rose-red lips.*

"Me kiss him?" Cole asked, stalking closer in consideration.

Warren used his forearm to imbibe Miles's thrashing. "If I do it, Victoria will ask for a repeat showing."

"I can't," Cole declared. "Jo doesn't share."

"Oh my God," came Riley Moore's exasperated groan. The wide receiver pushed through the gathering crowd of green. Lanky but strong, under Warren's restraint, Moore trapped Miles's shoulder to the unforgiving wall.

Miles swung before Moore could wet his mouth, letting his knuckles connect with the ridge of Moore's cheekbone.

A sweet shot of pain, of serotonin, the promise of a battle flooded him. Adrenaline thundered, evened Miles's breaths.

In fight or flight, Miles's natural response was kill.

Swearing to all that is holy, Moore clutched his face as Miles knocked Warren off for good.

He slapped Moore's arm. "Thanks, man. I really needed that."

"Fuck you," returned the receiver.

"What's the problem?" Cole asked again, ignoring the whine from Moore.

"I fucked up," Miles said plainly, shaking out his fist. "I figured out why I won, why I got the yards and ..." A fresh desire to beat Burton rose. "And I'm fucked."

"What, you skipped a jockstrap?" was Warren's guess.

"Stubbed your toe?"

"Bit of a live wire?"

"Swam with a shark?"

"I met a girl." The teasing stopped abruptly. His teammates perked up. A new foray of questions. *Who, where, when?* Moore's wet eyes grew round with interest.

"Doesn't matter," Miles said. "She hates me and I need her to win."

Warren snorted. "Get her back."

Cole was frowning. "You don't need a woman to win. You don't need any of your superstitions to win."

"I play with luck," Miles shot harshly. They'd argued the point before. "My entire career is luck."

"Sounds like you need to do some groveling," Warren mused.

Cole shook his head, wanted to argue.

Miles put a stop to it. "I don't have to grovel. We just don't get along. She's nothing like me. We're ... *Dios*, we're worse than opposites. She writes fan fiction."

"The fuck is that?" Warren asked the same time Moore asked, "What show?"

Coach Foss's whistle pierced the air, penetrated the inner circle. "Are you fighting, Santos? What have I said about it?"

Miles shook out his fist. "He tried to kiss me, Coach."

Foss aged another ten years, shut his eyes and blew out a long, fed-up exhale. "This job's going to kill me."

"Nah, Coach," Moore soothed. "It'll be the stress."

Coach jabbed his silver whistle at Moore's face. "Get consent first." Another whistle. "Locker room!"

As they shuffled down the tunnel, cleats like rain on pavement, Warren caught Miles's eyes to mouth, "Get on your knees."

***

AT THE LOUD SMACK of lips, Lauren's teeth ground together. Beside her, Maddie applied a third layer of Berry Peach gloss.

"Fat lip is worthy of an SOS," Lauren's sister told the mirror, dotting at her cupid's bow.

Kayla, lounging on the bay window like a sun-glutted cat, hummed agreement as she scrolled on her phone. "Let's find his Tinder and report him for misconduct."

Sharing the grimy, greasy parts of her date had gone over better than Lauren had planned. It helped that her lip was black and swollen, and her teeth felt like they were going to fall out.

After the first round of make-out lips over Raisin Bran, her sisters had calmed enough to listen, and promptly become irate.

The Peck sisters may quarrel, but they'd kill if someone hurt one of them.

"Mrs. Lopez set us up," Lauren reminded them, leaving Maddie to her detailing to flop on the couch. "And I'm not on a dating app and if I was, it wouldn't be Tinder."

Kayla glanced up from her phone, mouth in a line. She was the oldest of the Pecks and the most blessed. Hair shiny brown, eyes a swirling hazel. The tallest of the sisters, a constant reminder she had the upper hand.

"Oh good," she crooned. "We're back to sanctimonious. Why don't you go upstairs and tell Hannah what an idiot she is for trying to be happy?"

"Where is Hannah?" Lauren asked. The youngest Peck was a burst of sunshine to Lauren's grisly cloud.

Maddie smacked her lips again. "Mikey dumped her."

"Mikey?" Lauren rubbed her temple. "What happened to Joe?"

"Joe was eons ago. Mikey invited her to Paris. She bought three berets and now he's going with his stepdaughter he calls 'Baby.'"

Men. Lauren made a face, recalling Joe ending it for similar, intolerable reasons. At least Mikey hadn't asked Hannah to swaddle him. "Should I go check on her? Has she gone black hole yet?"

"No." Kayla unfolded from the cushioned window seat and pushed Maddie aside to check her eyeliner in the mirror. "We're going out tonight."

"On a Sunday?" Lauren asked, watching Maddie fluff her big blonde barrel rolls. "Is that smart? She should take some time for herself. Self-care and—"

"Wait two years until she gets headbutted by a tatted pervert?" Maddie interrupted sharply. "Because that's working so well for you."

"I'm happy," was Lauren's standard response to nagging. Whether it was true or not.

Happiness was like love. Say it enough, think it, hear it, and eventually you'd feel it. Whether or not your mind and heart agreed. You could convince yourself of love until every atom roared with it.

Until one day, reality struck, a wash of ice-cold water on your molten veins and your blood seized, your very composure shattered, ripped apart.

"And I don't know if he's a pervert," Lauren backtracked, feeling slightly guilty.

There was a chance she'd laid it on too thick in her storytelling.

But Maddie and Kayla just kept making excuses. *Maybe he really does like stripper food. Maybe he's shy. Maybe his little sister is a tattoo artist, and he offered his body for her practice.*

As if.

They were in La La Love Land again, conjuring fairy tales.

"Only perverts know every stripper in a five-mile radius," Maddie told her reflection, fingers flattening baby hairs.

"What does he do for work?" Kayla asked as she disappeared into the entryway, returned with her snow boots. "I forgot."

Lauren hadn't said. No way could she admit he was a professional athlete. They'd forgive him for murder.

It was the Disney princess in them to make excuses and cast blind eyes.

The curse of the Peck sisters.

Hannah, mourning the loss of another minute man she'd thought was her soulmate. Classic Aurora, love-at-first-sight crazy.

Though Lauren would prefer it to Kayla's diagnosis. The oldest Peck zipped up her new snowboarding jacket. A sport she'd only taken up a month ago because her boyfriend loved to shred. A new hobby, a new personality, sometimes even a new accent when she met a guy. Gave up everything she was for him.

Ariel.

Then there was Maddie, the fellow middle child, the one Lauren butted heads with most. Maybe because they'd both gotten Dad's frizz, but Maddie figured out how to tame it into lovely full curls that made her sparkling green eyes as bright as a dewy spring. And through highlight and contour and YouTube self-care videos, Maddie had taken the average height, dirty blonde hair, and small eyes and made a model out of it.

All to catch a man. Believing beauty was the key to love. An honest-to-goodness Cinderella.

How Lauren wished she could be afflicted with the same Cinderella curse. Even if it meant on her boring Sunday, she'd have to wear jeans, mascara, and lotion her elbows. It'd be better than the bitter truth harbored in Lauren's gut.

"Fiddlesticks?" Kayla asked Maddie, making a small grunt as she tore the tag off her pocket.

Maddie's nose wrinkled. "Too loud, and dirty. Let's go to The Hand."

"It's Sunday night," Lauren argued. "In the middle of winter."

"It's November, that's practically fall," Kayla retorted. "There's hardly any good powder. Après ski was dead at Stowe, and I've been trapped in snow gear all day, I want to feel sexy."

Maddie was nodding with unrivaled enthusiasm. "And Bo gave me a new necklace," she said, caressing the gold locket at her throat. "He wants to see how good it looks."

It looked like a collar. But Lauren would catch an earful if she said as much. "What if we stayed in?"

"And do what?" Maddie snapped. "Heavy breathe into our computers? It creeps me out whenever you're typing."

"I'm focused. It's Sunday." She grabbed for the remote. "We could watch"—Oh God, she'd almost said football, but she could never watch football again without her teeth aching—"60 Minutes."

Kayla shuddered. "60 Minutes ruined Halloween candy for me. No."

"Go ahead and watch it," Maddie goaded. "We didn't invite you to come with us. Hannah needs a rebound. Not a manic depressive tagalong."

"That term is outdated and offensive, and I'm not bipolar."

"No," Maddie announced brightly. "You're one polar and it's sad." The smug purse of her over-glossed lips showed she was proud of the clever jab.

Just as Lauren prepared to reiterate she was exceedingly happy—overjoyed really—Hannah crept down from the hall, heeled boots marking dots in the carpet.

The same carpet Lauren had taken her prom pictures on. The same carpet Kayla spilled a vodka slushie across in high school and got grounded until she got the bright blue out.

They'd all moved out of their childhood home at one point or another. Kids eager to spread their wings, but when their parents offered them the house rent-free while they sunned in Tampa, one by one the princesses skittered home, hauling along broken hearts, preparing to battle for shelf space in the bathroom.

The roommates were tough, Lauren often lamented, but the house was impossible to beat. Walking distance from her job, private bedroom, and the couch was already molded to fit her butt.

Not to mention, the pleasant monotony in knowing her neighbors, waving to the same people every morning, avoiding the same foaming-mouthed dog on the sidewalk.

"Do I need a coat?" Hannah asked, voice like a ghost, quiet, rasping.

The youngest looked most like Kayla, but not enough to be called twins like Lauren and Maddie. Light brown hair stick straight, rich round hazel eyes that hit you like bullets, even with the slight puffiness.

"That's what you're wearing?" Maddie's catchphrase speared the room as she took in Hannah's leggings and crewneck.

"I ate an entire carton of Ben & Jerry's. This is all that fits." Soft eyes skipped across the room, sensing hostility burning from the couch. "Lauren, aren't you coming?"

She sounded so genuinely surprised, Lauren half wanted to say yes. "No. I'm staying in and bettering myself as an individual."

Hannah nearly flinched.

Maddie waved a flippant hand. "She's on her feminist rant again after last night. Guy was a bad kisser."

"He headbutted me."

"Leave her," Maddie assured Hannah, guiding her to the entry. "Someone's got to take care of the house after we all depart, don't fight her for the spot."

CHAPTER FIVE

L AUREN SHOT OUT OF her dream with a gasp.

Brian's snicker echoed off her cubicle walls, peeling back the office quiet. She bolted upright, smacked the desk's edge with her knee, and pitched sideways.

In the crackling fluorescent light, she watched her abandoned coffee topple to stain the gray carpet with a wide black puddle.

"Shit, L, you good?" Brian asked, leaning over the plain white half wall with a grimace on his face.

The lack of care in his voice cut straight through Lauren's patience and sent her on a downward tumble. She'd gotten no sleep last night because she'd worried.

What if her sisters ran into Miles?

What if he hit on them? Took them home?

Not that she cared about what—or who—he did. It was the principle of the matter. Imagining horrible scenarios of Miles sweeping Hannah in a romantic kiss, Maddie giggling in his ear, trailing fingers over his tattoos. Kayla pretending to know what NFL stood for.

Not even the paint-stripping dissolvable government coffee could revive her.

"No, please," she mocked dryly, "don't help me up." Planting her butt on the hard carpet, she grabbed her mug and tipped it upright to save whatever sludge was left.

It wasn't drinkable when it was hot and steaming. Now it veered toward poison.

Lauren rubbed her eyes. "What time is it?"

"Best time of the day," Brian returned, flashing a—she guessed—charming grin. He folded his arms on her stubby wall to loom over her. "Closing time. Mary told me you were back here working your fingers to the bone, but I look forward to correcting her."

You look forward to correcting anyone. Doubly so if it's a woman.

"What are you doing here?" she asked, tone flat, detached, avoiding his chocolate eyes. "You don't work in this wing."

As the city electrician, he was usually out during the day, signing permits, watching TV on his phone in the government Chevy. Unfortunately, he returned in the afternoons to clock out, walking the dingy walls like he had a six-foot dick, and he just stopped Vermont from going supernova.

When really, he watched a stay-at-home dad electrocute himself before pointing out the outlet was still on.

Lauren had loved him.

She had loved him so ferociously, she'd planned their wedding. She'd named their kids. Sam and Aurora. And she'd told him. Showed him the ring she wanted, the dress she'd wear, the wedding night lingerie—naughty white silk. She spent hours on Zillow, searching houses in the New North End, close to his parents, something with shutters she could paint bright blue.

A Pinterest board for every room. She'd make their house a home, she had love to spare, to spend on aged walls and cracked windows.

Psycho.

The word reverberated in her head. *Crazy. Stalker. Psycho.*

You're obsessed with me, I can't breathe!

Without looking at him, Lauren fumbled back into her chair and woke her computer, watching the blue screen spin.

"I need expense reports filed, and you know as well as I do that Mary's useless after four o'clock."

"Mary's the accountant," Lauren informed him, like he hadn't been the one to introduce her to Mary when he got her this job. Like he hadn't tapped the fifty-four-year-old's butt and told Lauren she'd be lucky to look like that when she was forty.

Shaking off the memory, Lauren added, "She takes the expense reports. Not me. Give them to her." *And leave me alone.*

Brian loomed forward, smelling like frayed wires and her favorite lemon hand cream. The hand cream she'd bought him for Christmas because he'd liked it on her. The same year he'd gotten her thick, Snoopy dog pajamas so she'd stop trying to cuddle him in bed.

He stayed thin no matter what he ate. A patchy beard, trimmed close. Brian was a Dollar Tree version of Tony Stark with his glasses and tool belt and swagger.

Back then, she'd thought he was better than Tony—Iron Man—Stark. Pretended she was sleeping with a sexy architect. It'd taken years of focus to strip back her rose-colored tint. Count the age spots creeping in from his hairline, nails a little too long, bone poking out in his shoulder.

"Mary said you had a date. Is that why you're so tired?"

What Lauren really wanted to say was that Mary didn't know what she was talking about. That it had been two entire days since her epic fail of a date. That she'd only admitted to having plans on Friday because Mary kept inviting her to key night with her and her geriatric husband.

Key night.

Lauren had heard too many stories of Mary sleeping with a whole squadron of pilots to misinterpret.

She opened her email and typed: *change lunch hour to avoid Mary.* Sent it to herself. The mailbox dinged.

Mary was fun when she spoke of her six grandkids, but the other stories. Lauren couldn't eat leftover lasagna and hear about foursomes in the middle of her Wednesday.

"So did you?" he asked. It didn't sound friendly but pointed. He didn't believe her.

"How's your girlfriend?"

"You remembered."

Yes, she remembered. He brought her up every other day. The best girlfriend to exist. Ever. Amazing. Chill and cool and not like other girls. She didn't even know what Pinterest was. Drank beer and never got bloated.

"You keeping tabs on me again, L?"

Her teeth gritted together. She closed her browser to hide the red flushing her cheeks.

"Well, this has been great." She rolled her chair to the gap in her four walls, wholly prepared to hightail it to the ladies' room and scream.

"We should go on a double date," Brian continued, smiling, relaxed as he lounged on her things, fingers ruffling a sticky note reminder to reschedule with the dentist. Again. "That is, if you can get a lock down on a man. Shouldn't be hard for you."

Right. Because she was obsessed with finding a man. The point of her existence.

Brian saw Lauren as a caricature of the worst time in her life. Of being unconditionally in love.

She yanked a handful of tissues from David's cubicle next to hers, littered them across the wet carpet, and stomped over them.

Imagined Brian's balls splatting into the forty-year-old fibers.

"Snow tonight," he went on, lingering, overstaying, grinding on her composure. He scraped dirt from under his thumbnail, watched it fall into the crevices of her keyboard.

Her jaw clicked. "Then you should get home early. I know how poorly the truck handles in the snow. Had to dig for an hour to get out of our driveway."

"It was ice," he snapped. "No car handles in ice. Do you want to ride or not? I'm picking up my girl on the way too. Think you can handle meeting her?"

Lauren left the sopping tissues right there on the floor. She couldn't engage with him. Couldn't be brought down to those moments again.

Two years. Two years, she'd been sharing this office with him, listening to these barbs. She grabbed her purse and headed for the front hall. Stole her coat off the hook.

Suddenly a walk in the snow in the dark sounded pleasant.

***

MILES STALKED AROUND THE overcrowded living room to work off his nerves. He felt like a junkie, waiting for his supply, desperate, frantic, shaking with the need, wanting to scream for it.

His drug? Luck.

Tia Luisa ambled into the room, tan slippers dragging over the maroon shag carpet.

"Horchata," she announced, pushing aside a framed picture of the Virgin Mary to set his cup on the mantel. "Still your favorite, *hijo*?"

Miles's chest clinched at the word. At hearing it.

Tia's voice was so similar to his mother's, the same hint of accent, a slightly serious edge. Looking at her helped. Reminded him she wasn't family. Gray hair curled in crinkles around brown cheeks. Dangerously thick bifocals, a string of pearls designed for everyday clutching.

"Sugar and cream in a cup." He grinned, shaking out his palms. "Is there anything better?"

"There is nothing that can compete with a mother's recipe," she replied, sitting in the orange and green striped glider, gaze sliding to the street beyond her window.

Tia didn't have any children of her own. When Miles moved to Vermont—a real state, not a prank—she'd called him within the day. His mother's ex-sister-in-law.

He still called her Tia.

They bore the same sharp kind of affection, Tia and his mother. The kind that pinched and prodded, groomed until it was better, tighter, fit in the lines they'd drawn.

Tia's second husband, Ricardo, passed away last spring from a stroke. He'd been years younger than her. But Miles wasn't surprised when he saw the obituary. Luisa had worn him to bones and dust with her pruning.

Miles didn't know his dad. But he imagined, his mother's particularly venomous love had cast him out too.

But there was something about the familiar he kept coming back for. Tia chiding her soap operas in hurried Spanish, bundled in her chair in an ancient house in the Old North End.

The best horchata, the only good tostadas served in the entire state were within these paper-thin walls. He came for the culture.

And a bit of pampering.

"How are you, hijo?" She reached for him and Miles came to a crouch at her side, letting wrinkled fingers take his cheek. "How was your church?"

"God is good," he replied.

She drank her horchata out of a hand-painted teacup, complete with a matching saucer and spoon.

He wasn't surprised to see her add a clump of sugar to it. Maybe that's what killed Ricardo.

"Tell me about your date, that's why you've come." A slurp she pretended was a sip. "She's beautiful, is should not? That kind of light skin. It's something creams cannot give you. Flat like porcelain and hair so soft."

As if Miles would know how soft her hair was after a single date. It'd looked like a dense thorn bush.

"She's very beautiful, Tia," he assured, realizing just then, it wasn't an untruth.

"Nice too. You treated her well? Where did you take her? You have plenty of money, did you take her somewhere nice?"

"Yes, Tia, we shared drinks at a very high-end club with our own private table."

"Drinks?" Tia's spoon clattered to the saucer. "Girls want to eat. No drinks."

"I took her to dinner." He didn't mention where. "She's very nice, Tia. Very quiet."

"Yes. She is the one for you. I watch her across the street. She looks like a perfect match for you. I see you together. I see your babies already. Your curly dark hair, her white skin. Beautiful."

Babies. Miles didn't have time to empty his mailbox. But he knew not to argue. Lest he get a holy smack to the back of the head.

"The thing is, Tia." He sampled his horchata to stall and ended up finishing it. Wiping at his mouth, looking around the living room cluttered with doilies and plastic flowers. Crosses. Jesus on a football field.

He'd gotten her that one.

"I like her," Miles said, "but she left without giving me her number."

"You didn't ask for it?"

He didn't plan on her being the holy grail. "She was … overcome by our kiss at the end of the date."

"Miles. No. You don't kiss your wife on the first date."

Wife? How much did Tia know about him? Certainly nothing if she said the *W* word in front of him.

"Do you have her number? I'd like to call and see if—"

"You came on too strong," Tia informed impertinently. "You need to wait now. Let her come to you."

Yeah. He had exactly five days left to wait before he had to be with Lauren again, draining luck from her like a fucking vampire.

But explaining that to his Tia. To a woman who likened karma to blasphemy would be a lesson in instant consequences. The truth would wreck him, but a white lie …

"I can't wait," he beseeched softly, taking her frail hand and wrapping it with his, wishing he'd worn a shirt that covered all his ink to reinforce the imaginary halo on his head. "I think you're right, Tia. I think she is my … the future."

He walked around the W word to make sure Tia didn't reserve a church.

It wasn't entirely a lie.

Last Friday night, Lauren cemented herself as pivotal to Miles's future. He needed money, playoff bonuses, sponsorships that paid MVP prices. If he had to share a pair of handcuffs with her for the next two months for that, so be it.

"Please, Tia. She's special to me. I have to talk to her, convince her to—"

"I'm sure she has many men chasing her. Respectable men who do not kiss her right after they meet her. You need time."

The last time Tia dated was the '90s and he was a hairsbreadth from reminding her. He rose, feeling like a streak of black smoke in a dollhouse. "I know how to see women and I need—"

A smile curled Tia's lips. "I knew it would be a good match."

The door pounded.

Tia didn't jolt, black lashes dusting her glasses, she gestured for Miles to investigate as she sipped her horchata, pinky raised. "Take care of it. Then we discuss your courting."

Dios, spare him from that.

Quickly, he escaped down the hall and grappled for a new plan of attack. The truth would get holy water in his face, but—

Miles swung open the door. "We don't want—"

Jesus, Mary and Joseph.

Smoothed sea glass green eyes, a narrow nose, red cheeks.

"What the—?" Lauren pushed back the hood of her black parka, knocking snow off her shoulders. A shovel hung in her bare hand as she shifted awkwardly on Tia's front stoop. "Miles? What are you doing here?"

"This is my Tia's house. What are *you* doing here?"

"I am—" The red of her cheeks darkened as she looked over the shoulder at the freshly shoveled driveway. "I've been helping out since Mr. Lopez ... passed. Can you open the garage so I can get the salt? She usually keeps it cracked for me to crawl under, but it wasn't supposed to snow today. She didn't."

Miles blinked, a sense of unreality flooding him. Lauren was in front of him, covered in puffy black from her neck to her ankles, shaking and trembling, helping his Tia.

What the hell was she doing in a neighborhood like this? Mere blocks from Pink Persuasion? Old, run-down houses, cracked sidewalks, no streetlights.

Had she said she crawled into the garage?

His greedy, greedy mind answered all his questions with: *It doesn't matter, she's here. Luck has saved you again.*

Tensing his jaw, biting back a snap of *go home and lock the doors*, Miles pressed the garage opener.

As the metal rattled, Lauren turned to stride down the front path, wiping her hands of Miles.

Not this time.

He took chase, following her to the driveway, very aware that he was only in a T-shirt and jeans as falling snow melted onto his skin.

"I was looking for you," he said as he ducked under the rising garage door, watching as she moved through the dark garage like it was second nature. Taking the lid off a tan garbage bin to fish out an old Folgers Coffee can full of deicing salt.

"Can we talk?" he asked.

"Considering you're freezing your ass off for an apology, I forgive you."

He spread his feet to stop the shivering. "I wasn't going to apologize."

"Are you going to pay for my dental work?" she returned smoothly, stalking back to the uncovered blacktop, scooping a handful of salt and scattering it in front of her.

"It's too cold for salt," Miles said from the protection of the garage. "It's not going to work."

"It will in the morning, which is all that matters." Another handful. "I can lay it tonight and Mrs. Lopez can go to her Bible study in the morning without worrying." She worked methodically, chin tucked into her collarbone, ponytail whipping against her cheek.

She slipped.

Miles lunged and snagged her arm, a fresh slash of ice cold clawing his arms. "Are you wearing heels?" he hissed.

She'd been half a foot shorter than him at dinner, but the distance had narrowed.

"I came from work." She ripped her arm from his, digging for more salt.

"Stop that and talk to me," Miles insisted, yanking the can from her.

She slipped again and he had to pick between her and the salt.

Salt sprayed the night air as he hauled her into his arms. Course grains showered them, slipping into the folds of their clothes, burrowing into their hair, bouncing on the driveway and shooting into the snow-covered grass.

Her bulky coat compressed under his hands, allowing him to feel the full force of her shaking. Miserable.

She must be miserable and near death and she was still out here, in heels and bare hands clearing Tia's drive. Smelling like lemons.

"Great," she huffed, breath warm on his neck, moist air molding to his skin and sticking. "Now she's going to yell at me for ruining the lawn."

Twisting in his arms, she bent down, as though she was going to pick every individual salt grain from the snow.

"Stop." He caught her with determined hands, restraining her easily, taking her red, raw hands into his. In the falling snow, the whipping wind, in nothing but a cotton shirt, his hands burned hot over hers.

Yes. Miserable.

Reflexively, he drew her hands to his mouth and blew warm air onto the trembling fingertips, watching as a snowflake caught on the end of her lash.

He felt her tug and pull to get free and he chuckled at the attempt, thumb swiping over her torn nailbeds. "You're hurting yourself," he whispered, the fullest part of his lip brushing her finger.

She seemed to undergo a brief but savage battle with herself before her mouth twisted slightly, as if the touch insulted her.

"What are you doing? Let go," she snarled quietly, the patches of red on her face filling in with anger.

"I want you to go out with me again," he explained politely, blowing again on her fingers, rolling the rough skin between his. "That's why I'm here. I came looking for you. I want another shot."

"With me?" came her stony reply.

"Yes, with you." Dios, she was more difficult than he'd remembered. "Let's go on another date this Friday. We'll do dinner right away. More food than you can eat, anywhere you want, anything—"

Hastily, she ripped away from him, hands making tight balls. "Are you fucking insane?"

***

FIGHTING TO CONTAIN HER emotions, Lauren scooped a fistful of salt and chucked it at the patch of ice she kept losing it on. She would not fall into Miles Santos's powerful arms again. No matter how warm or comforting.

It didn't matter.

The man was insane. Asking her out? Didn't they both have bruises still? Ground salt stung her open nailbeds as she dumped the last of the repurposed coffee tin on the treacherous patch and went to the garage for a second helping.

"Did you hear me right?" Miles asked, a statue in the building snowstorm. Shock freezing him. "I asked if you—"

"I know what you said." She returned to the ice patch with a full tin, and sprinkled anew, gaze scouring his body. Did he own sleeves? Or think the tattoos were insulating?

"The answer's no."

"No?" he muttered. "That's it. No?"

What'd he want a handwritten note? "No ... thank you?"

He grabbed the bucket from her, flipped it over, and kicked the pile to splatter in every direction.

Lauren frowned at the clumps and clusters, the sparse areas.

He didn't care. Self-centered dick. He tossed the can into the garage, directly into the salt bin. Crossed powerful arms, and asked sharply, "Why not?"

She opened her mouth for a snappy retort and paused.

Was it possible he was onto something? Miles had a job, he was polite, he paid for her ride home, visited his aunt.

He was the most beautiful man she'd ever met.

And he was standing in the snow, asking her out. Lauren. The second middle Peck sister. The one with ten hangnails and a gag reflex to sour cream.

"See, I'm right," he said smugly. "You can't come up with a reason."

Oh, she wanted to slap the smirk off his face.

"That is why!" she snapped. The attitude, the presumption that women should fall to his feet. "We already went on a date and it was awful."

Miles seemed surprised by her review. "Awful?"

She nodded. "My mouth still hurts. I sucked on a frozen grape for five hours yesterday."

"I'd trade a split lip for forced impotence."

Her lips twitched with barely suppressed humor. "And you asked why? *That's* why. We're not good together."

He traversed the ice to stand in front of her, to conceitedly lower his head and say, "You don't know that. We went out once because we were forced to. What if we tried it ourselves? We could—"

"Miles, you took me to a strip club. You gave me a fat lip. You were late, you flirted with everyone but me. You told me you didn't want to date, we agreed it was bad. Why do you want to suffer more?"

"Because you're good for me," he replied.

Her stomach sank. Beast wanted a Belle. He was chasing the wrong princess. "Try again. I'm not a Goody Two-shoes angling to reform the bad boy. Talk to my sisters for that one. I don't have time for a pet project."

"Bad boy?" Miles muttered with distaste.

"Good boys don't usually tattoo their necks."

He jabbed his finger to the sky in victory. "Ha! I knew you were judging me in your little Miss Priss outfit." He caught the edge of her hood and yanked it up to cover her hair. "What's the first thought you had when you saw me?"

Beautiful.

Scary, perfect, beautiful. She'd wanted to play with his hair, she'd wanted to trace his tattoos. She'd wanted to scratch them off and see if she survived in the glow of his raw beauty.

But all that made her sound insane.

It was something she would have told Brian. Exactly what was running through her mind.

Miles stared at her with an odd flicker in his eyes.

She glanced away.

A bitter laugh from soft lips. "You thought I was trash." He rubbed at his chest and shook his head. "Every time, the truth cuts deeper."

"You leaned into it," she taunted. "Flirting, acting cocky and arrogant."

"Confident."

"Smug."

One corner of his lip curved up. "It's confidence when you can back it up. And I wasn't flirting. Men can talk to women without flirting. Even men with neck tattoos."

Protective instincts battled, those for herself and him. She hedged to embrace both. "I don't think you're trash. You're just not my type."

"Because of the tattoos and female friends." Sarcasm dripped.

"You're at home in a club!" She poked his chest. "You're a professional athlete, you make millions of dollars, you can afford to tattoo your body however you want and not worry about what people think. You've never been in love, you don't want emotions or entanglements and I have to think the only reason you're still talking to me is because I told you no. That's not a spark, it's reverse psychology."

"I need you, Lauren."

A flash of white-hot interest speared her chest.

She extinguished it with a single memory. "If I was the one chasing you, you'd be disgusted. You'd file a restraining order, call me certifiable."

"I'd stand with my arms wide open."

"You're lying." She allowed herself an internal grimace. Her voice was going shrew, cutting jagged and harsh. "I know you are. You don't want me."

His voice raised to match his frustration. "That doesn't mean I don't want to spend time with you."

There. The spark in her chest died with a hiss. Lauren sucked in a breath, made no effort to hide her confusion. "What does that mean?"

He scratched down the rigid line of his jaw. The flickering of Mrs. Lopez's porch light played over the layers of his hair, high-lighting the array of dark colors.

"I don't want you in my bed," he admitted. "You're right. We're not … compatible." A rueful smile. "But what about friends? I'll be your best friend, Lauren. Give me a chance."

"Why?"

He glanced at her hands, like they existed to torment him and firmed his jaw, seeming to wrangle his thoughts. Drew a deep inhale. "Look, I believe in luck—"

"Is this about the champagne? I'll drink a whole bottle to get out of this."

Sip. Puff. Pour.

"It's not the champagne. It's *you*. *You're* my luck. After our night together, I … I played the best game of my life. I have another game on Sunday and I need you to spend Friday with me." He stepped closer, smelling like fresh air and wet skin. "You're my good luck. You, Lauren. I need you. I've been going out of my mind trying to find you. I was about to bribe Tia. Please help me."

A plea.

A harsh yank on Lauren's locked-away emotions.

He didn't care about her at all.

Didn't think of her. Had meant it when he said bye.

She was a thing for him to use and he'd come to play on her emotions.

Too bad he was two years late.

The quickening snow felt warm compared to the ice banding her heart. "I'm not lucky."

"You were lucky for me." His hands cupped her shoulders, breath a cloud of white. "I have a certain routine before every game, and this week, the only difference was you. It's you."

She shook her head, ready to object.

"You are the reason. I was explosive on the field. Unstoppable. I ... I need you. Spend your Friday with me. Spend the next ten Fridays with me. Please, without you, I'm nothing. Average."

The glisten in his eyes was overkill. He'd never scratch the vault of her emotions. "You can't guilt me into dating you."

"It doesn't have to be a date," he said quickly. "Please."

"No." Then she was walking, crossing the street, slush breaking over her toes.

Her emotions weren't toys for him to play with, to break. He couldn't manipulate her like Brian had. He thought she was a silly girl who'd say "yes, sir" to his every whim. Who'd fall over herself to be with the dashing football player.

Lauren wasn't a princess anymore.

She was a villain.

Chapter Six

After the sun went down, Miles had little awareness of time. Only that it went far too slowly, the night sky dragging, suffocating the sun, wanting sin to rule.

Like every night, he was at Pinks.

Nursing his Coke, he stayed sharp, staring through every flashing light, listening to each high-pitched squeal, pinning it, assessing. Men murmured discreetly, tucked back in their booths, slugging domestics, exchanging greedy glances as they made filthy promises to good, hardworking women. A few hasty hand grabs made Miles tense. Set his teeth on edge.

"Calm down, cop, or Ralph's gonna toss ya."

Miles served up a mocking grin. "What about me says cop?"

Steph twirled near him like a ballerina on her own stage, tucking a glittery serving tray across her bare stomach. "You're not relaxed. Not drinking. You keep tossing glares and lifting your chin, an air of betterness about you. It's a boner killer."

"Good."

"Classic cop."

He trailed a finger across the interlocked pink Ps painted on the table. "We both know I'm worse than anyone in here." He sipped to cover the twitch in his nose. Her perfume smelled like peaches and vanilla. Reminded him he'd missed dinner.

"How are you, Steph?"

"Chasity," she reminded him, gesturing flippantly at her choker. Fake gold crystals spelled the name like a dog collar.

He wanted to rip it off.

But he didn't want to get his ass kicked out, so he played nice, curling his fingers into a wrecking ball.

"Chasity," Miles repeated with a croak. "How are you? How's work?" His eyes drifted to the stage, where a trio of women danced under waves of blue light, slow hip rolls at odds with the rap blasting through the speakers.

Chasity rarely performed on stage. Not these days. Not since Ralph took an interest in her. Asked her out. Kept asking.

She'd refused and was now relegated to serving drinks in spine-cracking heels and cheap underwear. Making half the cash she used to.

Miles pulled out a fifty. "Are you holding off Ralphie?"

"I can handle Ralph," she confirmed, cool, collected as she tucked the cash in her cleavage. "Compared to some of the regulars, he's as harmless as a butterfly."

He felt his jaw clench.

Steph tsked. "Don't give me the pouty sourpuss face. You and your white horse can rescue all of us but there will still be a line of girls fighting to get on stage the next morning."

It was the only reason he didn't keep offering exactly that. A new life. A better, safer life. Because it wouldn't stop the cycle.

Pinks would exist with or without Miles's intervention. So he did the next best thing, visited. Frequently, pockets lined, fists ready.

"Hey, sweet cheeks," a gritty voice slurred, hand slapping Steph's bow-covered ass. "I've got an open pole right here." A honk at his junk. "I'll show you how cash can rain down on those tits."

Miles was on his feet before the oaf finished speaking, hand locked around the man's wrist, rotating until the guy yelped. He spoke with a growl in his throat. "Couldn't you see she was talking to me?" He threw the wrist behind the intruder's back, pushed. "You say excuse me when you want to talk to her and wait until she responds. Got it?"

Panicked, breathing heavily, the asshole's free hand pushed lamely at Miles's chest.

"How much money you got?" Miles asked, pressing harder on the guy's joint, enjoying the sound of a faint pop.

"I-I don't know."

He squeezed, feeling a rush of power.

"I don't know!" the guy repeated, white faced and sweating. "Two hundred in ones."

"I'll take it," Miles whispered, tearing the cash from his struggling hand and shoving him away.

Steph's expression was flat disapproval.

It didn't change as Miles counted the bills into her waiting palm.

"Scaring off customers." She clicked her tongue.

"Does it matter if you still get paid?"

She tucked the wad of cash next to the others. "No." A sardonic wink. "I'm getting cable."

"Don't spend it on that," he admonished, returning to his seat, sending a hand through his hair, yanking. "Are you still by Mallet's Bay? Maybe you could save up for something else."

"I like being by the lake, and I just got window treatments for the trailer."

"If you let me buy you a car, it'd be a lot better."

"If I let you buy me a car, Miles." Her voice took on a familiar chastising tone. "What will I tell my brother? A rich wannabe superhero has a heart under all that black. Do you think that will go well? Think you'll be fine? Think I wouldn't get a handful?"

She turned back anything he offered: money, shelter, lawyers, education. Simply shook her head and soldiered on. The cord of frustration pulled tighter.

Miles was clenching his teeth again. A mantra started in his head. *Don't lose it. Don't raze the world. Don't explode.*

A year ago, he'd been steps from serious jail time. His manager, Victoria, had made him see the truth. He couldn't help anyone if he lost his job, the money. The more money he had, the more he could help.

He touched Steph's wrist, containing the adrenaline with a jumping knee. "You're always right, Ste—Chasity."

"I know," she returned flippantly. "Now I want to hear about the poor girl. Lauren, was it? What bad card did she draw to date you?"

He didn't know if Steph had noticed, or if Carissa had spilled, but strippers were better at unloading emotional baggage than therapists. "I fucked up with her."

"Ask me if I'm surprised," she mocked. "You don't romance a girl at Pinks."

"I wasn't trying to romance her, I was trying to appease my overbearing aunt. But ..." He let the rest spill out, the shitty date, their agreement to part ways, her knee in his urethra. The game. Salt in his eye. Her rejection.

He scratched his cheek, feeling pitiful. "Would you forgive me?"

"Of course I'd forgive you, cop." Steph ruffled his hair. And the gesture, the familiarity, the slam of his childhood crushed his chest, lodged a thick wad of loathing in his arteries.

Steph paused as though she felt the change in him. The heated iron prod sinking into his shot tissue, so hot it glowed red.

She looked right at the center of his pain. "You're sweet as a cupcake but ..."

Miles held his breath. This was it. The truth. The condition of their relationship, the thing that kept Steph away, made her smart to his mess.

"But all she saw was you being a domineering cop asshole. Women don't want to be chased."

"Yes, they—"

A thwack to his head. "They think they do," Steph informed promptly. "But they don't. Makes them feel too much like prey. Besides"—she cocked her hip, goose bumps visible along the curve of her thigh—"you're not trying to sleep with her. You just want time with your little lucky charm."

"So what should I do, wise one? She'll bring out a bat if I show up at her house and beg."

"Stop thinking of her as a woman."

"You want me to treat her like an object?"

Another smack to his ear. "Men," she hissed in the same pissed-off tone Lauren had used. "What if your lucky charm was a guy who didn't like you? What would you do?"

Easy. "Pay him to shut up and sit next to me every Friday until the season ends." A few hours in silence while Miles drained his luck. That's all he needed. No talking, no headbutts. Just a trade.

Dios.

Why hadn't he seen it before?

"You're a goddess, Steph."

***

AS LAUREN RETREATED FROM the bitter cold, she was blinded by brightness. Blinking, squinting, she unwound her scarf and fumbled for the coatrack.

Winter had come fast and hit hard. She'd barely made it out of the City Hall parking lot before the sky went black.

With the darkness came the marrow-bending cold.

"Who's car is out front?" she called as she kicked slush off her boots. "They're blocking the path, I had to crawl over the snowbank." She beat bright red hands against her coat, the skin sensitive and wet. "Did Brock sell his 4Runner? I liked that."

She unzipped her coat, ditched her work bag.

And got crickets.

"Hello?" Next came off her hat.

Dammit. If no one was home, what was the point of keeping every light in the den on? "Hannah?" Lauren called. "Kayla?"

Knocking frizzy hair over her shoulders, she finally shed her thick outer layer, and ducked into the kitchen. Empty.

A dark velvety rumble stopped her from checking the fridge, dragged her back ten steps. She turned.

"Lauren!" Maddie squealed. "Guess who's here."

Kayla lounged in the bay window, legs stretched for optimal viewing, a smug twist on her lips. "It's your date." The oldest Peck sister sounded accusing and victorious all at once. "The famous football star." She showered Miles with a slow, secretive smile.

Maddie stroked a looping curl, pulling it taut and letting it gently spring back. "She forgot to mention that part."

"I didn't forget," Lauren corrected sharply, wishing she had her coat on, wishing she couldn't feel sweat running down her spine, hair matted to her forehead. Wishing there wasn't a soy sauce stain on her sleeve.

The princesses had prepped.

There wasn't an uncurled eyelash or a dry lip. Maddie held court in front of a struggling fire, Hannah kept her back rigid on the center of the couch and Queen Kayla was a lazy tabby playing with her food from the seat of power.

And in Lauren's spot, in the comfiest chair with the best view of the TV, sat Miles Santos.

The prince.

A glass of water in his hand. No coat. Another overpriced, over-patterned T-shirt, familiar jeans. Dark brown work boots. Did he ever go home? Or was it an endless loop between The Peak and Pink Persuasion?

Settling narrowed eyes on her favorite chair, Lauren asked, "What are you doing here?"

"She has no manners," Kayla crowed.

"Are you sure you just want the water?" Maddie offered, twirling her hair more. Trying to reel him in. "We have tea and coffee, and Hannah drinks Red Bulls. They're sugar-free."

Miles's grin was slow and seductive. The fire flickering across his face made him almost sinister. A devil come to tempt. "I could go for something sweet. I'm afraid I've got a bit of an addiction."

He didn't look away from Lauren. In fact, he leaned closer, elbows lifting to the arms of his chair, perching there. "You're late. City Hall closes at five."

"She always works late," Maddie said as Hannah scurried to the kitchen.

The sound of her searching cabinets pulled Miles's grin wider. If there was a single piece of chocolate in this house, it was about to be found and given to Miles.

"Miles"—Maddie rushed to fill the silence, a cheery hostess smile painted her face—"how do you like Vermont?"

The thin edge in her sister's voice told Lauren she was furious. Apocalyptic that he'd visited without warning. Without giving her time to put on her Lululemon Aligns and perfume her hair in a cloud of coconut.

Miles glanced between the sisters, wheels turning. Smoking. Probably wondering how Lauren came from this lot.

"I've found everyone here to be extremely hospitable and one in particular lovely."

His gaze jumped from Lauren just long enough to wink at Maddie.

The ensuing giggle coaxed an eye roll from Lauren. "How are your balls?" she asked.

When he turned back to her, he wore a different smile. Not the same one he'd saved for beautiful women who were not his date, or the cocky grin, this was true amusement, teasing. And Lauren's breath caught.

Green eyes. He had green eyes.

Rich, dark evergreen irises like fresh-cut Fraser. She hadn't seen him in good lighting. Any lighting at all. And she understood why he clung to darkness. In the shadows, Miles Santos was the devil, a present of sin and danger wrapped with a black velvet bow.

In the glow of her living room, Miles was an angel. Pure, limitless green eyes. Long lashes fanning sharp, symmetrical cheekbones. The tattoos weren't a warning, faded lines drawing up his throat, they caressed him like beautiful memories, marking his skin where the clouds held him in Elysium.

She pinched her lips to keep from praying, to keep from telling him.

His head tilted, like he knew she was holding back. "Better than I deserve. How're your teeth?"

Being ground to dust.

"Oreo Thins, Raisinets, and shortbread cookies," Hannah announced her haul with a frown, twisting the orange shortbread box over. "These expired two months ago."

Because Lauren only allowed herself one a week. Because they crumbled in her mouth like falling snow, because the sugar and butter and flour melted on her tongue and wrapped her in a brilliant warm hug. Because if she had more than one, she'd have the box.

Thanking Hannah, Miles reached for those first.

"Do not eat my cookies," Lauren warned.

Kayla snorted her offense. "What is wrong with you? He needs calories. Football is taxing. I know because I played powderpuff in high school."

Lauren nearly exploded. "Don't you have a boyfriend?"

All at once, her sisters shot off explanations. "Not right now."

"It's an open relationship."

"He's not Miles Santos."

Princess fever was at an all-time high. Lauren had minutes, seconds before the fireplace started singing and Miles handed out tickets to a ball.

"I'm surprised any of them let you out of their sights," Miles said, smiling warmly at each Peck sister. Charming, handsome, chomping down on Tuesday's cookie.

Lauren snatched the box from his lap.

"Lauren! Have some manners," Maddie admonished, turning wide apologetic eyes to Miles. "She's not representative of the Pecks. Some of us actually know how to kiss."

"Maddie!"

"Lauren knows how," Miles said as if Lauren hadn't spoken. "She just doesn't want to kiss me."

"Who wouldn't want to kiss you?" Hannah squeaked.

Kayla bent forward. "I have a tattoo, you know. How far do yours go down?"

"Further than I should say," he replied wickedly.

"Enough!" Lauren stomped her foot, causing a cascade of perfect, buttery crumbs to sprinkle over the carpet. "Miles, leave."

"I will," he promised with a fake serious tone. "But first, I brought a gift for everyone." He stood, looking like a mountain in their small living room and pulled long glossy tickets from his back pocket.

It was happening.

The ball.

They'd buy gowns and comb their hair and Lauren would step on toes, but no one would care because she'd wear red, she'd wear red to the floor and paint her lips to match, she'd have wine and laugh with her head tossed back, she'd—

"There's only three," Hannah pointed out.

Lauren's fantasy shriveled. Her dress became a twig and her shoes fractured into shards of glass.

"Tickets for this Sunday," Miles was saying. "On the fifty-yard line, and I can get three more if you'd like to bring those boyfriends."

"I love football," Kayla gushed.

"We should all wear your jersey!" Maddie declared.

Hannah mumbled, "I'm single."

Lauren was stuck on the number. "Three?"

He tossed the tickets on their water-stained coffee table. "I didn't get one for you."

Right. He'd made his point. She said no to him and now he was going to spoil her sisters. Excellent revenge. Well executed. Hit exactly where it'd hurt.

"That's it." Lauren wrapped her hand around his arm, barely spanned the muscle. "Get out."

"He's our guest," Kayla snapped, holding a ticket like it was her precious. "You can't tell him to leave. We all pay rent."

She was right. Which only infuriated Lauren more.

Miles smiled as he sat back in his—her!—chair, looking like he lived there. Lauren's fury ratcheted to full-blown evil queen.

"Fine," she snarled at him, wanting to breathe fire. "Fine. I'll leave. Congratulations. You kicked me out of my own house."

CHAPTER SEVEN

MILES WAS A WIRED-OUT mess as he chased Lauren down a back set of steep stairs and took a hard left, shoulder catching drywall.

"Lauren, wait."

Dios, he was chasing her into the basement, like a fucking savage, a nightmare.

Stop, he commanded of his legs. *Stop this. Stop being a greedy bastard.*

Lauren slipped around a corner, a door swung. Miles shoved his boot in the jamb, slammed his palm on the wood.

"Five minutes, and you don't even have to look at me," he pleaded. "We can keep the door between us. You can have your phone in your hand, just listen for five minutes."

It was dark and dank in the basement, a low drop ceiling. Faint musty smell.

Fingers brushed his hand as they curved around the door.

"I'm not scared of you," Lauren told him, shaking voice betraying her. "I'm sick of you." A dim glow clicked on behind her, outlining her silhouette. The tucked-in shirt and oversized slacks.

"Five minutes and then you're gone? Forever. No more talking to my sisters either."

His eyes were slow to adjust, but eventually the scary, chained-up killer basement faded. He nudged the door open further. A bed with a light green blanket, plaster walls lined with movie posters, a narrow desk and a cluttered half bookshelf.

"You live in the basement?" Miles let himself into her room, his form casting big, intruding shadows on her walls. "Why do you live in the basement?"

Why did anyone?

Basements were for badly taped abandoned boxes with *winter '14* Sharpie'd on the side. Clear bins of Beanie Babies marked *save*. A place seldom used. A place to hide Christmas presents and forget about them.

Not a young, pretty girl's bedroom. Especially not one as uptight as Lauren. No way had the judgmental purse in her lips been born in the dusty basement.

Over the past week, Miles had spent all his time at Pinks peering into his memory to figure out the best way to convince her to help. What made her tick? What could he use for leverage? She'd mentioned sisters, and he'd stopped looking. The magic word to his plan, the key to her heart, her sisters.

He should have been thinking about what caused the frown on her plump lips.

Obviously, her room.

Sharp rapid clicks of footsteps on the main floor shook the ceiling tiles, rattled the sole lamp.

Checking her cuffs were buttoned, Lauren shrugged. "It's this or share a room with Maddie. Once we turned sixteen and her boyfriend started scaling the trellis for under-the-blanket action, I made the move. I didn't think it'd be permanent."

"Tia thinks you're a ghost, you're so pale." Now it made sense.

"It's better than sharing a bathroom with three other girls. I don't spend half my paycheck on Drano anymore."

Miles strode to her bookshelf, squinting as Lauren rushed to close her laptop, socks sliding over the cement. An oddly playful move from stoneheart.

"You're like a mole person," he accused, closing an eye to read a spine.

"You're being very dramatic." She pulled back a crooked drawer on her dresser. "There's just no windows. It's a basement."

"There's also no light," he said, spinning when he heard a door click, finding himself alone. "Is this the only lamp?" he called, warily appraising the squat jade green lamp struggling to reach the room's corners.

Dios.

He never thought he'd feel pity for the ice queen. But none of this made him conjure the image of Lauren straight-backed, with hard eyes, refusing a drink. The woman on their date had white sheets and clinically bare walls.

This room said a million things at once. Shouted it. Colorful ribbons dangled from the ceiling. Dried purple flowers wrapped in twine on her bookshelf. Spectacular and obscure quotes were pinned below pictures of friends, places, her family, forming a timeline of her life. Memories.

Assorted bobbleheads stood on risers behind her computer. Miles tapped the dragon's head, watched it shake.

When the door opened, Miles was caught with a finger prying open her laptop. "What kind of fan fiction do you write?" he asked, removing his hand, embarrassed he'd been snooping. "Ar-aragorn and the hot one?"

"Arwen?" Lauren scoffed. "No. No one cares about them."

"I do," Miles said. They were the only two he could half name. He tapped the dragon again, smiling at the stickers plastered to her laptop. "Let me guess, you're into the pretty boy? The elf. Orlando—"

"Legolas?"

"I'm right, aren't I?" He turned in time to see her laugh.

Lost his smile.

Bad lighting. A hint of a wet smell. A rising sensation of claustrophobia and Miles never wanted to leave. Lauren's laugh was a melodious sound, a cross between Christmas bells and a kettle's whistle, but he would've liked it if it were nails on a chalkboard when she looked like that.

Bright blue sweatpants, bare feet, an out-of-production Bills shirt that'd been slashed through to bare a patch of her stomach. Her hair was a wild mane, not the wetted-down hardness she'd had when they met or the pinned-back ponytail. Blondes and browns curled around her in a corona of sexy frizz, of bedhead and wandering hands.

This was the woman who pressed crocus and pinned them to her walls. Who ate shortbread and drank vodka, showered in lemon juice.

Her laugh trailed off when she saw his face, and he tried to school the lust lighting him up. Failed.

"It's not Legolas," she rasped, shifting between her feet, balling up the slacks she'd taken off.

"Tell me who," he asked, voice husky, and she laughed self-consciously, color filling her cheeks.

"It's embarrassing."

He wanted to move, to go to her side, to sink his hand into her hair. He tapped the dragon. It agreed. "You don't care what I think, remember? We're incompatible."

Nasty, dirty, filthy lie. His gaze dripped down her body, finding gentle curves and soft muscle. Nothing incompatible about spreading that body under him.

"Or did you change your mind?" *Say yes.*

"Alright." She threw her clothes into a white woven hamper. "I write about Sam and Frodo."

"Who?"

She shoved her face into her hands, collapsed onto her bed, and exclaimed, "The hobbits!"

"You write hobbit fan fiction." He was hard. For sweatpants and red cheeks and her one silky orange pillowcase.

"Say it with less judgment."

"I'm sorry." He laughed, wiping off his smile, turning, thankful the low lightning hid his increasingly obvious reaction to her.

Thought we were treating her like a man, he told his dick.

His best feature disagreed.

"Say something," she groaned, pushing up to her palms.

"I'm just wrapping my head around it," he said honestly, coming to grips that he'd been a blind idiot. "You're the first person who ever said fan fiction to me. I had to google it and sift through three billion results." He scratched his cheek. "You could write about anyone and you picked the slow, lame ones."

"They're the passionate ones," Lauren corrected in outrage. "The ones with feeling, the only ones completely unprepared and helpless and the strongest because of it."

"Passion," Miles murmured, laying out bait with his lowered tone. "Is that what you want?"

She winced, looked away, pulled at the comforter. "What are you doing here, Miles?" The abrupt change in her tone, the topic ended his arousal.

He crossed his arms. "Dropping off tickets to my Tia's pretty neighbors."

"I mean in my bedroom."

He flipped a wall switch, and nothing happened. "Did there used to be lights or—"

"I had plans to put them it and they fell through, OK? I've been busy."

"With Sam and Frodo. Perpetuating passion?" She bristled but he didn't press. "Explains the paleness. Tia wants to skin you, she hopes we'll have alabaster babies."

His eyes cut to hers, gauging her reaction. Hostile revulsion? Interest? Who was Lauren when she wasn't in suits, wasn't restrained in hair bands and buttons?

"Why?" She sounded genuinely confused. "You have the best skin I've ever seen."

"Well now"—Miles's fingertips brushed the bed—"what does that sound like to you?"

"If you're going to milk me for a compliment—"

"It sounded," he cut off, grinning, "like us getting along."

"I'm not giving you my Fridays, Miles. I'm tired after work. I don't want to be hanging out with you, going to the strip club, eating cheesecake, getting depressed."

"Dream date." He dropped to the edge of her bed and found it soft. Incredibly so, he sank and sank. "You don't have a headboard," he noted.

"Want me to come to your house and point out everything that's wrong with your bedroom?"

"Try. There's not a damn thing wrong with my bedroom. Strong, sturdy headboard, abundant lighting—"

"And a big mirror on the ceiling?" she finished.

"Skylight actually. But I like where your head's at." He winked at her, and her jaw sawed.

Spinning around, he got to the point. "I need your help."

"No."

"I'm not a man who gives up."

She stuck her nose in the air. "I'm not lucky. I'm the opposite of lucky. I'm sure you're a good football player. I'm sure my presence has zero bearing on your game."

Tilting his head, he drank her in, the sensual dip in the hollow of her throat, the soft chin, her lips. "Prove it."

Her head cocked. "You want me to flip a coin?"

He shook his head, still staring at her, refusing to be distracted by the quirk of her mouth. "Prove it's a fluke. That you're not the reason. Hang out with me again and if I play like normal, I'll agree with you."

Her eyes flickered, considering before a familiar hardened rejection sucked the thread of color from them.

Miles went to his feet. "Please," he said. "What if we had an arrangement?"

"An ... arrangement?"

"Four hours this Friday. I'll pay you." Handsomely. Then she could escape this dank cell of hers and stop cosplaying a snowflake.

"I don't need money."

"You're living in a windowless room. You need money."

"I don't live here because I'm poor. I live here because there's life. Maddie's hair curler setting off the fire alarm, Hannah's burnt maple cookies. If I leave, I'll be completely alone." There was indisputable fear in her voice.

Abruptly, she moved to the door, subtle shadows curling around her ankles. "Goodnight, Miles."

"Wait."

***

LAUREN FOCUSED ON MILES'S face as he loomed over her bed, hands not touching but hovering over the long body pillow. His dark eyes were slits, forearms tense but there was an intoxicating gentleness to his movements. As if he'd stumbled onto a flower bed and refused to shed a petal.

He was in her bedroom. Where she slept, read, spent time alone.

Where she'd cried when Brian dumped her. Where she'd plucked her left eyebrow into oblivion.

Funny, she'd be nervous showing anyone else her space, like she was letting them root through her mind, sort through the shelves of her heart, find it overwhelming.

But with Miles, there was no need to impress, no future. Lauren only felt a mild curiosity, no pain, as the running back explored her things.

Not even her sisters knew about her fan fiction addiction, but with Miles, it didn't matter.

She didn't care what he thought of her because he didn't think of her. And he didn't care what she thought of him. He laid it all out, guts and glory splayed across the pavement. No room for embarrassment.

His finger scratched down the seam of her pillowcase. "Please, if you don't want money—"

"Miles." She let her arms flop out, feeling like she was stuck in a loop. "I'm not the reason you won."

"I'll do whatever you want." He fell to his knees right there on the concrete floor. And then his powerful tatted body, his intensity, was hobbling over to her. No, not hobbling. A man of Miles's bearing didn't hobble or stumble, even on his knees, he commanded power, he crawled.

Lauren's throat tightened as his hands crept over hers.

Warm hands, always warm hands. Like fire-warmed mittens, like comfort and slow mornings. She sucked in a breath at the scrape of his scabbed knuckles.

Black lines streaked up his craned neck, looking like poles preventing him from lowering his chin from her.

"Anything you want," he murmured. "I'll do it. Just give me Friday."

She began to pull back from him, feeling his warmth travel and spread up her arms, across her stomach.

Changing to comfy clothes was supposed to send him home. Her ugly sweatpants a natural man deterrent, but his gaze held roiling intensity.

"Give me a list, a workbook of requests. Anything, Lauren. Anything, and I'll make it happen." His thumb coasted over hers, stroking, his breath was hot on her hip.

"Anything?" she repeated quietly, staring into the impossibly green irises, his voice was like an illicit cloud of drugging smoke. Before she could stop it, she had a hand in his hair tipping him back further. "Even sex?"

Silence.

The echoes of a sister brawl upstairs. Remote-ageddon.

"No." His voice sliced through the tension, a final answer.

Lauren felt ridiculous. Dumb. Embarrassed. She snapped her hand back and he was quick to catch her, thumb resuming an easy caress on her palm.

Unable to give her a break, he teased, "Interesting your mind went there."

Even on his knees, feigning submission, he wore power. "Is that what you want from me, Lauren? My body?"

She whipped her hands out of his. "Of course not."

In a slick rise, he swallowed the space around her, broad back blocking her light, drawing shadows into a thick curtain.

"You want to fly a plane?" he asked flatly. "I'll buy one. New clothes, I'll get you a mall. Archery? I'll be your target." Carefully, he breached the distance between them, stroked down her cheek. "No sex. Sex for me is the start of a timer and I don't want to hear a buzzer with you."

Because he wanted to use her.

Because he could get sex everywhere, but his luck only came from her.

"You can't be that superstitious."

He didn't say anything in response, just looked at her with pleading eyes, like she held the world in her hands and at any moment could let go, have oceans shatter and cities crumble.

He *was* that superstitious.

Truly believed she was the key to his success. Never mind that he looked like he could bench-press a Hummer, and possessed the reflexes of a leopard.

He thought he needed her. Had followed her, tracked her like a predator and when he had her cornered, fangs ready to strike, he rolled over to his belly, tail wagging.

She couldn't be considering this, could she?

Lauren stepped back and her spine aligned with the door jamb, the metal plate cold on her tenth vertebrae.

Miles moved with her, attached, his hand winding up to grip the trim above them as he held her waist. Arching into him was second nature. Inhaling the faint cling of processed sugar.

His forehead pressed down to hers, his eyes closed.

"I'll beg," he whispered.

Lauren tore from him, escaped backward into the hall, feet hitting the stairs until she collapsed onto them.

She *was* considering this. Was more than considering it.

Power.

Miles was handing her power, length after length, piling it in her arms yanked straight from his capable hands. The power of choice, the power of being the one who cared less.

She floundered under the press of it, heady from the concept. Her arms trembled, her breaths were short.

Power.

After feeling like a flag in the wind, getting shredded, raised and lowered when someone wanted a show.

He was in her house, hanging in her bedroom doorway, eyes dark, focus intense. On her. On her in sweatpants. He'd googled fan fiction. He'd found her.

Psycho, Brian would grunt.

But Lauren knew better, recognized more, saw and felt more than other people. Passion.

The field, his gameplay was his passion. And he believed to better it, he needed her.

That she was his destiny, his fate, a wide pool of luck he wanted to drown in.

Anything. She could have him beg, snarl the word, toss it between him and watch him bend and lick the floor. Not because he was insane or because he wanted to be humiliated, because he felt.

"No more strip clubs," she said, staring at her hands. "No more naked women or champagne."

"Whatever you want, I meant it. Four hours, we'll set a timer. Two-hundred and forty minutes, I won't drag it out a second longer.

Four hours of power. Of Lauren's choice.

And it would get her sisters off her back.

She imagined a domino fall of Peck girls when she explained she was booked every single Friday.

Brian's twisted frown when she told him to shut up. She had plans.

"Four hours." She nodded. Four hours where he couldn't run, where she couldn't scare anyone.

"Just." An arm dropped from the door, leaving him to hang on the frame like Achilles off the bow of his ship. "Promise me, you won't watch any of my games."

"Why not?" How would she know if her luck worked?

"Because you had no idea who I was when we met so I don't think you watch football and I want to limit moving parts. We'll keep our Fridays consistent and your Sundays football free."

A bit of her control yanked into his palms. She pulled back. "Fine, but my sisters get season tickets. I could use some alone time."

A taunting smile curved his mouth. "And what will you do in your house all alone in this dark room?"

She rose, feeling fresh, the lethargy of the day seeping out and spilling behind her. "What all normal luck blessed girls do in the dark." She poked the nose of a bear on his forearm. "Plan ways to make our four hours together intolerable."

Power felt good.

Narrowed eyes watched her fingers stroke the tattoo. "I knew you'd be thinking of me."

She laughed, pressing her shoulder into the door, crowded under Miles's width but she didn't feel like she was intruding, didn't second-guess.

His voice went husky again, made Lauren's heart stammer. "Do we have a deal?"

"Yes."

One second they were two, the next, they were one. Miles lifted her, spun, hands covering her skin, body warm and hard and rigid.

Too soon, he let go, smile showing white teeth. "I'll pick you up at eight."

As he strode for the stairs, Lauren admired the wide gait, the flex of his thighs.

"How much were you going to pay me?" she asked as he took the first stair.

"Ten grand."

"Ten grand for one season?"

He ducked down to smirk at her. "Too late to wonder, isn't it?" Then he was moving, walking, leaving.

"Miles?" Lauren called. "Ten for a whole season, or for a date?"

"Eight o'clock."

"Miles! Ten grand for a Friday?"

The door shut.

Lauren grinned, having gotten the answer.

CHAPTER EIGHT

MILES FELL STILL ON the Peck front stoop, unsure he'd heard right.

Lauren was bundled in layers and coats, a black scarf and knit hat, not a sprig of that wild hair free. He'd arrived early to make sure there was no possible reason she could complain.

And OK, if he caught her in a state of frazzled undress, all the better.

He'd never imagined she'd foil his dreams so effortlessly.

"What was that?" He put his ear closer to her mouth, hand raised to block the wind.

"We're shoveling." She zipped her coat until it pinched her chin, covering every inch of skin in faded black. "Rather," she continued, making sure her ears were completely concealed, "*you're* shoveling. I'll salt in your wake."

"Tell me you're joking."

"Aw," she mocked in a baby voice. "Big man can't handle a wittle snow?"

"You have four hours with me," he said. "Me. To do whatever you want."

"Wow, you really let that ego grow, huh? No kind of pruning or maintenance."

Shaking in the building nor'easter, Miles pushed inside the front door and tugged her zipper back down. "I can give you a massage. Take you winetasting. We could go car shopping, and you want me to shovel the driveway?"

The zipper continued down until it split. How many times on the drive had he wondered if she'd be in slacks or sweatpants?

Judging by the bright edge in her eyes, the white-ball-topped hat, she was through with serving him ice queen. Seemed she reserved that for potential suitors.

He sent a silent prayer to her exes, hoping they recovered.

"Our driveway only takes like thirty minutes. You're doing the whole neighborhood."

"The whole—This is not a good use of my skills," he rebutted, pulling down another zipper, parting her black fleece.

How many layers did she have on?

How many could he take off?

She slapped his hands away. "I don't want you for sex and I don't want you for money so I'm gonna be using you for those pretty muscles. Let's go. I only have four hours." She zipped back up the fleece, arched an eyebrow at him. "Do you have a coat?"

"No." If it was below fifty, he didn't go outside. He'd die.

"I don't have anything that'll fit you." She felt the hem of his gray henley and frowned. "Do you want to go home and get something warmer?"

And lose precious time? "I'll be fine."

"Hmm." She unwrapped the scarf from her neck and wound it around his. "There." Her hands coasted along his tattoos to adjust the curls at his nape, over his eye, across his forehead.

"Don't be a tease," he said as she wound a dark strand around her finger. He pinned her hip, hand slipping into the open gap of her coat. "Come on, I know you want to. Give it a yank."

He watched her throat bob. "And just because I want to, I should?"

"There isn't a thing you could want that I wouldn't." He brought her hand to his head, tipping forward. "Pull."

He should've guessed she wouldn't. No gripping his hair and testing the strength, she sent her fingers soaring through the curls, let her nails lightly scrape his skull as her lips parted in fascination.

Four moves. Spread her legs, bend his knees, send his hand down the back of her pants, and he could coax a cry from those lips, make the sea glass roll back into her head until she was ripping the hair from his scalp, grasping for control.

"Soft," she murmured, strokes gentle, meticulous.

Miles got the second zipper undone again. Stole a peek.

Simple clothes. A modest striped long sleeve meant to hide and distract. But on a figure like hers, it was nothing less than a mindfuck. Curves hidden in plain sight.

There was something about that Miles admired. A wolf in sheep's clothing. A fox skirting through tall grass, the brightest red hidden save for leaping flashes.

Daily, Miles was surrounded by flesh and skin, more curves than a switchback. He'd made himself a lion among wolves. Ferocious, bloodthirsty. But the curiosity of where his fingers would bend and mold on those black and white stripes drew his mind from the hunt. A high-necked tease constructed to make him suffer.

He swallowed a rush of excess hunger as he remembered the narrow band of skin on her hips. Lauren Peck was a knockout. Why did she hide it?

Maybe the better question was, who did she hide it from?

And where could Miles find the piece of shit?

"If I had your hair, I'd stroke it so often, it'd fall out," she said breezily, nails scoring his nape, drawing backward, pushing closer to him. She smelled like lemons and a wood-burning fire.

It was lucky, Miles supposed, that she mentioned his hair, and didn't drag him down a different road where stroking was only the start.

"I don't care," he replied, shutting his eyes to enjoy her sweet ministrations. "I'll grow it back."

Her hands stopped, retreated. Her waist slipped from his grip. "I'm petting you." She buried her face in her palms.

"I like it." He shrugged, easy tone earning him a glower. "Felt good. Let me know if you want me to return the favor. I'll grow my nails."

"You're … you can't be serious."

"Why not?" he asked, shackling down the vestiges of lust. "It feels good, I should return the favor."

The comment took her more aback than he'd thought it would. "Yes, well …"

"Shoveling?" Miles prompted when she didn't say more.

Thrust back into her torture plans, Lauren walked out the door, only noticing her undone layers when she had two feet buried under a fresh layer of snow. She didn't glide like the women at Pinks, didn't sway and swing, steps to allure, to tantalize.

Lauren scurried.

Each lift of her foot just high enough to bring her forward. Short, mediated steps executed at rapid fire, constraining her hips to a rigid line.

Nothing natural about her walk. It was trained the same way a dog flinched at a rolled magazine.

Gritting his teeth, Miles followed her into the winter night, tied the floral-scented scarf at his neck, and grabbed the blue plastic handle of the shovel.

The sky was an empty black, no stars, no clouds. The only reminder of the storm the three inches of white smoothing over the road. He dug the squared edge of the shovel into the driveway. Lifted. Threw.

"Aren't there snow removal services?"

"Yeah, but most of the neighborhood is retired and on a fixed income, which means they can't afford it."

"Which leaves you?" he asked in a disbelieving tone.

"They used to buy Maddie's overly sour lemonade and they always collected cans for me for school fundraisers. I'm paying it back. If you have a better solution, I'm all ears."

Another scrape, lift, throw.

"Excellent form." A teasing smile lurked in the corners of her lips. "Just do that another hundred thousand times."

"You know"—he inclined his head to her, giving another scoop, working a path between the cars—"that movie *Holes*. I get it now. I'm living it."

"No one will believe it," she murmured, staring at him with renewed intensity. "But I think you're even more dramatic than me."

Who wouldn't believe it?

Lauren had yet to do anything outlandishly dramatic. And he'd given her ample options.

Salt bit his ankles. Another scoop. Another throw, he found a rhythm as his boots crunched in the snow.

After her driveway came the neighbors. By the third house, he was sweating, winding Lauren's scarf back around her neck, rolling up his sleeves.

As he worked, he reminded himself of how desperately MVP would change not his life, but the dozens of women he looked out for. The threat of a short career kept him on edge. Not having the millions flood his accounts each year, going to Pinks with ones instead of hundreds.

League MVP would give him life after the Mountaineers. Coaching, talking head spots, post-career sponsorships. Three letters on his stat sheet would elevate him to a household name.

Shockingly, the four hours passed quickly. As he cleared thin strips of white off the sidewalk's edge, Lauren's eyes drooped. She was perched on an overturned salt bucket, her bare hands tucked into her armpits.

"Go inside," he told her as a tremor started in her back.

Her voice came back condescending, "You wanted four hours, you're getting it."

"I want four hours a week, pretty girl. You're not going to make it to next week if you sit out in the elements." He stopped, spearing the shovel into a snowbank, and folded his arms. His breath was a milky fog in front of him, pants making mushroom clouds.

A workout. On his Friday night.

Snow trickled down. Slow, big flakes from wafer-thin clouds. They had another fifteen minutes. Maybe he'd scrape the fresh stuff off her front porch.

"I was raised here, I know my cold limits."

"Why don't you wear gloves?" he asked, scowling at her hands. "Makes me cold just looking at you."

"In case I need my phone."

He didn't need more questions. He knew the explanation far too well. Wouldn't ask again. Bending in front of her, he enclosed her hands in his, and puffed warm air across her fingers.

"You carry pepper spray?" he asked quietly, wishing he could go back, wishing he could've been the older sibling, wishing he'd known sooner the dark reality.

"I have a penknife."

"Lose it," he instructed harshly. "A knife can be used on you. Pepper spray is best. If it gets turned around on you, it's not fatal. You know self-defense?"

"I took a class."

His hands snared her freezing-cold wrists, tightened. "Get rid of me."

***

LAUREN WOBBLED ON THE plastic bucket, staring into forest irises. Snow collected in Miles's curls, balancing on the arches and tumbling down to wet his scalp.

She didn't want to get rid of him. She wanted to pull him closer, she wanted to press the white flake on his cheek into his skin and feel it melt between them.

Each time she had Miles pinned, each time they entered a friendly rapport, he demolished it, smashed it to smithereens in mind-numbing quickness. Telling her to pull his hair, getting on his knees to beg.

This was the sharpest turn yet.

He didn't seem to realize he wasn't following the script, completely unaware that their conversation lacked flow. It jolted and recovered. It didn't give her time to plan and mitigate or defend. She had to react right there with him to keep from hitting the pavement.

"Get rid of me." His voice was low and menacing, a stranger on the abandoned street.

Lauren threw her hands apart and struck out with her leg. Her bucket pitched sideways. She yelped.

Miles had her spinning in the air, a solid warm hand sliding up the back of her coat to press them together. Snow on his eyelashes. Delicate white sucked into the black waves.

"Bad," he assessed, shaking his head, moving to put her down, thinking she'd given up.

She pulled his hair. Hard. Scratched at his skull.

His eyes dilated, irises swallowed by black and her lungs emptied as he squeezed her close. Before she could retract her claws, try something else, scramble free, he'd muttered, "Fuck," onto her neck, dropped her, turned, and reclaimed his shovel.

Another jolt, another whirlwind change.

What just—

Throat suddenly thick, she changed the topic. "I expected a lot more whining. Even a little foot stomping, but you've exceeded expectations."

"Do I look like I whine and stomp my feet?" His darkened gaze skated over her. They leveled that flare of … something quickly, back to teasing, like they'd never fallen off the edge.

"You look like …" She tilted her head, as if seeing him for the first time. Like she hadn't been watching his biceps swell, his shirt cling, seen the steam rise off his skin, and the bottom of his jeans sag from caked-on salt and snow.

"You look like a sweaty mess." She picked up her bucket. "Don't worry, with conditioning, you'll improve."

"My forty-yard dash is four point four seconds."

"If only speed cleared snow. There's another storm Friday." Her tone was unfamiliar, a lilt of teasing and confidence. She could say anything and he'd have to put up with it. How freeing to not mince words. "I already checked the weather."

"Wait, what? Next Friday?"

"This is your Friday night from now on. Santos snow removal." Her phone alarm went off. "Four hours." She silenced it. "And we didn't kill each other." She grabbed the shovel from his hands but he didn't let go.

"We're not done."

She let out a swift, shallow breath, reining in her fight. "It's midnight. That's four hours. That's the deal. I'm tired."

"Four hours"—Miles paused, seemingly considering the exact phrase he wanted. He threw her a beseeching glance—"and a kiss."

Lauren's throat closed.

Before she could control the direction of her thoughts, she imagined pulling him down to her, hands knotted in his thin shirt, stealing his heat, his lips on hers. Her toes pointing in sweet satisfaction, the sky clearing to show glittering stars—

No, stop. A ridiculous fantasy.

"We kissed last time," Miles said, as if he had to remind her. As if she could forget. His gaze wandered to her mouth. "I think we need to do that again too."

Panicked G-forces crushed her ribs into her lungs, stole blood from her brain. "Kissing wasn't part of the deal."

Kissing would give her ideas, demolish her defenses. Once had been enough to know she could do it. Kiss without attachment. Move on. But every week, a kiss. What if … what if she let it happen again?

What if her tiara came back? Melted onto her head, gold talons shredding her better sense.

"Barely a kiss," he was saying, reasoning, belittling as he unwrapped her scarf, caressed her cheek. "You asked me to kiss you before. Now, I'm asking."

"Miles, I don't think it's a good idea." She was only emerging from her Brian postmortem. Still raw, healing skin in certain places, vulnerable.

His palm stretched over her jaw, fingers stealing under her hat.

"Please." His voice was a building rumble, thunder sweeping closer. Disaster, and yet he smelled sweet. Sugar and snow, fresh air. "I need you, Lauren."

Before she knew what was happening, she'd said, "Quick," unsure if she was describing how she wanted him or how badly.

A hand on her waist. "Close your eyes."

She squeezed them shut. He needed her. She was needed. A kiss was nothing.

Gentle lips pressed into hers. The pro-running back with tattoos and sweat, with snow sticking to bare overheated skin kissed her like she was a phantom, not really there, like he was guessing where her lips began.

No lick, no suck, no pressure.

No jolt.

Easy, light. Miles peeled back, smiling, saying something. Snowflakes or goodnight, or petting hair.

Lauren couldn't hear.

The frayed end of a pink satin ribbon had speared her heart.

Chapter Nine

MILES SWIRLED THE LAST inch of watered-down whiskey around the bottom of the glass, thinking that the color was the same shade as Lauren's hair. As he tossed it back, he wished he had something better to compare it to.

Lauren, his good luck charm, his treasure. Contained. Wild.

Another game in his pocket and she'd proven her worth tenfold. Mountaineers were on a winning streak, heating up.

"Here she comes." Moore blew out a breath and shook his hands to get loose. A spread of gold rings clanging together. He knocked his elbow into Miles's stomach. "Any advice, lady killer?"

Miles finished his glass and slid it across the bar. He kept his back to the room, content to stare at the lined bottles and unlit neon signs. "Treat her like royalty."

Behind them, Asher Laughlin snorted.

Fuck, Miles hated that kid always bumming around. Moore was cool, young but fun, a good second on nights like this, nights when the edge needed taming. But Asher was a plain asshole.

Miles slid a disgruntled glare to the receiver, ready to ruin his white shirt. "Fucking problem with that, Laughlin?"

"Just find it ironic that's your advice." He ran a hand through pitch-black hair, looking bored. "You're railing the head of PR, yeah? Right in her office?"

"It's over, and I treated Sonja like a queen."

"Yeah," he grunted into two fingers of gin. "Queens take dick bent over their desk."

Miles glanced at the league darling, who remained rudely expressionless and then Moore, who seemed amused by the exchange. The men were different in every way. Moore was outspoken and free-spirited, quick to ingratiate himself with even the most surly players in the locker room. Then there was Asher, who stayed cold-hearted and detached in his treatment of the team, a constant threat he'd cut ties with the Green for better money, a longer contract elsewhere.

As much as Miles had his own drive, he had no self-sacrificing thirst like Asher. No compassion, no awe for the sport. He was a kite following a jet trail and when the wind changed, there'd be no goodbye before you were watching him dismantle your own defense.

Miles wouldn't spend time with him if it weren't for his friendship with Moore. For some inexplicable reason, the two were inseparable. Asher's dark cloud chasing Moore's sun.

Despising his crude language, defensive of his friend Sonja, Miles snarled to Asher, "What the fuck is your problem?"

"Boys, boys," Moore cut in jovially. "Let's not fight in front of my future wife."

"Treat her like a peasant, like a beggar," Asher told his team-mate. "Give her everything she wants and she'll follow you any-where, let you do anything."

Miles's temper crackled. He hadn't come to The Hand for a fight, but—

A soft throat cleared behind them. Asher and Miles unlocked horns to turn.

Lemons.

Soft blonde lashes swept down briefly, fluttered and Miles winced beneath a ripple of denial, regret.

"Hi," Lauren greeted quietly, expression revealing nothing. Not an eyebrow lift or disappointed smile, no hint of a taunt. Just a level chin as she stepped between them. "Just ... um. Excuse me." She turned her hips to keep from elbowing Asher.

Shame.

Miles not-so-subtly angled his way between her and Asher, ready with a tease, a hello, a what-the-fuck-are-you-doing-here, when she said, "Declan?"

The blue-eyed bartender turned, smiled. He ran a drying cloth around the lip of a martini glass. "The usual?"

Lauren's cheeks were pink as she nodded, wrestling her back pocket for loose bills. Actively pretending not to know Miles. Like she hadn't heard Asher's shit-brained comment.

There was a devilish glint in Moore's eyes, and the lanky receiver abandoned his lifelong pursuit of The Hand's beautiful owner to strike his gaze down to Lauren, lingering at the dip in her gray sweater, the hug of her jeans.

Jeans.

Miles had thought sweatpants were the height of Lauren's appeal, the sagging waistband that led to swinging hips. Wrong. Lauren in jeans was crushing. Denim curving and cupping.

"Oh, I have to know what a regular orders," Moore purred, too aware he had a face free of scars and tattoos. "Is there a secret menu?" he asked, letting loose a dazzling smile.

It was his schtick. Questions, flirting, the rookie would make her laugh and convince her to get air with him, invite her to a private stand-up show at his place.

"This one's mine," Miles told him, dashing any lewd plans. The words were sharp, harsher than he'd intended.

Lauren's eyes bulged but she didn't dare look, as the bartender slid her a full tray. Four drinks. Three looking fruity and tart with straws and sugared rims, fizzing. One vodka lemon.

A double.

"Whoa." Moore gave a swift, impressed whistle. "Where's the party and can I come?"

"Are you deaf?" Miles bit. "Did you not hear me?" He put the tips of his fingers against Lauren's back. Not too low, nor too high. The middle, the safety zone. "She's mine."

Lauren flinched under his touch, rattling the drinks on her tray.

"Miles," she chided, steadying a strawberry martini.

Finally. Acknowledgment.

"Lauren, say hello to someone you will never talk to you again, Riley Moore. And someone who doesn't talk at all, Asher Laughlin."

She tucked the tray into her stomach and looked up. And up.

Miles had never been insecure about his height. Six foot solid. He weighed more than Moore could dream to and maintained ten percent body fat. But as Lauren's head tipped back, extending the long line of her throat, he felt his shoulders drop back, his spine lock straight.

She glanced at Asher, and pursed her lips. "Football players, I take it."

"And drink connoisseurs," Moore flirted.

"One more fucking word," Miles snapped. The threat went unspoken. No one challenged Miles to a fight and walked away clean.

Moore raised his hands, dropping narrow hips to the bar.

"I'm taken," he muttered, searching for the dark-haired beauty who enjoyed saying no.

Taking Lauren's tray, Miles lifted it from her reach. "Where are you sitting?"

The Hand was the antithesis of the Vegas glamour he was accustomed to. Bare furnishings, thick planked paneling, boot-worn wood floors. Music loud enough to swallow conversations, quiet enough to drink in peace. Long pine tables covered the middle of the open floor, crowded with strangers and friends alike.

Not a single bedazzled G-string hung from the rafters.

Oddly enough, Miles liked the rustic charm. The smell of cedar, the stamping of snow off boots signaling a newcomer. It made him feel less alone.

Lauren led him toward the spotless front windows, glancing back every step like she thought he was about to hightail it with her drinks.

"What are you doing here?" he asked her back, taking a lick of her lemon. A rush of saliva filled his cheeks.

"Tuesday is trivia night."

Another swipe at her lemon was all he had time for before he found the end of Lauren's trail. The narrow row of Peck sisters using more hands than words to talk.

Between them sat a black placard with the number seven.

Miles grinned.

"My lucky night," he murmured.

Instead of pummeling Moore, he felt a sweep of gratitude to the rookie for texting him, telling him to play wing for his dream lady.

"No luck about it," Lauren retorted, sidestepping a game of darts. "What about you? Picking up bartenders or just acting like a possessive asshole?"

"If you thought that was possessive, settle in for a harsh reality."

She spun, walking backward, the stubby heels of her boots clicking against wood. A silent laugh made her eyes glow. "Oh yeah? Tell me."

He flicked his gaze up, missing the view of her denim ass. "Do you want any ink on that paper skin of yours? Because I bet 'Miles' would look stunning right across your pretty little throat."

Her heel twisted, she bumped into a metal support beam. "My throat?"

Lemon, he could taste it. "So when you look up with those big green eyes, everyone looking down knows who you belong to."

Feeling downright predatory, Miles advanced having found a soft underside to strike, intent on painting her cheeks red, making her forget Moore's pretty face.

Before he could shock and delight, before he could scare luck back into the corner, Lauren said, "Maybe we could get a little collar for me to wear every Friday. Put a bell on it."

Heinous revulsion poured into his veins. He nearly gagged under the sickening weight. A collar. Heart racing, sweat combing down his back, he swallowed, shook his head.

"No." He dug his steel toes into the floor, clenched his jaw. "No. I would never disrespect you like that. You're your own person. Shit, I'm sorry. I didn't mean it. You're not an object to me, you're—"

"Hey." Her fingers looped over his wrist. "It's OK, we were kidding around. It was a joke."

But it hadn't been.

He'd felt the possession heat his blood, felt the call of obsession.

Miles wanted Lauren's luck for him. He wanted to mark her, hide her, put her on a pedestal and take from her.

No one could touch his luck.

When the Peck sisters came within reach, Miles managed to smile past his self-loathing. "Drinks for the most beautiful ladies in the bar."

With a roll of her eyes, Lauren doled out the fruity cocktails, smacking the vodka on the empty side of the table and wrenched on her lemon. Juice sprayed her fingers, a seed sank to the bottom of her glass.

"Did Declan mention me?" the quiet sister asked, curving timid hands around her Bellini.

Lauren licked her thumb and gave a quick shake against the sour. "He seemed really busy," she lied. "I'm sure he'll talk to you later."

"God, he's so fucking hot," the mean one gushed, stirring the red martini. Her curls were big and shiny, so unlike Lauren's; if it weren't for the same green shade of their eyes, he'd never think to call them sisters.

"Don't blow it all on the bartender," the prickly sister—Kayla?—muttered. "There's a lot of talent tonight." Her eyes fixed on Moore's ass bent over the bar as he recited love sonnets to the goth owner.

Lauren stared at her glass, shaking the ice to stir, muttering something like, "You have boyfriends."

And suddenly, trolling for ass didn't interest Miles. Not even watching Moore get rejected for the fifteenth time. He didn't want to leave Lauren alone with the same sisters who sent her out on a date with him, made her ask for a kiss.

What if they tried again?

Picked a guy from two tables over. The nerdy one with glasses and a leather bracelet.

He couldn't stop the barbarian urge to claim and mark and since he couldn't—wouldn't—do that, he'd stay with her, cockblock. His luck wouldn't be spent on anyone else.

Eyeing the black placard, he asked, "How big can the teams be? Can I join?"

"Oh yes, we need a fifth," low-cut top with margarita said. "It's perfect. You can cover the sports category. We always write Lebron James."

"Hey, I got the one with Lamar Odom," the mean one interrupted. Maddie?

Lauren gave a derisive snort. "Only because he married a Kardashian." She tugged Miles's arm and nodded at the nerd table. "The Bro-Fucks always beat us because of that category."

Hipsters. Flannels and glasses and vegan leather belts. Another adjustment from Vegas. The assholes on the East Coast didn't identify themselves with spray tans and goatees.

"It's not fair," Kayla sneered. "I heard one of their brothers was a Bruin."

"So what," Lauren crooned, unimpressed. Like the Mountaineer beside her was chopped fucking liver.

He pulled out the long wooden bench, lifting it with Lauren still seated and slid next to her before dropping and dragging it back. "I'd loved to be your sports savant."

"Big talk, hope you can back it up," Lauren teased as she sipped her vodka. She pointed across from her to the timid Peck. "Hannah answers the history questions, she has a degree in American literature. Maddie's all things pop culture, and Kayla covers niche topics thanks to her plethora of hobbies." She went down the line, and knitted her fingers together. "So we're covered."

"And you?" Miles pulled her belt loop, sliding her closer until their thighs touched. And to push her, he snagged a taste of her drink, letting the alcohol and lemon burn his tongue. "What's your topic?"

Lauren watched his tongue flick the rind of her lemon.

Maddie slurped her martini. "She does all the nerdy stuff."

"Nerdy?" Miles felt himself grin.

"Technically, geeky," Lauren corrected, pulling the sleeve of her thick sweater into her palm. "I'm the only one who watches movies longer than two hours, which apparently makes me a geek."

"Movies are more than two hours now?" Miles blew out a breath and crept closer, wanted closer still. "You have so much wisdom to share."

A dinger sounded and the music dropped to a hum.

"Welcome to trivia night," a deep voice said. The bartender, Declan, stalked through the numbered tables, shuffling a stack of white note cards. "We've got our teams set up. Thank you for registering. Let's get into it."

A few excited shouts, a whoop, a whistle.

Maddie sighed dreamily. "He gets better looking every week."

Miles shot a dark look at the trivia host. Black hair, a spotty sleeve of tattoos. Tall, skinny, piercings cuffing his ear. He didn't get the fascination. But when he leaned down to mock ask Lauren if she could focus around Vermont's sexiest bad boy, he stopped.

Her gaze followed Declan's weave between the tables with rapt attention, examining him, watching as he perched on a stool, spread his knees, secured his boots on the metal rungs.

"So that's your type?" Miles mused.

Declan read off the first question, and Maddie claimed the pen, scribbling on the team's whiteboard and thrusting it—and her tits—into Declan's direction.

Thumbs up. Correct.

"My type?" Lauren made a face at her glass. "What do you mean?"

"I mean the bartender. That's why you went and got the drinks, you like him. Dark hair, light eyes. I'm surprised. He has tattoos."

"I never said I don't like tattoos."

Just his, evidently. And it rankled. "What's the change in heart?"

"It's not a change," she returned hotly. "I like tattoos, always have. I think they're—"

Another question.

Grappling for the marker. Scribbling.

Lauren lowered her voice to a rasp. "Sexy, I guess. But it's the men who get them that I don't like. Why do they spend all that money to drip in ink? To cover up mistakes, atone for sins, honor previous loves?" Her knee nudged his. "The men with tattoos have pain, enough to warn everyone of it in order to attract the right woman."

Her eyes drifted to his neck, and he felt it like a physical caress, a pointed fingernail tracing the lines.

She liked his tattoos. Not him.

Neither mattered. Still, he had to ask, "What's wrong with pain? Carbon gets crushed to make diamonds."

"Too much pain and you become unfeeling." She traced the rim of her glass. "You ever hear a diamond say, I love you?"

"Miles!" Hannah, Kayla, Maddie—one of them—interrupted. "It's your turn. Who's the Patriots' quarterback?"

"Tom Brady," Lauren rushed out, reaching for the marker.

Miles was faster, uncapping it with his teeth. "It's Baker Mayfield. Brady retired. They optioned Lincoln Wray for a while, but they couldn't cut the deal." He raised the board over his head.

Heard Declan's click of approval.

Correct.

He capped the marker. Found Lauren's irritated gaze.

"Lucky guess." He winked.

The game went fast. No breaks, rapid-fire questions until the final round between the Peck girls and Bro-Fucks, as Lauren had dubbed them.

For sudden death, Kayla was elected their representative by Kayla herself, even though Maddie made an argument for her to go.

Lauren swirled her third vodka. "You just want him to look down your shirt."

There was a chance the last round he'd gotten was overkill; Miles was used to the full-rage Vegas partiers. The conversation at the Peck table was dwindling.

Maddie hiccupped and pointed a pink-tipped finger at ... something. "I want him to do more than look."

He could appreciate the attitude. "I know a couple guys who would help you with that."

"No," Lauren hissed, squeezing his wrist. "No footballers. Not for them."

Kayla shouted, "Sean White!"

Hannah pulled a scowl. "We don't get football players, but you get one? That's not fair."

"Miles and I are not dating. We're friends."

Maddie chewed on a thin red straw. "Only you could be friends with him."

Miles smiled into his Coke. "Please, she turned me down. Stop rubbing it in." Gently, he pinched Lauren's hip out of sight of her sisters.

A new intimacy between them. Fleeting touches. One he couldn't stop, didn't want to. Kept caressing, stroking, fixing her hair, finding lint on her shirt.

Mine, his fingers said. *Mine. Mine. Mine.*

"Another double Grey Goose?" He pushed back her hair. *Mine.*

My luck. No one else can have it.

"Grey Goose?" Lauren sputtered. "I drink Svedka."

"You may drink Svedka, but, pretty girl, you down Grey Goose." He took her glass, stood.

"Hey," came a high-pitched greeting from a curvy brunette. "I heard you're unattached. I'm Kenna." A beer in her hand, no ring, a nose piercing. He'd clocked her when he walked in as an option.

Forgot about her the moment Lauren appeared.

He dipped his chin, feeling a tick in his jaw. "What can I do for you, Kenna?"

A finger on his chest. "I'm just wondering how far you live from here and if you ever get lonely."

Forward. Beautiful. She'd taste like pilsner and come twice before he even started.

"Sorry," he said with zero apology in his tone. "I'm with my girl tonight, but my buddy at the bar." He pointed at Moore. "He's the kind of company you want, trust me. He'll take you on a better ride than I can."

A bone for ditching the rookie and getting his heart stomped on by the owner's black leather boots.

"I don't know about that." Kenna's hips swayed.

With less levity, he told her, "You don't want this."

Because it was the truth.

Who wanted a possessive, distracted asshole?

***

LAUREN DRAGGED HER HEAD over to peer at the clock. Eleven o'clock. Eleven. On a Tuesday.

And Miles could take a woman home. Maybe to the alley. When she heard him sit, saw a fresh lowball slip in front of her, she blew hair off her cheek.

"Water, this time," Miles told her as he sat. "With lemon."

"You should say yes," she said straight into her glass, cheeks flushed. "You're not going to get a better offer from me."

Was she drunk?

On a Tuesday?

With Miles? Again?

Who was she?

She'd bitten a poison apple. Miles's hand was a spindle and she'd succumbed to dark, evil magic.

She felt the wrap of purple and black smoke, the drip into her system, slow and familiar. Because Miles Santos's charm, in the space of a week, was familiar. The I-know-I'm-a-big-deal-but-I'll-pretend-I'm-not-for-you toxic air he blew right into her mouth.

Sugar sweet and delivered like dripping honey.

Leave, she should tell him. *Leave me alone*. Say so and he'll do it.

Because *she* decided, she made the rules, she held the power.

But her lips were numb and her skin was warm. And she had ... something she wanted to ask him. Or tell him. Maybe she just wanted to sit quietly until he spoke.

He had her sisters eating out of his palm with his charm.

Hell, he could probably take her sisters to the back alley. Even Kayla. Her boyfriend, Brock, an unwilling victim.

"Funny," Miles said, pushing the water closer. "I'm not looking for a better offer. I like sitting here with you. Finish the water and I'll get another round, extra sour."

She snorted, fingers loose around the chilled glass.

Another round on a Tuesday at eleven o'clock. Surely The Hand would flip the sign in the door soon, flash the lights. Declan would scoot them away with a "You don't have to go home, but you can't stay here."

"You're not even tired, you should go with Kenna ... or invite her with you. Because I am about to pass out here." She slurped water and frowned when the ice didn't refresh her. And her words, they didn't slur, and her vision was sharp, counting single grains in the wooden table.

Not drunk.

Intoxicated with Miles.

"You look wide awake to me." His elbow touched hers.

Which meant the heat curling in her stomach wasn't the booze. Sucking on her teeth, she shrugged, moved away from him. "It's a clever ruse."

"Come on, I know you. You're a night owl. Just like me."

"Oh yeah? You just know that?"

"Yeah, Lauren. I know that." He swung his gaze to her and wrapped long fingers around his whiskey and Coke. The ice had melted. He'd made a big show of ordering it with Jameson, but Lauren couldn't catch a whiff of it.

"Wrong. I'm in bed at ten, snuggled up."

"And what do you do in bed?" His velvet voice made her toes curl, brought natural innuendo to the question.

Hammered.

She had to be. Because blood rushed to her face. "I don't know, I read."

"You read, write gay fan fiction, play a little body flute. I bet you're up until two every night."

She launched over the masturbation reference like it was a shark-infested moat. "Where did you get the confidence to assume my bedtime routine?"

"I'm a master of routine, Lauren. Of carving out time at night to have a better morning. And any woman who wears a button-down and flats on a blind date is regimented in her life. You had a plan before we met, an idea of how you were going to spend the night."

"You blew that."

"It wasn't my idea." A sip of his drink. The dark soda fizzed. "The only thing I have left to figure out is if you're the type who wears matching striped pajamas and a hair wrap or a big, holey T-shirt to bed." There was that rumbling voice again, caressing her, seeping past her skin to tickle at her cells.

"Neither." She finished her water, pushed it to Miles. "I just wear scraps of silk lingerie."

Shitfaced.

He sat up, sharp features lighting with interest. "No you don't."

Of course she didn't. Did silk lingerie even exist? But the fact that he knew, surmised as much, made her indignant.

"And why not? Why couldn't I wear little negligees to bed every night?"

"You could," he returned, settling into a dropped tone, husky and scraping. "But if you did, your room would have more lights. It'd have a damn mirror because no one, not even you, would want to miss a single angle of Lauren Peck in green silk."

She felt her nipples tighten, and she moved to cradle her glass to keep him from seeing. "I picture your house as a giant mirrored dome."

"A given. I still haven't found the kitchen." Teasing.

She could fall into it again, like before. But she'd fall under, drown, and wake up with clammy prince lips shoving at hers.

She peeled her lemon slice. "So you're seeing somebody at work?"

"No."

"Yes," she replied automatically. "I overheard your friend." His hot friend.

Were all footballers like that? Tall and dangerous and fun. A triad of seduction.

"You eavesdropped." His lips collapsed from their usual smile. "We were never seeing each other. Never exclusive. Sonja and I found mutual release best came with lunch."

She popped her jaw. "The rest of us just go to the local orgy siesta."

"Funny," he deadpanned. "But that's easiest for me. Most of my nights are full, so if I want to get some action, that's when it has to be."

What are your nights full of if not action?

The question hovered but didn't land. She'd seen him sweet-talk every stripper in Burlington. Yeah, she had a feeling his definition of action varied widely from hers.

"I don't date," he reminded her.

"Except me?"

"Have you met my Tia? She was raised on the old God. The vengeful one. If I tell her no, she'll start the rapture and I want a few more years before I rocket straight to hell."

"No shoveling in hell."

"Lauren Peck finding a silver lining." A wave of goose bumps followed his pleased tone. "What are we doing Friday?"

She leaned back, pulling her arms around her waist. The end of her fingers tingled slightly. She was definitely drinking too much for a weeknight, but she couldn't make herself stop.

Miles had played trivia with her sisters. Hadn't quit when they fought. Bought them round after round of drinks. Never once tried to flirt with them.

"You know what we're doing," she heard herself say. "Lake effect is going to be insane. Five inches of snow."

His eyes glittered with amusement. "If you think five inches is a lot, you need to raise your standards."

"Can I say anything without you making it sexual?"

"I can be silent."

"Laugh it up," she dared, an oddly pleasant chill chasing her skin. "You're shoveling, and I'm throwing salt like it's rice at a wedding."

His smile became smug. "And your plan B?"

A sudden laugh bubbled in her throat. "You can't control the weather, Miles. All the luck in the world won't stop snow in Vermont. Buckle down and do your public service."

He replied with answering amusement. "I'll do anything you ask, pretty girl."

Only because he had to.

"Maddie said you played a very good game."

"Two touchdowns," he said. "A good night with the help of my lucky charm."

"I'm not lucky."

As he finished his drink, he checked his phone.

"Honestly," he told her, standing, helping her to her feet. "I think the more you fight it, the better it works. So go ahead. Make me shovel. Deny our connection. Flirt with the bartender. I'll be at your place at eight." His eyes flashed to her lips, dashed away. "Cars waiting out front for you and your sisters."

Chapter Ten

Miles prowled around Pinks, going from room to room with a restless, punching stride. His head was clear, his reflexes honed, hands fisted, ready. The energy pulsing through him was different than the kind he found on the field, less panicked, less reactive. When he was here, when women were around, his power became a cold, dangerous thing. Scaled and snarling. It prowled in the shadows, poised to strike.

He looked out one of the small front windows. He'd left his car running outside. In case shit went down, no keys were needed, it'd go with anyone who got in.

His phone said it was 3 a.m.

He'd been so sure he'd sleep tonight.

"I overreacted," Steph repeated.

"Didn't I tell you to stay by the door?"

Steph didn't flinch when he spun to face her. "Didn't I tell you to stop using that tone with me?" She swatted the lace tie of her Little Bo Beep bonnet. "I called because you asked me to, not because I wanted to live under martial law. It was a break-in, it happens. Frankly, it happens far less than it should."

Meaning the lack of streetlights, the seedy corner lot, Ralph's flaunting online.

"This isn't a PF Chang's," Miles said, pulling the curtains tight across the dark window. "Here, vulnerable women are strapped with cash. Any break-in is an act of war."

Steph blew air out her nose, and left him to fume, pulling the bonnet free to reveal curled and sparkly red hair.

Petty theft was the least likely reason for a break-in. Steph knew it. Tripping the security cameras for a few hundred bucks in singles wasn't worth it.

The intent was far more despicable.

Neither of them could admit it. Even as the truth sawed on their arteries. The worst kind of terror. Fear crept down Miles's back, seizing the muscle, lighting him up with energy.

Sweat lined his hands.

Practice at eight.

He'd pace until then. Pace until the rage came to a simmer, until he could crouch on the line and focus on the ball, focus on plays and routines, things as pedantic as points and turnovers. Fumbles.

Fake things. Made-up rules. Penalties.

Nonsense.

In the real world, penalties came as scars, as drowning nightmares, toxic fumes pouring into a sealed garage.

Had anyone asked *her* to call if she needed it? Did she have a friend, an ally? Or was she alone, back against the wall, shivering with fear?

Miles didn't even know if it was her or the world that snuffed her flame. If the scars and nightmares smothered or if a hand did.

He'd subpoenaed the police reports, the body cam footage, her arrest record. Empty lines, sparse notes.

They didn't care.

His sister had been a whore to them. Less. A body. A druggie. Another Jane Doe in the morgue. There were bigger problems in LA than a dead stripper.

"Ralph's gonna be here soon," Steph said, hauling Miles's head above water. "He gets alerts when the cameras are moved." Her gaze was pinned to a shell of glassy black bolted above the door. An all-seeing eye. Steph knew every corner with one.

Miles made a face. "Do you think he's going to help you to your car?"

"No." She stalked to the carpeted back hall lined with doors to private rooms, offices. Bumping a hip on the last door to the left, she swung the dressing room door open, pausing for Miles to join.

Scared.

Steph had bags of bravado, but letting him into her space, that told him enough.

He stayed by the door, the only entrance and exit as she slid out of her heels.

Paint peeling metal lockers. Hello Kitty and green Monster stickers. Filthy words and phone numbers etched into the blue paint. Words of encouragement taped to the walls.

The Mountaineers' lockers were mahogany, smelled like fresh linen. A gold plate read Santos over his. His number was burned into the wood with the care it took the carve the Ten Command-ments onto stone.

"Ralph doesn't care if I'm safe, but he'll be pissed if he finds you here after hours."

"Tell him I'm your boyfriend."

"You don't act like a boyfriend. You're not territorial or swooning. You never touch me or get hard watching me." Steph dropped her shorts.

Miles faced the wall.

"See, you can't even look at me. Why would I date you?"

"Aren't you sick of men touching you?" he asked the gray drywall. "I don't see how you can date at all."

"It's different when you like someone, it could be the same caress, the same fuck that repulses and drives you. Why do you think I stayed with Dave for so long? It's hard to realize which you're feeling."

Rustling fabric. The dissonant creak of rubbing metal.

He tried to make his voice less volatile as he said, "I think you're beautiful, Steph, it's just—"

Her voice returned just as soft and low. "I know. You're not the boyfriend type anyways." A snap of elastic. "Covered. You can turn."

He put his back to the wall. "Maybe I'm a better type. One that doesn't get jealous. An evolved man who can let a woman make her own choices."

"The most evolved man in the world gets jealous if his girl's shaking her tits for cash." She'd put on Ugg boots and a black sweatsuit, hood pulled over her hair. Baggy. A disguise, hiding the curves, her smile. She tugged Miles's arms, unfolding them until they hung at his sides.

"You, cop, with your hero complex, all this protective macho bullshit, are not evolved. You'll be jealous one day. And let me tell you, Miles Santos, I wouldn't wish to be the unlucky girl who sparks your flame."

"Wrong," was Miles's bland reply. Steph couldn't get worldly on him. Not tucked away in peaceful Vermont. She hadn't seen half the horrors he'd witnessed any given night on the strip. In his hometown.

He wasn't at Pinks because he was a hero. He came to be the villain, a scourge on the patrons. An ominous presence that could strike without warning.

"What are you thinking?" she asked, tying the strings of her hood until only pink-lined blue eyes peered out.

"Carissa got a job at Nightingale."

"Yeah, well Carisa knows how to use the computer and stick her nose in the air. I don't."

"She could vouch for you."

"I'm happy here, Miles. Let's go. I hear Ralph's truck." They shared a look of exasperation for the pimped-out diesel. Floodlights, truck nuts, beer in the cupholder. She kicked her locker shut and flipped off the lights.

Moving through the dark, she told him, "You're not stronger than me."

Even shivering in her camouflage, Miles knew that to be true. "I wish you didn't have to be so strong."

Her hand found his as they stepped outside. She squeezed. "Tell Lauren about Sandra."

***

"I PAID THEM EACH an extra hundred to wait until eight."

Lauren looked over the street with complete bafflement. Every driveway on her road was being snowplowed. Simultaneously. Streams of white flying into hedges like a choreographed dance.

"This is Hollywood shit."

Hands in his jean pockets, Miles conceded with a dip of his chin. "I hired them for every Friday, until the season ends."

She blinked, mouth dry, amazed, shocked. Slid a look to Miles, leaning casually against the door of a canary-yellow car. No jacket, no scarf. "Jesus, Miles. You really hate shoveling."

"Your hands get cold."

She cocked an eyebrow. "That's a yes."

He opened the door of his car for her and with the click of a button, the engine roared to life, growling with power.

"I have an idea for date night."

Date?

Lauren made herself busy with buckling, knocking snow off her boots, unwinding her scarf. The leather was still warm from his drive over and not for the first time she wondered what his house was like. How far it was? What did it feel like?

Was it dark turrets and winding halls? The image he pushed to the world with his tattoos and smirks, or was it intricately beautiful? Cedar shingles and stepped, overflowing flower beds like a royal estate?

Both?

"Heated seats?" Lauren asked excitedly, wrangling out of her coat, desperate to feel the heat on her skin.

She wasn't into cars. Wasn't into driving. Especially in the snow.

She and Hannah split a fifteen-year-old brown CRV that lacked air-conditioning and an aux cord. A CD changer was jammed on disc six, giving the occupants their pick of tracks one through three of Sean Kingston or the rest: pre-pop Taylor Swift.

Miles's car hugged the ground. New and shiny. Screens where buttons would suffice. It purred under his control, lunging out of each corner like it had pent-up energy, was chasing down prey. A high-pitched squeal that Miles called the turbocharger rang when he busted through yellow lights.

It should've felt unsafe. Narrow roads, rolling terrain, fresh snow, and only the slivered moon for light.

But she felt untouchable beside him. Trusted him. His eyes didn't leave the road, one hand on the wheel, the other resting on the crook of his thigh, knees spread to cradle the sexy black steering wheel.

"Was this your car in Las Vegas?" she asked, folding her coat in her lap and leaning forward to make maximum contact with the heated leather. Her cream long sleeve was so thin, it felt like a hot stone massage.

"No"—a smirk edged on his mouth—"no, out there, I drove something a little more flashy."

More flashy than Laffy Taffy yellow? "A Corvette?"

He chuckled, as if she'd said, "A tugboat?"

"What?" she pressed. "A Ferrari? A Bugatti?"

"Warming up," he told her, swinging them in a tight left, molding her spine to the seat. "Ever heard of a McLaren GT?"

"I think I went to middle school with him."

Another laugh and her skin warmed everywhere. "Twin-turbocharged V8. Six hundred and twelve horsepower."

"That's a lot of words."

"She's in custom Raiders black and silver, sitting in my garage. Doesn't touch the roads unless it's a dry summer day. She's barely street legal. That's why I bought the Demon." He petted the steering wheel.

"Demon?" Her nose scrunched. "You wear a cross, why not call it Angel?"

"Sounds like a stripper."

She poked his arm. "You'd love that."

"Demon's the model, pretty girl. But if you think she needs a name, I'm leaning toward Lucky."

Her teeth cut in a line. Lucky. Right. She wasn't driving with a friend, wasn't on a date. The shoveling wasn't romantic, it was transactional.

In his life of owning cars that were useless most of the year, frequenting strip clubs, and getting propositioned on Tuesdays, Lauren was special only because she was lucky.

Only because Miles had equated her value in his head.

As the ride lost its thrill, Miles swerved into an abandoned parking lot.

Her question came like a blade, honed for one purpose. "Is this where you kill me? Cut off my foot to wear around your neck?"

No one would hear it. Big commercial buildings surrounded them with no windows, no lights.

Miles's hands wrung on the wheel.

Lauren squirmed in the leather, chastising herself for getting excited, being flattered. For being offended by their pact. "We're watching sausage get made," she guessed, adding warmth to her voice. "Going dumpster diving, doing a homemade escape room, breaking apart a gambling ring."

No laugh, no smile. The car shut off. Immediately, the cold crept in.

"Why are you nervous?" he asked.

Because she thought about him.

Because she had a shortbread cookie for dinner and instead of tasting butter and sugar, she felt the gentle press of Miles's lips against hers. She felt his hand unzipping her coat. She saw him heaving, sweating, muscles flexing as he cleared snow off Mrs. Castellano's bird mailbox.

And she felt helpless. Helpless and dumb and weak, like she was waiting in a tower for him to pick her up, gathering yards of hair for him to yank and rip at.

"I'm not nervous."

She was afraid of herself, of her feelings exploding and multiplying. She kept trying to stamp them out, destroy romantic thoughts with the heel of her boot but she was getting outnumbered.

"Hey." He closed her hand in his, warm rough skin. Dark green eyes locked on her. "You're the last person who should be scared of me, Lauren. I'd never hurt you."

That was the problem, wasn't it?

Because hearing it caused a field of clover to sprout.

"Then I'm out of guesses."

He let go of her to crack his knuckles. Sounding earnest, he told her, "You'd excel in an escape room. You're smart. You notice things others dismiss. I'll take all your ideas into consideration, but tonight, fuck your ideas."

A sarcastic laugh climbed up her throat. "Wow, I feel valued."

"You'll change your tune." Miles cracked the door. "Let's go. Leave the coat, we're going to get hot."

***

A FURNITURE STORE. ROUGHLY the size of a football field. Not that she'd ever been, but she assumed they were exorbitantly massive and could fit a hundred beds and matching nightstands.

Eight twenty on a Friday and Greenlist Furnishings' full staff was stationed in every department, waiting to assist Miles Santos in his shopping. He'd asked them to stay open, he'd requested privacy.

On Monday, Lauren would ask Mary to crunch numbers on how much this little excursion cost him.

"Lighting," Miles told the nearest employee, tugging Lauren's hand to follow, winding them through a display of Teflon cooking pans.

"What kind of lightning?" asked Jenny, his personal shopper. She weaved with him in her beige polo, a registry gun holstered at her hip.

"Overhead definitely." They skirted a wall of hanging area rugs. "Some high-quality lamps. But nothing big, just bright and lively. Something that'd make silk dance."

Not a date.

Looking over her shoulder, Lauren counted four, five beige shirts trailing them, saw her snow boots leave black rings, mouthed *sorry*.

She felt ridiculous. In her leggings and snow boots, following Miles like a depressing square of toilet paper stuck to his shoe. They passed couches and loveseats and benches, white chairs, thin chairs, chairs that would require a crane to move.

"Miles, what—" she slammed into his back as he stopped. Hands slipping around his torso, cheek catching shoulder blade. She shoved at the slab of muscle and wiggled her hand free from his. "What are we doing here?"

He ran his tongue over his teeth. "All week, I kept thinking about you living in a dungeon so we're going to fix it."

"You're buying me a lamp?"

"To start. We're going *Extreme Home Makeover*. But we've only got three and a half hours so unless you have seriously pressing questions, let's get started."

Surprise hit her in the chest. All this for her? Shopping, the store, the snowplows? For her. He'd planned it.

"We're decorating my bedroom?"

"We're gutting it. No more questions, just decisions. I told them your style was asylum chic in advance so we'll have plenty of torture devices to pick between." His lips quirked at the corners.

"Better than seventies porno."

"Hurry, pretty girl. I want you to fall asleep thinking of me." As he spoke, he gently ran his hand down her arm, pulling away the soft material to rejoin their hands.

Affection speared her. Her eyes burned so hotly, she closed them. Damn it. She needed a moment alone, time to compose herself, to shred petals and spray pesticides.

"Why?" She knew she shouldn't ask, knew Miles was trying to compensate her, return a perceived favor, but it was for her own good to hear the truth.

The long length of his lashes fused together under the industrial lights, and Lauren felt irritation leach from him.

"Because you deserve better."

Then they were moving again, leading the charge of employees. Time and time again, he'd stop abruptly, catch Lauren in his arms to ask, "This? Do you like it?"

He'd wait.

And she'd stare at the desk, the rug, the porcelain giraffe. Deliberate.

There were three answers, each more dangerous than the last.

Silent indifference earned a sharp dismissal from Miles, another tug on her hand.

No, returned an avalanche of other options courtesy of the Greenlist staff, notes were jotted, lips were pursed. Miles nodded, like he was committing each dislike to memory. *No string lights. No llama shower curtain. No jute mat.*

Yes was the worst. Yes cannibalized the display. Yes caused the price gun to beep, a large number to flash.

Yes meant it was hers. Bought and wrapped and stolen away.

Yes made Miles grin.

Lauren dreaded yes. Each yes felt like a punch in her guilt card. She wasn't lucky.

"You don't like it?" Miles ran his fingers down the gilded frame of a standing mirror, his chest inches from her back, she felt his warmth like building seismic waves, he smelled like snow and powdered sugar.

Lips at her ear, his voice was a murmur. "You don't like anything else? I thought you'd love this."

Of course she did. It was beautiful, detailed but not overdone, shiny without being tacky. And when Lauren looked into it, she didn't fixate on her flat hips or small chest. She saw Miles's decadent tattoos swirling over her shoulder, his brown curls touching her frizzy blonde mess.

"Well, I don't," she croaked.

She wouldn't like anything else. Nothing. Not a throw pillow more.

She had to protect herself, her sanity. Lock the feelings up. Axe any tender moments from her heart. She wouldn't do it again, the shredding of photographs, burning gifts, tearing through birthday cards and movie tickets.

"There has to be something you like," he said, thoughtful.

"There isn't."

"I don't believe you." A playful narrowing of his eyes. "One more thing, we're not leaving before one more."

"Fine." Randomly, she pointed above them to the biggest, ugliest chandelier. "That."

"We put that in your room, I'm gonna hit my head on it."

"Great." Now she did like it. A Miles deterrent. "If you're in my bedroom, you deserve to get smacked."

Black devoured his irises. "Spite is very sexy on you." He notched his chin to the wall of beige zombies. "We'll take the chandelier."

"I'm kidding," she said quickly, spinning, fingers knotting in his shirt. "I was making a point. It won't even fit in your car."

"Your joke cost me three grand, and I didn't even laugh."

"Three—" A cough. Her jaw unhinged.

Pleased, his lips curled into a full-fledged smile. "Pick something you actually like," he threatened, "or I'll do it for you."

His body heat cocooned her as he pressed his palms into the gold frame, trapping her, crowding her. Embracing her.

No. Axe it.

Her breath fogged over her reflection. The curve of his mouth touched her earlobe. "And I'll tell you right now, I'm thinking mirrors and spotlights."

"And chains?" Her dry tone echoed. But her heart hammered.

He arched a brow as though to say, "Maybe. You want to find out?"

Flustered, Lauren knocked his arm away and escaped his sugar trap. "Remind me never to come to your house."

"We did his house," Jenny interrupted, eyes narrowed. "And it's extremely tasteful."

A pocket of red dusted Lauren's cheeks. "Of course, it is—I didn't—I'm sorry. I haven't seen it."

"Yet," Miles added, laying his arm over her shoulders, her own removable tattoo.

Jenny stayed prickly. "He has excellent taste. You're lucky to have him assist you."

"So lucky," Miles agreed, hand winding in Lauren's tangled hair.

She pinched the budding rose on his forearm and shifted in his hold. Their eyes locked. "The luckiest girl in the world if you ask him."

His smile was a dark thing and in that moment, if Greenlist Furnishings went up in flames, she would not have been able to look away, and neither, it seemed, would he.

"We offer silver mirrors," a different, less irritated beige employee offered.

Miles shook his head, untangled them, and said roughly, "Everything for a bedroom that matches her style. Put it in the truck and send it."

Chapter Eleven

Miles glared up at the red and black wires, suddenly worried he was holding the equivalent of a Taser.

Fortunately, Lauren didn't seem concerned, not budging from her spot on the basement steps, knees raised, chin cradled in her palms.

"Use a wire nut."

He almost dropped the light fixture in exasperation. "Are you going to help or just comment?"

As if it took all the energy in the world, she slowly, achingly, rose to her feet, and clarified, "I was instructing."

Stealing the orange cap from him, she screwed the wire nut onto the exposed, frayed ends, creating a neat little cap. "There."

Lemons and flowers, her hair tickled his wrist, invaded his senses.

Again, Miles found himself stricken at the sight of her, standing in the dank hall of her basement, balanced on a paint-splattered step stool, she enticed him. Images of her undressing in his car, arching into the leather in her tight white long sleeve flew to the front of his mind.

He wanted to have her. Over and over again. *Mine. My lucky girl.*

He kept his arms raised, both of them, like he was hanging from monkey bars, their faces level.

A single flashlight—Lauren's phone—shone at the ceiling, bounced off the drop tiles and showered her in an ethereal glow. Light on the arches of her cheeks, the end of her nose, spiked shadows formed from her long lashes.

Footsteps above them, drawers opening, the dishwasher running.

"It feels like we're hiding," she whispered to him.

The Greenlist staff had left thirty minutes ago. Hannah and Maddie—or Kayla—watched with wide-eyed glee as box after box went through the front door and disappeared into the basement. Then the big items arrived, and Miles earned free Peck sister commentary on the headboard, the mattress, the dresser.

Naturally, there was a fight—or six—as Lauren magnanimously doled out her old furniture to her sisters.

Miles put his foot down at passing along the sponge-soft mattress. He'd send it to Cole's wife for their dog farm or whatever they were calling it.

A team of stylists and movers and designers arranged the room three times, even remade the bed before they debated another switch and Miles kicked them out.

It was nearing midnight.

It'd be another week before he saw her next. He needed to soak up his luck, to smooth Lauren's hair, watch her shirt ride up, and her toes curl on the steps' edge.

"Doesn't it feel like someone's about to shout, 'Got you'?"

Miles's grip tightened on the chrome-plated glass. "No," he countered. "It reminds me of seven minutes in heaven."

She made a pithy sound of sarcasm and tucked the wires neatly into the ceiling. "Never played."

"A shame." His voice was rough, he was drifting closer to her. *Hurry.*

Hurry so he could let go, could swipe back the hair from her cheek, lean in.

"I'm better at hide and seek."

He doubted it.

"And what do you hide from, Lauren?" That's what she was doing here. In the basement. Hiding. Pretending away the world. He couldn't see her but he felt the rise in her breathing, like a football's increasing whistle as it neared.

She screwed the cover plate into place. "There's plenty to hide from."

"Like a date?"

"Yes." No pause.

"Because you're happy alone?"

"Because," she sighed. "Because I'm not a masochist and some-times ... around certain people, all I get is pain so I'd rather hide."

"Who?" His question was a warning, a mercy. "I'll make sure you never have to hide from them again." It was his credo, his vow. To protect those who needed protecting.

"Valiant," Lauren mocked, lowering her hands. Lingered to murmur, "But you only get me four hours a week."

"I don't need more than ten minutes to break a jaw."

"Even that wouldn't solve this one." Her quiet admission surprised him. She rapped her knuckles on his chest. "Keep steady, I need a Phillips."

End of subject.

The pat, the dismissal. Steph mastered the brush off and Miles knew why, knew she battled memories as much as men, things he couldn't hope to challenge.

What chased Lauren for her to find solace in darkness?

Metal clashed, a lock jiggled as Lauren searched her plastic toolbox.

He cleared his throat. "You're good at this. I never predicted you'd be a wiring master."

"I dated an electrician," she explained tersely, the clatter increasing. "He brought work home and I picked it up."

The sudden jarring image of Lauren dating made his brain crash worse than a bee discovering a plastic flower.

He pictured her sitting rigid on a bed in slacks, her hair pinned down, eyes dead, lips pursed. A man beside her ... but when he tried to fill the features of Lauren's imaginary boyfriend, he began adding tattoos, bulky shoulders, dark curly hair.

"What about you?" she asked, returning with her tools, creaking up the ladder. Her hands worked in between his and between the tool fetching, ex-boyfriend hiatus, she was whispering again. "What would you hide from?"

"Nothing."

There were things Miles didn't want to face in the morning sun, but he couldn't hide from his problems. His reflection found him every time he washed his hands or put on his helmet. Sandra's eyes, her nose.

Shades paler, bruises under the eyes, creeping up her jaw.

He couldn't hide from the memories. Just run. "People should want to hide from me."

"Is that why you got the tattoos? To induce fear?"

"I got them because I like the way they look, pretty girl. And I think you do too."

"They don't mean much to me in the dark." She finished screwing in the light, dropped her arms to the ladder's top step. After a quick test, Miles followed suit. Helped her step down.

"Then by all means, let there be light so you can return to admiring."

"Hmm," came her response as she filled her toolbox. No denial. His body coursed with satisfaction. She *did* like his tattoos.

He could give her a tour of them, roll up his sleeves, unbutton his shirt, slip it off, shove the waist of his jeans down, press her palm against the black skin.

What would she look like as she touched him? Wild hair on end, a slight part in her lips.

An innocent image quickly debauched. Lauren on her back, unclipping her bra, knees cradling Miles's hips as he wrenched down her zipper.

"Done. Flip the switch." Lauren's dry command bleached his fantasy. She leaned into him, smiling. "I'm excited."

Miles was hard.

He puffed a laugh. "Me too."

Fuck, he had to go, leave before he stole too much luck.

"What if we turn it on and it still looks like a dungeon?" she asked. "What then?"

"We pivot to the backup plan."

"Oh." She chuckled, climbing down. "Tell me what the backup plan is and how many mirrors it involves."

"The backup plan," he started, jolting back to avoid her face near his still-growing erection, "is adding a third story to this house, and building your room up there."

Her next laugh came from the bedroom. He heard the mattress groan.

Miles became single-mindedly hungry, desperate as he searched for the light switch. Rushing. He wanted to see her in bed, head tipped back, lips spread—he found it. Flipped.

A scream.

A buzz of electricity. He saw Lauren in a flash of sparkling white and then glass exploded over him.

A shout from upstairs. Pounding feet on the steps. A flashlight in Miles's face.

"What did you do?" Maddie shrieked. "I was watching *The Bachelor*."

"Shit." Miles jolted at Lauren's curse, turned and found her inches away, plowing forward. He caught her, drew her into his chest. The beam of the flashlight hit her throat, the jumping pulse.

He swallowed. "We must've blown the breaker."

Hands clutching his forearms, Lauren shook her head no. "It'd be the whole panel if upstairs is out." Cold palms on his chest, resting comfortably. She wasn't tense in the dark, didn't stop the gentle caress of her fingertips. Her mind ran. "That means the heat's going to shut off. We have electric baseboards."

"It's Friday at midnight," Maddie snarled, flashlight on the ground as she texted. "We need heat."

Fingers drifted up his throat, around, tugged a curl at his nape. The sweetest torture, Lauren's wandering touch, Maddie's overstayed welcome.

Miles had a thousand ideas to keep her warm.

"I don't know how to fix the panel." Lauren's breath was on his chin. Did she know how close they were? Could she feel his hands gliding further around her?

"You know who to call," Maddie returned. "Do it."

The stroking stopped, Lauren's back went rigid. "He won't come.

"Yes he will." Stomping on the stairs, Maddie's fading voice. "I'm taking Hannah to Brocks. Fix this."

***

STANDING IN COMPLETE DARKNESS, Lauren felt Miles's gaze bore into her.

If he fumed harder, she'd be melted bone.

"Light," Brian snapped. He was speaking to her, she recognized the condescending tone. Moving slow to keep from lashing out, she pointed her phone, nailing Brian in the eyes.

"Not on me. The panel. And hold it steady."

After five years together, she could feel his eyes roll and steadied for the onslaught of a dozen similar times Lauren had failed him.

Remember when I asked for spring rolls and you brought home egg rolls?

How about the time you cried because I spilled microbrew on your dress?

And what about how you begged for me to stay when I left? Pathetic.

"Jesus, L, you can't be cold already. It's been ten minutes." He tucked a wire cutter behind his ear. "I left Miranda at home to help. Stop being dramatic. Put on a coat if you're freezing."

His use of her nickname suggested he was feeling territorial.

She wasn't shaking from the chill of the rapidly cooling house. She was shaking with pure, undiluted rage. Had been since Brian rammed his electrical bag into her arms and called her hopeless.

Every step down the stairs was a new teardown. Reprimanding her for trying to replace a light, for thinking she was smart enough to, for ruining his night.

"Leave it to the professionals. I actually went to college."

He kept needling, finding known sore spots and blowing salt inside. Making her feel small and stupid. Inadequate.

"Why don't I hold it?" Miles offered roughly, withdrawing from the wall like a phantom, hand curling around Lauren's wrist. White hot fury flashed briefly in his eyes before he blinked it away.

"No," Brian grunted, glancing up from the voltmeter. "She knows just how I like it, don't you, L?"

Yes stuck to her teeth.

Exactly how he liked it.

Lauren with a black sheet over her head. Lauren cooking, cleaning, doting, planning, loving.

She heard Miles's neck crack and thanked God again she couldn't see him. Hearing his boots grind on the kitchen tile, knowing his leg jumped with aggression was enough. He hadn't sat down, hadn't stood still since Brian bulldozed inside. He moved like a lion searching for a weak spot in the bars of its cage.

This, she could hear him snarl. *This is what you're hiding from?*

"How long you been doing this, Bryce?"

So much for not engaging. Her pre-Brian speech—warning—was hitting the fan quick. Couldn't he wait until after the power was on? Spare her the fallout?

Brian was doing her a favor. He'd lord it over her for the rest of her life and then some, but she needed his help. This winter was especially cold, the nights long. The risk of a freezing pipe was extra terrifying when the pipes were above her bed.

Plus, Brian was right.

She *should've* hired an electrician. But she'd been afraid they'd be the same. Reel her in, talk sweet and then call foul when she returned the favor.

Stupid to think she could do anything, teach herself anything.

"It's Brian, man. Keep up."

"Don't snap at him," she hissed, unable to swallow it down, let the bait dangle.

Brian removed the screwdriver from between his lips. "It's not a crowded room, L. And he can't learn one name? The name saving your ass?"

"You'll be well compensated," Miles gritted.

Under the shining light, Brian wet his lip suggestively. "I know I will be."

The implication was repugnant.

But not as cruel as the truth. She'd pay. In offhand remarks, reminders, and taunts, every day until she retired. *Don't let L turn on the lights. L would've frozen to death without me. L can't do anything.*

Her heart stuttered, stomach twisting almost painfully.

And if she fought back, he'd crush her with "You owe me."

So there'd be no biting back, only swallowing her words, lowering her chin and forging ahead, burning through minutes until she could get away.

"No," Miles returned sharply. "I'll be paying your rate."

"I'm not a joke handyman. I'm the city electrician. I don't make house calls. L's an exception because she needs help."

"Help" was said with reticence. As in psychiatric help. As in meetings and courtrooms and straitjackets help.

Miles's arm curled around her waist. "She's never mentioned you."

Brian pushed her hand higher and wrapped copper wire around a screw. "Yeah, but she told me all about you. Trying to make me jealous. I know what her game is."

She was wound so tight, a flick to her temple would shatter her.

Frozen, heart cleaving, the light trembled. Her hands clenched into fists, nail digging into the soft flesh of her palms. She was falling down the tower steps, tumbling, crashing.

Her nightmare overtaking a far-off dream and shredding it.

Her nasty secrets, worst moments, the most awful words she ever spat laid out in neat rows.

Before today, before now, Lauren had been unperturbed to show Miles her quirks, told him the embarrassing, awkward stuff, the save-it-for-marriage moments because he didn't care, because he couldn't leave. No reason to be embarrassed.

Brian wasn't a quirk or a mistake.

Brian was a reflection of her. The epitome of who she was, what she was. Another vapid, shallow, useless princess. Written by a man and born to one goal. True love. And she was the worst of them all, she was—

"Tell him, L."

She wanted to bury herself.

And she wanted to tell Miles the truth. Shake out every horrible detail so he understood, but there wasn't a single path that didn't make her anything but utterly pathetic. A sob rose and gathered in her throat.

Brian finished securing the panel door to the wall, pocketing his flathead. "It's something. Seeing L date again. She took our breakup real hard. She mention the ex? That's me."

A wide hand slid up her shoulder, around her neck. Miles's thumb smoothed her jaw, the heat of his chest at her back could've been a supernova and she wouldn't have moved.

In his velvet voice, he murmured, "She only told me she was waiting for an upgrade."

Brian jumped on that in an instant. "You took her to a strip club, right?"

Lauren was never speaking to Mary again.

For a moment, she thought Miles would tackle him. His hand hardened to bruising, his tall form rigid, tense, poised to attack.

And Lauren was not a princess. Because she wanted it. Relished the idea of Brian getting pounded into mincemeat.

"Yes," Miles said, no layer of offense in his tone. His thumb slid up and up, made a gentle circle in the tender skin beneath her ear.

"They have excellent chicken," she defended weakly.

The mocking smile and triumphant glint in Brian's beady eyes sent her back a step. "I have a feeling you'd do anything for him, L."

He threw a breaker on.

A hum.

Flickering lights over their heads.

"Fixed." Brian sneered. "You'd let him take you anywhere, L. Don't forget, I know you."

"Knew me."

Another breaker.

The hall lit up.

"You'd let him do anything to you." Brian's mouth twisted into a skin-crawling smirk. "It's the only reason a guy like him is still around."

The disgust in his words seemed to spark Miles's temper. "I do whatever Lauren wants to do."

But Brian was on a streak, vicious glare ripping her apart. "You don't seriously expect me to fall for this, do you?"

He flipped another breaker.

The living room lights sparked to life. "Him, L? Really? When you're not even over me?"

***

MILES FLIPPED. HARDER THAN a coin on game day, he flipped.

He was going to kill this guy. Pummel him. Not stop at black and blue, he wanted Brian red and white. Bones and blood.

His grip hardened on the counter, old toast crumbs sticking to his skin.

He hated Brian the electrician.

Another thrown breaker.

Another.

Another.

The house became bright enough to sit atop a Christmas tree.

Smug as all hell, reeking of fake musk, Brian smirked. "All better." He clapped his palms together. "Don't try it again, man. If it was easy, everyone would do it. It's not like playing a game."

"You think professional football is easy?" He was going to stomp him like a wasp, take the stinger in his steel and break it in half.

"L, get my bag from the hall."

Miles's ribs punctured his lungs when Lauren turned. He recognized the bland, pinched face, the falsely cold eyes. The mask she wore to face down her rivals. Just missing swipes of black paint under her eyes.

"Excuse me." Even her voice was the same. Edged, empty.

Miles ground his teeth to hold his rage in check and let her pass.

The minute they were alone, Brian muttered from under his breath, "Women."

It was strike or get out of range, so Miles pushed out his own breath to trail Lauren, not bothering to lower his voice as he took her elbow, "You fucking dated that guy?"

"Yes." She didn't stop walking even if it meant dragging him. "And if you could stop antagonizing him, that would be great for me."

That tone. That fucking tone. He'd go back. He'd go back to the night they met and rip the buttons off her shirt, mess her hair up, tell her that he;d read a fan fiction about Cole Seeder and now he couldn't look his teammate in the eyes without wanting to call him master.

He wanted to order her sparkling waters until she screamed at him. Until she slapped him. Until the fire broke through.

"Stop antagonizing him?" His voice was not his own. Mean and mocking. "He's treating you worse than dirt beneath his shoe. I haven't begun to antagonize him."

"Do not, Miles."

He laughed. Laughed at the warning. Laughed at the incredulity. "He deserves it."

"But I don't. I see him every day And if you make him angry, I'll never, ever be rid of him. And he knows"—her throat bobbed with emotion—"he knows we're not dating so stop trying to make it seem like we are. It's embarrassing. He's right. It makes me look desperate."

"He's not fucking right, Lauren."

Quiet, stilted steps down the hall, into the living room.

"Where'd you put it?" she called to Brian, back in that voice, an unfeeling coating tainting each syllable.

Miles hovered at the limit of his sanity. He and Lauren … they'd decided they weren't a match, they'd clashed and made sickening black smog. But the idea that Brian dismissed them as well? That he saw them, blinked and said no?

Acid burned in Miles's stomach.

Who wasn't a match for Lauren? Beautiful, smart, thoughtful. Fucking funny with her laconic wit.

"Christ, L," came Brian's squawk. "Can you do anything?" Lumbering steps toward them.

Miles's patience split, two elastic threads launching backward with enough force to cut and welt skin. And he made a choice. A statement, a damning answer.

Sending his hands into Lauren's hair, he took her mouth with his.

It was not sweet or kind.

It wasn't a peck or a brush.

He poured his wrath into her lips, made her taste the thrashing passion with nips and sucks. Clutching her into him until she couldn't move, couldn't shiver without him feeling it, he devoured her, savoring her gentle curves laid against his bulk.

Lemons. And not the slightest bit sour. No hint of her glacial heart either as her fingers snuck into the pocket of his jeans. A handhold, a rope in the ocean to keep from getting sucked in the waves.

He dominated her with the same brutal focus he kept on the field, blacking out extraneous sound, non-pertinent information.

He wanted her against the wall. Pressed to it. Then he could nail her shoulders back to taste her neck, lick up her throat as he pulled her legs up around his hips. He'd bend his knees to lift.

If only he could pull himself from her mouth. But he didn't want reprieve. He was crossing the twenty-yard line, not even a safety left to feint and he didn't slow.

Punishing tongue, he split her lips apart, and groaned at her waiting, hot tongue. Fingers gripping onto her ass, another hand possessively at her nape.

A tremor broke across his back as he let her tongue touch his, explore carefully while he kneaded her thigh, brought it wide enough for him to slot his thigh in between hers, to find heaven.

Their first kiss, he decided. This was it. Not the headbutt, the church kiss.

This, the languid brush of her tongue on his, the scorching heat roaring in his veins. The biting cold of her hands.

His Lauren was not cold, not frigid, she—

Whimpered against his mouth.

A breathy mewl that throttled him, struck him so quickly with blind lust, he tore back and yanked her into his chest to keep from seeing her swollen lips, her hazy eyes, from teaching the wall a new trick.

Swaying in the kitchen's threshold, Brian stared. Fists lightly clenched as Lauren's breath teased Miles's throat, her hands knotted the fabric at his back.

A full moment of silence preceded any sound.

Miles shared a slow, cocky grin. "Sorry, Baxter. Didn't mean to distract her. But I couldn't help myself. I don't have to tell you how addictive she is. You were looking for your purse?"

"My electrical bag."

Brian didn't move from his spot, so Miles nuzzled into her tight curls, smelling lilac and lavender, jasmine. "Bill me whatever you think you're worth. I won't even notice it," he kept his voice pitched low, erotic.

When it became clear Brian was too stunned to move, he extracted himself from Lauren, kissed her cheek and grabbed the ex by the shoulder.

"It's time to leave," he said. Midnight had long passed. He gentled his tone to say, "Lauren?"

No ice, but no heat in her eyes. She watched him like a butterfly had landed on her nose, and she wasn't sure if she hated bugs or not.

Are you OK? He longed to ask. *Did I overstep?*

Did you like it?

Do you want more?

Could you feel how fucking hard I was?

Am.

"I'm out of town this weekend, but I'll be at trivia on Tuesday."

She blinked.

"Sound OK, pretty girl?"

Her head tilted up, to the side, confusion and surprise and ... wonder? Offense?

"I'll miss you," he added, trying to knock her from her stupor.

Her brows knitted together.

Miles shoved Brian to the door, sweeping his bag from the living room carpet and forcing it into the prick's arms. Shoved the electrician outside.

He took a moment to admire the early, early hours of a Vermont weekend. Smiled. "Let's go, Brett."

He'd taken to covering himself in the blackest ink made, and now for the first time in his life, he wondered how he'd look with a stripe of glistening white.

That's all this day was. White, an empty canvas. Blankets of snow softening the metal edges of cars, of rooflines. Pillowed white hedges and fluffy domed trees. Perfect white reflecting the moon's blue glow.

Snow. He'd never stop marveling.

He'd seen it in college, played in it, swore at it for wetting his hands, blurring the field. He'd wished to get back home. Back to the desert, to dependability.

What would snow look like in the desert?

The Peck sidewalk was pristine, the driveway matte black. He needed to tip the shovelers. They'd done an excellent job. Hell of a lot better than he had. Should he get Lauren and show her? Otherwise he'd miss the annoyed look on her face and—

"Leave L alone," Brian snarled, pounding down the steps, punching hands into the sleeves of his coat. "You're just gonna hurt her."

Miles's response was a slow smile and a subtle shake of his head in disbelief. "Yeah, between the two of us, I'm not the one who gets off on hurting women."

A gentle push on Brian's shoulder sent him flying backward, ass hitting dry pavement.

It'd be effortless to destroy him. Registering the look of fear on his face, he'd just realized he was the prey to Miles's hungry predator.

No matter, Miles didn't hunt to live.

"It's time you left my girl alone," he said roughly. "If you want to talk to her, speak to me and I'll relay my own interpretation."

Silence.

He feigned a step forward. Brian flinched.

"Do you understand?"

The lamb rose on shaky feet, too dumb to see the wolf. "She'll love me always," the prick sneered. "She'll always come back. Keep calling, missing me, wishing she was mine. You can push me around like a compensating asshole, but you'll never have what we do. History."

"Yeah, I have something better." Miles clasped the scruff of Brian's shirt and forced him into the driveway, not stopping when his feet stumbled and dragged. He slammed Brian's chest against the garage door, pressed in with his knees.

"I've got a future with her. Dare to talk to her again and you won't have a future at all. Don't come again. She won't call."

Chapter Twelve

Miles slowly eased from his knee and stood, feeling every vertebra crack into place. He cleared grass from his palm.

There was silence in the stadium, and no one dared to break it. Warren Rose retiring.

Even notorious loudmouth Burton Kilbride hadn't spoken. Which meant this was as serious as it was shocking.

Leaving after only two years with the Mountaineers.

Why?

Trying to piece it together, Miles sought out Cole, Warren's closest friend, to search for a hint, a tell, but the tackle was impossible to read, arms folded, mouth set.

He seemed ... less surprised? More surprised? Damn Viking vault. He'd get nothing from Cole.

They'd won, they should be celebrating. *He* should be celebrating. Fuck, they should all be celebrating him. Miles Santos had played another flawless game.

He'd sunk his teeth into Lauren, and he'd replaced his blood with pure dashing luck.

Was it because of their kiss?

Or because he thought of her every time he ran? Licking a lemon, arguing with her sisters, her ass in those jeans.

Her ass in his hands.

Each clawing step, every time he slipped through a gap in the defense, the memories flashed.

More than memories.

Lauren teasing a shirt up her ribs. Lauren crawling across her new bed. Lauren squeezing him as he whispered into her ear, "That's it, pretty girl, take it."

Addiction was too weak a word.

Miles suffered a crippling dependency on her.

"The announcement will go to press after the last home game," Warren continued to explain. The entire team was huddled around him, every man on his knee at center field. A thank you for the win, a quick bond before the team split to interviews, to buses and families. "This is the last time I'll play in this stadium and I'm damned thankful you all made it a win. Let's keep it going. I want my last season to be my longest."

No clapping or whistles.

Burton gave a grunt of agreement, but he clawed into the grass, digging into the roots, prying.

Their quarterback was leaving. In his prime. Abandoning them. Half the team had come, signed on to play for him, for Warren Rose, the man who put his team before himself.

"Ye haven't even been sacked," Burton said, ripping up grass-roots. "And yer quitting?"

Hearing the harsh Irish accent spill into Burton's voice, Miles tensed, body on autopilot, ready to subdue an extremely mercurial bull.

Warren eyed the burly tight end. "I'm not hurt. I'm getting out while it's good. Before I have two metal knees."

"That's the dumbest thing I 'er heard." Burton pushed to stand, barging forward to glare down at the quarterback. "Ye get out when it goes to shit."

"Why now?" Miles had to ask. Why when everything was working? When his payout was so close. "We could make the playoffs."

"We will," Warren corrected, standing, helmet swinging in his grip. He looked over the team, every face feeling the confidence of their leader. "We *will* go to the playoffs, and next year, I'll watch you win it."

"Don't watch. Play with us. Hand me the ball. Come on."

Cole was on his feet now, more cleats on the ground, bodies getting closer. The giant lifted his chin, and everyone waited. "There are more important things than football."

Burton was about to rip off his beard. "Name fucking one!"

"Victoria," came Warren's calm response, accustomed to the outbursts of his oldest teammate. "I want to spend more time with her. She's busy and if we're going to have a family—"

"Fucking A. Yer family planning? Ye haven't even married her."

"Is Victoria pregnant?" Miles's voice was that of a little boy barefoot in a hall, asking why Mommy is crying.

The quarterback adjusted and readjusted the sit of his ball cap. "No and she never will be unless we get some time together."

Burton scoffed again, muttering obscenities, denouncing parents worldwide.

"I'll be around," Warren told his team. "As much as before. Even if I wanted to escape your ugly mugs. I have no choice. Victoria works with half of you."

Warren Rose peeling the numbers off his back, laying the football down for his girlfriend. For love.

For Miles, football was an escape, an energy burn and a means to an end. Money. Cash money to spend on the people he deemed deserving.

Often, he entertained the idea of quitting the sport to start a women's shelter, to full-time babysit Steph, to become a bodyguard, but he couldn't imagine giving the rush up for love. For something so flimsy and flighty.

He and Victoria could break up in a year and Warren would have nothing, no one.

Asher caught the horrified state on Miles's face and smirked. "He your good luck charm too?"

Burton steamrolled Miles's reply. "Everybody thinks yer a dick."

Moore readied to bite back, his skinny legs stretching, but Burton always lifted a hair taller. And no one had the balls to fuck with Burton Kilbride, a man with nothing left to lose.

"Fucking try it," he dared the rookie.

The wide receiver grinned, slinking back, knocking a hand on Asher's arm. "Yeah, stop, or Miles will start taking Warren on a date every Saturday and I don't want to see the two of them slurping spaghetti."

Miles grinned. "We'd let you play with the meatballs. If you're good."

"How's the girl?" Cole's rumble sent Burton scattering.

Something happened between the two of them last season, a fight or worse. Whatever had, Miles noticed, it made the Irish madman skittish.

"Lauren?" Cole clarified after a second's thought. "Are you going to bring her around? Jo could watch the games with her. She has a whole row to herself."

"Nah, Lauren doesn't watch."

"Not a fan?"

"Not allowed."

A noise, a *hmm* in the back of Cole's throat. "Thought you were interested in a woman's choice. Or did I peg you wrong?"

"Our situation is working right now. The deal is I get Friday night and she spends Sunday alone."

"Situation?" Cole asked as the team split up to shower, to shake hands and give sound bites. "Jo would crucify me for using such a word."

"Yeah, Santos. Weren't you saying you treat them like queens?" This from Asher.

"We're not dating," Miles returned sharply. We have an arrangement."

Cole nodded thoughtfully. "Jo and I had an arrangement."

"My arrangement is a lot different from lifelong marriage. It's one night a week."

"Two," Moore butt in. "Unless that wasn't Lauren you spent Tuesday with."

"The more time I spend with her," Miles explained, "the better luck I have."

"Luck," Cole mused. "You're close."

"Close to what?"

"To realizing the truth." He stepped into Miles's space, smelling like sweat and sod and a bit of the Mass smog. "To realizing it's not luck that's making you quick on your feet."

"Enlighten me then, fifty-four. What's the secret from an all-American?"

Burton snorted. "I'm the dumb one and even I know there's another four-letter word for it."

"Lust," Miles deduced.

Burton grinned. "No. Not that one."

***

LAUREN KICKED HER HEELS off under her desk and stretched her toes. Lunch had been, oh, five hours too short. At least it'd been painless, forking her leftover Chef Boyardee mini ravioli with a chatty Mary, who disclosed every second of her weekend.

Yes, she had found the backs to her alien earrings, and yes, Mr. Mary made her walk funny after Friday's bondage night, and yes, she'd tried the doughnuts from Lucy's. Too dense.

Like most days—every day—Lauren applied minimal effort to the interaction and less when she returned to her cubicle. Cracking her neck, she logged into her computer and fun task of the day: ordering fresh printer ink and six reams of eight-and-a-half-by-eleven in sad government white.

"I know that face."

Her fingers froze on the mouse. Her mood plummeted.

A macabre chuckle. "Yup. That one too."

She didn't look up. "Are you out of office supplies, Brian?" Assuming he knew how to use office supplies.

"I want answers, L."

"Yeah, well, I've got none of those."

And she wasn't being facetious.

Over and over again, she'd sought reason, grappled for sanity, an answer as to why Miles had kissed her.

OK, so she knew *why* he'd kissed her: Friday, luck injection.

But why'd he have to make it so …

Earth-shattering?

Stomach-twisting?

Fantasy-inducing?

Dirty?

Yes, dirty. Why'd he have to use his tortuous tongue and his big, warm hands? Why'd he have to taste like mint and metal, his skin scorching under her touch?

"What are you and tattoos doing together? He's not your type. He's a fucking bully, L."

Lauren stared at her desk, the screensaver a series of blue dematerializing squares. Her hands balled, her bare feet drilled into the scratchy carpet. "Did he hurt your feelings?" she mocked. "Do you want me to put him in a timeout?"

"Jeez, L. First, you tell me you'll never love anyone like me. You don't leave me alone for two years. Fucking obsessed with me and now you're dating a punk who threatened me? The love of your life?"

"I don't love you anymore."

If she kept saying it, he might hear it.

"Am I supposed to believe that you love him? Miles fucking Santos? He's from California!" Said like California was the entrance to hell itself.

"You have something against successful men?"

"Think, Lauren. For once, think. Why is he even with you? I'm trying to look out for you here. I know how sensitive you are."

Her fingernails sunk into her palms. "I *am* thinking."

"Then you know once you say no to him, stop whoring yourself out, he'll dump you. Why else would he want you?"

She knew exactly why. And it was too embarrassing to say aloud, to tell her ex they weren't dating. She was a vessel for imaginary success.

Brian thought Miles was playing with her emotions.

No. She handled that all on her own.

Miles didn't care if she had emotions, or thoughts, or ideas. He just wanted her slotted into his routine, four hours so he could keep buying fast cars and loose women.

The tiny, tiny bubble of wonder in her chest, the shimmery rainbow orb of maybe-he-likes-you popped, sprayed soap in Lauren's eye.

She could be a cardboard cutout and he'd kiss her after four hours.

Brian stalked around the cubicle, breaching her white walls to perch on her desk, fold hands over his knee like a snotty teacher ready to lecture.

"He's going to use you up and toss you aside. I don't want to see you lose it again."

"Then look away."

A sharp click of his tongue. "You're just like your sisters. You complain about them, but you're no better. You're delusional, living in your head, it's not realistic. You need a fucking wake-up call."

"Leave it alone, Brian."

"I'm offering help, I'll be your wake—"

But she was past listening. She jerked to stand and kicked her chair back to get in his face. "Don't insult my sisters. Ever."

"You do it all the time."

"When we were dating!" she defended. "I confided in you, worried with you because we were in a committed relationship for five years. I was sharing my feelings—"

"Christ, your feelings, I don't miss those."

"Out!"

Lazy in his movements, he slid forward, let his hand drag over her calendar, thumb the marked game days. "I'm not cleaning up your mess when he drops you."

When had he ever once helped her clean up a mess?

She chased him out of her sad little square and yanked the calendar from its spot, sending silver tacks flying. "I'm sick, I'm leaving."

"You think he'll even show again?" Brian called as she stormed down the hall, his question trying to wrap rope around her ankles, drag her back, bring her to her knees.

No. He'd done his job already.

Reminded her of who she was, how far she hadn't come. Cold, she was supposed to be cold and calculating, find a smart match and then let feelings develop.

She texted her sisters first. The group chat. **Under the weather, not making trivia. Find replacements.**

Next came Miles. She hadn't used his number yet. Their texts blank and open, waiting for first contact. NASA at the ready.

Feelings, she had *feelings*, and they hadn't so much as texted. No *I'm home* updates, no *watched that video, hilarious!* No emojis because words were too much.

Suddenly, texting felt as intimate as putting pen to paper, sealing it with wax and a squirt of her perfume.

She zipped her coat, used her hip to open the door and closed her messages. Called him.

"It starts at six, right? I'm not late." He sounded like he'd just woken up, throat raspy.

"I'm not going tonight," she told him, wrapping her scarf tighter as she walked home, watching the sidewalk for slush piles. "I don't feel good."

"Do you need a doctor? I have contacts that—"

"I just need sleep," she interrupted quickly. "If you want to go, by all means. My sisters will be there."

"Compete without my lucky charm? You must be terminal if you think I'd do that."

"OK, fine." She didn't want to tease tonight. She faked a dry cough. "Bye, Miles."

"Wait, are you walking home? Stay on the phone with me."

"I don't want to talk, I'm—"

"Sick. You told me, but please, pretty girl. At least until you're past Pinks. Until you have the key in the door."

"Miles—"

"You don't have to talk. Don't even listen. Just stay on the phone." There was a pause, movement, fabric and water. Then his voice became an echo. "Your fingers must be freezing." The water stopped, his voice muffled and clogged. "Tia thinks you'll catch your death for walking, but she's like me, anything under fifty is Arctic."

He spat. More water.

Brushing his teeth.

He *had* been sleeping. Because he stayed up nights. Busy.

"My manager said I'd acclimate, but she's fuck wrong. I got a heated mattress. You ever try one of those? Don't answer. I love it. It's—"

"Home," Lauren choked out. She jiggled her keys into the receiver, still two blocks from her street and hung up before he could say more. Before her lie unraveled.

Brian was right. He had the horrible tendency to be right. To announce it and remind her.

Whether or not he knew the truth of her deal with Miles, he was right. She liked Miles. Her feelings had bloomed, blossomed, were thick vines creeping up, encasing her heart. Stupid overwhelming feelings.

The one thing she couldn't trust.

She took the long way home, avoiding the walk past Pink Persuasion's blacked-out glass, hands numb as she strolled the neighborhoods where she used to roller-skate and chase the Creemee's truck for a vanilla maple waffle cone.

She wanted the cold to seep in, wanted it to kill like an early winter frost. She wanted green vines so brittle she could snap them with a single thought.

On she went, one foot in front of the other. She passed the Luft's mailbox. Forever deformed after Hannah clipped it with their dad's Impala. The sidewalk she painted a chalk dragon on. An apple tree she'd foraged to make apple sauce for Brian.

She'd loved Brian. So much that her heart had changed, grew new branches, beat differently.

And Miles was a better man than Brian. He never flirted with her sisters. He understood her jokes. Never made fun of her, not even with the most embarrassing stuff. He asked questions when he didn't understand, he was curious and interesting and fun.

How did a princess fare against a king?

Fifteen minutes, an hour later, her fingers were too numb to turn the lock on the door. She used them like little crab claws, twisting awkwardly, bouncing on her feet. Yelped when the door swung in.

Scarf, coat, mittens, hat. Left in a pile by the door. Maddie would complain. But not until morning.

Lauren would be better by morning. Detached after she practiced locking away her feelings, sending them into the back of her mind, remembering not to trust herself.

The doorbell rang.

She poked an eye at the peephole, expecting the mailman. Swallowed. Opened the door.

"Didn't we just talk?" she asked. "I'm not going."

"We talked two hours ago," Miles corrected, not waiting for an invitation, filling the vestibule with his powerful body, eating up the space. No coat.

Never a coat.

He lifted a ceramic tan bowl in his hands. "Two hours and twenty-six minutes. The exact time it takes for Tia to make fresh chicken tortilla soup, the healer of all ailments, and for me to buy a movie." He retrieved a DVD from the back pocket of his jeans. "Fantasy, over two hours."

Lauren took the plastic case, squashing the swell in her heart, the little voice in her head chirping, *he remembered, he remembered! We love him!*

"*Pacific Rim*," she read, flipping over the cover. "Sci-fi and fantasy have nothing in common." She glanced up to explain but found she was alone.

"Nothing?" Miles groaned from the kitchen, opening cabinets. "They can't have nothing in common. A thousand years ago science was fantasy." He found bowls, spoons, and with full hands nodded to the stairs. "Down."

When she stared, he took it as a signal, striding into the basement, expecting her to follow.

What other choice did she have?

"Have you seen it?" he asked as he flipped the lights on in her room.

Making it as bright as the sun.

Or near enough.

She'd never get used to it. The ceiling seemed taller, the walls straighter. Her new white desk. The twin bookshelves. Her fancy—sturdy—new headboard and a mattress she shouldn't have accepted but would legitimately commit murder to keep. It didn't feel like hers, it felt like a hotel, like she'd unpacked her suitcase for a couple of days, and tomorrow she'd toss the towels on the floor and put a twenty next to the remote. *Great stay. Will recommend.*

It felt especially different when Miles set the bowls on her comforter, and kicked off his heavy tan boots. "Lauren?"

"What?"

"Have you seen it? *Pacific Rim*?"

Twice. And the sequel.

"No." A liar. A dirty little liar and she couldn't stop it, couldn't suck it back.

Why are you here?

Because she was sick? Because he'd worried? She pictured Miles in the Demon racing to Tia's, asking for help.

No, a dark voice intoned. He doesn't want his luck going bad.

A punch to the stomach.

"Awesome." He sat on her bed, stretching out to get the remote from her new nightstand. The new remote for her new TV. New mounted TV.

"Sit down." He patted the bed next to him. "You have to eat before it gets cold or it won't work."

Yes cold. Only cold.

"Are you a bed eater?" he teased softly. "Or just a sink eater? We can go upstairs and fight for the drain spot."

"Bed's good," said with the same flair as *she's dead or you have chlamydia.*

Careful to sit in the farthest corner from him, she accepted the steaming, spiced soup. Watched robots and kaiju go full battle royale death match, and all along thought, we're sharing a bed.

And she was so fucking screwed.

***

"WHY'D YOU LIE?" MILES asked as Lauren spat toothpaste into her sink.

She was beautiful like this, hair tied at her nape, neck arched, bare feet, face pink from hot water. Youthful, it made sense he took luck from her, a fairy handing out wishes.

He pushed higher on her bed, adjusting the pillow at his back but he didn't kick up his feet. Felt like it would cross a line. Imply an invitation.

No implications. He wanted a full-blown offer.

"I haven't heard a sniffle or sneeze."

She wiped white off her lip. "I'm having an aura."

"No, you're not. My sister got those. Knocked her out flat. You're playing with your toothbrush."

She set the toothbrush down and peered at her reflection, considering, blinking. Miles wanted to look, wanted to see what she did, what brought the hollowness to her eyes.

"Some days I feel too much," she admitted quietly. "And today was one of them. I wasn't sure if you could handle it."

"I can."

"Then I can't," she countered, throwing out her floss. "I can't handle these days. I feel more … than a normal person. I feel too much and no one ever knows how to react when I get that way. It's better if I just stamp it out, lock it down, freeze—"

"And you have no trouble with that? Swallowing your feelings?" *Going icy, losing your energy, yourself? Becoming first-date Lauren? Becoming Brian's punching bag?*

"Are you trying to feel less, Miles?" Her hip rested on the pedestal sink as she watched him through the doorway. Her head cocked. "Let me guess, you're tired of being horny all the time?"

"Do you think that's who I am?" he asked, pushing to sit upright.

They'd eaten soup, split a shortbread cookie, finished their movie. Fuck, he didn't know why he was still here. Still lingering, asking questions.

He didn't know why he'd come in the first place.

She'd let him off the hook, canceled. He was free to join Asher and Moore on the hunt, try and sober Kilbride enough to go fisticuffs.

He'd made his mom's soup for her.

His mom's recipe.

A recipe he'd stolen when he left. The last remnant of her lazy cursive.

He didn't cook, not for himself. But from the moment Lauren's voice cracked, his ass had been in the kitchen, gathering ingredients. Bone-in chicken, corn, cumin, half the habanero in the recipe. A quarter of what Sandra liked. Extra lime.

Then he'd been on her doorstep, shivering, lying about the soup as he fought his instincts to check her temperature, lay her down, fan her forehead and warm her feet.

Stayed.

Overstayed.

She'd changed into a massive white Race around the Lake 10K T-shirt that someone had doctored with red Sharpie to say Rage the Blake 1K. Shorts may have gone underneath, impossible to tell without asking, or worse touching. She'd washed her face, tied back her hair, rubbed a lemon-scented cream into her palms and brushed her teeth.

She'd thrown the hint at Miles and he let it smack his chest and shatter on the floor. If she wanted him gone, she'd need to say it. Need to make him leave.

He'd previously thought her beautiful, but in clothes she liked, graceful movements efficient and smooth, in her space, doing mundane tasks, she was nothing other than striking. Long neck, sharp nose, the full lips.

He'd sported a half chub for most of the movie, and now, a hard sudden thrust of desire surged.

He fluffed a pillow over his lap. "Do you think I'm horny all the time?"

"Of course not. You're also mad. Like when someone touches what's yours and you're, I presume, happy when you're playing football. The rest of the time? Horndog USA."

"For your information, on the field I'm horny and mad."

"Double jeopardy," she remarked dryly.

"You're kidding, right?" He leaned forward, hands crimping the blanket folded across her comforter, the same green of her eyes. "If I looked at you with the same lens, you know what I'd see?"

She spread a different, thinner lotion on her face, white and shimmery. "What?"

"You don't have any feelings." As a drop of white slid down her chin, Miles felt swift lust quake down his spine. "You're stone cold. You feel nothing."

"I told you—"

With that, he went to his feet, moving, circling, shocking her into silence. "Fuck, Lauren, you called your piece of shit ex-boyfriend to your house in the middle of the night and let him talk to you like you were less than a dog. Worse, you rolled over. You took it. You let him do it. You didn't care at all."

Her voice tight and quiet, she said, "I cared."

"No, you didn't. You wouldn't have said a thing if I weren't there. Same as when we met. A block of ice, incapable of empathy."

"I care too much!" She clutched the skin, her arms shaking, elbows bending and catching, chin tucked. "Too much," she repeated, voice no more than a rasp.

Oh fuck, was she going to cry?

White-hot anger snuffed his lingering erection and panic stomped on the ashes.

"That's the problem, Miles. You think I didn't cry myself to sleep on Friday, Saturday, Sunday? Why do you think I canceled tonight? I had to see Brian today, had to listen—" She swallowed, lifted her gaze. "I hated having him here, in my house. It's already so tainted with him and now this, all this new even feels wrong. I work with him. Every day. And I thought it would be a dream. A white-picket American apple-pie fucking dream. Walking into work together, kissing in the halls, picnicking in the park at lunch. I had all these plans for us."

"I was going to—" She stopped herself, sent a last glare at the mirror and put her toothbrush back behind it, leaving it to hang open as she staggered and fell against the towel rack.

"I thought I was living in a fairy tale," she croaked. "And when I told him that, when I told how much I loved him, how happy I was, that I was devoted and excited and lucky—" She choked on a laugh. "I believed our little problems, Brian's comments, his taunts, I believed the power of love would fix it, smooth the humdrum of office life, add color to our dullest winters."

Miles almost crashed into her dresser, felt the walls shift their orientation, feeling sick as Lauren dropped her arms and made fists of tiny, delicate hands.

His hatred for Brian penetrated his bones, became part of his DNA.

"He laughed in my face," she continued, eyes iced over, a defense mechanism. "He told me the truth. That I was fucking insane. It was one-sided. I'd been making it all up in my head. He never loved me and I was obsessed with him."

Miles's stomach seized as her voice leached of its usual softness, not stripped bare but clouded in a sheet of protection.

"Every day I see him and remember exactly how much I feel. More. Too much. An unhealthy amount. I'm in my head, I'm living out fantasy scenarios. Jesus, Miles, first Brian and now—"

She jolted, silent again. A tear trekked down the bridge of her nose.

"Now what?" He felt tile under his socks, cold, slippery before he realized he moved.

"Nothing."

"No, you used my name and his in the same sentence, so you better finish it."

"I forget, OK? Sometimes I forget we're nothing more than a transaction. That you're here to take your pixie dust from me and go shake it during a game that I don't even get to watch." A shake of her head, a flush heating her cheeks.

"You don't like football. You don't want to watch me play."

"You don't like fantasy!"

A minute, two passed. She was right. He hated magic and wizards and robots, but he liked it with her.

He opened his mouth to explain, to apologize, to eviscerate Brian, but Lauren spoke first.

"Of course, I want to watch you play. You're my friend." She groaned slightly and pursed her lips as though trying to suck the words back. "But that's what I mean. I think of you as a friend. I think you come here because we like each other, because we get along and it's not true. I'm doing it again right now, because I'm not locked in, I don't have the walls up. So yeah, I didn't want to see you tonight. I wanted to be alone. I wanted to fucking reset. I wanted to—"

She scrambled to stand and Miles moved to stand behind her, feet eating half the fuchsia penny tile. The aqua walls of her bathroom made him feel like he was being swallowed by a flower and he didn't care. He'd photosynthesize to get this right. He planted his hands on the sink, knuckles white enough to match the porcelain as he locked Lauren between his biceps. Not touching.

Not now.

Too raw, too wrong.

He closed the medicine cabinet so they had to face themselves in the mirror. Lauren's dewy skin, red eyes, and tangled hair. She looked like she'd been sprinting, sounded like she'd been screaming. And behind her hovered a monster. Tattoos, thick dark hair, ruthless narrowed eyes.

Slowly, gently, he wrapped his fingers around her chin, lifted and held her there. Stepped forward, pressed tighter, a shark nearing until she met her own gaze. He stopped just short of contact.

A tear skated down her cheek, dumped onto his fingers, and continued down his arm.

Miles was fucked in the head that he held her there, crying in the mirror, thinking about how good she looked with his arm holding her, his hand on her hip, scrunching cheap cotton.

How could he have ever thought her less than beautiful?

"We *are* friends, Lauren. It's not in your head. I'm your friend."

Another tear, faster.

Caused by him. All of this. If he'd kept his distance, given her space. But he'd been greedy. He caught the tear with his thumb, sent it on the same path down his arm.

"Will you tell me how you reset?" Another captured tear. "Please."

She sniffled. "You'll make fun of me."

A frown tugged at his brows. "When have I ever made fun of you? If I ever have said anything like that, tell me, and I'll deliver an apology to the likes of which you've never seen."

She tried shaking her head and he firmed his grip on her. "No. Tell me when I've ever treated you like fucking Brian treats you. I would never. Not just because we're friends, because you're a person."

Her fight fled.

Under his fingers, her jaw went loose, then her eyes closed and all at once she fell into him, her head on his chest, her ass on his thighs. A sob escaped her throat.

And drove nails into the cage around his heart.

He held her just like that, perched in the bathroom, his body no more than a rock for her to cry against as the reality of her world consumed her.

As she felt.

Miles never swayed, never looked away as she cried, her neck staining red, cheeks becoming a blotchy mess.

He smoothed her hair and whispered into the line of her cheek, "We're friends."

His arm stayed secured to him, fearing a strong wave might whisk her away. "We're friends," he told her, lips moving down the column of her throat. "It's not in your head, Lauren. You're my luck and my friend."

A featherlight kiss on the delicate dip between her neck and shoulder. "It's real. Your feelings are real. They're the same as mine. Don't let him and his problems cast a shadow over our friendship." He stroked over the pulse in her throat.

In time, the sobs slowed, became sniffles, became knuckles in her eyes, wiping and drying.

"Tell me what you were gonna do tonight."

Her cheek rested against his chest, his heart and then she was spinning around, looping her arms around his middle. Hugging him.

Mumbling into his chest and hugging him.

When was the last time he'd been hugged?

It caught him off guard. He forgot how it worked, arms and hands, and did he turn his head or nestle it onto the top of hers? The feelings that flooded him were so inappropriate, so inexcusably wrong, he struggled under the weight of them.

It couldn't be that the last time he'd hugged—it couldn't.

"Fuck."

He broke from her hold, pushed to suck down air, sat on the bed, put his head between his thighs.

Lemons and then, "Are you OK? What happened?"

He squeezed his burning eyes shut, tensed his entire body.

"I'm sorry. I didn't mean to—"

He reached out and snagged her wrist, gave her a strained smile. "It's not you."

She eyed him for a long moment, as if weighing his sincerity. He bent forward, straightened his back to bring their faces level. "See, you think I'm either mad or horny"—his voice shook—"but I've got my own fucked-up feelings. And you hug me and—I think the last time I hugged anyone was at a funeral."

"Your sister's?"

He tore his eyes away from her as sand filled his lungs. "Did you look me up?"

"You mention her in the past tense."

He sucked his teeth and crossed the room, drew in a breath to gather his bearings.

Lauren watched closely, a cat tracking a leaf falling helplessly to the grass.

He hugged her. With his arms and chest, their thighs pressed together, he held her tight, inhaled lemons and toothpaste and the eucalyptus of her lotion. Hugged.

Hand spanning the back of her head, face buried into her neck. "Friends, Lauren. You can't overthink else. I'm—" His voice thinned. "We're friends."

She stayed loose against him, hands a knot at his spine.

Impossible to tell how long they stayed like that, interwoven, inhaling, feeling, if the wetness on his chest was tears or drool or a bit of both.

Together they parted, hands slowly raking over skin, caresses and strokes and space. Lauren's eyes were glassy. Gorgeous.

"Dream date," he teased, tucking hair behind her ear. "Bland soup, dead sister, and a movie you've seen a dozen times."

"Twice."

"You were quoting it. I saw your lips moving at the end like a backup actress."

"I have a good memory for useless information. The epically clichéd monologue of *Pacific Rim* included." Traces of her tears remained, swollen eyes, red tip on her nose but like the sun breaking through clouds, she smiled for him. "I would've been writing. Maybe reading at first. But by two o'clock, I'd have five new chapters up and posted."

"Frodo and Sam?"

"They feel so much, and they aren't afraid to show it."

Passionate, Miles recalled. He stroked his thumb over her cheek. "What's your username?"

The sunshine smile burst supernova. "You will never know." A push on his chest. "Goodnight, Miles."

He couldn't stop his hands from caressing the soft skin of her jaw, her neck. Smooth, beautiful. He tipped her chin up, watched her eyes dilate, heard her breath quicken. And he kissed her.

Slow.

Deep.

Lazy.

His mouth toyed with hers, tongue coaxing hers to play. She tasted a little of salt from her tears and a wild burst of fake peppermint. Yes.

A cold shaft of wrongness knifed him.

Friends, was all he could think.

First, he took her on an awful date, then he lured her into this arrangement. And now he was trampling the exact sentiment he'd promised. He pulled back from her.

"Goodnight, Lauren." A kiss to her temple. "Go make some hobbits do the dirty."

Fighting his natural desires, he charged up the stairs, down the hall, out the door, and stumbled past the sidewalk into the snow.

Froze there.

The sun was rising, a dusky pink and orange swirl spilling onto a snow-white canvas.

He'd spent all night with her, missed Pinks.

But it wasn't the worst realization.

It wasn't Friday. He didn't have to kiss her.

Chapter Thirteen

Miles stared as Lauren twisted in front of him, golden light brown hair flowing over her shoulders.

He wanted her.

There. He admitted it. Couldn't afford not to when it screamed in his head all hours of the night.

Miles wanted her, wanted this woman who was so much better than him.

He snagged her arm and reeled her back home. The smack of her palms on her chest was muffled under the pulsing music but her smile was a spotlight in Nightingale's low lighting.

Friday night. Their time together and he'd taken her dancing where they first met. Hoped it would haul her out of the desolate swamp she'd waded through on Tuesday.

Tuesday.

Her lips on Tuesday.

Salt and mint and clutching hands, the heat vibrating the air.

Fuck.

He spun her away, let their arms extend, watched her hair double in size.

He'd kiss her tonight. Kiss her and stop. Stop, because if he did more …

It was obvious to him, and Carissa and every guy who gave Lauren more than a passing glance that *more* meant *all*. Meant locked doors, and sweat and licking, sucking, meant making Lauren chant his name as he tasted her sweet oasis. And because it was Miles, because Miles was fun and free, because sex was as rewarding, as fleeting as a fresh set of downs, he'd leave her there. Thank her, call her a good friend.

And she'd go in that cave and shut off. Block him out, spikes raised, mote filled, trebuchet loaded.

He wouldn't be able to see her again and his luck would dry up. Steph's income stream would become a trickle.

Nightingale's butter-smooth tile was thick with bodies, breaking fire code and not a one cared. At six feet, Miles stood above most heads but even he could only see the faint glow of the bar's backlighting, nothing else.

They'd gotten drinks, cheers'd, sampled and promptly lost them on a table or a wall or—his hip felt wet, maybe he'd spilled them.

Did it fucking matter?

Lauren was in jeans. Tight jeans that reached all the way to her belly button and clung, holes on the thighs, at the knees and a shirt he'd have called a wash rag had she not wiggled herself into it.

No bra, no straps on her shoulders at all.

Jeans in a sea of bare legs, dresses, and leather and Miles had hit the jackpot with jeans.

There was no hope for talking. Miming and mouthing were the only viable option. And he missed it.

Wanted to ask what made her eyebrow quirk, her hips swing, what sent the delighted twinkle into her eyes, the same spark that made her chew on the corner of her lip.

Later. He filed the questions for later, for the car ride home, the walk to her door, for her bedroom while she was putting her hair up, sliding under the cotton sheets, in the morning as she stretched.

Fuck. No.

He spun her again, far and wide, so she didn't feel his reaction to her. If she got close, she'd realize exactly what was happening to him. That he'd been hard since she shimmied out of her coat in the car, laughing, wiping sweaty palms on her thighs, saying, "This is insane. What if I get cold?"

"You won't," he'd assured.

If she did, he'd warm her up.

Though now warming her up without jabbing her with his erection would require a lighter, a bottle of whiskey, and a sacrificial couch.

She'd turned the air vents to her skin to wash off the goose bumps. "I've never been dancing before. Other than at weddings. But not like this." She'd stroked the goose bumps on her arms. "This is Maddie's shirt."

Blasphemous.

Lauren deserved to dance every damn day. Bouncing on her toes, throwing her hands in the air, screaming along with made-up words to songs she clearly didn't recognize.

Miles would take her every Friday.

He'd pick her up with flowers—crocus, the ones in her room—drive her six blocks, wrap his arms around her as they ran through the parking lot and unleash her onto the floor. While he sat and watched.

But she didn't want to dance alone.

So Miles stayed with her, making an ass of himself, bobbing and nodding, smiling.

In his heart of hearts, he faced reality. The worst thing imaginable.

He'd do the fucking Cha Cha Slide for Lauren Peck, lead YMCA choreography, stumble through a quadrille.

"You thirsty?" he called, tugging her back, angling his hips away to put his mouth at her ear. "Do you want a drink?"

Her arms wove around his neck, her breasts, her stomach, her everything attaching to his side. He felt her stretch onto her toes, her fingers gloss hair over his ears and it was a lightning bolt of desire.

"I'm never drinking again," she told him. "Only this, until my feet give out."

If that was the case, he'd carry her.

"Good choice?" His hand swept around her waist. "Better than shopping?"

Lips against his ear sparked ecstasy in his veins, lit a fire under his skin that burned brighter as she grabbed his shirt, two fists in the fabric.

"Dream date," she pulled back to smirk. "Gold star for the horny, angry brawler."

He didn't argue. No sand in sight but skin galore. Miles got to touch and feel and watch every curve on Lauren, see sweat bead down the indent of her back. Her gorgeous full hair was damp at the crown and sticking wayward strands to her forehead.

And it did nothing to diminish her appeal. Nothing could. He was going to punch through his zipper.

And just like she wanted, there was no pressure to talk, only companionable silence in a lively space. Music and wine.

Her mouth brushed his jaw. "Do you think I'd let you get this close to me on a first date?"

"You think you could keep me away when you're in those jeans?"

She pulled back to laugh, lips pouty, moist, so much skin he'd never seen, her clavicles, the sweet swell of her breasts, the slope of her shoulders. Bare. On display for him to eat up.

A jolt sent her sideways, a groan as a wide body elbowed her in the back.

Miles reacted, catching her, slotting her at his back and wrenching the bastard's arm, throwing him backward.

"Fucking watch it," he snarled.

"Whoa, man." The dope swiveled, struggling to balance three beers in his palms. "My bad, didn't see her."

"No shit," Miles snapped. "You're piss drunk, stomping around. Get the fuck out of here, sober up."

Delicate hands curled into his back. Heaving.

Under the raging music, a muttered apology came.

One of her hands slipped down the back of his jeans, knuckles touching his tailbone.

"Miles!" she shouted.

He heard her groan again, but pictured it in a different setting, his mind mismatching memories. A groan in her bed, under him, writhing.

He twisted, took her face in his hands.

Fuck he was throbbing. Her knuckles grazed against the line of his throat, fingers splitting to follow the separate curls of black. "I'm fine, I overreacted. He didn't meant it."

"Doesn't matter what he meant. He should be fucking aware of himself, he's a big guy and you're—" Smaller than Sandra. Thinner, shorter. Took one self-defense class.

"It's OK, I've got a bigger guy who's aware enough for both of us," she teased, voice low and sultry. "So bring back horny Miles and dance with me some more."

She knew?

Of course she did, his hand sealed them together, the magnificent friction on his length.

Move back. Push away. Get free.

He pressed them tighter and she gasped. A lovely sound, needy and wanton.

Her fingers flexed against his skin and she was pulling him in by the gold chain at his neck. "It's almost midnight," she said, swinging her hips, forcing his to move in sync.

Midnight.

At midnight, it'd stop. End with a kiss.

Could he stop? Her hands were frigid on him.

She jolted.

He yanked her tight, ready to pummel another jackass.

Lauren squirmed in his hold, phone screen casting a glow on her face. Her mouth parted and the hazy sweet curve vanished. "It's Hannah."

Over her shoulder, Miles read **SOS**.

"We have to go," she shouted, pushing through bodies, throwing elbows, doing a half-decent impression of Miles breaking through the line, pivoting, spinning, charging through gaps.

In four minutes, Miles was buckling into the Demon, peeling out of the parking lot.

"Which hospital?" he asked, shifting to third, shooting downtown. "I'll drop you off and meet you inside. Then—"

"No," Lauren stared at her phone. "Left. Go left. Take me home. I'll get my car and pick her up myself."

"I can get her. Tell me what's going on."

"Fine. It's an SOS, that means she needs me. I'm the one who saw the message, so I'll find her. She's outside some bar in the New North End according to her dropped pin."

"Did something happen? Is she hurt?" He shifted to fourth, fifth. "Should we get EMS?"

"No. An SOS just means she needs help now. Not necessarily unsafe, just unwell. Go right." She pointed to a streetlight. "Does that make sense?"

For as much as hated the police, he still managed to say, "Why don't you call the cops?"

"Because she doesn't need cops. She needs her sister. It's usually me. Maddie's getting beauty sleep and Kayla's spending the weekend at Killington Mountain. Another right, right here."

He threw the steering wheel, panic in his chest. A sister in danger. "How often does this happen?"

"It's for emergencies."

He downshifted through an ice patch, and clung close to the rail guards. "How often, Lauren?"

"I don't know, once a month."

"And how often are you the one answering, going out at midnight to unknown dangers?"

She didn't respond.

He hit the steering wheel. "Once a month. Got it." He was going to kill her. "Once a month you drive to a pin on a map because of a single text. Once a month, Lauren? Are you fucking kidding me? Who knows what's out there? It could be a creep waiting to hurt you. Worse."

"This isn't Vegas, Miles, or LA, it's Burlington. We make teddy bears and maple syrup."

"That shit happens everywhere."

"Slow down. I see her."

Fuck, Miles hit the brakes and pulled over to where Hannah waited, shuddering in the snow.

"Wait here," he demanded, but Lauren was out before he could set the parking brake. He watched as she rubbed her sister's arms, pushed her hair back, lips moving quickly.

Miles felt pangs of longing as he watched them talk, nod, hug.

Hug.

He honked. "Get inside."

Throwing back the front seat so Hannah could slide into the back, Miles vibrated with anger. Horny and mad. Maybe Lauren wasn't off about him.

Because right now all he wanted to do was yell at her and fuck her, stamp his possession over her, give her a long list of rules to follow. *No going out. No SOS. No getting out of the car, no work.*

"I'm so sorry," Hannah burst, sobbing, words a muddled slur. "I just"—she hiccupped—"really needed you." She cried more, red hands shot from the dark back seat like killer vines, tapping icy digits against Miles and Lauren's arms.

Lauren dragged Hannah's hand to the vents. "You didn't interrupt anything," she soothed. "Besides, Miles loves being overprotective. You've made his day. Hero box checked."

"What happened?" he grunted, spinning out the wheels to get back on the road.

Blubbering drunk, Hannah spouted vowels and sobs, smelling of baby powder and gin.

Lauren's voice squeaked through the noise to explain, "She was flirting with a guy—"

"Daaayyyve."

"Right," Lauren agreed. "She met Dave and he asked her out after he bought her a drink and he got mad when she took too long to answer him, and he got—" She paused, her hand gliding over his knee and squeezing. He'd been bouncing it, trembling. He wrested the steering wheel, pushed into fourth. With a tight smile, he forced himself to relax.

Thumb stroking, Lauren finished, "He got pushy. She texted and left."

"I'll go back," he promised. "Does she remember what he looked like? Distinguishing features? Is Dave his real name?"

Lauren glanced back and cringed. Miles looked in the mirror and found brown hair like a net in front of the littlest Peck's face. She snored.

"She's really drunk," Lauren noted. "She probably won't remember this."

"That's fucking worse."

"You think I don't know that? She's my sister. You think I like her being out alone? Drinking? That's why I set up the SOS. For this. Save our sister."

"You should not be the one picking her up."

"Who else is going to? You?"

"Yes!" A pause, the both of them panting. Hannah gurgled a limerick. "If you let me, I'll answer all of them."

And he meant it.

This was the wrong thing to say, he deduced from the silence that followed. Silence that extended for the length of the drive.

Was she offended?

Impressed?

Had he ... overstepped? A knot formed in his throat, cutting off sound, cutting off air.

No. No. They were friends. She was his luck, his pretty girl, and

...

He wanted her. What precisely he wanted, he wasn't sure. Her body, no-brainer, serve it to him hot, cold, wet, dry, he'd eat like a king, but he wanted her protected too. He wanted to be her shield and if he was hers, then dammit, he'd have to be one for the entire Peck clan.

In a pink fur-trimmed robe and red shower cap, Maddie waited in the front hall of the house. After a scream for Miles to leave—which he ignored since he was carrying Hannah—she calmed, got a briefing from Lauren and hurried Hannah to her bedroom.

Once again, Miles was in the house he'd vowed not to enter, next to the woman for which he'd vowed the same.

As if no time had passed, no SOS, like picking her sister up on the side of the road was normal, Lauren stepped over errant gloves and scarfs and boots crowding the floor to hang her coat on a narrow hook.

"I'll see you next week."

"Lauren." He caught her hand, straightened, focused. "You're forgetting something." He kissed her. Quick, still radiating with anger.

Then Lauren moaned, "Miles," and it became more. Less than he wanted, but more.

No mortal man could ignore such a plea. He swung her around to cage her into the door, meshed their lips together, tongue driving and rolling with hers exactly how he'd imagined, greedy, deep.

When that wasn't enough, he worked up the skimpy fabric of her shirt. One of her hands lifted, nails digging into his hair, scraping his scalp. His body quivered with bottomless need. His bones chafed. He wanted to taste her everywhere. He wanted—

He yanked back.

He wanted to keep her in his life.

And Lauren wasn't a woman for casual sex, for casual anything. Breaths sawing, he smoothed the curls. "If Hannah remembers anything, I want to be the first to know." He stepped back from her, grabbed the door. "Night, pretty girl."

Chapter Fourteen

HE SMELLS LIKE CIGARETTES, Lauren thought as she ordered from Declan. Miles smelled like sugar, like cavities and blood. Like she'd bit into a sucker so hard, she split her lip, but kept eating. He tasted like …

Sex.

She wiped her hands on her jeans. Jeans. She'd worn her jeans. Jeans she'd worn to a club, jeans she'd worn ten, eleven times in the last year and now were regular in her rotation. What was she doing? Vying for Miles's eye to gaze over with hunger. Insane.

Trivia. With her sisters.

Why was she nervous?

Because Miles and she were on the cusp of something. Something important. Something that he didn't want, something she kept trying to drown. Friends. Be fine with friends.

You could have had more, a mocking voice told her, *but you blew it with your freak out, with your tears, with your teasing.*

Lauren couldn't give her heart only to see it dropped again. She was tired of being the source of love, of believing in more, the power of magic. Over the past two years, she'd watched her sisters give chances like breaths, forgive as easy as waking up.

She'd seen depression, anger, rage mount and grow in her home. Hate fester on the remnants of unrequited love.

They were friends.

She was his rabbit's foot.

And it twisted her up in knots.

His damn ritual, his mouth and hands messing with her head. Anyone would like kissing Miles. Feeling the heat of his hands, the scratch of his calluses, the skill of his tongue.

He was a good kisser. Obviously. He was great at everything he did. Got all the good genes, all the charm, the ease, the confidence. And he smelled good—like cinnamon sticks and candy canes—and he held her like a knight would a damsel.

In return, Lauren had … feelings.

Not a match. They'd agreed. Signed, sealed, delivered. No pair. Not in this lifetime.

Still, it had thrilled every atom in her body to see him bristle at Brian.

Then again, Brian had a knack for that. He'd pissed off her sisters, her parents, Mary most days.

She was not a princess.

This was not a love story. Not a fairy tale. There was no ball gown, no tower, no extravagant garden maze. Tomorrow, she'd be in her slacks, her gray button-down, tie her hair in a knot and spin in her chair developing back problems for the sake of office supplies.

One day of a thousand in her future. Another drop in the bucket of the rest of her life.

Mary would retire.

A new Mary would hang the lights on their nondenominational tree, take them down on Valentine's Day. Brian would marry his girlfriend, grow a spare tire, lose his hair. And Lauren would watch the clock click down to five as she searched catalogs for cheaper pen ink.

Real life. Paperwork, phone calls, Brian Junior.

Her life was sweatpants through and through.

"You're drinking a rum and Coke," a friendly voice accused. Blonde, thirtyish, a mustache indicative of a *Top Gun* addiction. "No." He shook his head, planting exposed forearms on the bar. "Amaretto sour."

She must've scratched her nose, frowned, given him a sign of life because he tried again.

"I know." His fingers snapped, the rolled sleeve of his flannel slipped past his elbow as he nodded to Declan.

The drop-dead gorgeous bartender strolled over, each step a lesson in patience is a virtue as women swooned behind Lauren. Not her.

Not when he smelled like cigarettes. And his hair was a little too dark, frame a bit narrow. No leather jacket tonight, just a plain white T-shirt, giving him an old-school soda shop vibe, a bruiser from *Grease* with a comb waiting in his back pocket to slick his hair to an oily sheen.

Declan folded his arms, showcasing the sleeve of black animals and words, lyrics. A shame to cover only one arm, stop at the wrist, the shoulder.

"What'll it be?" he asked, giving Lauren's companion an up-down.

"Two bourbon Mountain Dews, please."

Black brows arched at Lauren, Declan doling out two beats to object before he scooped ice into cups.

None of The Hand's staff could be accused of being overly friendly, and Declan was certainly the least. Unless you were on fire or underage, he was minding his own business. Aloof.

Precisely why Maddie was frothing at the mouth to have him.

"I know it sounds bad," blondie defended, sporting a toothy smile, fiddling with his button. "But you have to try it. It's refreshing and very flavorful. You'll never go back."

"Wow." Lauren had no other response except to peer behind her, send a charade SOS to her table with bulging eyes.

But Hannah was on her phone, Kayla massaged her temples, and Maddie was adjusting the sit of her sticky boobs in the window's reflection.

"I'm Michael. What's your name?"

Confused, Lauren cocked her head. "Do you want to talk to my sisters? Because I'm not a messenger and Hannah's not really ready—"

Michael followed her gaze and a puff of air escaped his lips. "There's more of you."

"Our parents aren't quitters."

"Sisters," he muttered. "I didn't see them."

If he hadn't seen the three prettiest girls in the bar, it made sense why he was talking to her, but he didn't leave. Didn't shout *psych* to Declan and direct focus to Maddie.

Beguiled, Lauren gave Michael a once-over. Nice smile, his sneakers pointed at her, he had a wrinkled collar and a fidget in his hand.

He was buying her a drink.

The jeans.

Flirting. With wide eyes, Lauren caught up, blinked, switched their interaction from stranger danger to potential love interest.

He was handsome, really, kind of in the way Brian wasn't. Where Brian was thin and severe, Michael was rounded. Soft, wide nose, flat brown eyes. A smile fit for a college brochure, projecting *I can do my own laundry, put down the toilet seat, and I'm not a serial killer.*

"Are you here for trivia?" he asked, a bit of a Boston accent. "I'm subbing for a friend tonight."

Yes. The flannel. The nerdish vibe. "You're here with tea"—Bro-Fucks. Not their name. What was their actual name?—"team three? I'm team seven. I'm Lauren."

"Lauren." Another ingratiating smile. "What were you about to call them? Team Geek? Team Flannel?" At her silence, he chuckled. "Worse? Oh you have to tell me."

"In my defense, your team beats us every time. And we really want drink coupons."

"It's bad, isn't it?"

"We call you the Bro-Fucks."

Another laugh. Slightly infectious. She felt herself roll into it, follow along. Easy. Flirting was easy. Nice.

"OK, yeah." He wiped at his eye. "That's harsh. But know that I am only a temporary Bro-Fuck."

"Do you guys have a name for us? Or are we so bad, they haven't noticed the competition?"

"They mentioned the Swifties, and I think that has to be you. You look just like her. Before she went pop. Curly blonde hair, green eyes, beautiful." He leaned in closer, elbows sliding along the polished wood. "Plus my friend said you were the one who listed every member of the Fellowship faster than him. It really rankled his week."

Declan dropped two off-greenish drinks in front of them as well as a tray of her usual order.

Michael put the puke-colored glass in her hand, the fizzles tickled her nose.

"Try it," he encouraged. "One sip. Trust me, you won't taste the bourbon."

"I don't really ..." She trailed off, watching bubbles roll off the ice.

"It's breaking bread for the war," he reasoned. "The elves would have done it."

"No, the dwarves." She frowned, a blush working over her, but Michael laughed and agreed, hit his glass against hers.

This was not fantasy.

This was reality. This man, nice and kind, he'd bought her a drink, compared her to a celebrity. He knew Tolkien.

She could refuse to drink, explain. And he'd apologize profusely, he'd order her a tequila sunrise and offer to throw himself off Mount Doom.

Her fingers curled around the glass.

There'd be no pressure, no hurt feelings, no seven years of bad luck, no deal, no strip club.

She hadn't even thought to ice him out, to stay protected, he'd slid into her space undetected, stepping through the holes Miles had slit open. Left gaping and raw.

Sensing her hesitance, Michael refrained from drinking. "What if we made a bet?"

She gave what she hoped was a dashing smile, put on her geek face. "Lay out your terms."

***

MILES'S GOOD MOOD DETERIORATED the moment he stepped inside The Hand. A fact Burton would have his balls for.

Because his good and now bad moods swung with the whim of one woman.

There wasn't time to pound the snow off his boots or wave to the Peck sisters. Plans to ask Kayla about snowboarding in between interrogating Hannah and telling Maddie he hadn't seen her shower cap evaporated. Idle chatter, bonding, when two weeks ago he couldn't tell them apart without name tags.

Up in smoke.

Because the prettiest Peck sister, the smartest, the funniest, the brattiest, most beautiful sister had her hand in some schmuck's grip.

The smile melted off his face as hers grew.

As she laughed.

For a mustache.

"If we win," the blond moron was telling Lauren, still pawing at her hand. "You give me your number and if we lose, I'll give you mine."

"Hmm." Lauren tipped her head, sea glass eyes alight. "And how do I know you won't sabotage your own team?"

"For you? They can all rot. The Bro-Fucks die tonight."

She knocked her glass with his. "Deal, just don't tell them their name."

"Deal."

Miles shot from unhappy to vehement rage to a maelstrom of whirling red and black, when Lauren sniffed her drink and raised it.

He was there, removing it from her hands faster than the D-line could strip a ball, ditching the toxic green mess on the bar, and pressing the tips of his fingers into asshat's chest. Shoving.

"Are you trying to kill her?"

The interloper spat sickly sweet green into his hand. "What? No."

He peered around Miles's body and no—Miles moved to block Lauren. No looking at his girl. He had two inches and a hundred pounds on the himbo and he sure as shit was going to use it to his advantage.

"She can't have the fucking bubbles, man. She has asthma. You want her to go down right here? Now tell me, are you consciously a threat or too dumb to hear no?"

"I didn't know. She—"

"Blame her," Miles snarled. "Fucking try."

Cold hands pinched his hip. Because she couldn't talk? Because her lungs were struggling? Her throat closed?

How did asthma work?

He spun around. "Do you have an EpiPen? Do I stab you with it?" He touched her cheeks, her forehead, brushed back hair and felt her pulse, searching for signs of distress, for coughing, choking.

"She didn't—" the guy said, crowding them.

"Leave, now," Miles grunted, peeling back the buttons of her long sleeve to check for a rash, a witch's mark, something that said imminent death, something he could fix or heal.

"A doctor?" he asked, voice like sandpaper. "What do you need? Can you talk? Nod?"

Lauren's hands overtook his. "Miles," she said, swallowing back a laugh. "Hey, I'm good. I'm not hurt. Nothing bad is happening." She pressed his hands to her ribcage and inhaled deeply.

"Thank Dios," he muttered, dropping his forehead to hers. Situation handled, Miles flipped onto his heels. "Who the fuck do you think you are pressuring her to drink when she clearly can't?"

"She didn't tell me." The blond kid rushed out, dodging Miles's advancing steps. "Lauren—"

"Don't look at her."

Mine, his inner voice said, *mine. Not yours. Mine.*

A door slammed into the wood and the gentle rock music cut off as Riley Moore's dream girl stormed toward them. A blaze of dark voluminous hair, emo clothes, and combat boots. A steel bat dangled in her fingers.

"We have a problem here, boys?" She said *boys* but it sounded like *whiny, useless fuckers.*

Five foot and inches, she managed to stare the three of them down. The bat swung a lazy circle. Deadly eyes skewered Miles, as if she clocked him as the biggest, ugliest threat and siphoned her influence there.

"Because if we have a problem," she continued smoothly. "I have a solution."

The metal bat slammed onto the bar, ringing. A warning bell.

Glass rattled. Declan steadied a bottle of bourbon from toppling. Didn't look up from the dishwasher.

"No problem," Miles told her in that same cool tone, a tone that suggested chaos if not respected.

"Good." She collected her bat, swinging the wrapped hilt into her palm, the tip jabbing Miles's side. On purpose, no doubt. "I don't tolerate problems in my bar. Tip your bartender and run along." Even as his ribs crunched with pain, Miles held her stare.

Declan muttered something like *overkill* when the scary brunette hopped up onto the bar, thick black boots stretching over the wood.

Beside him, Lauren dug into her purse.

Miles stopped her, throwing a fold of fifty singles in front of Declan. He always kept cash, too much cash. Ignoring the mouth-breathing doughboy, he claimed the Peck tray and led Lauren to the windows.

"EpiPen?" Lauren questioned, steps short and stompy, face aglow with red. Anger? Embarrassment? Asthma?

"Were you going to drink that?"

"An inhaler. I need an inhaler. It's not a bee sting."

"Were you?"

"A sip maybe. I mean … it was …" She slid around a table, turning to face him as she announced resolutely, "Yes."

Yes.

So she'd risk herself for some dude at the bar but not Miles. Why? What was so great about an ill-fitting flannel and short teeth?

Probably doesn't have half your issues, that recurrent voice peppered. Probably didn't yell at her to drink, didn't come in hot and cocky when they met, didn't stalk her.

Which made *him*, not Miles, *him* with the wallet chain and soft hands, the good guy. The better man. A man who believed like Lauren did.

Fuck.

Overwhelming thoughts told Miles to take Lauren, to kiss her, here. Now. Right in front of everyone.

But he wondered what'd she say. How she'd react.

She hadn't taken a sip for him. Hadn't seen a reason to. The risk wasn't worth the reward. They hadn't swapped numbers. She hadn't worn jeans. She'd laughed at how terrible their paring was.

And shred his soul, he didn't give a shit. He wanted her luck for himself. His eyes, his hands only.

Wrong. So fucking wrong.

"I want you to be careful, Lauren." He slid the tray onto table seven, and pulled out the bench for her. "Tell people your limits or they'll run over them. What if you had an asthma attack and I wasn't here?"

Hannah plucked up her Bellini. "If she did, I have her inhaler."

"So do I," Maddie echoed, laying a napkin under her martini. "It makes my purse lumpy."

"Really? Lauren asked, genuinely confused, fingers paused on her lemon.

Kayla rolled her eyes. "You never do, somebody has to."

Family. Sisters. In five minutes, they'd be at each other's throats over which was the seventeenth state added to the union, but they'd come back here. To trivia. Fight and answer SOS calls and carry inhalers.

Pain clawed into Miles's ribs.

No wonder Lauren believed in the power of love. Felt love, gave it so easily. She was flooded with it.

"I want one too," he croaked, taking his place at Lauren's side.

"I have a spare," Kayla offered.

Lauren waved a dismissive hand. "He doesn't need it. I bring it when it's just us."

He dragged a hand over his face, feeling barbs slice his stomach. Right. She didn't want him to care for her. Scratching his cheek, he peered at the rafters and exhaled a sardonic laugh.

Overstepping. He was doing it again.

Licking the flesh of her lemon, Lauren slid him a glass, muttering, "Rum and Coke."

Absurdly, when he drank, he found it absent of any alcohol.

She'd noticed. And instead of asking, pointing it out, ordering him a plain soda. She'd made a special request, kept up his rugged drunk appearance while delivering what he wanted.

He wanted to tell her right then. Tell her everything. How all the reasons they shouldn't be together didn't fucking matter. He'd try for her, with her. On his knees through glass, he'd try.

Instead he drank, sucked air through his teeth, turned his head to avoid the onslaught of lemon wafting from Lauren's lips.

He needed her to win. He needed to win to protect Pinks. To hold leverage and money. Power.

Even if he didn't, what did it matter? They'd fall apart sooner or later. Days, if Miles knew himself.

So there'd be no Lauren for him.

"Let's get after it, trivia night," he exclaimed, voice tight.

The stringent smell of an Expo marker wafted as Kayla blocked off a corner for the tallying points.

"I have a good feeling about tonight," Lauren told the table, ditching the yellow rind in her glass.

They won.

But it was Tuesday, so they didn't kiss.

Chapter Fifteen

Lauren woke with a groan, reaching out to smack her phone into silence.

But it was quiet.

Here it was. The end materializing. Her mind scrambling to bits harder than eggs in a smoking skillet. Expected after Tuesday. After Miles had given her *the look*.

Not the panicked, terrified look he had when he'd thought she was hurt, that look had stunned Lauren into prideful silence as he checked every patch of skin for injury, ready to peel it off her and graft it onto himself.

No. The *other* look. The one after Maddie kissed Declan's cheek and Kayla took a selfie with their drink coupons.

Lauren had turned, vodka rousing red in her cheeks, excitement calling her heart to hug, kiss and hold. Then the look. The step back.

With evil intent, the look stole her smile.

Set mouth, clenched teeth, forest gaze indifferent. She could read his mind, *you're crazy. I don't love you, I don't like you. It's in your head.*

Declan flipped The Hand's sign to closed.

There was no hug, no kiss.

More of the look.

Trudging to work Wednesday morning pitted her soul. Wasting away in her hollow cubicle, ordering Brian cheap conduit, ignoring his "This should've gotten here yesterday" comment.

It slid off her back like snow melting from the mountaintops. Finding any path down, uncaring if the streams wore the rock and soil.

White walls, gray carpet, a black stain. Repeat on Thursday. Ate leftover lasagna at her desk, butt numb. Not even Friday could peel away the aftereffects of the look. Not when Miles texted he'd be late.

Her reply had been immediate: **Come over whenever.**

As if she had too, didn't care.

She felt alone. Lonely. Lonelier than before she'd had a friend. Feeling too much.

She tugged the comforter higher on her shoulder and shut her eyes. *Stop waiting for him. Close your eyes. Count sheep.*

Behind her, the mattress dipped, a cool breeze crept under the sheets.

"Go back to sleep," a velvet-soft voice whispered.

Miles Santos was in her bed.

Lauren might never sleep again. *There.* She lost her mind. Officially.

She drew back the covers to splash water on her face, to slap her cheeks—

"Go back to sleep," Miles repeated, hand slinking over the curve of her waist to hold her still, thumb timing circles over her T-shirt.

The heat his touch erupted—not imaginary. He felt warm and heavy.

"Shh," he cooed. "Don't get up. It's late. You need sleep."

"You scared me," she rasped, voice thick from disuse. "I can't go back to sleep now."

"Shit." His hand stole more ground until his elbow laid in the small dip under her ribs. "Sorry. I had to see you."

Because he needed her luck. Because he was superstitious and dumb.

"You didn't have to get in my bed."

His chuckle caused the hair behind her ear to flutter. Sugar and blood. An ache bloomed in her core.

"I'm tired," he whined quietly. "I had a long night. How was your day? That's all I care about now."

Now that the clock had started, he cared. T-minus four hours of Lauren time. She dug deeper into her pillow. "It was fine."

"Fine?" He sounded skeptical.

"Good."

"Good?" Like he didn't believe her.

"It was another day, Miles." She pushed onto her elbows to glare at the dent in her pillow. "I woke up, went to City Hall, came home. A day. Fine. Good. Call it what you want. It's every Friday for the rest of my life."

With a teasing edge, he said, "I know, that's not true."

Fire back, give him something to play with. But she couldn't. Because she had a feeling it was the truth.

At her side, Miles cleared his throat. "I'm sorry I was late tonight. It couldn't be helped."

She didn't ask. They weren't friends. "It's fine," she muttered, dropping to her stomach, facing away from him.

"Go to sleep, pretty girl," he said again, warm moist breath dusted the back of her neck. Was he sharing her pillow?

A cold foot touched hers and she jerked, hissing. "Too cold."

"It won't be," he informed slyly, arm wounding around her middle. "If you help me warm up."

"Warm up by stealing my heat? No." She wiggled away, trying to build a sheet wall between them.

He grinned. She didn't know how she knew it, wasn't looking at him, her eyes were still adjusting to the darkness, but she knew it. His sexy grin.

In three pulls and pushes, Miles got Lauren to her side, hip and shoulder in the mattress. Instead of sliding forward, molding himself to her body, becoming the big spoon, his hand explored, left the safe zone of her waist and trailed down to play with the hem of her shirt, found the bare skin too high on her thigh.

"Miles," she scolded, squirming. But he was shushing her again. Lips brushed her nape.

"Come on," he coaxed, voice like a silk shadow. "This always helps me after I spend the day sitting." His fingers dug into the meat of her thigh, squeezed. "A little blood flow," he whispered into her ear, "and then you'll fall right back to sleep."

The heel of his palm circled her skin, drifted down her thighs to the overtight muscle in her calves. His hand encompassed her entire ankle, thumb stroking the soft skin behind the bone.

Through flexibility he didn't deserve to possess, his other hand joined, working the muscles of her legs, kneading, massaging, pushing her right to the edge of pain and straying back, stroking.

Was she awake? Was this real?

Yes, because in Lauren's head, in her dreams, she'd never be this patient. This tame. Wouldn't quiet the moans scratching up her throat, wouldn't seal her teeth against gasps. Her hands would be in his soft, beautiful hair, pulling, stroking.

"How's it feeling?" His breath on her shoulder now, palms sliding just under her T-shirt to wrap around the front of her thighs, grip and grab.

He didn't stroke and rub as much as taunt the muscle. Choked and released. Flexed it and let go. Never too hard.

"Just like that." Velvet words dabbed down her spine. "Relax."

Wetness pooled between her thighs. Before she knew what she was doing, she'd spread her legs, tipped her hips so we could better reach around her thighs, grab at her like handles.

"That's it." His breaths came faster, blankets falling off them. "Let me take care of you. I'll make you feel good."

His words shot blazing heat through her, hacking into her cold, bitter heart.

A friend, she wanted to tell her goose bumps, her hammering heart. A friend giving a friendly massage.

A friend with big hands moving her just as he wanted.

"Your skin is so soft everywhere. If you weren't burning up, I wouldn't be able to tell what's you or the sheets." He stroked higher, reaching the curve between her ass and thigh. Didn't pause, didn't ask permission.

And she didn't do anything but moan as he took two handfuls of her ass, as his thumbs angled inward, spread her wider, caressed.

Could he see? In the dark, could he see the wet stain on her pink boy shorts?

"Fuck, Lauren." The tone—

She gasped, flipped around and rose to her elbows, panting. What the hell was she doing?

This wasn't what they did. He was ... oh my God.

"Miles," she gasped.

His hands were raised like guilty weapons. But she was pushing up, knocking them aside, taking his face in her grip, angling. A black eye.

Blood dried on the corner of his mouth. Glitter stuck to his eyelid, the arch of his cheek.

He'd been in a fight. A bad one.

Eyes hard, he stared right at her, lips pressed in a flat line. The look.

The ivory tower, the rose gardens, her frilly ball gown gnarled and twisted, grew boils and sores. The tiara stung her scalp.

He'd gone to the strip club and slunk straight into her bed.

***

MILES SHOVED UP TO the headboard, grateful the lack of windows helped to cover the worst of his injuries. As he flattened himself against the steel-framed wood, he scratched a finger over his face. Fat lip, blood. Swelling under the eye.

Regret washed through him, a cold rain in his blood.

He'd ruined it.

He smelled like fake strawberries and wore a cross section of blood. This was it. She'd cut him loose.

"Is it yours?" she rasped into the dark, sheets strung around her waist, hand at her mouth, appalled, disgusted.

There was no going back so Miles closed his eyes, left his tone bored, lifeless. "I don't know what—"

"Is it your blood?"

"Some."

"Who else?"

"You want a list, pretty girl?"

Fed up, her tone changed from concerned to indignant. "Get up," she hissed, throwing the comforter back.

Miles's heart lurched at the impending doom. The lights snapped on.

Two sharp inhales.

She'd forgotten pants.

His eyes stuck to her legs, glued to the bare thighs, the underwear he'd mistaken for thin shorts were near transparent cotton. His heart hammered hard enough to make his hands throb as he pressed shaking palms into the mattress.

She stood there for a moment, unmoving, then cocked her hip. "C'mon, let's go."

He flipped his eyes to hers. Fuck, he should have thought about this before he'd gone in with the wrecking ball. The collateral damage, the disgust, the revulsion—

Were missing. Her gentle gaze raked over him calmly from head to toe.

Of course she'd be kind to him when he least deserved it. Make him the villain.

"Right." He tossed his feet to the floor, stood, embarrassed to find his stance shaky. "I'm sorry. This wasn't how—" He took two steps to the door and Lauren blocked him.

"Where are you going?"

"You're kicking me out." He hardly recognized his own voice, low and strained.

"Don't tell me what I'm doing," she returned sharply. Catching the ends of his fingers and tugging forcefully, she knocked him sideways, bare feet kissing the penny tile. "Take off your shirt."

"What?" He shook free of her grip. "What are you doing?"

"We're cleaning you up," she explained, leaving no room for questioning. "But first we have to ... assess your wounds."

"Wounds?"

Her skin flushed dark enough to distract him from the blue walls. "Shirt off," she demanded, "and tell me what happened."

Confused—fucking stunned more like—Miles grabbed the back of his shirt and pulled it over his head, the bend making his ribs sing with pain. That's what a size twelve to the lungs did. Three on one, he'd been bound to catch a hand or fist, the very tip of a knife.

Normally, nothing the physical trainers even noticed. But there'd been a woman in the mix, and getting her safe left him open for cheap MMA bullshit.

"Either you tell me," Lauren threatened, folding his shirt, staring at the cross over his right pec, "or I'm going to make up a story and it'll have dragons. So ... you were at Pinks and ..."

Her tender sea glass gaze floated to his stomach, and her folding became bunching, wringing.

Wondering if there was bruising, he looked down, but the tattoos covered any discoloration. It was just him. Muscle cut into the standard squares. A dark trail of hair low on his stomach.

"A dancer was catching flack," he smoothed the hard truths. Poppy getting groped, crying for help.

"And you stood up for her?"

He'd thrown down, good and nasty. But admitting he was thirsty for the fight wouldn't solve any problems.

"Am I right?" she pressed.

"You're always right about me. Nailed me day one. Mad and horny."

She made an amused sound, reaching out to touch the pads of her fingers to the outside of his eye. "You're spreading a bit of both to me. Pants off."

His heart stopped.

She smirked. "Shower. You smell like Kandy with a K. It's going to be cold. Hannah showers at night."

"Is that my punishment?" he goaded, blocking the bathroom door from her as he undid the buckle of his belt. "A cold shower?"

"It's the start. Next you'll get the blood and body oil off my bedspread. And if I said cold, I meant frigid."

She was right. The water burned it was so cold, spiking icy drops against his skin. He stayed there, in it, shuddering, hands cupped over his balls, waiting for Lauren to yank back the curtain liner and throw in the toaster.

Nothing.

He washed quick with her geranium shampoo and hopped out. Not wanting to get her towel wet for the morning, he dried as well as he could with his shirt and stepped back into his jeans.

In the bedroom, he found the bed stripped clean.

"Sit," Lauren commanded, patting the mattress.

He followed orders.

Tipping his chin back, she coasted exploring fingers along his jaw, tested the sore skin around his eye. "Is that why you go there? To pick fights?" she asked, clearing wet hair from his forehead. "Why'd you have to go tonight? Miss our time together? Do you—" Her throat bobbed. "Do you know how it feels to be second to the strip club, to getting bloody? I thought your routine was everything, eight to midnight. But I guess that's unless you need a lap dance."

She lifted his hand in hers, found the split knuckles. Glared.

He curled his fingers around hers, closed his hand. "Steph asked me to come, said there was a group coming in that was especially rowdy."

"Steph is …"

"Important to me."

She stumbled a step back. "She's important."

"Yes," he confirmed, commandeering her wrist to spread her hand over the base of his throat. "Finish your assessment, Nurse Peck."

"What are you thinking? You have a game on Sunday and you're fighting? Is she so important to you that you'd risk your job?"

"They all are."

She flinched and a stab of guilt struck.

Miles took her chin in his hand. "You are too."

"Because I'm lucky." She sounded annoyed.

"Yeah." He exhaled hard. Lucky. That's the reason he gave her. Why he was here. But—"You'd be important to me even if you were a black cat under a ladder."

"You wouldn't be here if I wasn't lucky. We wouldn't know each other. There'd be no Fridays. What if I said I can't see you next Friday? What if I made you leave right now and you lost? Would you come back or would you hate me?"

"I'd understand if you wanted me to go."

"Then leave."

Like clockwork.

He rose to his feet, water skating down his spine. "My sister—," he murmured, voice low. "She passed away ten years ago. It was just the three of us. Me, Mom, and Sandra. She was the oldest, the wisest." His throat thickened, voice strained. He couldn't do this.

But he had to. Needed her to know why he was an absolute asshole, why she should feel good about making him leave.

"We were raised Catholic." He touched the ornate cross hanging at his neck, the matching one inked on his chest, nail scraping the ruby in the center. "Mass every Sunday, confession on Wednesday nights. We sang, we pot-lucked, we prayed the rosary before bed. Sandra was beautiful. Green eyes, long hair. Everyone thought so, especially in her church clothes. And she started dating this guy when she turned seventeen. I can't even remember his fucking name, only that he wore a cross."

He pulled at his chain, the cross he'd torn from the asshole's neck. "One day, Mom found them both in Sandra's bed and she flipped. My sweet mom who lived for Jesus, took one look at Sandra and axed her out of the family. I remember the way she threw Sandra out, grabbing handfuls of her hair, shoving her down the stairs. She wasn't even allowed to grab her shoes. Mom locked the doors, put the chain up."

"Oh, Miles." Lauren's voice shook with dark emotion, her eyes welled with tears.

He looked away to finish. "She must have pounded on the door for hours before she gave up. I tried to see her the next day when Mom finally let me out. But I couldn't find her. I was fifteen. Her boyfriend didn't care, called her a whore when I asked him. The first guy to ever punch me in the face."

The first guy Miles had ever put in the hospital.

"For weeks, I looked, heard rumors. Mom acted like Sandra never existed. Wouldn't look at me if I shouted Sandra's name at her, showed her picture. Then, five months later, we get a call from the LAPD, asking us to come downtown. Mom refused so I go. Sixteen, I walk in, already have a record for pretty theft, and they send me to the morgue to identify Sandra's body."

"No," Lauren choked. "No. Miles."

"She wasn't wearing something that a stripper wouldn't. Bruises everywhere, eyes bloodshot, I hardly recognized her. The coroner thought she might've been choked to death." He struggled to get the words out. "There was no investigation. No one cared about another dead stripper. I paid for her to be cremated because I didn't want anyone to see her like that. In those clothes, skin black and blue."

Arms wrapped around him, stroking, rocking. "I don't blame her," he croaked, tears streaming.

Gently, Lauren cleaned his cheek, mindful of the bruises.

"I don't blame Sandra for finding work. Using what she had after one mistake, one wrong move." He felt his voice waver. "She was just trying to survive and some bastard didn't let her. Didn't think she'd had it hard enough already, hadn't lost enough dignity. For one mistake."

A few minutes passed before Lauren calmed enough to say, "Steph reminds you of Sandra."

"They all do," he gritted. "Every dancer, every bartender. I've offered everyone a path out. To take them away. They don't want to be beholden to another man, they've got pride and dignity. So yeah, I go to Pinks every night and I spend hundreds of thousands of dollars there and I fight whenever the opportunity arises to make sure nobody fucks with them."

"Why can't you call the police?"

"You know what would've happened to seventeen-year-old Sandra if someone called the cops? She'd be the one arrested. If they even cared to show up. A record. Prison time. She'd be back on the pole before she ate her next meal."

"I'm so sorry, Miles." She was wound around him like a warm blanket, hugging, holding, melting into the gaps on his rigid form. "Don't go. Don't leave tonight." Lips touched his shoulder, fingers danced over the cross. "Kayla keeps sheets in the hall closet. Let's take those and curl up."

He dragged hands down his face, feeling wrecked. When was the last time he explained Sandra? Wednesday confession?

"I'm not staying here," he said. "I have to go."

"No, you don't." She moved with him to the door. Tears streamed down her cheeks. Her voice wobbled. "Take your luck from me. All of it. I don't know anyone more deserving."

Then she was crashing into him, lips warm on his, slightly wet.

How many times did he have to kiss her when she was crying?

And how big of a monster was he for pulling her into him, for taking what she offered, slipping his tongue into her mouth, penetrating her safe haven, twisting their tongues together and sucking until they were panting. Until she whimpered and it went straight to his balls.

He yanked back, stepped away, kept her from closing the distance. "I'll get the sheets, then I'm tucking you in, and leaving."

"Wait, let me get you some Advil and ice."

"Dios, Lauren," he joked, voice straining, thin, fake. "Quit keeping me up late, I've got a game Sunday."

"Stay," she repeated.

"I'd never push my luck."

Chapter Sixteen

Lauren was in a state of pure shock as she blocked the front door from her sisters. Saturday night playing goalie. Glorious.

Backing up into the wood, hand steel tight on the knob, she shook her head. "You're kidding me. Should Hannah really be going out? She pulled an SOS last week."

Flashes of Miles; his face picking Hannah up, white-knuckling the steering wheel, vowing vengeance. Sandra. He saw Hannah as Sandra. All of them.

Maddie didn't look up from her phone. "So what?"

So what? Lauren gave a humorless laugh, feeling like she was shouting into a void. "So take a fucking break!"

The phone lowered, Maddie's perfectly trimmed eyebrows pulled together with a frown. "You think we don't want to take a break? Don't know how easy it would be to take a two-year break? We would love to. Just sit in our rooms in sweatpants until Prince Charming appears out of nowhere."

"Miles isn't—"

"He is," she snapped, getting nods from Kayla and Hannah behind her. "You got lucky and you're still blowing it. Don't be a bitch because we're brave enough to put ourselves out there."

"Being concerned is not bitchy."

"We know what you say about us," Hannah sputtered, the two braids at her temples swinging out like antennas. "You think we're idiots for dating."

Lauren's hand went lax on the door, she stepped around pink muck boots. "No I don't. I think—"

"You think because we want love, we're ruled by our hearts." Maddie threw her rainbow scarf over her shoulder. "Move, or Kayla will put a sleeper move on you."

Everyone except for Maddie rolled their eyes, jumping to correct her. "She learned tai chi."

"It's a peaceful practice."

"I'd never put a sleeper on her."

Maddie huffed her annoyance with another flagrant scarf throw. She stomped her Sorel wedges. "Move."

One last beseeching plea, Lauren said, "Hannah was nearly molested last week."

"Yeah and the bartender saw it and asked me out," Hannah interjected, smiling like she'd taken Cupid's arrow in three spots. "He said someone as beautiful as me needs protection."

"And you fell for that?"

Harnessing her eldest sister energy, Kayla wrenched the door from Lauren's grasp, letting blistering cold sweep into the entry.

"See," Kayla said in a haughty tone. "Bad things happen. But if you keep trying, so do good things."

"That's ridiculous," Lauren countered. "If you threw a knife in the air a hundred times, you wouldn't get stabbed every time, but you'd still bleed out."

Maddie pried smooth curls from her coat, half listening. "Have you told Miles you like him?"

Taken aback by the switch in topics, Lauren frowned. "We're not dating."

"I didn't say you were, but if any of us was hanging out with him, and saw the way he looked at you, how you looked at him. We'd tell him. Take the risk for such a big reward. We wouldn't live in limbo, wondering, torturing ourselves. Before Brian, you would've told him by now."

Before Brian, Lauren would be in love with Miles by now.

The thought hit like black ice, sent her careening.

Love.

It wasn't a feeling, it was an emotion. It held weight, came with strings and baggage and it could be beautiful, dressed up right, cared for, dusted and attended to but it could also rot, and it never disintegrated, it stayed with you, love gone bad, a fifty-pound sack tied to your heart.

A big risk.

Shrinking back into the coat hook, Lauren muttered, "It's more complicated than just telling him."

"It's simple," Maddie returned in a matter-of-fact tone. "Take the risk or be miserable. Keep living the same day over and over, a shell of yourself. You don't have dinner with us anymore, you drink through trivia."

"We thought Miles was helping," Hannah murmured. "But ..."

"But you're still suppressing," Maddie finished. "Mary told me Brian picks on you and you let him."

Lauren's gaze snapped up. "Where do you talk to Mary?"

She lifted long maroon coffin fingernails. "We go to the same nail salon. It's the only place that does decent acrylics."

Right. She should've guessed.

Cold air continued to seep inside, dying Kayla's cheeks red, reminding Lauren it was Saturday afternoon, her free day and she'd yet to shower, put on a bra. "If I tell Miles I like him, then it's over because he doesn't like me. The end. I never see him again. I did the all-or-nothing thing with Brian. I gave all and he gave me nothing."

The withdrawn faces said they'd all done it. Some more than once. Smoke over and over and over.

"You survived," Kayla said into the silence, pulling the door wider. "Come with us. We're not going drinking, we're going to the library to pick Maddie up a nerd. She's trying something new."

"He has glasses," Hannah squeaked as if she'd delivered juicy gossip.

"Nothing wrong with nerds," Maddie defended, tone sharpening. "I used to live with one." A knowing nod to Lauren.

She didn't correct her with *geek*. Not now. This one got a free pass. She had something bigger to say. "Miles doesn't like me. He thinks I'm his good luck charm. We have to kiss every Friday if he wants to win."

A pin drop would shatter eardrums in the silence.

Again, Kayla was the first to recover, saying, "The Mountaineers are undefeated."

Yeah, Lauren had figured.

***

IT WAS THE NIGHT before game day and Miles was—to no one's surprise—disobeying curfew. Unlike most weekends though, which involved boobs and booze, he found himself in the Rose family room.

No couch, no chairs, not even a flatscreen in the center of the lake house. But there was a massive wooden desk and a wall of file cabinets colored to mimic the rainbow.

"Me or Warren?" his manager, Victoria, had asked when she'd answered the door in a silky black robe that matched her hair. She didn't bother to hold it over her chest or tug it down her bare thighs. Not when Warren leaned over her shoulder, looming in nothing but matching black briefs.

Frankly, it was more covered than he was used to seeing either of them. Victoria's affinity for short, low-cut dresses, Warren's shower stall across from Miles's in the locker room.

"You," Miles had said. Warren had nodded once and disappeared into the house's state-of-the-art kitchen.

Now, Miles cleared his throat as he fidgeted by the window, peering out to see the crescent moon shimmering over the lake.

"When did you know you were fucked?" he asked.

Victoria made a sound of consideration, fingers bouncing on her forehead, probably missing her bangs. "Usually midway, when Warren's sucking—"

He sliced a miserable look her way.

That's all it took. She focused on him for the first time since he'd showed up on their porch. And the effect of those blue eyes searing his soul was discomforting.

"What happened?" she demanded, arms folding. "Should I be entering fix-it mode?"

"It's nothing field related."

"Good because Cole is on being actively, knowingly drugged by his wife on the daily and Burton's getting fines on fines for his flagrant disregard for hygiene. I don't need another falling Mountaineer."

Falling. Yes. That's what it felt like.

The air whooshing out of his lungs, his stomach left twenty stories up, a scream or a laugh, a cry clogged in his throat. Backward, falling backward, no idea when he'd hit, just blue skies and sun and smiles. In the back of his mind, a nagging reminder that it'd end soon. Splat.

"Frankly"—Victoria moved to sit by him on the bay window—"I'm not sure Warren could handle it if you fell apart. It's his last season and you're playing so well. He needs you." She tied the belt of her robe, cocked her head. "So do I. Because you're going to get a big fat bonus this year, which means I am getting a proportionately big fat bonus."

"Glad I can help."

"Glad I could pick out a star player. Although"—she threw up her chin, blazing blue eyes slitted to look at him. A dark pink nail poked his cheek, forcing his black eye into the light—"I thought we were done fighting. Who gave you the bruiser?"

"You don't want me to tell you."

"Was it someone at Pink Persuasion, Burlington's most exclusive—and only—gentlemen's club?" She had an all-knowing tone. "Where you spend approximately six nights a week? If you think I'll be disappointed, you're wrong."

He lifted his brows. The one rule Victoria had when she signed him was to stay out of trouble, to quit the clubs and brawling, stay on a clean path.

"Oh come on, Miles." A gentle chiding. "A professional football player in the strip club every single night? People talk."

"I thought you didn't want me there."

"I've kept tabs on you, but they've loosened. You haven't been arrested so who am I to judge what jiggles your jolly?" Striding across the room to her desk, she perched on top of it.

She looked a little too comfortable in that position, leaving Miles to wonder there was a reason there were no papers or pens on it. Probably the same reason Warren had looked like he had to go work off some energy.

Miles had to ask, "Is this your sex room?"

Her smile was feral pleasure. "Sex house." She rapped nails on the desk. "You didn't come here to ask about my sex life. I talk about that enough at the stadium."

"Heard Warren's retiring."

"That's why you're here at ten on a Saturday? You want to retire too before it goes out of style?"

No. He wanted … he wanted to watch Warren and Victoria together. He wanted to study and take notes like he was watching a film. Learn something. But he was falling, there wasn't time.

"When did you know, Victoria?"

She cocked her head, black hair slipping over her shoulder.

"We're the same. You and me. We've got certain … appetites."

A nod, she leaned back as Miles paced in front of red, orange, yellow, green cabinets all the way to pink, and looped back up rainbow road.

"When did Warren ruin it for you?"

"It being …"

He sliced her an impatient look. "If I have to spell it out, we're not as similar as I guessed."

"Fine." She uncrossed her legs, palms curving around the edge of the desk. "Immediately."

Dread scorched a black trail down his body.

"Yeah," he muttered, pausing at yellow, scrubbing at his jaw, his neck. "That's what I was worried about."

"Why are you here, number seven? With a black eye, looking like a kicked puppy, asking about my great love affair?"

Love.

He felt it slash at him.

"It's been a month," he replied, stalking to the window, cupping his hands against the glass. Yeah, a perfect view of the fucking lake. Might as well be a painting.

Life here with the Roses—because though they hadn't married they were undoubtedly the Roses—was picturesque.

"A month?" she asked.

"It's been a month since … You know?"

"I don't." Deadpanned.

"A month since I met her." He turned back, brought his hands together and threw them apart to spill. "It's too soon. It's too much."

"Don't expect me to agree. I was gone for Warren in a week. He says he was quicker but he just wants to beat me at something." Her legs swung, like she couldn't contain her happy. "When you meet the person, you know."

"But I don't believe in a person."

"That doesn't make sense." A shake, a furrowed brow. "Is she the one who hit you?"

"No. She's got tiny doll hands. It's … it's … love is so"—he held his hands out and shook them like he was getting the last Snickers from the piñata—"it's so fragile. I feel like … It's like I'm holding a sheet of the thinnest glass in the world, so delicate a raindrop would shatter it. And I'm a fucking running back, I'm a wrecking ball. What's the point in admitting it if it's going to break?"

"You don't have to admit it," Victoria told him with a shrug. "Don't. But it won't change shit. You'll still feel everything the same. Love doesn't have to be fragile."

He scoffed.

He knew how fragile love was. A mother's unconditional love was enough to move mountains until your sister made a single error.

Love was the most damn fragile thing to exist. Why else did people cry over love, forget themselves, get depressed? Lauren knew how tenuous love was, how painfully it ended. How abrupt.

He wouldn't get anywhere with Victoria. She hadn't felt the sharp sting of spoiled love. Yet. "I'll see myself out."

"Wait," a low drawl said. Warren leaned by the door, a slice of pizza in his hand, the gentle curve of his smile told Miles sound traveled in the Rose house.

Warren blew on a slice of pepperoni, as though this were a normal occurrence. Midnight naked snack with guest.

"Sometimes," he said when his lungs emptied. An inhale. "Sometimes it's better to make the risky play." The quarterback opened the door, ignoring Victoria's call to stop him.

Miles looked to his captain, his leader. Nodded.

Pulled his hood up as he stepped into the cold winter night.

Risking it. Risking it could lead to a game-winning touchdown. Or a torn ACL.

CHAPTER SEVENTEEN

MILES PEERED DOWN AT the short, musty staircase and then glanced back to Maddie. Her face was smug, brows raised, and for the first time since meeting the Peck sisters, he was struck by how different they each were.

Maddie had Lauren's hazy green eyes but the eyebrows were higher, her nose slightly upturned, lips thinner.

The greatest departure was their mannerisms. Through the faded beam of moonlight streaking into the hall, Miles had known who he was dealing with from silhouette alone. Cocked hips, lowered chin, slightly pigeon-toed.

Maddie dusted her nails against her matching nightclothes to confirm Miles's suspicion.

"It's about time," she said smartly.

Then she was gone, winding down the darkened hall of the Peck house as if she hadn't witnessed a break-in.

An unsuspecting ally in the dangerous game he was playing.

Inhaling deeply, Miles took the stairs two at a time.

Quietly, he opened Lauren's door and felt his heart seize. A small amorphous lump lay square center in the bed. With only the glow of her blue computer charger for light, he removed his boots, careful not to let the steel toes smack the floor, and crossed the room.

Ignoring the voice in his head that said people got shot for less, he peeled back the corner of her sheets and settled into the bed. If someone crept into his house, his literal bed, he'd be trialed for aggravated murder.

Lauren? She flopped onto her stomach, lips parted. Hadn't even woken.

The protective side of Miles wanted to throttle her, show her how ill-equipped she was for certain dangers.

Dangers like him.

Instead of teaching a lesson, his hands roamed forward, brushing the soft fabric of another T-shirt he couldn't wait to read.

"Pretty girl," he whispered, brushing hair behind her ear. "Pretty girl, wake up."

It wasn't too late, eleven or twelve. He was usually up until three but Lauren was lost to her dreams.

"Lauren." He prodded her hip.

"Mmm," she moaned softly. "Miles." A rustle of the blankets. "I was having a dream about you."

Give me every detail, he thought as he played with a knotted lock of her hair. "Are you sure it wasn't a nightmare?"

He leaned closer to hear her hum a yes. "Mm-hmm, you snuck into my bed because you missed me."

"That's not a dream, pretty girl. That's happening now."

"No," she croaked, kicking her legs from the sheets. An exhausted groan. "No, you're here because it's Friday." She yawned, her entire body shuddering emphatically. "It's Friday, which means you're here to load up on luck so you can make my sisters fawn over you on the field."

He sent a smile to the pillowcase. "Open your eyes."

"It's dark, what's the point?"

"Only that it's Saturday and I've spent all day trying to stay away from your bed and now I need consoling for failing my only goal." His fingers glided up her waist, higher, lifting with her rib cage, the side of her breast. "I'm full on luck, I'm here for Lauren."

Slowly, her lashes unfused, fluttered apart to tickle her brow bone.

Fuck, she had long, beautiful lashes. Willowy down to each individual lash, long narrow limbs, perfectly proportional, no curve extraneous. The sleek lines of a sports car, finely honed, each subtle dip packing a punch for speed and efficiency.

She fell to her back, sighing. Instinctively, his thumb poked the hollow in her cheek. "What's on your mind?"

Please let it be the same thing that's on his.

Another twist and she was facing him, cheek nestled in her pillow, eyes a sliver of sweet, faded green. "I should get a security system because I'm getting used to waking up with someone in my bed and next weekend you have an away game."

Better than the lascivious thoughts prowling his head.

She was thinking of the future, next week with him. Bending forward, he pressed their foreheads together, noses scraping. Lemons and lilac and peppermint. Subtle scents Lauren corralled into a stampede.

"I'll make sure no one else gets in your bed."

Spend his final breaths ensuring it.

"You can't promise that."

A dark chuckle parted his lips, his grip firmed on her waist. "Oh I can, Lauren." He wedged closer, sliding across 800-thread count to nudge his jean-clad thigh between hers.

"Don't forget"—he curled more hair around the rim of her ear—"I'm a very powerful man." No bragging, just threat in his voice. "I make half a million dollars every time my cleats hit turf, so if you wanted me to, if you let me, I'd post trained guards at every window and door to guarantee I'm the only one crawling into this bed with you."

A short intake of breath was her response.

The shock should have stopped him, but he rampaged onward. "Hell, if you don't stop me from doing it, I might hire them anyway." From day one, he should've made calls. Ex-military. Pros. Armed. A few discreet extras to trail the sisters.

Fuck, he was considering this.

Sloppy hands scrunched his cheeks, brushed his jaw. She made a grumpy sound. "I have baby hands."

He took her fingers and pulled them to his mouth, kissing each cold pad before soothing the abused nailbeds with his tongue. He felt a smile brush his mouth. "What are baby hands?"

She made a squeeze motion. "When you wake up and aren't strong enough to make a fist or be useful."

"Don't wake up then." A lick down her thumb, her thighs clenched his. "Go back to sleep. Keep your hands very baby."

"Why are you in my bed, Miles?" Her finger trailing down his forehead, as gentle as a feather. "Are you hurting still? In pain? How's your eye? Your lip?"

"Healed."

"I'm not blind. Unless you got a face tattoo, your eye is darker than yesterday."

"I feel like a million bucks, pretty girl."

Softer this time, she asked, "Then why are you here?"

"I never finished your massage yesterday. Let me get you back to sleep. It won't take long, you won't notice me."

"Hmm," she murmured, relaxed again. "I always notice when you touch me."

Fucking good. A rush of male satisfaction bled into him.

Of its own accord, his hands veered to her legs to clutch the muscle. Firm, then gentle. A mirror of her soul.

Fragile.

She was so utterly fragile.

A feather-light moan hit his ear, and she pushed higher up on the bed, shoulder coming level with his eyes as he floated focused hands along the soft back of her knees, across her thighs.

"You—" She sounded breathless, ragged; nails scraped his skull. "You have a game tomorrow."

She hadn't worn shorts tonight either. "Yes."

"Shouldn't you sleep?"

"There's nothing else I'd rather be doing right now."

"Hmm," she concurred throatily. "Nothing like putting your baby-handed lucky charm to sleep."

"Nothing comes close to the way my blood hums when I'm touching you, Lauren. Smelling flowers in your hair, feeling your skin under mine, being near you when you have a sleep-thick voice, and I pretend we just woke up together. I didn't know the effect you had. But pretty girl, you're DEFCON one, you're acid rain, sandstorms and rockslides You'll kill anyone who gets too close."

Surprised, she pushed to her elbows, and Miles sent her back down.

"Relax," he instructed, begged. "Let me touch you, I need this."

"Miles—"

"Please," he countered, more pleas on his tongue.

"If you start this"—her hands tangled in his hair, pulled at the roots until their eyes locked in the shadows—"you'll finish it. Completely."

"I'm talking about a massage, helping you get back to those dreams."

"I'm not tired." She rolled, thighs still clenched around his and drew him forward, down, over her.

Hovering on braced hands, he felt the tickled caress of eyelashes on his cheekbone. Her voice was a drug he hadn't yet tasted and craved.

"I want you to finish what you came here for," she whispered. "Not why you told yourself you're here. I want you to show me the truth, all of it."

***

IT WAS EASY FOR Lauren to be brave in the dark while she has half delirious from strong warm hands working every bend in her body. Demands and honesty, revealing questions, she didn't fear the consequences in the shadows. There wasn't enough room in her brain to consider the moment after this.

Waking up with Miles's velvet voice murmuring, "Pretty girl."

She'd never had a nickname like that.

Would've proposed to Brian on the spot if he'd called her it just once.

Pretty girl sounded like fresh honey dripping onto her skin, like a beautiful and protective shield covering her imperfections. That's how Miles made her feel.

He was watching her. Or maybe she held him like that, facing one another, gazes locked. The break in his voice had sliced the sleep out of her. A tranquilizer to her carotid wouldn't put her down.

Hovering over her, curled hair dangling in the space between them, he was exquisite. Freeze him, dip him in plaster, and she'd have the feature piece of any museum. Beautiful, breathtaking, bold.

Except for his eyes. They were fierce. Smoldering like a bull trapped in a ten-piece metal harness straining to hold him. The tremor in his throat, slit eyes, chest rising, skipping, falling with half breaths and sighs.

He squeezed her ass, then his fingers fell inward, moved to where she was already too wet. Too wet, too damning, too telling.

But in the dark, it didn't matter. Her knees gave way with a slight part.

A groan filled the air.

His, then hers. As his finger slipped under the seam of her panties and stroked at her very core.

A rush of air through slotted teeth. "Somebody this wet usually wants to get fucked, pretty girl. Tell me if I'm wrong."

Her legs quivered. Jesus. She'd known Miles got around. The way he walked, held himself, those fucking tattoos, his little smirk. The way he said *fucked*, like the word itself was carnal. Lust and sin with a drugging effect. Lauren wanted all of it. Wanted to lie down and let him rage and break over her, a hundred-year storm to shake the mountains.

She wanted to slide down her icy front walk and let his words pelt her like snow and hail, leave stinging bruises. Experience every part of him. The gentle, the rough, the gritty.

She craved him exactly as he was. Pure, undiluted Miles.

"Take off your pants," she gasped as his lips touched her shoulder.

Yes. So easy to be brave in the dark.

"Fuck." His hands gripped harder, fingers parting the lips of her sex, spreading wetness. He kissed her or she kissed him. However it started, they both lost grip. He rose up, claiming her wrists and pinning them against the headboard, making her grip the slatted wood.

"Hold on, baby hands," he teased as his knee came between her legs, rubbed and added delicious pressure for her to writhe against.

Again, their lips met, chased, followed. Long and deep, consuming.

Faster, she thought, *now*. Bust the zipper, give her something to clench around and she'd come. That quick. Shatter in the echo of minutes of foreplay when she was strictly a thirty-minutes-and-a-good-book kind of girl.

"Already panting for me," he murmured, thigh giving friction to her core, jean and cotton. "Should we get your inhaler, pretty girl? Is it my turn to play nurse?"

She dug her heels into the mattress, grinding air, hips lifting. "Play Miles."

"How long have you thought about this?" Wet, open-mouthed kisses trailed up the line of her jaw, her neck where he sucked hard and fast. Floated away and started again, bruising her skin. Hickeys, marks.

Places she couldn't hide.

Didn't care. She wanted his marks, skin to match his. Black and white. Little signs of proof that the dark wasn't a corner of mind. It was real. She could be brave and Miles Santos could kiss her neck, rock against her like an obsessed man.

"How many times, Lauren?"

"So insistent." Her chuckle sliced to a growl when he drew back, stole pressure from her core. "Never," she answered quickly, moaning when he came back to her, covered her, sucked on the hollow of her throat.

He sounded offended when he repeated, "Never?"

"Not once." He and her in bed, it wasn't a possibility. Anything past a kiss had blurred outside the realm of her imagination. Miles Santos didn't want her.

"I'm not doing my job right if you're not already imagining me deep inside you."

His next kiss was a shot-for-shot preview of what she'd failed to imagine. Teasing lips, nip of his teeth and then drowning depth as his tongue penetrated her mouth to curl with hers and suck.

He tasted like fresh spring water and fake spearmint. Like he'd fished a mint from a bowl at the bar and ground the chalky candy into the crevices of his molars. Washed it down with an ice cube.

Cheap and gritty and she drank it like Grey Goose, let it ease down her throat, numb her extremities. Gasping into him, wishing she could get lacquered in the taste, she arched, pushing at his hair. Soft, perfect hair, she never tired of toying with.

"Pull my hair," he said, barely got it out before his lips attached to her neck, sucking on a spot that bubbled her blood, right at her throat, pulse vulnerable to the ministration of the flick of his hot tongue.

"I fucking imagined it," he told her sternum, dragging the collar of her shirt down. "From that first fucking kiss, I imagined it. Ripping those hideous buttons off your shirt, tearing your belt off to spin you around. Spank you as I bent you over the Demon."

More yanking on her shirt, stretching, fabric biting her skin. "Your bra drove me insane."

"You've never seen my bra."

"You're cold all the time and it makes me so hard seeing these peaked." His hands came together to crush her breasts.

There was no need for padding, hardly need for her cheap Target bras, and Miles revered them, fantasized about them.

If possible, she grew wetter, squirmed. Was this even sex? Sex with somebody who knew how to do it? It was horrible.

Tortuous.

No more foreplay, no more confessions. She ached mind, body and soul, desperate to be filled. No more clenching around nothing, trembling with frustration.

"Hurry," she rasped, still playing with his curls.

"Do you think I'm not?" he countered, pulling her shirt up, shaking his head at the image.

Lauren couldn't remember if it was a Thanksgiving 5K freebie or one from Kayla's ex who was too into Michael Bolton.

Sliding down the bed, he rolled the fabric up her thighs to sit above her hips bones. She arched to get rid of it.

He bit her. Right on the exposed bone, sending pain down her legs and flooding her panties. Hands on her calves, shirt pooled on her stomach, he massaged again.

Another groan. What was he doing to her? Making her feel languid and wound. It wasn't fair. She thrashed under him, unashamed in the dark, just pleased as Miles's hand returned to her core, pressed.

His groan rattled her heart.

"I want to—oh *fuck*," he hissed, knocking her panties aside to stroke her. "I wanted to spend hours on this. Just kissing you. Only kissing you, tell you—" He cut himself off. "Why'd you have to be so goddamn wet? Why'd you have to want me back?"

"How could I not?" Words freed in the shadows.

He groaned something into the swell of her stomach and bit there too before sucking. A mark for each place he visited.

She pulled his hair. "Miles."

He didn't stop, sucking, licking, biting, waging sensual warfare, his fingers finding the knowledge to end her or strike peace. He caressed around her aching clit, avoiding, tempting.

"How do you smell like lilacs, Lauren?" He sounded mad as his fingers worked circles over her. "How do you always smell like lilacs when I've used your shampoo and it's gardenia. Will it be lilacs in heaven?" he asked, tapping at her core. "Should I find out?"

She yanked his hair when he ducked between her legs, massive hands spreading her ankles. She pushed against him, wanting bruises there too, hoped he held her tighter. Everywhere. Enough black to rival Miles.

A sweep of his thumb pushed her panties aside and then his mouth latched to her clit, flat tongue wetting, stroking. He sucked.

Lauren's body bowed and she cried out. Oh God, he'd leave a mark there, right *there*. Writhing on the mattress, ankles pinned, she gasped, "Miles, yes!"

Determined, eager, treating her like she was leaking ambrosia, he kept sucking, kept tickling with the tip of his tongue, expanding her definition of pleasure.

Her hands yanked on his hair as she ground into his face, marveling at the slight rock of his hips, like he was meeting her, thrusting into her with everything.

"This," he said, kissing high on her public bone. "This in particular, I thought about. Imagined how you'd taste a dozen ways. Sweet like shortbread, lemon sour, maybe the sting of vodka. How fucking wrong was I? Salted lilacs." He chuckled, thumb flicking up her calf. "Is that an ice cream flavor?"

"Ben and Jer—," she cried out as he sucked again, hard. Pulled back before she reached a peak. Hands shoved her knees together and then Miles was ripping her panties down, off, pulling her wide, blowing cold air onto her hottest part.

The lights went on.

A shriek. Lauren clamped her legs together. "Lights off!" she demanded, unraveling her shirt to regain modesty.

"Open your legs," Miles returned, tone gentler but no less of a command. He kneeled at the foot of her bed, hair wild from her hands, lips glistening wet, eyes glazed as he unbuttoned his jeans.

Every tooth of his zipper echoed, the sound was erotic, made Lauren want to follow his command, but—"Turn off the lights."

"You can't possibly think I have a good enough imagination to picture true beauty. Spread those legs and let me see."

She rose to her elbows, hair tumbling into her face. His jeans fell to his thighs, catching on thick, bunched muscle, and holy—his cock had slipped out at the fly, his fist clamped tight on the tip. He dragged down, revealing more and more.

And more.

Her throat went dry.

"See how badly I want you?" He stroked back up, wiping at his mouth, taking her wetness and using it as lubrication. "Spread your legs, pretty girl, and I'll share."

"Jesus, Miles, I'm not ..."

"Not what? Finish it."

"Not like you. I don't do this much. Sleep with people I'm not—" In love with. "Intimacy is sacred to me."

"I won't do anything short of religious." He kicked his jeans down the rest of the way, the boxers too, lost his shirt. "If you disagree, I'll put an X right here." He slashed at his cross tattoo. "I'll denounce it, retract every vow, but first allow me to get on my knees and show you proof of faith."

"Jesus, Miles."

"I'll denounce him, too." He smirked. "Just to keep his name off those lips. Say mine again."

Another stroke, her lungs emptied. "Miles."

"I haven't touched anyone since we met, since you spilled into me and jerked back like I was the devil risen. Spread and show me the holy land."

She wet her lips, croaked, "Doesn't Santos mean saint?"

"I'll change it to sinner." He stepped forward and spread her knees with those wrecked knuckles, hissing at what he saw, chewing on his busted lip. "Fuck."

Were they looking at the same thing? The light brown hair neatly maintained, wet, so wet the bed beneath her was too.

"I have so much to confess," he murmured, thumb spreading her folds as his fist slid down his tempting rigid length. "So many dirty thoughts. I am a sinner, Lauren."

Lauren. Not pretty girl. Lauren in the lights.

"Touch your nipples," he instructed. "My hands are full, and they're begging."

Barely cognizant of her hands, she felt pressure on her stiffened peaks. Moaned as she cupped and pinched, pretended they were his hands.

In the brilliant glow of her room, he watched her knead while he thrummed her, stroking himself, calling back the desperation until she gasped, back shuddering, frantic for more.

He looked like a saint, ruined like a deity.

"The minute I enter you ..." He thrust inside her with his finger. Sucked his teeth, a shake of his head. "*Dios*, the second I fuck you, I'll hear the angels, see the gates."

She wanted to laugh but he twisted inside her, added a second finger. She panted instead.

"I've heard people go blind from such brightness. Is that what you'll do to me?"

She thrashed on the bed as he plunged deep, gasping, "I'd never—*fuck*—never hurt you."

His jaw went tight, the lines of his beautiful tattoos stretching and collapsing into new patterns, ones just for Lauren to see.

He thrust again, adjusting his grip, head rolling back as he stroked himself, clearing a drop from his tip. From his lips came the Hail Mary.

"*Dios te salte, Maria llena eres de gracia, el Senor es contigo. Bendito tu—*"

She came. Right there, on his hand, around his fingers, silent scream in her throat. Not making it past the second verse, back bowing, fingers tweaking her nipples.

"Miles," she'd gasped and moaned, rolled in her mouth. His name its own prayer.

As she languished in the receding wave, Miles retrieved a condom from his jeans, tore it open and slowly, eyes scouring her body, rolled it on. "Will you take me to church?"

If she said no, if she had a moment's hesitation, she knew he'd stop. So her answer was fastidious and direct. "Fuck me now."

Being brave in the light wasn't so difficult.

A smirk. "God is a woman." His hands wound around her ankles and tugged her down the bed he'd bought her, hauling her back from the headboard he'd picked out.

Limbs loose, excitement built in her chest. Along with strands of panic. Could she be too wet? No. Certainly not as the end of his cock rubbed against her. She'd underestimated his size, the width. A cry escaped her throat as he pushed, stretching her, shattering her concerns, her self-consciousness. She drew her knees to her chest high while he dragged her to the edge, pulling her onto him as he stood, rigid, abs like pulsing stones.

Sacrifice, sacrilege, sacrament. Here. Now. Immediate pain for long-term betterment. She cried out his name when he made it to the hilt.

Hands rough, sloppy at her thighs. Praying again. Spanish. She didn't recognize it. Longer, spoken from memory, quick, fast. Started again.

He bent over her, arms curling around her, mouth sucking the side of her breast, pushing even deeper, unlocking a new angle in her hips.

"*Como era en el principio, ahora y siempre. Como—*"

"Oh God," Lauren gasped at the first gentle rock of his hips into hers, at the shot of heat bolting up her spine. "I'm going to hell," she said into his neck, clawed at his back as if his tattoos were handles.

He crushed her tighter into him, hands on the inside of her knees, flattening them to the sheets as he took her mouth in a vicious kiss.

"Let's go together," he croaked. "It'll be worth it."

That was the only warning before he pulled out and pistoned back inside her. Naturally, Miles did nothing slowly. He was muscle and mayhem as he plunged into her, over and over, driving her to the cliff, escorting her to edge, telling her to peek over the side, his hand in hers.

Wind on her face, a fall to the death. And she'd leap the moment he said she could.

His voice in her ear, whispering how much he loved her tits, how good she felt, how she made him feel.

Real. This was real.

Lauren detonated, skin pulling taut, dying pink as she clenched and pulsed. Bared under naked light, headboard smashing the wall. Miles pounding into her, groaning, telling her to let go, telling her she was his. Repeating it. *His*.

She felt herself squeeze and tighten and pulse.

With a roar, Miles exploded over her, teeth scraping her collarbone, sinking.

When the shuddering eased, Miles moved tenderly, caressing her thighs, adjusting them to be on their sides, curling her leg around his hip.

Like that, they lay. Him pulsing inside her, legs looped around his back, hand stroking his hair.

The devoted words of the Hail Mary dusted her neck in between Miles's lazy kisses.

She loved him.

Real.

***

LAUREN SLEPT LATE AND woke up to bad news.

She was alone.

Completely alone.

After ... God, she'd been more than one person last night. Falling asleep with the lights gleaming and Miles still inside her, big body cradling her, velvet voice coaxing her to dream.

At some point, hours, minutes, he'd woken her with a deep, sensual thrust, her thigh locked around his waist, his mouth on her ear, tongue tantalizing sensitive, untouched skin as he begged her to let him atone.

Never in her life had she felt as complete, as needed.

They'd been bodies in the dark the third time. Hurried, desperate, him behind her, thighs glued together as she bucked into him, his hand covering her mouth, earning a hickey on his palm.

Hickey.

Lauren shot out of bed, and waddled to her bathroom on the balls of her feet. Sore, deliciously sore. She flipped on the lights and shut them off. Sank to the cold tile floor, accidentally knocking a towel off the rack and sending it over her shoulders.

Tenderly, she pressed fingertips to her mouth.

She looked like she'd stumbled free from a car wreck, the jaws of life had ripped open her shirt, glass had stung her eyes red, and the seat belt had wrapped around her like a snake and constricted, leaving trails of purple bruises holding her body.

A smile spread dry, swollen lips. Her feet kicked against the ground. Giddy.

Deep conditioning, extra jojoba oil in the hair and it'd still have knots for the week, but ...

She looked well and truly fucked.

And she liked it.

Liked how Miles's desire spread across her skin, hugged to her ribs, peppered her thighs.

He'd been thorough in his claim of her. She coasted light touches over the black circle beside her navel. Dark. Would it outlast the others? How long? Would Miles get to admire his handiwork on Tuesday? She couldn't wait to show him.

Did she finally understand the purpose of crop tops? She could slice and dice a T-shirt for him, wear it to trivia with her jeans—

Wait. Trivia wasn't part of their deal.

Not the routine. But he'd come for three weeks.

Pushing to her feet, Lauren ditched the towel on the vanity and put on her Sunday best. Blue cargo pants and a black crewneck with holes cut out for her thumbs. Balled-up socks in her hand, she charged upstairs and stopped, surprised to see Maddie and Kayla in the vestibule, layering hats and mittens over bright green sweaters.

"Look who emerged from her cave," Kayla mocked, struggling to shove her wool-socked foot into her boots. "I thought Sundays were your hermit days."

"Oh please." Maddie rolled her eyes. A thin green scarf hung loose on her shoulders, white earmuffs resting over a green beanie. "She came to show off. She had a late-night visitor."

Kayla whipped around, her boot smacked the wall. "What?"

Slamming a hand over her neck, Lauren glared at Maddie. So much for sisterly love. "Want me to bring up your overnight guests?"

The eldest Peck sister's eyes hadn't finished scanning Lauren tip to tail. "He made a mess of you," she mused, walking one-booted to the stairs and patting Lauren's puff of tangled hair. "You'll have to shave it."

Lauren knocked the probing hand away.

"Can you please tell him to come at a respectable time in the future?" Maddie asked, situating her curls to fall messily under the muffs. "The idea of him sneaking around in the dark freaks me out."

"He's six foot and like two hundred pounds. He doesn't sneak anywhere," Kayla rebutted, hopping on one foot.

"I think that's what Lauren likes about him," Hannah noted as she strode into the hall, gathered in a robe, wearing her own post-Saturday-night glow. "Brian treated her like she was invisible, and when you're with Miles, it's impossible not to stare at who he's drooling over."

"He's more than a body," Lauren said, casually scratching her neck to hide the mottled skin.

"*He's more than a body*," Maddie mocked in alto, sparking a round of bullshit.

"I don't even notice his huge beefy muscles."

"I put a bag over his perfectly symmetrical cheekbones when he talks."

"What tattoos? I only see his heart."

Lauren dropped the act, planting hands on her hips. "None of you are funny."

"Isn't the game about to start?" Hannah asked, pitying Lauren's strife. "You guys are never going to make it."

Maddie shrugged, patting gloss on her lip. "It already started, but it lasts forever, we haven't missed anything."

"You're not going?" Lauren asked Hannah.

"I'm tired," she replied with a knowing smile. "But you can have my ticket."

A ticket. To Miles's game.

He'd already busted their routine.

And she wanted to see him. Missed him, wanted to see him smile and run and excel, do what he loved doing.

She put on her socks. "Let's hurry."

Chapter Eighteen

As Lauren waited for customer service to come back on the line, she wondered how many hours she'd spent listening to the same mildly depressing muzak.

And why she was tapping her feet like she was front row at *Hamilton*.

The noise cut off sharply, but instead of a voice, it was a dial tone.

Lauren cursed under her breath, struggling upright, grabbing the phone to redial, and found Brian's grubby finger on the end call button.

"I'm out of conduit," he told her.

Clenching her jaw, she pushed his hand off. "I've been waiting for thirty-one minutes, what the hell?"

"This isn't office balloons and tampon buying, L. I won't be able to do my job tomorrow if I don't get a hundred yards of rigid metal conduit."

"I put in an order but it will be weeks before delivery."

"Go buy some in the meantime."

"No, Brian. You should've come to me sooner, and Mary before me. This was your oversight. It's your—"

"It is not"—his voice raised to smother hers—"my job to count—"

"Brent," Miles's smooth voice cut through the office chatter. Lauren's stomach fell through the floor. "I told you to leave my girl alone."

Heart hammering, palms sweaty, Lauren couldn't believe her eyes as the man who dominated the field, brought a stadium to its feet with two touchdowns, stalked lazily, indolently into her cubicle. Jeans, a white thermal, tattoos leaking out. When she blinked, she saw him doing the sign of the cross on his knee in the end zone.

The fans called him *The Blessed*. New this season.

Another blink and he was Miles, her bad date, licking his lips, counting the buttons on her shirt.

How was this the same man who called her on Sunday night as he lay in an ice bath to ask her about dinner? The man who left her on speaker and listened to her crunch through a bowl of Fruity Pebbles, sore, overtight muscles seizing in the ice, water sloshing as they discussed their worst and best fortune cookie fortunes. He'd never gotten seven as a lucky number.

Didn't order Chinese anymore.

Lauren admitted to faking an MSG allergy because Brian considered carry-out date night food. From there, the topics grew odder. Skateboarding was way harder than either of them thought. Coffee was a terrible and effective stimulant, but no more effective than a slap in the face. Nickelback only had bangers.

She'd eaten four bowls of rainbow shapes just to keep talking to him, dreading the goodbye.

And on Monday, while she was recovering from a stomachache, he'd called again. Ran on the treadmill while she replied to comments on her latest Frodo-Sam post.

"What are you doing here?" she asked, jolting to stand, eliminate the space between them. "I thought we were meeting at The Hand."

"It's snowing. Think of your cold baby hands." Completely ignoring Brian, Miles licked the pad of his thumb, smirking as he stroked it down her throat.

She tipped her head, confused, feeling the wet line like ice pressing into her.

He smirked and murmured, "There it is," then his arm was looped at her waist, and his mouth was sucking at the previously concealed hickey.

Glancing back at Brian, blushing, she squirmed.

Miles tugged her tighter, sucked harder, laughed into her skin. Her toes curled, heat whipped over her. God he was hot.

"Does anyone get to come in the building now?" Brian groused.

Lauren turned, still wrapped up in powerful arms. Miles paused his worship, shoulders falling back, rising to his full height, hand smoothing hair down her back. She narrowed her eyes. "Yes. This is a public building. Literally anyone can come in."

He sputtered, "Only if they have a pass. Where's his badge?"

Hand massaging the roots of her hair, Miles's attention on Lauren's mouth as he said, "Sweet Mary said I didn't need one." He used a single finger to turn Lauren's face back to his. "Don't engage with him. When you argue with an idiot, there's no resolution."

A snort. "Says the guy who short-circuited her entire house. How am I the idiot?"

"One," Miles gritted, deep green cutting Brian where he stood, "you're picking a fight with a man twice your size. Two, you can't take a hint when two people are ignoring you, and three, I'm sure my pretty girl complained about this since your truck has aftermarket wheels and a decorative fender, but you've got a tiny cocker. Considering men think with their dick, your IQ must be in the single digits."

"I don't have a beef with you. I was talking to L. About work."

"I'm not finished," Miles snapped. "Only a complete dumbass would let Lauren go. And then dare to talk poorly to her in front of me."

"You're into this?" Brian asked Lauren, eyes bulging with rage. "You see how he's talking to me?" The disbelief was so thick, she almost cringed.

She'd had a similar thought. "I do. You should leave, he's got a killer right hook."

A cool laugh, Miles's hand curling hair behind her ear. Though his focus on her again, his voice didn't lower. "I don't know how anyone could taste you and keep themselves away."

Oh God, another whisper, another caress and they'd be re-playing every position on the low-pile carpet. Next to the stain. Tangling their hands together, interlacing their fingers, she told him, "I have to lock up and then we'll go and get the first round."

"Let me help," he murmured, tracking the knot in her throat as she swallowed.

She nodded, feeling a little dizzy, feeling lost. "Brian was just leaving," she muttered over her shoulder. "Bye."

"Congrats," her ex spat. "You found somebody as fucking insane as you. I give it a week."

His pounding footsteps had barely quieted when Miles took her mouth, tasting her, tongue slipping between her lips. He cornered her into her desk, locking her hands at her sides, pressing tight—pulled back abruptly. Raised a dark eyebrow. "Killer right hook?"

"Practice up if you don't, I'm not a liar."

"No, pretty girl. You aren't that."

***

MILES FOLLOWED LAUREN THROUGH the network of drab, square, white-walled offices as she shut off lights, computers and coffee pots. How anyone could maintain their humor, their life in miserable windowless halls of flaking paint, brown carpet, and drop ceilings, Miles couldn't fathom.

It was a place dreams found their end, goals and ambition were the main source of sustenance and he should be itching to escape before the posted signs about trash rules choked him out.

But he didn't. He continued trailing the blonde woman in black slacks, a neatly fastened cream button-up, and a brutally dark hickey on her neck.

A new unfamiliar feeling sprung in him. Longing.
Missing.

He'd missed her on Sunday. On Monday, he'd stayed away because her absence leveled him so completely, he'd feared he was sick. Two PTs had confirmed his heart rate was normal, his vitals were great. One accused him of being gone for the poor girl.

What did she know? She was in sports medicine, not neurosurgery.

It was just—he'd never fallen asleep inside someone before. Didn't know it was possible. Yet. He already knew how he wanted to sleep tonight.

Following blindly through the maze, a plaque caught his eye and he jerked back to read on the door: City Electrician.

"Is this Brian's office?"

Lauren lifted her brows, unplugged a chunky overloaded power strip. "Can't you smell the Axe Body Spray?"

"I smell oil because dude's a snake." Miles closed the door behind him, the click raising a brow from Lauren. Much like the man, the room was lacking any good qualities. Low ceiling, fluorescent light poles, the desk was too small to properly hold two people and there was a messy stack of papers on top of the only file cabinet.

He didn't want to, fought the image flashing, but he pictured Lauren and Brian bent over leftover spaghetti, discussing weekend plans. Lauren leaving her sweet cubicle, with the tropical forest calendar, colorful sticky notes, the orange cup of highlighters, to lock herself in a cell with a monster.

Brian should be kissing the ground Lauren walked on, professing endless apologies, but he had the insane ego to insult her, intimidate and oppress Miles's good luck charm. Red-hot anger swirled to a tempest in Miles's stomach.

Forcing the thoughts away with a lock of his teeth, he watched Lauren bend to unplug a light-up bobblehead.

Done eliminating fire hazards, she shut off the light switch. Miles stopped her, fingers catching her wrist, spinning her into him, brushing back thick hair to gaze at her throat. "You covered up my marks. Are you embarrassed by me?"

Her cheeks colored deliciously. "No, I like them," she assured quickly, mindful of the way he was walking her backward, heels dragging on the carpet. The whole of her body shivered as he delivered another lick down her neck. "I like when you make me yours. I love it, but it's not exactly work-appropriate."

"I think it's very work-appropriate, especially when you're working with fucking Brian."

Miles was still watching the circle of purple and blue as she spoke. "It wouldn't have the desired effect, he'd accuse me of doing it myself with a vacuum and creativity," she said. "He doesn't believe you could ever want me. He's made that abundantly clear, asking over and over why you spend time with me, implying ... "

His gut clenched.

"I haven't told him," she assured in a hurry. "At first, I didn't want to jinx it and now, he doesn't get an explanation to my life."

Jinx him. Because Brian was a fuckwad but his confusion had been warranted. She thought luck was the only reason they spent time together. Not anymore. He'd traipsed through City Hall on a Tuesday afternoon, not ten minutes after practice because he couldn't wait the hour to see her.

"I don't know how he could possibly think that. You're the most desirable person I've ever met."

She shot him a disbelieving glance. Then her thighs hit the desk's edge.

His hands pressed against her hip bones, pulled her into him to give friction to hard-as-granite dick. Aching since he'd uncovered his mark on her, tasted the lilac on her skin, smelled lemon on her hands.

It was no secret, he liked sex. Didn't make him an anomaly. What man didn't? It was as satisfying as a good long run or as great as a touchdown. Sex with Lauren was neither. More than an adrenaline rush. More natural than a run, less serious than a touchdown.

Her eyes widened as she dug her fingers reflexively into his stomach. "How are you hard right now?

"You clearly dressed with me in mind. Black, thick pants"—he swatted her ass—"twelve buttons, each tighter than the last." He ducked his head to whisper in her ear. "It's fucking intoxicating, you're not playing fair."

"I recall you not liking this look on our first date."

"I like the way you look mine." He tipped her head to the side to kiss down her throat, biting and sucking the skin. No tattoo for her, he wanted hickeys. An excuse to bite her, taste her, strip her and stare.

Head angling back against the shoulder, she moaned, fingernail scraping over the V of his T-shirt, grazing the tattoos. "What a match we make," he whispered against her lips. "My pretty girl sporting battle black."

"Black and white."

"I'm brown, but I'll fly you to the beach so we stay a matching set. Suck these perfect tits until you've got as much black as me."

Her laugh wrapped him in a warm blanket. "Since day one, you've wanted me at the beach."

His hand came to hold her throat, tongue at her ear, soothing a bite to the lobe. "Me and you, naked, skin tight from sun and salt water, bodies molded in the sand."

"Sticky."

"Yes. My hands on your sweet pussy as I fuck you good and deep, slow, waves crashing." He nipped the curve of her neck and shoulder.

She elbowed him. "You're being a tease."

He broke back from her. "I'm not." Stalked around Brian's fucking desk and fell into his chair, heard a creak. Slapped his thighs.

Lauren stared down at him quizzically, pushing back a straggle of dirty blonde hair from her right eye. The very edge of straight white teeth sank into her lower lip.

"Tell me, Lauren." He undid his belt, zipper, then the button of his jeans. "Are you wet right now? Sticky for me? From one little kiss, a dirty word?"

"This is my job," she said tersely, looking behind her, around, as he unzipped himself and split his jeans wide. Oops, he'd forgotten boxers.

Her swallow was audible as he freed his hard cock and gave it one familiar stroke. "Answer the question."

"I work here," she reiterated, body very still.

"No," Miles crooned, voice low, mouthwatering. "Brian works here. You are about to fuck me."

Her breath caught in astonishment. "I'm—"

"On his desk," he breathed, fighting to stay in his chair, not splay to his knees in front of her. She had the lead here. Right now. This was about her. "And we'll see then, if he understands that we're together."

On the other side of the door, wheels sounded, a door slammed shut.

"It doesn't lock," she whispered.

"Don't worry," he soothed, dampening his dry lips with his tongue. "If he interrupts, I'll keep going until you finish."

Her face was completely red, but he was distracted by the sight of her mouth, plush silky lips that promised to bring him salvation. The effort to keep from reaching for her caused his hands to shake. Fuck, he was hard as steel, ready to shoot.

So uniquely hard for her. His pretty girl who wanted him with the lights off, but made demands like a dominatrix.

Nervously, she tucked curls behind her ears, another glance at the door, and then she was fumbling with her pants.

"Stop," Miles coaxed her to him with a finger. "Allow me."

Like a newborn fawn, she teetered to him, with shaking legs and big, dilated eyes.

Unable to fight himself, he grabbed her by the belt loop and yanked her across the last two feet. Stripping her from the waist down, and clamped his mouth over her hip, the dip beside it. He lifted and then she was bare-assed on Brian's desk, blush spreading to all over.

His voice turned predatory. "He ever touch you at work?"

"No," she huffed, as if no one in their right minds had ever considered an afternoon delight. "Of course not."

"Insane." He ran his hands down her thighs soothingly. "I couldn't work a day by your side without having you on every surface." Seated, he dragged the chair to the desk, all business as he took her knees and draped them over his shoulders. He bit the tender skin of her inner thigh. "I'd get nothing done." Using his middle fingers to part her open, he bit his tongue. Did a prettier pussy exist? One as pink and wet and tight?

"I'd do this all day or be too busy thinking about it to work. I'm already too busy thinking about it."

Barely finishing his thought, he stroked his tongue over the hard bud of her clit, lapping at the sweetness and sucking to drive her half wild.

She moaned his name and clutched his hair, back arched so far, three buttons of her shirt burst to reveal the taut muscle of her abdomen.

Mine. Mine. Mine.

Lapping at her, laving, desperate for more buttons on the floor, more exposed skin, he asked, "Will he notice if you come on his desk?"

Her head thrashed wildly. No.

Mine.

Blood scorching, heart hammering, he licked her again, sampling leisurely at first, enjoying his favorite food, quickening, speeding, his tongue worked her, lips and mouth and teeth, racing as he felt her climax draw closer, as his cock leaked.

On his shoulders, her knees shook, her hands were tight fists on the maple desk.

"You—oh *fuck, God*, you"—she panted, trying to talk, scratched a pointed nail through his curls—"you sound—"

He sucked harder, slipped his thumb inside her, giving her body a reward to pulse around. "Hungry," he finished for her, eyes flashing to the fragile arch of her throat, streaked with pink. Teeth scored her hip again.

"Hungry," he repeated. "Thirsty, fucking feverish."

"Jealous," she croaked, the word breaking across the room. "You sound jealous."

Jealous didn't begin to cover it.

He was murderous. Fucking Brian having her, touching her? Knowing he'd never had her here, like this was the only force soothing him from fucking her right in front of him.

A savage, a barbarian. Hedonistic and disrespectful.

He pressed his thumb deeper into her, twisted.

"I'm not jealous," he lied with a rasp. "I know you've never been this wet for him. Never risk being caught spread open for anyone but me."

Her response was a moan, eyes hooded, staring, completely mesmerized as he withdrew his thumb from her, sending the pad up her navel, streaking a line of ambrosia, chasing it with his tongue.

"I know because I only get this hard for you." A kiss to her waist, her hip, her thigh. Teeth clenched to maintain restraint, he fell back in his chair, dug in his pocket and hastened to put on a condom, Lauren's curious gaze followed every roll of the latex.

He slid forward, spread his knees, cock bouncing, overeager. "Come sit on me."

She pushed up, knees drawing together, blocking his favorite vista. "Not on the desk?"

"Next time," he groaned. "Tonight, I want you to ride me with full control. I want you to find your pleasure in this prick's room."

A gasp. "Miles."

"You ride me, pretty girl, or I'll fuck you against the door until it collapses so everyone hears."

The slight widening of her eyes told him however she answered, she wanted both. Vixen.

Mine.

Bracing on the desk, she slid forward, feet dotting the carpet and then her knees were sliding on the outside of his thighs. Clenching at the plastic arms, Miles chewed on his lip as gentle fingers stroked his collarbone, lingered, followed the Roman numerals inked there. The chair creaked.

"Sandra's birthday." The needle on bone stung less than her tender touch.

"Beautiful," she murmured. "You're so beautiful."

"You're—" He hissed as Lauren lowered into his lap, trapping his length between their stomachs. A thousand failing descriptions dying on his tongue. *Gorgeous, beautiful, striking, killer.*

They still had shirts on, he hadn't unlaced his shoes.

She touched the tip of his cock, smoothed the bead of moisture down the side. The war ended, his hands grabbed at her thighs, he thrust into her palm, frantic, lifting her hips.

A painful noise escaped his throat to keep from slamming her onto him. "Take it," he urged, shoving his heels into the floor. "Sit. Take control."

All at once, she did, shoving, sending her hips down, swallowing him in her tight, wet core, squeezing.

"*Oh*," she moaned. "Oh my God." Eyes closed, breaths stuttered and skipping, she clung to him, arms wrapped around his shoulders, hot breath in his ear.

She took him so well, like she was made for him, the elegant spans of her legs cradling his brutal thighs, delicate wrists and elbows bending around him like he was the only heat she'd ever felt.

He was going to come. Buried in her, one thrust. He was undone, hands pressing on her thighs, thumbs digging into her hips. "You got to move, baby."

A slight retreat of her hips was the only relief granted before she sat again. Hard.

The groan torn from him echoed.

"Quiet," she chided, the vixen coming to play.

He smothered his next noise with her lips on his. Chasing her as she rose up and dropped again. His arms cinched her waist, helped her lift, slammed her down.

Helpless gasps flew from her mouth, nails bit into his shoulders. He went for his marks, dove to suck and bite, darken with single-mindedness as his hips thrust up to meet her. The back of his mind told him to stop, ease off her, to quit making paints of her skin, but ... it felt like this, this thing between them would only last as long as her skin purpled. And he was terrified of it fading.

Black and white.

No, he was trapped in delirious, roiling gray as she rode him. As his name proliferated her lips, as her back arched, her hands grabbing the desk for leverage, hair tickling his knees. Gray, muddy gray, where time and place were indecipherable.

Banishing the feelings building in his chest, Miles licked his fingers and sent them to her bundle of nerves, stroking firm circles, making her quiver around him.

"I've been thinking about this," he rasped, watching her bounce on him, sweat beading in the hollow of her throat.

"Yes," she hurried to agree, pushing forward, wrapping around him again, holding like she'd missed him, hips slowing. "I didn't know it could be like this."

Made two of them.

Grinding into her, tensing his abs to give her clit pressure, he slowed her further, both of them too close to the crest. Too quick. He hadn't even fucked her against the door yet.

Greedy, his hands reached around her ass, fondling as his hips drove as deep as they could, as Lauren mewled. He spread her cheeks. Her yelp pierced the air as his thumb pressed into her ass, filling her, overwhelming her. Green eyes squeezed shut, her pussy clamped down on him, wringing.

"Fuck," Miles groaned, as he filled her mouth with his tongue, every part of him in all of her.

Mine.

He pistoned up into her. The crest raised higher, a new, undiscovered peak. He sucked on her lower lip as she tightened around him, pulsing, slamming down, riding with total domination. Mouths entwined, tongues swirling. His hand in her hair.

"*Fuck.*" He bucked out of the chair, swaying as blood returned to his feet as he lost control, trapping a dangling Lauren against him as he pitched his hips into her, ramming up as he dragged her down.

Sweat gathered between their skin, the crook of his elbow and her bent knee, the curve of her ass and his palm. Tension built in his spine. Sweet and blistering. He shoved his thumb deeper, bit her shoulder.

They came together on a hard, rough thrust, her nails clawing his shirt, his teeth caught on her bottom lip.

He didn't bother cleaning up.

He let Lauren down to stand and watched with carnal delight as she stepped into her panties, pussy still wet and glossy.

The condom went in Brian's trash as Lauren found her pants, tucked in her shirt to hide the missing buttons.

He kissed her forehead, turned off the lights and with his hand on the small of her back, led her to his car.

A sense of devious pride rolled over him as he opened the door to The Hand, guided her to the bar to order drinks for round one. Strawberry martini for Maddie, Hannah's Bellini, Kayla's margarita, and Lauren would be getting extra lemons tonight.

The redness hadn't quite left her yet, and she wore the hickey on her neck like the finest pearl necklace, chin raised to show off the opulence.

"You're beautiful," Miles said, drawing her fingers into his, nodding to Declan for their order.

Lilacs and lemons rolled into his side, Lauren's perfect mouth opening. Dropping. She froze, attention over his shoulder.

Steph had her hands up, neon red hair unmistakable. A darting glance between Lauren and Miles and the stripper blurted, "I'm not fucking him."

***

IT WAS A RELIEF, Lauren supposed, to hear it aloud. In fact, if she and Miles were really going to try this, whatever *this* was, it might help in the beginning if every beautiful woman he knew voiced a similar sentiment.

Would give Lauren peace of mind.

She didn't think Miles was the type to juggle women—more the guy who parted on a good note when his tastes changed—but ...

Steph—formerly known to Lauren as the stripper Chasity—was a stunner.

After uncomfortable introductions, Lauren told Steph, "I know." She tried to look earnest as Miles gaped at her, half the bar eavesdropping. "Or at least, I didn't think you were." A glance to check in on Miles.

Still staring, still horrified.

They weren't exclusive. Miles didn't promise or vow to be hers except for four hours each Friday. But given they'd talked every day this week and he'd been inside her twenty minutes ago, she was feeling confident in her answer.

Assured in his frantic desperation for her, the thirst with which he groaned against her skin, the smiles he hid in her hair, the way he'd clutched at her as they slept, like he was scared she'd float away, out of reach.

You felt confident two years ago, an insidious voice hissed in her mind.

The Disney princess in her was crowning, her idealistic fantasy dying everything rose pink.

"Sorry," Steph said, leaning in, lowering her voice, seeming to naturally lean toward Lauren, or maybe avoid a fish-mouthed Miles. "That's what girlfriends yell when they see me. Like I'm the reason their boyfriends are hanging out at Pinks, because I'm a nymphomaniac demon who should take the blame for their indiscretion."

"That's bullshit," Lauren remarked, and Miles's mouth snapped shut.

"Lauren—"

Steph nodded, brows lifted, saying in a bitter tone that matched hers, "Utter bullshit."

The both of them shifted to stare at Miles with brilliant smiles.

"He's gone brain-dead," Lauren told Steph.

"No, he's rebooting. Like Batman and Bruce Wayne are in the same room and the game's over."

"Like Pippin in front of the Palantir."

Another shared smile.

"Steph." Miles cleared his throat. "You remember Lauren."

"We already went over it." The redhead's grin was full of mischief. "And I'd never forget your girlfriend, Miles, I showed her picture to Andrew on door two so she never has to pay the cover when she comes to drag your drooling butt out of the Ruby Room." A wink in Lauren's direction.

"Oh," Lauren said, hooking on *girlfriend*, thoughts grinding to a halt. "We're not. That is to say, I'm not his girlfriend—"

"The fuck you aren't," Miles ground.

Lauren's heart clogged her throat.

Luckily, Steph stayed cool. "I didn't exactly hear a question in there."

Miles leaned over, lips curving against Lauren's ear. "You telling me you let any guy fuck you like I do?"

Her cheeks went pink and she shook her head.

"There," Miles said. "Settled. And Lauren knows why I go to Pinks, OK? And it's not your shining personality."

"My shining personality got a five-hundred-dollar tip last night."

"Tell me it wasn't from the buck-toothed brute."

"Who else would pay me that?" Steph's voice was easy, smooth, rounding out the edged rage in Miles's tone. They reminded Lauren of Maddie and Hannah. Outlandish and protective. A strong layer of love, a safe feeling to say whatever you wanted without losing each other. Miles had earned that, deserved it after losing Sandra. And she had a feeling, from the initial terrified look on Steph's face, Steph deserved it too.

Instead of feeling jealous or possessive at their easy repartee, she felt glad. Glad he got to be friends with someone who could've been his sister.

Behaving more like himself, Miles's hand drifted back to Lauren's, fingers lacing. "You should stay away from him," he advised.

Steph's snort said what she thought of that sentiment. "He uses bifocals and wears a medical bracelet. He's my favorite client."

"You're off tonight?

"Yeah." She nodded behind the bar, sending Declan a small smile. "Caught up with a friend."

Lauren lunged for Steph, catching her hand, treating her like she would her own sister, or if she were Sandra. "You know Declan? I need to hear everything. My sister Maddie is obsessed with him, she can talk to any guy but can't even order a drink without stuttering."

Steph stared at Lauren's hands on her arm, glanced up at Miles as if offended. Oh.

She'd come on too strong. Too much.

She melted backward, retreated, frantically buffing pink from her eyes.

Steph yanked her back, eyes soft, watery as she tapped Lauren's hands with purple dip nails. "You won't believe half of what I have to say," she whispered, eyes shining with ... affection? "But TLDR he's not the reformed bad boy he pretends to be." Her fingers lingered on Lauren's, the look, it *had* to be affection, so sweet, eyes tipped, tender smile. "I'm heading out. You two enjoy your night."

"Wait," Lauren blurted. "Do you want to join our trivia team?"

She smiled, and wow, she was beautiful. Red hair, blue eyes. Everything Lauren wasn't. "Thanks but I'm off to home. Not many nights I get to bed before midnight."

Miles's hand shot out to catch Steph's shoulder. "Your car's in the shop."

"I'll—"

"Oh, Miles will drive you," Lauren volunteered, already turning in Miles's hold. "Let's go."

Chapter Nineteen

Miles's worlds had collided and there was no crash, no explosion, far less carnage than he would've guessed. His seedy nightlife had met his good luck charm and ... they'd argued over who got the front seat.

Miles vetoed the both of them cramming in the back.

One hand on the wheel, the other on Lauren's thigh, he checked the rearview mirror. Steph sat in the middle seat, legs crossed, picking at her fingernails. "I can get your sister Declan's number if you want."

Twisted around in her seat, legs on top of each other, back bent awkwardly, Lauren asked, "I thought you and Declan were together. He gave you a look."

"You're sweet," Steph cooed, ratcheting forward, hair ruffling at the blasting heat. "There's no *together* for strippers. No decent man is OK with the way I pay bills."

Miles hung left to curve along the lake and Lauren tipped, grabbing his bicep to steady. "I'm sorry."

"Don't be," Steph returned, foot pressing into the back of his seat. "I'm not. I've got bigger problems."

"Like what?"

Miles's eyes flicked in the rearview mirror, warning Steph. Throwing Lauren into the deep end was a bad idea. And Steph's drug-dealing abusive little brother wasn't wading into warm waters, it was baiting the sharks.

Fuck, Miles didn't even want Lauren to dip her toe in and now they were heading to a sketchy trailer park when they should be naming the planets.

He didn't want Lauren involved with his mess. Didn't want her to hear it, watch her eyes well with tears, her chest cave, that soft, pained breath. Her capacity for empathy couldn't take it.

Twice her size and he'd grown up in it, and still some days it was too much, made him want to scream and fight and fuck until he was cold and empty.

"Bad spray tans, sticky singles, shitty ex-boyfriends."

"Steph attracts losers," Miles said, steering the conversation from her real problems, sticking to a truth but only a palatable one.

"Hmm." Lauren nodded. "I get that."

Steph's immediate reaction was a pointed laugh. "You date losers too?" she asked, barely restraining a grin as she watched Miles in the mirror.

Laugh it up, he wanted to say, *I don't care if she calls me a loser, as long as she calls me* her *loser.*

"Oh yeah," Lauren went on, missing the interaction. "The whole family has bad luck. I call it the curse of the Disney princesses. Our fatal flaws when it comes to dating."

"You must be Cinderella," Steph crooned.

"God no. That's Maddie. I'm Anna and it's terminal."

Watching for his turn, Miles asked, "Which one is that?" Sandra had liked Jasmine, and Ariel. He didn't know the others.

"From *Frozen*," Lauren explained to Miles's consternation. "The one who fell head over heels in love with a guy who just wanted to use her. Me. All the way." To Steph, she added, "My ex Brian wanted a maid and cook and warm body. Not me. I thought I was curse-free until he pulled the plug and called me delusional for loving him."

A sharp intake of breath. "Asshole."

"Understatement," Miles chirped. An asshole got a fist to the stomach, Brian begged for a boot to the face.

"Thus, the princess curse. It's terminal. My other sisters, Hannah and Kayla, are Sleeping Beauty and Ariel."

"You're not Anna," Miles told her, wrenching the steering wheel. "Brian was a villain, you're not cursed."

Out of the corner of his eye, he saw her gaze slide to his necklace, watch the gold on the black ink. There was a minute Lauren was lost in private contemplation before she said softly, "It's not just Brian."

Miles felt his heart plummet to his stomach and it took surprising effort to silence the argument building in his throat. He stared hard at the road, ignoring the hot touch of her gaze. Not just Brian. Because Miles was using her.

"I'm Elsa," Steph exclaimed into the tense air, voice bouncing off the leather. "No, man. I just want a palace in the middle of nowhere. Maybe I should set you up with Declan."

He jerked the steering wheel, crossing over the centerline to throw Steph sideways. A cough. "Not now," she added. "When you two are clearly together."

Silence fell. Lauren turning around in her seat, taking her hand from him to adjust the vents. If she expected Miles to agree right after she called herself cursed, she was wrong. She was pure undiluted luck. He'd never been happier, never played better since meeting her. And she thought of herself as a harebrained princess?

Was he the villain she'd fallen for? The beast?

Not an hour ago, he'd fucked her in her ex's office, blind with jealousy.

Yes.

The road bent to shape the cove into Mallet's Bay, where docks sat high on the ice, left to rust until fishermen returned in the spring. Though it was still Lake Champlain, the view from the Rose's house was very different from that of the trailer park.

"Lakeview," Lauren cooed as they pulled next to a single wide. Not condescension, no judgment, it was like she couldn't see the weeds piled at the shore, the wide holes in the ice people used to dump discriminating materials. "Best sight in Burlington."

"I think so," Steph agreed, unbuckling, slipping forward to squeeze both their elbows. "Thanks for the ride."

"Wait." Lauren jumped, pulling out her phone. "Give me your number. I'll add you to the SOS group."

"Steph has me. I watch out for her," Miles ground.

"I know and I can too, like when you're playing or traveling to away games."

Denial clung to the tip of his tongue. But Steph was already entering her information. He hated it, wanted to grab the phone and smash it, dump it in the lake. Hated Lauren stepping into his dark world.

"Thank you, Lauren, for including me."

A beautiful smile from his pretty girl. "Any friend of Miles is a friend I'd like to have."

Briefly, he wished his sister could've met Lauren, felt included, felt normal, be invited to trivia and driven home. Would Sandra have used an SOS the night she died? Would Lauren have found her body, sobbing as she covered it with her coat, dialed the police?

A deep inner conviction clawed his chest. No, it'd be worse. Miles would've had to identify two in the morgue instead of one.

***

"DISQUALIFIED," LAUREN SAID, SCANNING Hannah's text. "Maddie took a phone call during round one and the Fuck-Bros said they were cheating."

Miles's response was a terse, "They earned their name. Drop you at home, then?"

As he rounded a corner, Lauren realized he'd been taking her home before she even spoke. He never wanted to return to The Hand. Maddie's call was a well-timed excuse.

He cut down a side street, shot past a row of parked cars battered with snow from the plows. The doors of which would have to be dug out before anyone got to work. Lauren tried to sympathize, to luxuriate in the heated seat, to relax, to shut off her mind. But an innocuous energy thrummed in the car. Emanated from where Miles was coiled in his seat, and she wasn't precisely sure why. What she'd done.

"Are you mad because she's your friend?" she asked carefully, voice cracking as she broke the silence. "Brian didn't like when I tried to hang out with his friends. He said we were a couple, not conjoined twins."

"Fuck. Do not compare me to Brian." The contempt in his deep voice made her want to shrink away, but his skirting the question sent her backbone straight. Not delusional, right. He was upset with her. Mad. Angry, ready to drop her off, send her home, come back on Friday.

Lifting her chin, she said with as much dignity as she could, "I thought that's what you wanted. To help protect—"

Miles shook his head, seeming to barely resist the temptation to let go of the wheel and shake her. "And how are you qualified to protect Steph?"

"I can drive a car just as well as anyone. Pick her up when she needs it."

"She's not running out of gas on a highway. Steph's life is drug dealers, and perverts and stalkers." In a harsh tone, he went on, "What are you gonna do when her addict brother goes on a bender and kicks her out, or when a drunk waits for her in the parking lot at Pinks, hoping for an afterparty?"

She opened her mouth. Her voice lost.

"Exactly."

Given the stubborn line of his jaw, it was clear he believed her to be just as useless as Brian had. Can't change a lightbulb without male supervision. Can't realize someone's not into you. "I'd call the police. What would you do that's better? How are you more qualified than me? Have your vigilante license? A record of—"

"Yes. I have a record for beating Sandra's boyfriend to a pulp because even at sixteen, Lauren, I had a hundred pounds on you. Now I have even more and I know how to use them. If someone tries to mess with her, they go through me."

Lauren laughed. "You're not a superhero, you're a football play-er."

Fingers wrenching on the wheel, Miles stared at the pattern of the road lines. "I'm neither. I'm a fighter. Football pays the bills but I'm bred to fight."

"No. You're not." He was sweet and thoughtful and though he'd clearly been in fights, how many she couldn't wonder from the scars on his hands, the way he'd reacted blank-faced to his black eye, it didn't make him a fighter.

It made him a protector.

He could tattoo every inch, get piercings, more chains, drip in gold and metal and ink and he'd never be a fighter, never override his instincts, the hollow look in his eyes when he spoke of violence. Fighters were vengeful and brutal. Brian was a fighter. A hundred and forty pounds soaking wet, but she'd seen in his sneer, understood the way he wanted people under his thumb, wanted to yell, how he yearned for it. Fed off conflict.

"Yes I am, Lauren. Why do you think I started playing football? I wanted to destroy every guy who ever joked about my sister being a whore without going to fucking jail for it."

"If that's your reasoning, Miles, then call me a brawler too. I'd stand up for my sisters in any circumstances, to anyone who tried—"

Miles's head ducked and twisted away as if the movement could block out her defense. The muscles in his arms knotted. "You shouldn't have to protect them."

"That's rich coming from you. Protecting every woman you meet."

"I can. That's the—"

"*Me too.*" Even there, even in her insistence, hearing the smack of her hand on her thigh, she sounded small. Delicate. Hated it.

"With your one self-defense class? Can't you see where I'm coming from? I don't—"

"You don't *what*? What, Miles?" she pressed. "Can't figure out a non-hypocritical way to say it's OK for you to help but when I do it, it's not? That's the same kind of bullshit Brian—"

"*Stop* comparing me to him."

"I will when you stop acting like him."

He pulled over hard, the Demon's wheels crying over the rumble strips, and then frozen grass, the front bender dug into a snowbank. The car jerked into park and then Miles's hands were on her face, cupping her cheeks, angling her to look at him. "Goddammit, I don't want you hurt," he hissed, eyes wild. "I can't stand the thought of you being hurt, and this ... my world, I've made it fucking messy and if I was smart I'd stop with Steph and Pinks to keep you from it but I can't because I'll never stop. If you get dragged into this because of me ... don't you think I've pictured it? What could happen to you? You in the parking lot at night?

You in the morgue?" His voice quieted, trembled. "I'm a big guy, I can take it. But you—"

"Strength isn't always about muscle."

"It is when you're dealing with this shit, Lauren. These guys ..."

She heard her voice raise, felt her knuckles tighten. "I won't abandon someone because there's risk. We're the same—"

"I wish you would," he murmured, the raw words cutting her off. "You look at me like I'm good, but I would ... I would leave Steph completely, ditch every girl at Pinks. Stop going, mind my own fucking business if I could get five more minutes with my sister."

"No. No you wouldn't."

He shook his head.

She stopped him, hand on his chin. "No you wouldn't, Miles."

"Yes," he answered with a soft grunt, tears in his eyes. "Yes I would. For you too."

It struck her right in the heart.

Silence, his hands brushing back and forth under her eyes, a lone tear dragging down his skin.

"Is it because I'm your good luck charm?" Her voice was a shadow facing the afternoon sun. "Because you'll lose without me?"

He flinched, shoving a hand through his hair. "You know it's not."

"Then what," she pushed, kept pushing. "What is it?"

He set his teeth, still brushing over her cheek, his eyes stuck on the movement, glued to the spot.

"See, Miles," she ran a hand through his curls, stroking, caressing. Pulled back. Away. Took step after painful step down from her vine covered tower. "This is what I mean. You'd protect me and I'm just a deal to you. It's ingrained in your system to help anyone and—"

"You consume my thoughts," he told her, still using that raw tone, the one that peeled back his armor. "I can't see a fortune cookie without laughing, I can't step inside my house without wondering how your eyes would bulge, if you'd laugh and say it's what you pictured or if you'd touch the walls and shake your head, look at me with a surprised glint. I'm in the locker room reading about Sam pegging Frodo, every gory detail because I'm looking for you. Because when I can't have you on the phone, when I can't be in your bed, stalking you in your office, I'm searching AO3 tags, waiting for your voice to fill my head."

"I'm not pop—"

"Three million results. Three million weirdos like you and I want to call you my girlfriend and I've never once had a girlfriend because I've never once wanted one. Wanted another person I loved taken from me. Because they all leave. Sandra was snuffed out, my mother changed her mind. Dad did both."

Lauren couldn't breathe.

Miles panted, gulped down breaths. Steam caked the windows of the Demon. As his cheeks got the barest hint darker, as he sucked in oxygen, Lauren suffocated.

The windows fogged entirely, and she shivered in her seat. She felt cold and hot and she wanted someone to tell her to climb faster down from the tower, to run along the steep stone steps, burst into the garden and sprint without ever looking back, go into the woods and be alone. Safe.

But she felt herself waiting, opening the pages of a great story and seeing Miles's name there, feeling in her bones that he was coming for her, he was so close. It didn't matter how long she stayed locked up. He was coming to her.

He leaned over and unbuckled her seat belt. "I'll leave once the living room light's on."

"What?" Lauren's thoughts drifted back to her, and she wiped at the window, smearing translucent stripes to see her house. The sidewalk shoveled, always shoveled with Miles watching over her. She hadn't realized he'd taken her home.

Was dropping her off.

"I thought ..." She turned to look at him. "Aren't you coming in?"

"No." His hands were upturned in his lap where he watched the lines of scars, turning them over and scowling, fisting healing wounds. "We had a fight. You don't want me to come inside."

She couldn't think of a better reason to invite him in.

Carefully, she unbuckled his seat belt, gently helping it roll across his chest. "Come inside with me. I have shortbread." She pulled his face to hers. "I'll share."

"You're mad at me," he insisted, avoiding her gaze. "We're fighting. I'm overprotective, a caveman, I'm not evolved, I'm a brute. You don't—"

"Why would I ever be mad at you for caring about me?" She tucked errant curls around his ears. "Come with me."

Slowly, his eyes dragged to hers, tension between his brows, a heavy wariness drowning him. "Are you sure?"

"Yes," she smiled. "but we'll have to be quiet. It's a weeknight."

Miles was shaking his head again. "Why would we be loud?"

"Oh." Lauren kissed his cheek, her heart bursting. "It's fun seeing you be the innocent one."

Chapter Twenty

There were twenty-eight reasons Lauren was surprised to see Brian. But the main ones, the most concerning reasons, were that she was in the women's bathroom and she wasn't wearing a shirt.

It wasn't like she was moonlighting in the toilet or even expecting anyone to know where she was. She'd gone to the farthest bathroom in City Hall. Known for its odd red walls and missing paper towels.

The one with only a single unclogged stall and absolutely zero toilet paper. Empty always.

Perpetually.

Today it was as busy as Lake Street at rush hour.

She couldn't remember the last time she'd wanted to pretty herself up. Especially after a long week, but she'd wanted to surprise Miles. Not be wearing the button-down he'd seen, not have her hair in a low ponytail, or her main perfume of spilled coffee and vellum.

She wanted to make his mouth drop, and then she wanted him to taste her wild berry lip gloss.

See where the night took them.

They'd spent every night together, dinner Wednesday, dancing at Nightingale yesterday, tonight she wanted to relax, lock her bedroom door and turn on the lights. Because despite the time they were spending together, Miles hadn't touched her, not more than hands and a kiss goodnight.

And Lauren wasn't coping well without his powerful touch, his expert fingers.

Her nipples tightened just thinking about him.

She covered them with her palms and yelled, "What the hell are you doing in here?"

Cheeks splashed with tears, Brian's face was a splotchy red, eyes lifeless as he hovered there, staring, shoulder holding the door open.

"Get in or get out," she hissed. Couldn't believe she was saying it. "I'm not flashing the whole office." For a split second, she considered retreating to a stall as Brian lugged his feet into the room. But why should she retreat? She'd done nothing wrong and it wasn't as if he hadn't seen her naked before.

"She's leaving me," he cried suddenly, back hitting the wall, knees buckling until he was splayed on square white tile. Sobbing. Snot dripping from his nose. A hiccup. "She's. Leaving. Me." Words between pants. He was barely intelligible.

Reaching behind her to grab her yellow long sleeve, she asked, "What are you talking about?"

Twisting the fabric, finding the opening, a peek to see his eyes closed, watch a ritual thump of his head on the plaster. She yanked it over her head.

"Miranda!" he burst.

"Miranda ..." Shoving hands through the sleeves, she pulled her loose hair free, tucked the front into her pants, and turned to look in the mirror. Too colorful? Or perfectly cheery?

"L!" Brian cried. "Are you listening?"

"What else would I be doing?" she muttered, twisting to stare down at him, hands on her hips. "What about Miranda?"

"She doesn't want to be with me." Back of his hands in his eyes. "She found somebody better, said I was only a placeholder." He rose to his knees, half walking, half crawling over never-mopped tile, hands grasping Lauren's arms.

She slapped at his fingers. "Do not touch me," she hissed, tossing her reflection an exasperated look. "Sit down."

He sat right there, butt and boots and contorted face, like a sad, well-trained puppy.

"Mary told me you were in here," he said, calming down, pants leveling. "She said you know. But how can you know what this feels like? Miranda was the one. I want to throw up."

Miranda, yes. The girlfriend hotter than Lauren, cooler, better. The woman Brian actually *loved*. "Why did you come to work when you're such a mess?"

"She texted me!" he growled, throwing his phone at the green stall door. Watching it swing. "She's moving out, told me not to come home tonight." He dropped his hands in his face, rubbed his eyes. Ugh. Those were never cleaned bathroom floor hands.

There was maybe nothing sadder than watching a grown man sit on the floor, legs akimbo, hands plopped down in his lap, struggling to breathe he was bawling so hard. Maddie and Kayla, hell Miles would tell her to soak it in, take a selfie with him, to feel vindicated.

Hannah would cy.

Lauren ... she just felt sad. Sad for him because she'd been there. She did know. She'd been him. Wasted all of her vacation time on a cry trip to her basement. Painted her nails black with a Sharpie, watched only the part of *John Wick* where the dog died.

She'd been a sad masochist. Behaving like a wrecking ball smashed through her heart, swung at her organs, demolished her sense of identity. Painful and hard, she hadn't seen an end to it. Hoped for numbness, the opposite of overwhelming hurt. She'd loved Brian so much.

"Does it ever go away?" he asked, clawing at his shirt, tears streaming down his face, wetting his polo. "Have you ever felt like this?"

That he could ask—

She tore her gaze from him, bending over the sink to check her lip gloss in the mirror. "Of course I know how you're feeling." A pucker, a smile. A frown. "It's how I felt about you."

"You didn't feel this way," he ground out, a child on the floor having a fit. "I *love* her—"

"I loved you," she snapped. How could he not understand? "I loved you this much, maybe more, and you threw me away."

"Miranda loved me back."

Lauren strangled the bitter laugh in her throat. "Did she?" she taunted. "She dumped you over text."

He flinched, recoiled.

Felt like she'd smacked an ice cream cone from a toddler's sticky hands. "Look"—she came to a crouch in front of him, awkwardly patting his shoulder—"you're going to love people who don't love you the same. That's kind of the end of the story. It doesn't change or fix your feelings, and it won't make you love them less when they look you straight in the eyes and say they never loved you."

"Are you still in love with me?" His hand covered hers, clammy, cold, bony.

"Fuck no." She yanked back. "I'm not twenty and an idiot. I found"—she stood, fingers going to her lips—"someone else."

She had. Miles was her someone else, her someone better, and she might be his good luck charm, his flavor of the month, but it didn't matter, didn't change her feelings, nothing would.

"Is Miranda gonna come back. Is she—"

"No, she's not." Lauren almost smiled. Brian blubbering in the bathroom, asking her for advice. *Delusional*, she wanted to croon, *you're crazy. Miranda never liked you, you made it up in your head.*

But feelings weren't decided in the head. They were a function of soul and body. Your heart decided and it was up to your brain to cope. To decide what to do next. Share your love or keep it locked away. Either option didn't change the flush you got at the mention of their name, the comfort from smelling their neck, from hearing their voice.

"How did you"—hiccup—"how did you fix it? How did you get over it? How'd you *stop*—stop the feeling?"

She hadn't. She'd tried, gone numb, banished all feelings, fought for cold, lived a stoic life, but she'd never quite managed it. Never successfully lingered in that desolate state. Time passed and she'd fooled herself into thinking she was heartless.

But she wasn't. She'd fallen in love with her sisters again, worried over their safety, their problems, fretted like an old maid for two years and then ... Miles.

Miles Santos with his smug overconfidence. Nightingale, the strip club. Champagne.

She could taste bubbles on her lips. "There's no way to stop it," she said, using the edge of her discarded button-down to wipe off the gloss. "You can't stop loving just like that. You need time." Time to think, time to recoil, rebuild. Time to crawl step after grueling step back up into that tower. Because no one locked you up. No one dared you. *You* put yourself up there, past the trellis, in the cold stone to wait. Because the feeling of love—whether you think you're free or trapped—is like being rescued. Having someone see all your flaws and forgive them, like them. Sharing secrets, telling them what you thought about while you were waiting. Every odd thought, every tick and habit you developed. You show them the spiderwebs draped in the corners of the room. The tick marks by the bed post. How you painted the dresser and started making a rope tie bridge out of your sheets when you finally saw him. When he threw a ladder on the portcullis and dropped elbows in the window. Smirked.

And you fell, the stairs collapsed under you, twenty floors of stone and mud turning to dust from one smile. And you have scrapes and bruises and you'll get a headache every year thinking about the fall, how hard it was, how the world slid out from under you, but you'll barely feel them. Not when hands touch the pink skin, lips kiss over it, arms encircle you.

She looked in the mirror.

Her eyes seemed brighter. Skin clearer. Cheeks a constant flush these days, all the way across her nose. "You don't get to pick who you love. You just have to keep going, and hope you get to feel it again."

Brian's sobs echoed off the tile, became a wave of sadness.

Karma.

Lauren offered him the the sleeve of her discarded button down. "My recommendation is to take some time off for yourself to feel bad and then try again."

"I don't want anyone else. I want Miranda."

"I thought that too and I was an idiot for waiting so many years, thinking there was nobody else out there I could love. Don't wait two years, Brian. You have a receding hairline." Because she sympathized for him but she also hated him.

Best of luck would never come from her, but *How's it feel?* seemed harsh so Lauren split the difference, shutting her mouth, stuffing the shirt into her bag, leaving.

"She didn't ever love me." Brian was gasping for air again, angry and desperate. "Just like I never loved you."

No, she'd never wish him luck. Folding the sleeves of her top to sit at her wrists, she said, "It doesn't make your love any less real. Channel it elsewhere."

"I can't."

"You *can*," she gritted, picking him up under his shoulders, spinning him, pushing him from the women's room. "Get a salamander, name her Mandy." She stopped outside his office, her tone drier and drier. Opening the door, she flicked on the light. "Request time off," she added, looking over the desk, his chair. "And sorry for having sex in your office. Try not to think about it."

That was it.

She was striding down the hall, a streak of yellow in government beige, a wave to Mary in the front office. Double doors.

Miles, leaning against a growling Demon, wearing only a black floral henley. He smirked. "No buttons."

She strode right to him, eyes locked on his, and put her fingers in his waiting palm. "No buttons," she confirmed, taking hold of his collar, pulling him down.

He kissed her until her fingers shook over his skin, until she was sending them down, digging into him. Fingers in her hair, holding her to stay longer, to spend more air on him. Her lashes fluttered as she clung to him, reaching around him, pushing him into the metal of the Demon.

"No buttons," she repeated, wrapping herself into his arms, sliding her head into the crook of his neck. "Brian got dumped."

"I'll get the champagne and in six hours when it's flat, we'll toast."

"Old, flat champagne. You spoil me." She glanced in the driver's seat and saw a folded paper bag. Smoothed his hair flat, and watched the curls bounce back. "Movie night?"

"Dinner. Buffalo mac and cheese."

Her favorite. She sagged against him. "You do spoil me."

"It's a bribe. What if we went to Pinks tonight? Steph's been having some trouble and I want to be there before her shift because the bouncers don't come until eleven. She sounded scared on the phone. Her boss is coming on to her."

"You don't have to explain it to me. Let's go to Pinks."

"Yeah? Last time I took you, you kneed me in the dick."

"I was hangry. Forgive me?" She swept the point of her tongue across the pulse in his throat and he made a soft, guttural noise that set fire to her brain. "Food," she breathed on his skin, "is an excellent distraction. Really puts a cap on my internal rage."

"Maybe while we eat, you can tell me and Steph about your new fan fiction."

"Can you please stop telling people about that? The only reason I told you was because I was trying to push you away."

He slid his arms around her and set his forehead against hers. "But my AO3 account just got approved and I've got piles of gay porn to go through unless you give me a hint. BabyhandsCrocus? Shortbreadlover401? PeckProblems?"

"Santosisking102."

Laughing, he pinched her thigh. "Now I know you're lying. That's my username." He nipped at her throat. She knew exactly which spot. "Come on," he murmured, "let me feed you, make you laugh and order you vodka while I suck the lemon on your fingers."

She heard her heartbeat thrum in her ears. Her cheeks burned from smiling.

"I love you, Miles." Slowly, she slid her hands up his chest to lace her fingers over the back of his neck. "I love you. I think I have

for a while but talking with Brian—it made me want to tell you."
Saying it wouldn't make it worse or better, but saying it felt right,
felt like the dust was settling from the tower's wreckage, cuts were
healing, bruises fading. Didn't matter what he said in return, felt
in return, she wasn't ashamed of her feelings. She was solid in this
and she didn't need a response to know it was time to share.

His shoulders were stiff, arms tense as he gripped the edge of
the Demon's roof. Grinning, feeling light as air, she shuffled back,
kissed the side of his neck and opened the door, sitting, giving
him time. She rolled down the window when she saw him shiver.
"Hurry up, food's getting cold."

CHAPTER TWENTY-ONE

MILES HAD BEEN UNPREPARED for this. This feeling. This infuriating ache that made him smile.

He carried it around like a ten-pound gold chain hanging around his neck. A sick, ironic ruby-encrusted cross banging against his heart, and he couldn't take it off without severing his head. Couldn't even ignore it, didn't get used to it.

For three days, he waited for her to flip, to turn on a dime. They'd fought, she was done. Cut him out and then … she didn't. She hadn't. And a riot of feelings swallowed him.

She didn't care enough to cut him out. It was one-sided, these feelings building in his chest, they didn't match hers and he was so fucking thankful. So glad she'd held him back, pushed him away, locked her feelings up, glad like a bastard that Brian had wrecked her, ruined her from loving again. He saw a future.

Then she switched the play, no more running. Miles didn't have the ball, he didn't have the route, he was ass over head on the line as Lauren snatched a ball in the end zone. Game over.

I love you.

Then she'd said it again, like he hadn't heard her, as if she hadn't ruined his eardrums.

Again when he jokingly offered to dance for her on their table's private pole. Again when she'd kissed him goodnight, fingers in his hair, lips hot and hard, tongue swirling, intoxicating. Lemons and lilacs, her soft cheek sliding against his stubble as she whispered it, closed the door to her house.

They were in love.

Game over.

Now came the wreck and ruin, the tiptoeing, the fear, the waiting.

So much, he liked the feeling. Too much. He never thought he'd crave love again. But this was Lauren. And when she said the words, his body split into leaning in and running away, pinned him in place.

Lauren's love. How'd he end up with it? The kid from LA with a rap sheet. The kid who ran out on his mother at sixteen.

As Saturday melted into Sunday, as he added peanut butter to six scrambled eggs, the chain tightened around his throat. Now, he felt it claw up his neck, slicing into his skin, cutting off his air. He had to breathe past it, gather the strength to fill his lungs.

Miles knew what love was. Bleeding out. Watching someone put the bandages away.

Love was as thin as a razor's tip, as delicate as a summer breeze, as short-lived as snow in Vegas.

He never wanted her to feel it. Not for him.

He could drown in it, suffer it alone, battle the madness of love, but the both of them …

"Man, you going to shower?" Moore's voice cut through Miles's thoughts. He stood from the bench. *Fuck*. He had to shower. His routine, his ritual, his carefully formulated way to win.

Pregame shower, air dry, double taping his left palm. He went through the motions, waited. Something bad was going to happen. He could feel it. Feel the chain carve grooves into his skin, scrape off the black lines reaching up his throat. In every beat of his heart, he could feel it, a rubber band being pulled too taut. Another inch, another millimeter and it'd snap.

The welts on his skin would be the least of the injuries.

Through muscle memory, he stumbled through warm-ups. Ate the crust off a sandwich, choked down cookies 'n' cream bars. Said his prayers. Washed his mouthguard in soap. Then he was on the field, grabbing the ball from Warren, slipping through the gap, sprinting. Not breathing.

Down in three yards. Three fucking yards.

"Do it again," Foss shouted from the sidelines, gum near flying out of his mouth.

Again, Miles agreed. Black turf beads dug into his elbows, sweat dripped down his back. He tasted soap and he couldn't breathe.

Warren helped him stand, righted him until steady. "Shake it off," the QB said, yanking the jersey back over Miles's right shoulder pad. "One down isn't a game. On to the next."

They set again, all in the line. Miles bent. New run. One bad down. Not a bad game.

Hut. Snap. Miles snagged the ball, sprinted. Hit.

The crowd cheered. A home crowd, confident in him. Forgiving of a small error. They knew how lucky he was.

Snap. Miles cut his route, got the handoff and exploded, thighs burning, hands slapped his, tried to stop him, force him back. A spin, pivot, new gap, a straight arm shot him out of bounds, sent him into a sea of seething orange yelling for him to get back. Leave.

Two yards. Two yards with the backtracking, Miles tossed the ball to the refs and stalked across the field. Fourth down. Special teams ran onto Mountaineers turf for a punt. He was done. Choking, he yanked off his helmet the second he was off-field, slammed it into the ground. The crowd cheered. A home crowd, screaming for the defense to work.

Better, he needed better. He needed MVP, he needed playoff bonuses. He needed money to protect Steph, the girls at Pinks.

To spoil Lauren.

He turned, dragging hands through his hair, ignoring Burton's swearing as the tight end kicked over a Gatorade dispenser, splashing red. One possession. One bad possession, he'd turn it around. He pushed air from his lungs, inhaled, looked up, away from the game to clear his head.

His knees locked.

The family section was small. Victoria sat in neon green, taking pictures with her phone. Cole's wife, Jo, in a nest of empty seats, picking dog hair off her jersey.

Three rows back he saw not blonde, not brown, but somewhere in between. A shade that matched everything, that haunted his dreams.

Three women in a line, each with similar delicate bone structure, high cheekbones, pointed noses, one with naturally rosy lips.

One not like the others, one that stood out for the shine in her eyes, the wild throw of her untamed not-blonde-not-brown hair.

A meaty hand clamped down on his shoulder. "Quit hogging the ball if yer just going to run for two," Burton growled.

Miles could barely hear it.

Lauren in the stands. Lauren watching him. Wearing green. Sitting in the family section.

"Ye hear me?" Burton kept badgering. "I'll get it done if ye won't."

Miles shoved the Irish prick off him. Lauren watching. Coming. Betraying.

He'd expected it.

The chain snapped on him. He could breathe.

They lost.

***

LAUREN PACED THE PLAYER parking lot. The passes Miles got for her sisters, they opened a lot of doors. Snow fell around her in earnest, making the sky hazy and blurred, forcing her to squint and glare as the Mountaineers filed from the stadium.

It was only his silhouette, but she knew it was him instantly. He walked a little wider, hips nocked forward. Charging ahead in her puffy coat compressed under her folded arms, her hands were numb. Night had come swift and early. December had arrived.

"Miles," she called. "Miles." Voice lost in the wind and snow. She kept moving, steps light, shivers wracking her back. It was hard to see his face, to tell if he'd heard. Then all at once, it got so, so easy.

Flat, detached hatred. "I told you not to come," he said, tone lifeless, bone dry. "I asked you, Lauren. For *one* thing. One thing in this. Don't come."

He kept a shell of air between them as she moved, avoiding her touch. A slick camel dress coat hung past his knees, his wet hair frosted in the snow.

She smothered a stunned laugh. "It's in your head, Miles. I'm not your lucky charm. It's not me or your routine."

"Then how do you explain that?" She missed the monotone as rage and disgust curdled his velvet voice. "Twenty-one to seven, Lauren. First loss since I met you." A hard stare, and then he was moving, leaving, a panther moving through the fog of the Amazon, slinking, muscles tensed.

She had to run to keep up, skating around staff in bright orange shirts shoveling, others clearing windshields. The biggest storm of the year, throwing snow at the ground, watching it pile and amass.

"Miles." She grabbed for his hand, trying to twist him, but he was no easier to move than a mountain with deep roots. Instead of pulling him to her, she clung, another snowflake clinging to him. He treated her as such, ignoring her, weightless, insignificant, like she'd fall off or melt away eventually.

"Miles, this is the second game I've been to. It's not me. I had to know. I had to see if it was real."

He was shaking his head, keys in his hand, hitting the start button. The vibrant yellow of the Demon was hidden under white but the engine cut through the scrape of metal on asphalt, the lingering rumble of voices. Jaw tense, nostrils flaring, he wiped the windshield with a bare hand. Trembling, not from the cold, no Miles wasn't cold under her hand. Never.

Trembling to restrain himself?

"Did you hear me?" she asked, voice softer, wishing for one calm night, one non-magical snow-filled night. Wishing her story wasn't *Frozen*. "This is my second game and you won last time."

"Why did you come?" His hand over her wrist, removing her. Green eyes near black, he watched her. "You're lying."

"I'm not lying. Ask Maddie or Kayla—"

"'Cause they'll tell me the truth over you."

"Can you just trust me?"

"What?" he snarled. "Because you love me? So I have to trust you now? Because you said those pretty little words without thinking and suddenly you get to do whatever you want? Treat me however you want."

She felt his words like a slap. Worse. Like sheets being ripped off her, cold water thrown over her languid, sleeping form. Skin going tight, burning at the cold. She pulled back.

"Fuck this," he grunted, opening the door and slamming it to knock off the snow. To burn off anger.

"Stop, please." She swallowed back a sob. "We need to talk about this. You shouldn't leave a fight without solving it."

"Tell me the solution then." She stared, silent, cracks scoring through her heart.

"Right," Miles returned, a mean chuckle. "The deal's off. I don't need your luck anymore. You've ruined it."

He sat in the driver's seat and Lauren threw her body in the gap, hip knocking metal and leather. "Don't leave mad."

Like she was no more than a gnat, less, he shoved her to the side, as easily as if the pavement was ice beneath her. "Please," she begged. "Where do you need to be other than here?"

"Where do you think? I'm going to go drown myself in strippers—"

"That's not you, Miles."

"Get a fucking lap dance, pound back some patrons. Watch women fall over me."

"Stop this. That is not you."

"Neither is losing." He slammed the door, narrowly missing her elbow. Then the car leaped, power, all coiled power unleashed, snow kicked into Lauren, whipped at her cheeks, shoved down her coat as bright yellow revealed itself, as he drove from the parking lot, wheels spinning.

Her heart was not in her body. Her body was resistant to the cold, hollow. Cement scratched at bare knees, her ball gown tore, gashes in the bodice, strips missing from the back, open skin. She felt her body bow, felt her fall forward on cool cement steps. Stairs she couldn't climb. Not as she lay bleeding, open, not as her tiara slid off, gems scattering as the gold broke.

"Hey!" a bright voice shouted quite aggressively. Lauren snapped out of her mind, back to the parking lot, back to shivering and shaking, back to Miles's snarl echoing in her ears. Before her, a Range Rover idled, painted the brightest red she'd ever seen. The passenger window rolled down, a woman bent over the center console, hand raised. "Hey, did you meet Miles like five weeks ago?"

Caught between her broken castle and the tundra, this woman chatting like she was on fast forward, Lauren was having trouble making sense of anything.

"Yes?" She drew her arms around her torso, holding together the imaginary ribbons of her torn dress.

SOS.

Her heart knew the Morse code, dialing it into her ribs, hammering each letter, cracking bone. *SOS. SOS.*

Save me.

"And that's him," the woman went on. "who just drove off right in his little sporty I-have-a-big-dick car, right?"

Slowly, Lauren's gaze returned to the woman in her neon SUV. Black hair cut sharp at the neck, blue eyes that could rival Frodo's, bright red lips, creamy skin. Each color oversaturated. Hard to look at. Beautiful. "Yes?"

"Great." She slapped the leather seat beside her. "I'm Victoria and you should get in."

"Excuse me?"

"I'm not going to kidnap you and sell you on the black market. Promise. Girls lifting girls. Women together forever." She waved flippantly. "All that. Trust me. I have credentials, but if we're going to follow him, you need to be fast or we're never going to catch him."

A dumb idea. Miles would kill her for getting—

No. Miles had left her.

Lauren ripped the door open, climbed into the seat, and buckled her seat belt. "I know where he's going," she said. Then, "You said Victoria?"

"Yes, and you're the one," Victoria returned. " I'm his manager." A flick of her wrist, bright green nails and the fans threw heat as she blasted them out of the parking lot. No signaling. The rear wheel caught the curb.

SOS.

"Ignore that," Victoria instructed, hand waving again. Lauren clutched the door handle. "I'm a great driver. Better even in the snow." She changed the radio from AM to FM and adjusted her seat heat level as they sped through a yellow lights, wipers slashing through snow.

Lauren was going to die.

"What's your name?"

"Oh I'm Lauren. I'm Miles's—" her voice caught. She didn't know how to end that sentence except, "I love Miles."

"Well, no doubt that scared him shitless. Though rushing to the nearest strip club is not the response I had to the love bomb."

"It wasn't a bomb. We're dating. He called me his girlfriend." A sharp left. Lauren's seat belt locked on her chest. Her stomach flipped. Tires over the centerline.

"Not your bomb." She flipped back the car's ashtray. Plucked a loose M&M free. "His. Realizing you're in love suddenly, it's scary. No it's terrifying," she corrected, pulling up to Pinks' front door.

Lauren didn't say thank you. She was rude and hasty, jumping out of the car, sprinting through the snow.

Behind her, Victoria called. "Be patient!"

Ironic as they'd rushed here, as Lauren sucked down stale perfume-soaked air, eyes fighting to adjust from all white to seductive black. The place was mostly empty, they'd just opened, dancers mingled across the room, strung across chairs in little rodeo outfits. Lauren saw red hair, turned. Ran straight into Miles's back.

Powerful hands caught her, moved her away. "Dios," he gritted. "Can't I have a fucking moment of peace? What are you doing here?"

"What are you doing here?"

"Getting a lap dance in a private room," he said, pulling a wad of cash from his pocket. "From whoever looks the least like you."

She snatched the money. "You don't do that, Miles."

But he was already storming across the lacquered wood floors, drawing the eyes of every woman as he broke past the stage into a hallway marked Red Rooms.

Maybe they didn't watch him, but her chasing after, wet shoes sliding on the floors, cheeks stinging from the cold. There necks went back-and-forth. Miles hard steps, Lauren's frantic chase. Her frizzy hair, puffy coat, squeaking sneakers. In a strip club on a Sunday. Let them judge.

Coat sliding off his shoulders, Miles sidestepped into room two, and Lauren jumped through the door before it slammed. Sweat and sex and a bucket of cologne. Pink couch arched around a narrow stage. A gleaming blue pole centered the room.

Loud grinding music, different from the pop and rap played for the stage shows. Low lights.

"You're not what I ordered," he growled, dropping sore muscles onto the tufted blush pink couch, looking like an ad for Dolce and Gabbana, tattoos, perfect face, dichotomy.

"You want a lap dance, Miles? Fine." Lauren could hardly believe what was happening as she tore off her coat, threw it right at him. "Have your lap dance."

Little by little, the distance between them shrank. When she got within two feet, in arm's reach, close enough to see frost on the end of his lashes, he shook his head. "Put your coat on. You're out of your league here."

Five weeks ago, cursing Maddie in the line at Nightingales, she would've agreed. Would've left, battling back tears, ran home and hid. Today, she said, "No I think *you* are."

Ignoring his scoff, voice a malicious hiss, she continued, "I can't think of anything you'd despise more than getting ground on by some girl in this club, so I'm going to not let you destroy yourself right now." She kicked off her sneakers, cold wet socks. None of it sexy, no finesse as she peeled and pried off layers of clothes.

Miles stared, legs spread, fists on his thighs. He stared, jaw set, eyes impossibly dark. Any lingering green winked out by the lights, by his anger, by Lauren in her bra and underwear.

"Stop."

An unheeded demand, too late, too soft, conflicted.

Her shirt landed next to him. Her bra didn't match her panties. Her skin was cold, covered in goose bumps but she staggered for the panel by the door. Turned up the music with shaking hands.

Low, shaking bass.

"Why did you follow me?" he asked harshly, as she turned, as she stepped on stage, walked a circle around the pole, pulled her windblown hair from its tie.

"If you want to fight," he baited, watching her fingers curve over her stomach, caressing. "I'm in the other mood."

Good, she thought. Looking at him, imploring him as she ran her thumbs down the straps of her bra, feeling her pulse hiccup as Miles fixed her with the darkest glare she'd ever seen.

She smiled and spun, stepping off the raised platform to walk heel-toe to him, to the couch he sat at like a king. She kept her back straight, her chin high. She could do that. Had confidence when it came to Miles. Because even at his most vicious, as he snapped and snarled like a cornered lion, he watched every part of her, devoured her.

His eyes closed, tongue wetting his lower lip, ribs spread.

"Look at me," she murmured.

He obeyed, nostrils flaring.

But he fought her still, kept his voice rough to ask, "How could you come when you knew what it meant to me?"

"Because I love you." An obvious explanation in her opinion. She teased her left strap down the curve of her shoulder. "Because you saw me on Tuesday, kissed me and you kept winning. And I had to know how much of my luck was real."

"A test."

"A reward. Seeing you on that field, watching you succeed—it makes me crazy. Because you don't believe it's you out there, sweating for the money, pushing and working. You call it luck and for the life of me, I don't understand why."

His jaw went tight, eyes darted away. "Dancers aren't chatty."

"Fine," she huffed, turning around, smoothing her hands down her hips. She swiveled. She wasn't a dancer, especially not to the thumping, dripping pulse of the music, but she knew what he liked. Innocent touches turned carnal. Hands petting her thighs, turning inward, pulling away at the last second.

Stretching her arms over her head, she bent her knees just so, angled her body forward, wiggled until he saw every seam of her panties.

Her hair was a mask down her back, big and growing as she moved and sweat. She twisted, marveled at his violet gaze, loved how it clung to her. Quickly, she undid her bra and stepped between his knees. Steadied shaking hands on his thighs. Stroked up, fingers hungry.

"Is this what you wanted?" she murmured. "You wanted to be danced for?" Her knees parted to grip the outside of his hips, slid down the pink polyblend. Lauren inhaled the familiar scent of Miles's soap and skin.

She ground against him, waiting for him to answer. *Really* answer. Admit he didn't want it, admit he blew up, admit the truth.

Riding over his clothed lap, she pulled on his hair, pushed her breasts against his mouth. Waited. Music like white noise to Miles's silence. To his rigid body under hers, furious, livid, angry. So many things at once. And she was loose, aching for him, spiraling and spinning. She knew his answer already, why couldn't he say it?

"Is this the fairy-tale ending?" he seethed, inches from her face, grabbing her hands and holding them like a vise, shaking her.

"Your dream date?" He pushed with another shake, hot breath on her face.

Fury filled his face but that was all hardness under her legs, pulsing against her. "Happily ever after," she whispered, grinding slower.

"Stop trying to make us work. We don't work. You're—" he hissed as she broke free her trapped hands to spread cold palms over his chest, kneading, undoing buttons of his shirt. Buttons. With her.

He panted like a bull on her neck, sweat beading at his temple. "We lost."

"I'm not your luck, Miles. I never was."

"It's all you were."

She ignored the sting, let it ricochet off. He was just lashing out. "You're mad. Take it out on me." She could take it, could help him. "Do whatever you need. Do it to me."

His mouth landed on hers like he wanted to fuse them together. Slamming against her, hand in her hand, teeth knocking, noses smashing, foreheads clashing.

Dream date. Yes.

One of them in buttons.

A bad kiss.

The best beginning. Once upon a time.

She didn't hesitate to respond, kiss back, wrap herself around him, press against his heat. Big swallowing kisses, lips like life rafts on drowning seas. His hands roamed, desperate and frantic, diving and twisting. One hooked at her waist, hauling her forward, the other on her shoulders, shoving down.

Friction. As his hips lifted.

There and gone.

Warning bells ignited. Died as his hand tangled into the thin cotton of her panties. Before she could tense for intrusion, prepare, his finger was inside of her, two. She made a desperate sound into his mouth, trying to breathe his air. His hand moved, readjusted. Then both of her holes were filled with him.

His voice was no more than a rasp as he said, "Didn't think you'd be wet."

Teeth down her throat. A third finger inside her, finding rhythm, her legs splaying further apart, victims to Miles's desires.

She clutched at him, lungs filling, hands stumbling down the placard of his shirt, wanting skin, wanting art at her fingertips.

"No," he growled, hitching her higher on his fingers, a new angle for his intrusion. "You don't get to touch me. I'll fuck you with my clothes on right here like the whore you are."

The flush of embarrassment coated Lauren at his words, his labored breathing. *Whore*. And she'd clenched for him. Liked it. A sick perversion made OK by the timbre of her love's voice.

Patience. He needed patience. He was mad, hurt, acting out.

And so, if he wanted to get even with her, if calling her a whore bandaged his scars, she'd let him. But she wouldn't let him destroy them in the process.

She moaned, his fingers plunging into her, driving her too high too fast. She grappled for his belt, ripping through it, the zipper next, started prying down his slacks, reaching for his steel-hard length, gripping, stroking.

She didn't need to ask why there were condoms in the room, a candy dish of vice. Not now, she just took one, opened it quickly, rolled it down as he sucked on the skin under her ear; whispering vile, filthy things that made her blush, made her wet. Uncomfortably, painfully wet around his fingers.

He stood, hauling her with and then set her down. Confused, Lauren sucked in a sharp breath, reached for his neck, lips wet, stinging. He stopped her. Turned her. Bent her down over the seat. Pink all she saw as strong hands dug into her thighs, her ass. He didn't even take her panties off. Just shoved them aside before he thrust into her. Hard, deep. A cry leaped past her lips, her body bucking at the shock, the sudden spread, knees giving out. All her weight on her hands and stomach.

His hands curled around her thighs, pushing her apart, pushing him deeper. A stab of pleasure, the burn in her abdomen became a throb as he retreated and thrust again, as he slowly fucked her.

"This?" he rasped, bending over her, his heat crowding her, buttons on her spine. "You *like* this? This is what you love? No." He rammed into her, intentionally brutal, knuckles, broken, bleeding knuckles wet on her shoulder kept her down, her cheek in the fabric, warm from where he'd sat. Every thrust pounding. She gasped with each surge, panting, building tension between her legs.

"You thought you loved this? *Me*?"

He was breaking before her, hips faltering in his pace, hands gentling and tensing like he kept forgetting to be mean, to keep his mask.

"You can't make me not like it," she hissed, lips muffled on the fabric, her hands reached back for him, capturing his wrists but not moving them, pushing or pulling, just holding. Over her shoulder she watched his glazed eyes strain, his chin tense and bunch.

Black slacks, a navy button-down. He was handsome dressed up, tattoos twisting free of his collar, like flowers poking through cracks in the sidewalk.

Voice firm, Lauren unleashed the truth, "You can't make me not love you. This won't do it, Miles. It won't work."

He seized her hair, pulled her back to him, arching her, hips grinding roughly into her ass. Thrust again. Her moan followed, her ache rich and full. And she gave it heft, let it use all the air in her lungs, let it compete with the music, with his anger. Head tipped back on his chest, she watched him. "You can't spend your whole life running."

The tension broke from his face. His hand glided between her legs to find her clit, teasing gently, touch possessive. At war with himself.

Yet his voice was utterly soft as he commanded, "You're going to come right now. Prove that you love me."

Teeth sunk into her shoulder. And she did. Right there, hauled against him, satin pants on the back of her bare thighs, cuff links tickling her navel, she came.

He followed, a roar in his throat, a last slow, deep thrust. Then, he let go of her. In the throes of her orgasm, she collapsed forward, muscles lame.

Empty. She had become so empty.

"No," she groaned, turning on the couch, rugburn on her shoulder as she twisted. Saw Miles stumble backward, eyes wide. Watched as he shoved himself into his pants, condom still on. Zipped. Rushed to the door.

She swallowed the knot in her throat. "Wait!"

He was gone.

Chapter Twenty-Two

"Miles! Hey, Miles!" Steph's voice sounded like it was in a vacuum. Hands were clutching him again, different hands, not gentle hands, no lemon, no tremble. Hands that he didn't like, not Lauren's hands.

He could barely see the hands, anything, except a flash of red. Fuck, was he crying?

Crying and he felt like he was going to throw up, felt like his body was revolting. "Room—" His voice was hoarse, low. "Room two," he told Steph, told the hands that were too warm, too rough.

Breaking free, so good at breaking out, running, he charged forward, aware of the wetness on his cheeks. He crashed into a table, rushed onward before it toppled. Glass shattered behind him. Miles felt like a feral animal let loose in a maze. *Get out, get free. Breathe.*

He was a monster.

A monster in the worst conceivable way. In every way he'd claimed not to be. Territorial, possessive, heartless. He'd fucked Lauren, treated her like less, used her, when all he ever wanted to do was love her.

She'd suffered by him, held on to him. A monster. He couldn't look at her cheek, rubbed red, at the pale green glistening. The last time. The last time he'd have someone love him, the last time he'd deserve it. Now it was gone. Lauren knew the truth. Love destroyed.

I won't let you destroy yourself.

She'd laid on his coals to protect him. Burned skin and bone to keep him from hating himself.

Too late. He hated himself the moment he didn't stop her, the moment he lost the game, saw her in the stands. Hated how it didn't work. She'd broken her word, broken their bond and he'd forgiven her in the span of a blink.

"Miles," Steph was shouting. He pushed out the door.

Blistering cold. Praise Dios, there was cold. A blizzard raging. Ice and snow and brittle wind. How he hated snow, detested the cold, refused to spend time with it. A California kid.

He understood now, running through the parking lot, he understood why people lived here, craved white. The numbing effect. He made it three, six, twenty steps down the street when his knees buckled, brought him into the snow, the hard-packed earth beneath. No coat, he'd forgotten it.

Snow up to his thighs, soaking into his suit, more sliding down his nape, a snapped button on his shirt, seeping into his Italian shoes. Bite and claw and kill. Fuck, he wanted to scream. Fuck me. Fuck this. Fuck love.

Fuck snow. It took too long to kill the feelings. He couldn't do this. Love was not supposed to survive. Lauren wasn't supposed to look at him like that, after he'd ...

A monster.

Love was fragile and sacred, and since he was sixteen Miles had only used himself to break. She couldn't love him. She couldn't. She didn't. She was—

Miles.

He kept hearing it. Her voice curled around his name, looking up at him, tears in her eyes.

Miles.

No more MVP, no more bonus, no more late nights in Lauren's room, no more hitting his head on the steps down to the basement, no more watching her brush her teeth, no more smelling lemon on her fingertips, watching her hiss when she drank. No more feeling her hands count his tattoos, no more taunting smile, the little tease crafted to make him laugh. No more love.

Not for him. A monster, Steph had been right, and the minute Lauren figured it out, realized it wasn't a phase, that he broke and pushed and fought, she'd leave him, take his heart with her.

He wanted her to. Days ago, he'd thought she'd go, when he growled at her in the car, when he showed exactly how unevolved he was, making unreasonable demands because he was terrified to see her hurt. She'd laughed.

Today, she'd realize. The Santos's, they weren't worth loving. They were the kids you kicked out, left on the streets, they weren't worthy of forgiveness.

"Miles Santos," Lauren said. "Get in this car, *ahorita.*"

No not Lauren.

Dripping wet, shuddering, Miles lifted his head, long strands of hair fuzzying his view.

Tia Luisa was yelling at him.

Still his mind ran. Why did Lauren chase him? Why didn't she kick him out when he'd gotten in her bed that very first night? Why didn't she call him a sick fuck at Nightingales? Why couldn't she understand who he was? That he would break her. Shatter her into a million broken pieces beyond repair.

"Get in this car," Tia Luisa snapped again, brake lights dying the snow behind her red. Barely aware of the snow packing to his body, Miles lumbered to his feet. Tripped. Made post holes through the snow until he was climbing into the front seat of his Tia's hatchback.

The fabric seats were too warm, too comfortable against his icy hands.

"You're going to get a cold," his Tia scolded, signaling into the street. "What are you doing in a place like that, hmm? You don't go to places like that."

"Tia, I do." Left, then right, a straight stretch. Lauren's walk home, Lauren's cold hands.

"No, you don't," Tia returned.

He was so tired of people telling him who he was, what he did. "Yes I do, Tia. I do go to places like that. Because Sandra went to places like that, because it's the only place in this entire state that I can feel close to her, feel like I'm doing something for her because I couldn't before she was killed."

Tia looked at him as she parked in her driveway, set the brake. "Get out."

"I don't want to." Maybe his wet clothes would turn to ice, and he'd freeze here.

"I didn't ask." Tia used a tone of admonishment. "I need help. You will help me."

The car turned off and he wanted to … just be cold again, to feel blood slow in his veins, to lose the ends of his fingertips. Cut them off.

"*Ayudame hijo*, the driveway is slippery."

***

IT WAS HOT AND Lauren was wheezing as she crawled across the dirty fabric of a strip club couch. Bare skin rubbing, breaths sawing.

At least it had to be hot. Why else would she be panting, gasping for air, feeling like she'd run a marathon? Sweat tracked down her back, wet marks from Miles's mouth on her shoulder. She didn't shudder or shake.

Never in her life had she felt both hot and numb. Numb came from negative ten degrees, came from watching Maddie get prom-posed to while you bought your own ticket. Numb came from Brian invalidating her feelings. She'd never felt numb like this. Not because of her pain, but his. Miles.

Losing his sister, watching his family dissolve, sending himself down every pathway to find violence and end it, he'd been hurt.

Was she too late?

He'd become so damaged. He thought he didn't deserve the love she offered. He didn't know how to respond. So he'd become what he hated to try and send her away, to prove he didn't deserve it.

Numb, she was numb for him. Numb like coming home on a cold night and finding no fire burning in the hearth, no dinner simmering on the stove. No one at all, when you expected a home and got a house.

Fighting to fill her lungs, numb and hot, Lauren rested her cheek on the pink fabric. Shut her eyes, her torso still draped over the arm of the couch, blood cutting off in her legs.

He'd run. Always running. Ran after his sister, ran after the ball, ran for Steph. And he'd stopped with Lauren. He'd sat, he'd rested. She ached for him to rest.

She ached for him, she—

The door opened, and Steph hurried inside a striped triangle top and red skirt the same shade as her hair.

Lauren couldn't say hi, couldn't find the energy to cover herself. Numb, she gasped for air, hand clutching her chest. Her lungs squeezed.

"Oh God," Steph croaked as she closed the door, locked it.

A lock. Lauren hadn't thought of that. Hadn't been doing much thinking at all. Only fixing the crushed look on Miles's face.

"What do I do?" she asked, voice a tremor as she turned off the music and kneeled on the floor, acrylic heels squeaking against the tile. "What's wrong?"

Wrong. Yes, something was wrong. Lauren knew something was wrong.

Steph floated Lauren's discarded shirt over her back, covering her twisted, wet panties, shielding her.

Lauren's lungs burned.

"Inhaler." Lauren's voice was hoarse, barely a whisper, throat thick, spots in her vision.

Steph jumped to action, searching the room. Hands in Lauren's jeans, her coat.

No. Lauren hadn't brought it, she didn't have it. She wanted to tell Steph to call her sisters, but she'd surely die if she exhaled now. Ripping up Miles's long coat, Steph dug into the pockets and shrieked with success, stumbling forward to press the nozzle into Lauren's parted lips, she depressed the pump.

They waited, and slowly Lauren felt better, wrapped her hand around her inhaler—not hers, on the one Miles carried with him. The one he'd had to have put in his pocket after seeing her in the stands. A sign he hadn't stopped caring for her, thinking of her.

She took another puff, felt less numb.

Up close, Lauren smiled at Steph's palm tree charm necklace, the small anchor drawn under her eye in black. Attention to detail, Maddie would laud, is so important.

"This isn't Miles," Steph assured shakily, blue eyes wide with pity. She brushed Lauren's hair off her face.

"He wanted a dance," Lauren croaked.

Her eyes widened as if the notion was beyond reason. "Miles would rather hang himself than have us dance for him."

Pants dropped onto the couch beside Lauren, then her bra, her coat. Steph worked quickly, folding Miles's coat, keeping the inhaler out in case Lauren would have another break. There was a serene focus to her, Lauren observed. It detracted from the sheer white stockings, the navy garters. She worked like she'd done this before, stepped inside the door and cleaned up other broken-hearted naked girls.

No wonder Miles worried.

Pushing up, feeling stronger, marginally better, Lauren accepted Steph's help into her jeans.

"It really isn't him," she insisted. "I don't know what's gotten into him. But when I see him, he's getting a Steph handprint on both cheeks."

Clasping her bra, Lauren shook her head. "He doesn't want me to love him."

"That's ridiculous."

"It's true. He thinks love stops cold turkey once you mess up." She remembered the look of awe on his face as she invited him inside after their fight. The confused glances when he'd snuck into her bed. "And instead of waiting for it to happen, he's trying to control it. Trying to make me stop loving him before it becomes real."

"Do you?"

Could she ever not? If he could pack her inhaler while pissed off at her, she could love him as he ran. Would. Because mistakes were just that, temporary issues, accidents. But love was so intentional. Each caress, each murmuration.

She put her shirt on, rolled the sleeves. "Through every mistake, I'll love him."

"Oh Miles doesn't deserve you."

"He deserves much more than me," Lauren countered, wet socks on her feet. She laced her shoes. Steph's hands swept down Lauren's cheeks, drying her skin, brushing her hair back.

She wondered which of the two of them would stand out more on the street. Sailor Steph looking magazine-worthy or Lauren, hair wild from Miles's hands, bite marks on her shoulders, red swollen eyes, trembling lips.

Steph smelled like strawberries. "Should we get your sisters?" Steph asked. "I can text the group."

"No," Lauren said, reaching for her coat, fixing the inside-out sleeves. "No I have to get Miles. He's not in a good headspace. He thinks—he knows I betrayed him. I did, but only because I love him so much." One mistake.

"You can't," Steph said, fixing Lauren's other sleeve, eyes darting to the door. "Not yet. We need to get the tape first."

"Miles is more important."

"Lauren." Steph grabbed her shoulders, made her look into bottomless blue eyes. "These rooms are under video surveillance so whatever you and Miles did"—she glanced at the glass dome above the door—"my boss Ralph will see it."

"That's—"

"He's never liked Miles but once he sees it, God, Lauren. Blackmail would be the best option."

"Blackmail for—"

"Cash, what else. Miles works his ass off. We have to fix it."

Lauren's stomach dropped. Twisted and shriveled. She hadn't just stolen his win streak, she'd stolen his livelihood. "Where are the tapes?"

They were up together, a new mission now that they were dressed.

Steph cracked the door and peered into the hall. "It's still early," she whispered. "He probably hasn't seen it. We can grab it and ditch it." A silent pause. "OK, I'll get the tape, you stay here."

"No." Lauren snagged the only thing she could—Steph's bra strap. "It's my mess. I'll fix it."

The red-head turned, a smile flashing. "Together then."

The door swung open and Steph made running in heels an art form as Lauren slipped behind, delving deeper into Pinks, down the hall, past private rooms three through eight and straight into one marked *Off Limits. Staff Only*. Stickers that said *Toxic, Guard Dogs Inside*, another supporting the NRA.

Steph bust inside like it said *Free Shortbread*, hauling Lauren to certain death.

Pitch-black. Panting nervous breaths. "I know the switch is here—*Oh!*" Steph hissed. Glass shattered.

The wall turned blue. No. Screens, one on top of the other, a dozen powered up, the whirr of computer fans, or spinning hard drives. "Is this fucking NASA?" Lauren asked, searching for a mouse, a keyboard, a tower of some sort. She'd expected a VCR with an eject button, not White House security.

She glanced at Steph, red hair purple under the glow. "Any hints?" she asked, crouching down to follow wires, hoping for a CD deck to free.

"I still don't understand Reels. I don't know what any of that is," Steph hissed.

"How many cameras are there?" She squinted at the bright screen. "None of them are labeled." And they were rotating, screens flipping between rooms. "What's the point?"

"Miles isn't the first rich guy to slip. Ralph bought a second house with what he discovered in this room. Can you find it?"

Lauren tried to take in the information, her stomach plummeting. She could figure this out, she could figure anything out, she just needed—

"You bitch," a deep voice came from the door. A big man, wide in the stomach with a dense black goatee scowled at them. "Telling my secrets when you're in my office, baby? After how good I treat you?"

"Ralph"—Steph's voice was wafer thin—"baby, I—" She sprang into action, a gazelle in five-inch stilettos, leaping for the door, driving it closed right in his face.

His answering roar rearranged the vertebrae in Lauren's spine. "You cunt! You get out right now. I'll fucking kill you and your bitch friend."

Plastering herself to the door, Steph pushed back, hand baring the handle from moving. "Hurry," she demanded.

CHAPTER TWENTY-THREE

"I WILL NOT QUESTION why you were in the snow. Why you can't take care of yourself. Why you don't have a coat, why you want to wreck a nice pair of pants." Tia raised thin eyebrows at Miles, not asking a question.

Miles stayed silent. He didn't want to talk. Not anymore. Not ever again. He wanted to—

What had Lauren said? Angry and horny. Not far off. He'd fucked and now he craved nothing but a fight. Blood and pain and vengeance. Knuckles in his cheek, a foot in his back. He wanted to break through drywall, smash glass with his skull. Yes, he wanted to wreck and ruin and destroy. Be the beast, the villain, the deceitful prince. He wanted to prove how he wasn't right for Lauren. Wanted her to see it with no love fog.

See him be a fucking mess.

Congrats, asshole, his conscience mocked, *you did it. You fucked her in a strip club while you called her a whore.*

No going back.

Exactly as he wanted.

No waiting for the other shoe to drop, he'd thrown his boots through the subfloor.

"You look faint." Tia not so gently reached up to slap his cheek. "Come to the kitchen. I made flautas for you. Your mother's recipe. Good for blood pressure."

He sunk deeper in the carpet, watching the old woman skirt around a Noah's ark replica.

"What do you need help with, Tia?"

"Think I'll let you walk into a blizzard?" she snipped, tongue clicking, passing a pair of giraffes. "No. I need help eating flautas."

"That's not help."

She pulled out a wooden chair at her breakfast nook and pointed. "Sit down," she commanded in a voice only wielded by Catholic, God-fearing widows. The same voice had struck him in the pews at Easter mass, *be silent or Jesus won't rise.*

Or on Christmas day, during the second entirely Latin verse of "Oh Come All Ye Faithful," "Stop fidgeting or no presents."

A voice he hadn't heard since his sister died.

In under a minute, he found himself, Gautier suit soaked to the bone, sitting, knees bumping the underside of the table, a steaming plate of memories in front of him. Smelling like garlic, cumin, lime, a fresh pinch of cilantro, a mouthwatering marinated beef.

His mother's hurried Spanish, black hair freshly colored, stains on her fingertips. "You think Lauren would love you if she knew what lay in your soul?" his mother would ask. "The fear, the possession? Your need for control, your terror of the future? You sat and watched your sister leave. You loved Sandra, and you watched. Love is cold and mean, and—"

Tia's harsh English broke into his daydream. "Good for fertili-ty," she informed, nudging the plate closer, opening a tub of sour cream. "Your mama would want me to tell you now that you're in love."

"Mom didn't want babies. She made that clear when she tossed Sandra out."

"Oh no," Tia said, adding a fork and knife, a cloth napkin with fresh stitching on it. "Your mama wanted grandbabies so badly."

"She shouldn't be allowed to have them, she couldn't take care of her own kids."

Slowly, Tia sat beside him, pushing the plate until it hit Miles's stomach. "I never had kids, hijo. But I know mothers love their children incredibly deeply."

"But that's not—"

"She loved Sandra so much."

"She kicked her out." He shoved the plate away. "She sent her to die."

"I know she regrets it every day. Every second, she regrets it. She loved—"

"No, she didn't—"

"Why do you think she made Sandra go? Because she loved her so much. She held to very high standards. And it broke her heart to see her perfect daughter have a flaw." Miles's jaw clenched. "*Te amo, hijo*, but I sent you on a date you did not want because I wanted more for you. Better. I pushed, because love is ... love can be expecting more, because you want to see the best for them. Your mama wanted the brightest future for Sandra, worked hard for it, left your daddy, raised you in the Church. She meant to teach Sandra a lesson. She never expected Sandra to take it as goodbye."

"She killed Sandra. Love killed Sandra."

"No, Sandra didn't have faith in her mama. Trust to return. Didn't believe love forgave."

"She was seventeen! It wasn't on her!"

"*Si, hijo*, and your mama had her when she was the same age. A tragic, costly mistake. She still lights a candle in Sandra's name. We pray for her when we talk. Could you forgive her? For wanting better?"

Up until an hour ago, he'd have said no. "I love like my mother." He cut into the flauta, watching the cheese run, stomach revolting. He shoved it into his mouth, tucked it in his cheek. "I expect too much and I punish for it. My love is callous and breaking, bitter."

"No—"

"*Yes.*"

"What have you done, hijo? Why were you in the snow? If it is Lauren, she will forgive you. Those girls are good. I set you up right."

"I didn't make a mistake, Tia." He felt Lauren's skin compress under his hands, watched pink marks appear, the skin pinch white. "I did it on purpose. I made sure she couldn't love me."

"Love judges, but it forgives," she pressed. "Ah, there she is. Go to her."

Miles followed his Tia's gaze to the window, swallowing the lump of corn tortilla left his mouth, pushing back from the table.

Maddie was charging outside, flinging a scarf around her neck. "That's Maddie, Tia."

"It's Lauren," Tia insisted, looking puzzled. "The pretty one. Maddie's the shoveler with the elbows, the frown. She has a boyfriend."

"No, Tia. *That's* Maddie." He pointed. Recognizing her by gait alone. "Lauren, my Lauren, she's the shoveler."

"No—no. I set you up with the pretty one."

He looked back through the glass. Tia had them confused. Had set Miles up with—No fate, no divine intervention. A confused old woman had flung Lauren in his path. Luck. Strangers in masks at a ball.

"You did," he agreed, brows furrowing as Hannah scurried from the house, yelling something to Maddie. Kayla next, zipping her coat, throwing her arms over her head.

They were fighting, shoving snow off the old CRV. Maddie yelled something. Hannah was on the phone. Kayla launched into the driver's seat, shouting at Maddie, who screamed for someone to get a shovel. They had to be loud to be heard from Tia's kitchen.

"Hurry up!" Hannah cried.

Miles ran for it. Wet pants, sleeves, his suit jacket freezing into a solid sheet of ice as he raced across the street, leather shoes trudging through the snow. Thick waves of white, wind kicking it off the ground to make ice vortices. Make the night bright, change the dark sky into a dull, flat gray.

"It won't start!" Kayla cried from the front seat, kicking at the pedals.

Maddie, who was frantically shoveling out the tires didn't look out as she yelled, "Get the other keys then, start the Impala!"

"It's parked in," Hannah called, clearly disgruntled, scaping the back window of the car with a long blue brush.

Maddie threw her shovel. "*Fuck*!"

Up close, Miles saw a sort of tube braided into her hair, the ends wrapped in socks and she wasn't wearing jeans or a skirt or anything fancy, just pink sweatpants. Unpolished, frantic.

"What's wrong?" Miles demanded, jumping over the curb. "What happened?"

"Lauren," Maddie said, staggering forward to clutch at his shirt with wet, bare hands. "She sent an SOS. It's Lauren. You have to—We need your car."

Holding her scraper like an axe, Hannah ran to them, phone in front of his face. "She's at a strip club! She could be killed!"

"Do you have jumper cables?" Kayla called.

Maddie shook her head, shouting back, "We'll just use his car."

He almost said *Lauren doesn't want me*, but then ... it didn't fucking matter anymore. It didn't matter because Tia was right.

Miles loved her so much, and if she could forgive him for this, he vowed never to give her something to forgive again.

Even still, she could hate him and it wouldn't matter. He'd make sure she was safe. Now and forever. He'd follow her for the rest of her life guaranteeing she'd never suffer again.

His fault.

An SOS. He slapped his pockets for her inhaler.

Gone. He'd left without his coat.

Nasty, coiled fear filled him.

He looked at the car, not starting, turned to the Peck sisters yelling at him, demanding keys, help. Not hearing any of it.

He ran. He was born to run.

It was hard in the deep snow. High knees and a long stride helped as he sprinted down the sidewalk, curved and dashed for the street, ran in the tread marks of tires, packed snow he could push against.

Cars honked, lights blinded him and he might get hit, but he'd get to her quicker.

"He's running," Hannah shouted somewhere behind him.

Kayla and Maddie were yelling, "We're coming."

Looking back would slow him so he didn't. Didn't have time to tell them to stay off the road, to call the cops, to not put themselves at risk. Not that he could tell a Peck sister not to protect own of their own. Lauren would fillet him at the mere mention of it.

He ran faster. Quicker than he'd ever moved. It was his job. This was his life. Running, charging, pushing. Running from LA, from his mother, running after abusers, running into trouble. All his life he ran. But it only felt important now. it only felt useful in *this* second. When his run became a chase.

He'd never run again if he could just get there fast enough to save her.

Feet screaming in his dress shoes, Miles tore free of his blazer, ditched it on double yellow lines behind him. The buttons sheared on his shirt, busting wide, flapping. The ends of his pants were heavy with slush, slashing at his ankles. Snow wet his hair, pelted his skin.

His heart was in his throat as he cut into Pinks' parking lot, ran around the Demon, sprinted inside.

Heard it.

Yelling. Not Lauren's, but worse. So much worse.

"I'm going to string you whores up, you hear me? This is the last time you bitches misbehave. I'll make an example of you." Ralph, Steph's suiter, her stalker, her fucking tormenter and boss. Ralph. He was shouting.

One look at Poppy pointing, hiding behind the bar in the main room and Miles charged to the back, kicked open the door to room two.

Empty.

Cleaned out.

Lauren was gone. His coat was folded.

He cut back to Poppy, to ask, to question, but before he turned for the stage, he found Ralph pounding hits fists against wood. "I'll make you scream, Steph!" the owner threatened, spit flying from his mouth. "And the little whore too."

Miles lost it.

Chapter Twenty-Four

"Switch with me," Lauren demanded, scrambling over the wires, around the rolling chair, an overflowing trash bin of Takis Blue Heat.

Straining on her heels, sliding inch after inch down the door, Steph nodded. *"Hurry."* Her voice was muffled under the ferocious pounds of Ralph's barrage.

Lauren had never heard such nasty things come out of a mouth. Foul, disgusting threats in quick succession.

"You have to find it," Lauren rushed. "You find it, I can't." She wrapped a hand over Steph's on the door, holding it rigid, slid next to her in the buzzing blue light. Once her shoulders were tight on the flat wood, Steph launched forward, hands slamming the keyboard and mouse.

Lauren could feel every fist hit the door. Felt it threaten to throw her back, crush her against the wall. Hardening her spine, she lifted a foot and planted it on the cabinet across from her, kicked back until her other foot left the ground. Until she was a human doorstop.

If he wanted inside, if he wanted to do a single one of the nasty promises he spewed, he'd have to wait until her legs quit, snapped.

Then he'd have to take her arms, her teeth. She'd protect Steph until she was just skin and broken bone. They hadn't found lights, hadn't found the recordings. Hadn't figured out an escape. But they would. Lauren would make sure.

"Phone." Steph was frantic, body trembling with adrenaline. "Where's the phone?"

"You fucking slut," Ralph screeched. "I'll skin you for this."

"Pocket," Lauren gasped. "Jeans."

Steph found it, turning on the flashlight, unleashing a spread of white. Lauren couldn't help but picture Steph underwater with a spotlight, white in drowning dark blue. Helped that she'd dressed like a sailor. Not Elsa. Ariel. Red hair. Fishnets. Dreaming about a different world.

"I don't know," Steph croaked, clicking the mouse, staring, blinking quickly. "I don't know what any of this means. *Fuck*. I don't know computers. Do you know computers?"

"I tried!" Lauren hissed back, barely finishing the word before Steph kicked her stiletto straight into a screen. Blue cracked, splintered, faded. "Not the screens, the rest!"

"Right." She was panting, dropping to her knees and ripped wires, slamming drives to the floor, making a pile fit for an electronic dump site.

"Chasity, you—" Ralph's scream was cut off by his own, "What the fuck?"

A renewed effort hit the door, made it leap open an inch and slam shut. Lauren pictured his body being thrown against her, imagined the wood cracking. She lost her ability to speak, fighting to hold back a cry as she straightened her knees, became a spanner bridge between Steph and Ralph, holding her breath, adrenaline whipping at her limbs to push.

Another slam. Her leg twisted. "I'm gonna fuck your corpses!"

"Call the police," Lauren gritted. "Right now. I'm done waiting. Do it."

"Not until we have the tapes," Steph responded in sheer panic. She sent the spiked end of her heel through black metal. "Miles can't—we can't ruin Miles."

Lauren imagined the police watching Miles bend her over, tell her to take it. "I'll protect Miles," she said, knowing she couldn't, knowing it'd wreck him, but understanding that it wouldn't hurt him more than seeing Steph injured. "Right now, we need protection." Steph needed protection.

"I promise, I'll—"

The door shot open, Lauren's legs crumpled, she cried out. Kicked. Slammed wood back onto the jamb. Steph doubled her efforts, destroying, smashing, the room grew darker, quieter.

The shouting stopped. Replaced with grunting and growling. Probably preparing for a big push. Lauren didn't know how much more she could thwart. If he threw his entire self against it, would the door even hold? She pictured the hinges shearing, her legs breaking, wood smothering her as he charged inside, clawing for Steph.

"Help me." She pushed harder, feeling each grain of the wood like a ridge on her headboard. "Help me, I can't hold it."

Steph rushed to her side, legs spread, hands shoving the door shut, barricading. They couldn't keep it up. Both of them were shaking.

"Fire," Steph hissed through her teeth. "We could burn it, I have a lighter."

"There's no escape in here. We'd have to get past Ralph. He'd let us burn."

"*Fuck.*"

The slamming continued, but not on the door. Under their combined effort, it stayed secure, in place. Solid. Defensible. Two of them strong. But Lauren heard it. Heard a body hit the wall. Knew they couldn't keep it up.

Lauren took Steph's hand and squeezed. "I'm sorry," she said. "I'm so sorry I got you into this."

"Gladly," Steph replied, eyes wet. "Gladly for treating me like a friend."

"Family," she corrected, holding her tightly, bracing for Ralph's next onslaught, knowing they were at the end. Something would break. The door, their legs, the drywall next to them. And they'd be exhausted when it finally gave, legs numb, arms weak, they'd have to fight.

A fire. Maybe a fire *would* work, to protect Miles.

Shrieks began on the other side of the door. Following by muffled shouting. Ranting from Ralph.

Silence.

Steph's breath shuddered beside Lauren, her hand squeezing tightly. The door bounced. Lauren gasped. They uncovered strength to push back harder, tighter, cutting off all circulation. The end. Looking at each other in the dark, their eyes were full, hearts determined. *For Miles*, Steph seemed to say, withdrawing a black Bic from her cleavage. Lauren nodded, heart a rampage in her chest.

A tap came between Lauren's shoulder blades. A careful knock. Almost timid.

Lauren's breath caught. Steph's face shone in the glow of a small flame. A trick. Ralph was tricking them, pretending to be tired, giving up.

"Pretty girl?" came Miles's velvet-smooth voice. "Pretty girl, come out please. I have to see you. Please pretty girl."

Steph was the first to step away from the door, to turn, press parted lips into the small glowing seam. "Miles?"

"Steph," came Miles's desperate voice. Lauren heard fingernails on the wood behind her head. "Steph, is she there? Tell me she's there. Tell me I made it."

Lauren's mind kept saying trick. *Trick trick trick*. A voice modulator. He was being held at gunpoint, Ralph had knocked the door down, this was Lauren's coma dream. She'd texted her sisters SOS, not Miles. He'd left. Ran.

Blue eyes questioned Lauren. And she felt numb, so numb again, fight leaching from her muscle. She shook her head.

"No," Steph said, nodding silent communication to Lauren. "She doesn't want to come out."

Fists on wood, not pounding, but breaking into open palms. "Please, Dios. Please, Steph, let me. I need to see her," he rasped. "Just ... tell me she's OK. I need to know she's OK. Now. Tell me.

"You left her," Steph growled.

"Lauren, pretty girl, I'm so sorry. Please," he begged. "Please, I'm sorry."

Steph took Lauren's arm, whispering. "We can stay in here. We don't have to go. Destroy the tape, call the cops."

But Lauren's legs drifted to the floor, wet socks squishing in her sneakers. Miles. He'd come. Real. He was calling her pretty girl. She released the handle, wondering what his face would tell her, needing to know if it was twisted with anger, thunderous and powerful, or if his lips were drawn down at the sides, if those forest eyes shimmered with fear. Horror at history repeating. Losing another person close to him.

Or could the soft tones, the whispers, the thick stretch of his honey voice mean something else entirely?

She pulled open the door, preparing for heartbreak. And it happened. The remaining shards of her heart cracked and split. Miles was on his knees in the low-lit hall, hands pressed into his eyes sockets, grinding, murmuring. Blood leaking down his wrists, an endless flow from busted knuckles.

Steph gasped.

Lauren turned to figure out why and—her stomach lurched. Ralph's body was strewn on the floor, face down, arm twisted.

"Did you kill him?" she whispered.

Miles jerked up, eyes like fire. She braced for anger, for the speech of how she was weak, how she needed protecting, how she'd messed up, all of which she'd agree with right now.

He crawled.

Crawled on the grimy tile to her, slipped trembling hands around her ankles, his forehead dug into her thighs.

"Did you kill him?"

"Are you hurt?" he asked, callused hands running up her calves, feeling, searching for a knife hanging from the skin, for tape holding her together. "Tell me you're not. Tell me—"

"I'm fine, Miles." Of their own volition, her hands sunk into his hair, tipped his head back.

Tears. Tears dripped down his cheeks, made pink trails of the blood splatter.

"Please," he croaked, chest heaving, gasping. The pulse in his throat made his tattoos dance like flames in the wind.

From her pocket, Lauren retrieved the inhaler and set it between his lips. She didn't press it, he didn't need it, but it distracted him as she'd planned. "Why'd you have it?" she asked, voice timid. The muscles around her mouth quivered

"You're safe," he murmured against the plastic, breaths deepening. "You're safe."

"Why were you carrying this, Miles?" She flipped it in her palm? "Why'd you run with this in your pocket?"

Damp curls stuck to his forehead, dripped water down his jagged nose. Hands gripped her calves, massaging, she wasn't sure he knew he was doing it. "Today has been the worst mistake of my life, Lauren. I love you so much, hearing you were in trouble—fuck I can't. Don't ... You terrified me."

She crushed her fingers around the inhaler, thoughts becoming a poison. "You don't love me, you got scared. I'm sorry for scaring you. Nothing happened."

"*Nothing happened*?" He yanked and her knees buckled, fell until she straddled his thighs, his arms hauling her into him, pressing their heart together. Forehead against hers, he stared into her eyes. "Nothing happened?" he whispered into her ear. His entire body trembled, the strong muscles of his thighs, powerful hands quaking like a newborn.

Her numbness melted off her like water rolling down her skin.

"I—to you. I did—" He kept stopping, kept trying again. Gave up, the words too horrible. "Forgive me. *Dios*, forgive me. I can't ask for it but it's all I'll ever desire. I'm *so* sorry. I'll never ever touch you in anger again, never touch you. Period. Just let me love you. Dios, Lauren, let me love you. Please."

"Miles." Lauren's heart was confused. Her brain casting a million scenarios. Concrete dust on her knees and palms, a broken dress, a crown being laid on her messy hair. Polished, crisp legs bending, kneeling to meet her. Her prince had found her in the ruins.

She sat frozen in his embrace for a breathless, undecided moment before melting forward into him, winding her arms around his waist. "I love you. There's nothing to forgive."

He took her in a ferocious kiss. Mouth tasting like dried tears and ice, his shirt wet and cold under her hands.

"I'm so sorry," he murmured, kept murmuring, "I'm so sorry I thought—*fuck*, I knew—I thought we were all the same. All the Santos's. I thought you'd leave when I messed up. I knew it. You'd end it, come to your senses, wake up. And when you didn't ... when you agreed to help after I chased you to your bedroom. When we argued, when that Fuck-Bro flirted with you, I was fucking up and you were steadfast. And it gave me faith. In you, in myself, gave me hope and peace, longing. You give me hope,

Lauren. And then more time passed, I made more mistakes and I waited for you to leave. I waited."

"And you got tired of waiting."

"Do you know what it's like to be in love and know it'll kill you?"

She shoved her head against his chest, marveling at the strength and breadth. "Yes. Miles, I do."

"Pretty girl, strong girl." He brushed his nose into her neck, inhaled. "Why don't you ever leave?" he asked, fiercely, clutching at her with desperate fingers. "Why don't you see me and leave?"

"I see more than you can," she whispered. "I see your heart, constantly making attachments you write off as duties, I watch you work tirelessly to force help on people too proud to ask. I see how you honor Sandra with every action, and Miles"—she tapped his heart—"you love your mother still, her cross on your heart. You do nothing without intention and you let people think you're a philanderer, a miscreant."

"I'm a monster. I want to be better for you. I'm done trying to end this, done sabotaging, because I can't imagine a single day without you, Lauren. You're not my luck, you're my fucking life, the air I breathe. No inhaler could fix me without you. And it's selfish."

"You're not selfish."

Rough knuckles lifted to her cheek. "Look what I brought you into. Look where you are."

"I'll sooner die in my cubicle than any danger you bring and at least I'll be happy. There's color here. You brought me color with your midnight tattoos and gold chain. You staunched the numbness from killing me. Life without you is beige and gray. The same thing every day. Putting my head down, muting my feelings. I don't want to write about other people's passions, I want to have my own. You make me want to stand up for what I want."

She laughed softly, feeling her heart swell and heal. "I don't know how to fight or run or remember my inhaler, but I'll bring that fucking ring to Mordor." She felt tears in her eyes, and then Miles was kissing her again. Yes. The feel of his arms around her, his tongue in her mouth. A kiss. Their first Sunday kiss. Her body locked against his as she tasted desire, fear, love in every movement.

"I'll keep messing up," he said against her lips. A shake of his head. "What if you get tired of forgiving, what if I push too far? *Whore*, Lauren. I called—"

"I quite liked that, as it turned out." A blush flooded her. "We forgive each other. I made you shovel an entire street, I made you shower in the cold, I made you drink an entire bottle of Dom Perignon when I definitely could've had a sip."

"I thought you'd be safer without me. That for once I'd done the noble thing."

"How can you expect me to be safe without you?"

"You'll never be rid of me now." What could've been a tease, played like a dire threat.

A soft throat clearing interrupted them. Wiping her eyes in the hall, actively eavesdropping, Steph said, "I don't want to ruin this because I *love* what's happening, but do we have zip ties or a ball gag handy? Because I don't want him mobile when he wakes up." She kicked Ralph's calf.

"There's rope in the car." Miles rubbed his face, as if suddenly exhausted. "We'll hog-tie him."

Lauren felt herself smile. Smile. Happiness in a decidedly dark moment, a bud of a young flower unfolding on a damp forest floor. Adrenaline pounded through her, she felt so wrung out on emotion, the back of her tongue was painted in sharp wicked flavors. Loss. Fear. Defeat. Relief. Love. Humor.

Color. Passion. Never a dull day with Miles.

Just as a laugh tickled her tongue, all hell broke loose.

The Peck sisters had arrived. Hannah, surprisingly quick, ran, the metal edges of her shovel whacking the walls, a war cry on her tongue. The bouncer—Teddy—was shouting at her, running after. Maddie had keys slotted between her fingers like daggers and Kayla was there too, attached to the back of the bouncer, wailing on his shoulders, snowboarding thighs clinging for life.

Miles hauled Lauren up with him, not letting any space between them, moving in front of Steph.

"What—" Hannah staggered to a stop. Maddie's keys jabbed her back. Kayla and the bouncer hit the wall, tangled as the massive bald man tried to flip her off.

"Teddy," Steph called. "Stop. She's fine."

"We're here to rescue you," Maddie announced, soundly deflated. Her attention went to the body on the ground, lingered. "We're not as fast as Miles." She had on pajama pants. Her heatless curler dangled down her back, her coat was buttoned wrong. Each sister had wet hair and shivering frames.

Lauren felt new emotions build, felt her voice thin as she asked, "Did you all run here?"

Slowly, the shovel's tip lowered, Kayla released her kung fu grip on Teddy's, and Maddie frowned. "Duh, you sent an SOS. The car crapped out. It was Miles's idea to run."

Lauren looked at him, "That's why you came back—"

"I was coming back," he said steadfastly, "Either way. No matter what."

Steph hummed in the back of her throat. "He can get mad, freak out, and forget his worth, but he's loyal. Who do you think sent me to check up on you?"

Protecting her, even when he was trying to destroy them. Lauren nestled further into his side, tipping her chin back to kiss him. "How could I not love you, Miles?"

Chapter Twenty-Five

L AUREN WAS IN A rush and stressed to the nines as she strode through the construction site, pushing back a wide panel of thick plastic. "Did you get the cash sent to Poppy? She couldn't pick it up."

Steph popped up from her chair, more covered than Lauren had ever seen her. A turtleneck, corduroy bellbottoms, a heavy-duty face mask and plastic safety glasses. She pushed bright orange headphones off to dangle at her neck. "What?"

"Did you pay Poppy?

"I paid Poppy," Miles's voice came from the door.

Both women turned. Steph made a face. "You chose black?"

Lauren's breath caught. Her heart soared. Black. Yes. A fitted black henley that made his tattoos look like webbing on his skin, dripping around thick arms. Dark curls had grown in the past month. So much so he'd started wearing a headband under his helmet.

The only thing he did before every game.

Because Lauren liked the curls, liked pulling them, sifting them through her fingers, playing with them while he cuddled her and fell asleep thirty minutes into Thursday movie night.

"I also shared a few words with her boyfriend," he added, lifting his eyebrows. "And what do you know, he agreed it's important to respect Poppy's career. She'll pick up her check next week."

"Good work, cop."

The nickname earned a glare. "Thanks, brains. All platitudes are owed to the boss."

"Not your boss," Lauren corrected as Miles wrapped a hand around her hip, kissed her neck. "I'm the building manager. We're all bosses."

Building manager. The same job she had at City Hall. Similar in no way. No ink, no semi rigid conduit, no cubicle or red bathrooms. Now she negotiated for discounts on ball bearings, interviewed dance teachers for the weekly pole class, helped the dancers manage their finances, and yes, there was a fair amount of vodka ordering and lemon stocking.

No beige.

Miles tapped his knuckles on her head. "Where's your hardhat?"

"The one that says, 'Miles's property'?"

"I do own the building." Bought before it hit market after Ralph's blackmail scheme came to light and he left town, deed still in the safe.

"It's date night, I don't want to mess up my hair." Her work look had changed considerably. Slacks still. Until spring hit and she could torture Miles in a pencil skirt, but no buttons. Never. Instead, a tasteful heathered-pink T-shirt that read *Pinks*. The rebrand of Vermont's only gentlemen's—and ladies on Thursdays—club.

Construction had begun in earnest last week. While Miles was running for a personal best in Buffalo, Steph and all four Peck sisters demolished every stained mark on Pink Persuasion's dirty walls. No more private rooms. A dance floor was being added, elegant locker rooms with showers and nap pods.

Eliminating the stripping part was unthinkable. If they did, another place would open, one where the dancers weren't given voices, offered respect. There would always be need of a strip club in Burlington, and in Pinks, there'd be no question of safety.

And though they were closed for the next month, Steph—new events coordinator—pointed out that if the dancers didn't get paid weekly, they'd be forced to find new, shadier avenues to eat, support their families, and pay their bills. Miles was singlehandedly bankrolling salaries with his playoff bonuses.

For the first time in her life, Lauren thought of work after she left, she arrived early and her cheeks hurt when she left. Upon delivering a very classy cookie bouquet to Mary, the gossip queen agreed to help develop a finance plan for Pinks and entered early retirement.

Brian was still on an extended leave.

"When are the bouncer interviews?"

Twisting until she was cradled in his arms, head under his chin, Lauren answered off the top of her head, "Next week, after practice. I know you want to come."

"Yeah, he has to pick out the ugly ones so he doesn't worry about you and all that meat," Steph retorted, blowing sawdust off her tarp covered desk.

A work in progress. But soon their office would be a sanctuary, aqua walls to offset the bright logo, matching desks, chairs with actual lumbar support. Windows. A wall of them, out of budget but splurged for upon Miles's insistence. Steph approved.

"No," Miles said over Lauren and she couldn't see him but she almost heard him stick his tongue out at the redhead. "I trust Lauren entirely. But it's better if I tell them she's taken from the get-go. Don't want them coming to work for the wrong reasons."

"You're terrifying, Miles." Steph droned. "You could scare us all into six more weeks of winter." A frown. "Shouldn't Maddie be here?"

Their interior designer. Kayla and Brock were handling demo, Hannah brought baked goods daily and even Tia Luisa had stopped by, told Miles to plant lilacs down the front sidewalk. He and Lauren had barely held it together, they wanted to laugh so hard.

"She's working on the basement today." The basement. No longer Lauren's room. Since it was only a few blocks away, the Peck basement would become a crash site for employees too tired or drunk or scared to drive in the snow.

"Ah," Miles's breath teased Lauren's ear. "I do miss the dungeon."

Living with Miles was humbling. No mirrors on the ceiling, no torture rooms or sex swings. A split ranch with twenty-six acres. Well-kept. Heated floors, a garage filled with outlandish cars. A small but growing collection of movies Miles brought home.

Steph's phone rang, and she swore. "This is actually Declan. I asked him to pre-vet some of the applicants. I'll take this outside.

You guys should not stay in here. Paint fumes, dust, probably mold. We need to check for asbestos."

As they watched Steph hurry out, covered tip to tail, Miles mused, "I'm still learning the real names of my employees and she's talking building codes."

"She might be a genius," Lauren agreed. "I taught her Excel a few weeks ago and yesterday she coded us a website." She dropped her head back on Miles's chest. "I don't think anyone's ever given her a chance before. She wants to prove she can do it."

"She already has." Miles gathered her hair up to kiss her neck. That spot. "I'm still gonna make fun of her for the time she confused URL and urinal."

Siblings. Immature, bratty, loyal, caring.

"How's your day been, pretty girl?" Velvet smooth, his voice curled around her.

"Excellent," she murmured, spinning, working her arms around him. "When are you leaving for Florida?"

The Mountaineers had made the playoffs as a wildcard. And even if they lost to the Buccaneers, there was already chatter about how far they'd soar next year.

Miles knew.

He'd told her repeatedly that it would be his best year yet, because she'd be in the stands watching. "Wheels up at six. I'm gonna miss you," he said, inhaling her skin, dragging her shirt down to lick at her shoulder.

"Not like I'll miss you," she warned, already feeling the pang of separation. "We ordered a TV to watch the game, I'm an ESPN Plus subscriber, can you believe it?"

"You know just how to get me hard, pretty girl."

Laughing, she pushed him away.

He stopped her, trapped her against him, hands enveloping hers, pink knuckles, black palms. "Marry me," he whispered.

"Miles ..." Her voice wavered. Every time he asked, she got lightheaded, off center. "We talked about this. You don't want to get married."

He spun her to look at him. "I want to marry you."

"No you don't. Because what if you wonder if the only reason we're together is our rings? A once-spoken vow? The fear of being smited for getting a divorce?"

"I don't want to get married in a church, Lauren. I just want to be married to *you*. I don't want God mentioned once. Just you and me. I want us to share a last name. I want a beautiful, tasteful ring on your finger, and I want a gobsmacking enormous diamond on mine."

She laughed.

"Marry me," he urged against the skin of her neck. "Please. We'll do it in the off-season. A summer wedding. Cole got ordained for Warren."

"Warren's not even engaged."

"Cole's thoughtful. The three of us in The Peak, you in white slacks."

She slapped his chest. "I'd want my sisters to come."

"Bring them."

"And I'd want Steph and Poppy and Candy. And you'd hate yourself if you didn't invite Burton, and Riley, and—"

"Don't say Asher." He cut off. "So what? You want a wedding of football players and exotic dancers? We can bring a casket for my Tia to die in while the guests arrive."

"You said you didn't care about God."

"You are my God. I'd marry you in a mosh pit of clowns, bare-ass naked."

She grinned. "Dream date."

"Where you want, whoever you want, whenever. Just say yes and tell me your username."

"Oh!" She was grinning now, holding onto him, cheeks burning, eyes near wet. "I get it. *That's* why you want me to marry you. What's mine is yours."

He tugged on her belt loop, mashed their foreheads together. "Fair's fair. I'm bringing twenty mil to the marriage pot, I just want one measly username."

"Maybe when you get to the big B, I'll share."

"You're cruel. Cold."

"I've heard it before." A smirk "Sure you want to marry me?"

"It's all I think about," he said honestly, a sigh against her skin. "Want to hear my vows?" His voice rippled with sudden intensity.

Lauren's throat clogged. She imagined the tiara with a long white veil.

"To honor you," Miles began. "To cherish you. I vow to protect you, and let you protect me too. I vow to fuck you whenever those sea-green eyes look at me like I'm too good. I vow to replace your walkathon shirts with *my* walkathon shirts." She laughed. "I vow to take you on your dream date. Wine and music and I won't speak until you're drunk, begging for mac and cheese. I vow to put your name forever on my skin, in the biggest spot we can find."

Tears in her eyes, throat thick, she whispered, "Right across your forehead."

He didn't blink, didn't laugh. "If that's what it takes for yes."

"I don't need my name on you, I already know it's on here." She poked at his heart. "I love you, Miles. I'd give up eternal life to be with you, just like Arwen did for Aragorn, but give me a year first. A year to plan a wedding of chaos, to mentally prepare Tia. Then I'll wear my one true ring."

A nod on her temple. "I'll take a year." He stroked her hair, holding her tight, making her feel like she could live and die in his arms and never want for anything. "Hey, pretty girl ..."

"I'm not telling you my username."

"Not that," he said. "But before you agree, I should've told you earlier."

Lauren pulled back at his serious tone.

"I've never actually seen *Lord of the Rings*."

Thank you for reading.

www.ingramcontent.com/pod-product-compliance
Lightning Source LLC
Chambersburg PA
CBHW021215220726
48287CB00015B/1390